CARNAGE UNENDING

More Warhammer 40,000 from Black Library

• DAWN OF FIRE •

Book 1: Avenging Son
Guy Haley
Book 2: The Gate of Bones
Andy Clark
Book 3: The Wolftime
Gav Thorpe
Book 4: Throne of Light
Guy Haley
Book 5: The Iron Kingdom
Nick Kyme
Book 6: The Martyr's Tomb
Marc Collins
Book 7: Sea of Souls
Chris Wraight
Book 8: Hand of Abaddon
Nick Kyme
Book 9: The Silent King
Guy Haley

• DARK IMPERIUM •

Guy Haley
Book 1: Dark Imperium
Book 2: Plague War
Book 3: Godblight

Gahzghkull Thraka: Prophet of the Waaagh!
Nate Crowley

Gahzghkull Thraka: Warlord of Warlords
Denny Flowers

Brutal Kunnin
Mike Brooks

Da Big Dakka
Mike Brooks

Grotsnik: Da Mad Dok
Denny Flowers

CARNAGE UNENDING

A WARHAMMER 40,000 ANTHOLOGY

DAN ABNETT - CHRIS WRAIGHT - GUY HALEY
MIKE BROOKS - NATE CROWLEY - RACHEL HARRISON
DAVID GUYMER - MARC COLLINS - STEVEN B FISCHER
JUSTIN WOOLLEY - DAVID ANNANDALE

BLACK LIBRARY

A BLACK LIBRARY PUBLICATION

'Ork Hunter' first published in *Words of Blood* in 2002.
'Wulfen' first published digitally in 2013.
'The Glorious Tomb' first published as an audio drama in 2014.
'Sarcophagus' first published digitally in 2015.
Blood Rite first published in 2019.
'Road Rage' and 'Mad Dok' first published digitally in 2021.
'Packin' Heat' and 'It Bleeds' first published digitally in 2022.
'The Price of Morkai', 'Consecrated Ground' and 'Hell Fist' first published digitally in 2023.
This edition published in Great Britain in 2026 by Black Library, Games Workshop Ltd., Willow Road, Nottingham, NG7 2WS, UK.

Represented by: Games Workshop Limited – Irish branch, Unit 3, Lower Liffey Street, Dublin 1, D01 K199, Ireland.

10 9 8 7 6 5 4 3 2 1

Produced by Games Workshop in Nottingham.

A CIP record for this book is available from the British Library.

ISBN 13: 978-1-83609-296-4

Printed and bound in the UK.

For more than a hundred centuries the Emperor has sat immobile on the Golden Throne of Earth. He is the Master of Mankind. By the might of his inexhaustible armies a million worlds stand against the dark.

Yet, he is a rotting carcass, the Carrion Lord of the Imperium held in life by marvels from the Dark Age of Technology and the thousand souls sacrificed each day so his may continue to burn.

To be a man in such times is to be one amongst untold billions. It is to live in the cruelest and most bloody regime imaginable. It is to suffer an eternity of carnage and slaughter. It is to have cries of anguish and sorrow drowned by the thirsting laughter of dark gods.

This is a dark and terrible era where you will find little comfort or hope. Forget the power of technology and science. Forget the promise of progress and advancement. Forget any notion of common humanity or compassion.

There is no peace amongst the stars, for in the grim darkness of the far future, there is only war.

CONTENTS

ORK HUNTER

DAN ABNETT

Keyser, who they call the sergeant but who wears no rank pins I can see, calls a halt. He gets up on the limed trunk of a massive fallen cypress and stands, sniffing the air.

We wait, thigh deep in the stinking soup below.

The wet air seems to fill my lungs with steam, and I want to cough, but the Skinner nearest me, a lean brute with charcoal-blackened eye-sockets and piercings down his ears, fixes me with a savage glare as if he can tell what I'm thinking. Keyser waves three scouts ahead, and that leaves thirty of us, twenty-two Skinners and eight Jopall Indentured. I'm halfway down the file, the swamp water bubbling and oozing around my legs, dust flies swirling round me.

The silent halt seems to last an eternity. There are spiders in my hair. I can feel them.

Captain Lorit, looking as out of place as the rest of us Jopall in his white-flecked, jade green fatigues and white peaked cap, wades forward. 'What are we–' he begins.

The Skinner they call Pig, standing to the captain's left, surges forward and takes my commander in a choke hold, clamping one greasy paw across his mouth. The captain struggles, wild-eyed, and Pig tightens his grip. The reason for Pig's nickname is self-evident – slabby and fat, with vastly developed muscle groups stretching his tattered tunic, he has a face ruined by scars and a ragged snout of flesh where his nose was bitten off.

Pig's muscles tighten further and the captain begins to turn blue. We Jopall look on in silent disbelief.

Keyser drops his hand and the Skinners un-freeze and move again. Pig releases the captain and throws him, gagging, face down into the water.

Keyser's jumped down off the cypress by then, and drags the captain up with one hand.

'He assaulted me! That man assaulted me! Put him on a charge!' The captain spits out weed and slime, indignant. Keyser doesn't put Pig on a charge. He punches the captain in the throat and silences him. The Skinners laugh, an ugly sound. Pig snorts, a far, far uglier noise.

'I thought we covered this in basic back at Cerbera. When I signal silence out here in the Green, I mean silence.' Keyser's voice is as sharp and taut as a wire. He says this to the captain, who is too busy grovelling and vomiting in the liquid mud to listen attentively.

He turns to the rest of us. 'We've got a scent of the 'skins. Close by, no more than a kilometre. Arm, load and follow. No noise. Especially you skinbait.'

That's what we are to them. Not Imperial Guard, not fellow troopers, not noble soldiers from the Jopall Indentured Squadrons. No matter most of us are from good, up-hive stock, no matter our comrades are even now defending the walls of Tartarus Hive against the Invasion.

We are skinbait. Nothing. Lower than scum.

For these Skinners set the value of scum. There are juve-gangs from the Tartarus underhive I'd have more respect for.

It is my considerable misfortune, mine and the other members of my squad, to have been sent to Cerbera Base to undergo jungle warfare training with the ork hunters just as the war for beloved Armageddon began. There is no hope of rejoining our company or hive. We are stuck for the duration, seconded to one of the most notorious units of 'skull-takers', the so-called Keyser's Skinners.

Once in a while, from very far away, we hear the thump of artillery or the scream of ram-jets. Open war is being waged in the lands beyond the jungle, far away. It may as well be on another world. Word is Yarrick himself had returned. Oh to be part of that!

Oh to not be part of this... I believe the Skull-takers have been fighting the feral greenskins for so long, they have begun to mirror what they fight. The least of them are painted and pierced, the worst have implanted tusks jutting from their jawlines. All have ork finger-bones, teeth and ears dangling from them as grisly trophies. They have no official chain of command. They respect no rank or authority other than their own. I have been told they elect their leaders. Think of that!

We edge forward now, slopping through the pools of mire; thick, sticky fluid like mucus. Dragonflies, with stained-glass wings as wide as a man's arm span, cross the glades, beating the air louder than the blade-fans of the air-cars in Tartarus' elite district. Skaters as big as my hand skitter across the sheened water.

Pig tells us we're wading through sap, sap drooled out of the fleshy cycads and root-ferns all around. He snorts again. It's hard to catch my breath, the air is so humid. The Skinners though... they move so silently. They disturb nothing. They make no ripples, leave no trace. Their damn boots never get stuck in the mud-pools. Their sleeves never catch on thorns. Fronds never whip back as they pass. Bark doesn't snap as they climb over it. Even cobwebs remain miraculously intact, as if the Skinners were never there.

For coarse brutes, they move with unimaginable care and enviable skill. We Jopall blunder like fools amongst them. I spent four weeks last summer on a covert training course at the Hades Hive Guard Academy. I did well. I thought I was good. How... how in the name of the Emperor who watches us all do you not make a ripple when you wade through water?

We stop once more, and I lean against the bole of a giant ginkgo. Something has laid a clutch of wet, yellow eggs in the fabric of my jacket cuff. The size of rice grains, they glisten. I shudder and make to wipe them off.

A dirty hand grabs mine and stops me. It is the Skinner with the blackened eye sockets.

'Don't touch them. Rot-wasp eggs. Be thankful they chose your fancy jacket to lay in and not your ear, or your genitals, or your tear-ducts.'

He scrapes the eggs off me with the blade of a rusty shearknife.

I look at him, bewildered.

'You wanna wake up with larvae munching out of your nose? Eating out your brain?'

I shake my head. Who would?

He chuckles.

'What's your name?' I ask.

'Deadhead.'

'No... your real name.'

'Er... Rickles,' he replies, as if he has to think about it. Then he turns away.

'Don't you want to know my name?' I call after him.

He turns back with a shrug. 'No point remembering the name of a skinbait who'll be dead by tonight. I'll never use your name anyway.'

Anger puffs up inside me, dry and fire-hot despite my sweat. 'I'm Corporal Ondy Scalber of the Jopall Indentured, you scum-sucker! Remember it! Emperor help you that you do ever have to use it!'

He grins, as if my forthright attitude has impressed him.

But he punches me in the mouth anyway.

We press on, the ever-quiet Skinners silently punishing every clumsy stumble of us Jopall. We reach a glade where the vast upper canopy is broken and sunlight streams down bright as lasers. There are flowers here, floating on the frothy, weed-choked water, huge flowers with shocking pink heads. Vast insects too, slow and drowsy, buzzing the air like chainswords and dripping nectar from each hideously limp proboscis. A pallid white serpent with vestigial limbs slides through the murk between my legs. My friend, Trooper Rokar, starts to whimper. He has just discovered that something unseen and submerged has gnawed off the cap of his boot... along with two of his smaller toes.

I was in a scholam with Rokar. I pity him. His injury. His weakness.

The scouts come back, two of them. We never see the third again. They confer with Keyser for a while. Then he tells us, low and mean, there's a nest nearby and we must fan out.

Rokar is whimpering even more now, and begins to climb up into a tree. The captain tries to call him down. Rokar shakes his head, refusing, terrified.

Keyser gets him out of the tree. He throws a stab-knife and impales my old friend through the sternum. Rokar drops and hits the ooze with a wet slap. His body sinks.

'He was no use to us anyway. A liability. Worse than a liability,' Keyser tells the captain.

The captain is speechless with rage and horror. We all are. I don't know what to think or feel any more.

I am sent on the right hand side of the fan advance, with

Deadhead and Pig, and another Skinner called Toaster who hefts a heavy flamer unit. Trooper Flinder of the Jopall is with us.

Pig stops us under the shade of a horsetail and smears foul smelling grease over our skin from a dirty pot. Now we smell as bad as the Skinners, and I notice for the first time that they are caked in the stuff. It isn't just dirt. It's deliberate.

'It's skin tallow,' Toaster sneers as he explains while checking the hoses of his sooty flamer. 'Now you won't smell of soap and humans.'

Pig has just daubed us with ork grease, blubber fat from their pestilent bodies. My stomach turns over.

We edge onwards. Flinder and I try to be as silent as the Skinners. Our efforts seem laughable. Then Deadhead stops me again, and points down at the gossamer skein my shin was about to break. He traces it back to a clump of flowering moss and gently exhumes a clutch of stikkbombs, wired to the cord.

Keyser appears.

'Good work, Deadhead. Good eye.'

'Wasn't me who found it, sir. It was Ondy there.'

I look round, delighted to hear my name used.

'His shin, anyway,' Deadhead adds, and he and the Skinner boss laugh out loud. Curse their filthy hides.

We crouch in sap-water for half an hour, not daring to breathe. Bird calls and insect chirrups wing through the air. Some of them are natural, some are disguised signals. I can't tell them apart.

Deadhead waves us on.

As we cross a deep culvert of mud and slime, I see movement in the far tree-line. I've always had a good eye. It's the one skill I'm still proud of. I make something pustular and green amid the Green.

So I don't hesitate. I raise my lasrifle, and fire a stuttered burst.

Something big and green and tusked and monstrous slumps out of the foliage, its chest cavity exploded, and drops into the mere.

Then hell breaks loose. There are 'skins all around us, throwing themselves up out of the ooze, spitting out the hollow reeds they were breathing through. They are lean, malnourished, pale things, with jutting teeth like anthracite and deep-set eyes like diamonds. They howl and whoop. They stink. They wield heavy cleavers, cudgels and crude sidearms.

We're all firing. Gunfire explodes from the other elements of our formation. The wet air becomes cinder dry with ozone from the laser discharge. Las rounds pepper through the leaf cover and fill the air with sap-vapour.

Toaster triggers his flamer and wastes the curtain of foliage before us. Swine-shrieks issue from the raging fire, piercingly harsh.

I fire, on full auto now, dropping 'skins around him. A rusty cleaver takes Flinder's head off his shoulders in a welter of blood and frayed tissue. I see Captain Lorit lifted right up out of the water on a primitive spear that transfixes his gut. He screams, piteously, flailing his limbs.

I had fixed my bayonet hours before, as per the Skinners' briefing. Now, with las rounds expended and no time to change the clip, I stab and gut and slash.

Deadhead is nearby. He has wrested an ork lance from some dead grip, and is splitting skulls and whooping like a 'skin. Toaster fires again, his belch of flamer vaporising a tide of charging 'skins so that nothing but their fused skeletons slump in the steaming water, dribbling molten fat.

I impale a charging 'skin on my rifle-blade. It howls and pulls towards me, dragging the weapon out of my grasp. There is a plate-metal hatchet in its massive paw already wet with human brain tissue.

I pull my autopistol and blow its face apart.

'Throw! Throw!' yells Deadhead, tossing me a clutch of stikkbombs.

We hurl them together into the densest part of the 'skin press. In the flash-wash, slivers of shrapnel flutter back, stippling the water with a million separate impacts.

The orks turn and melt away, as if they were never there.

We regroup. Five Skinners are dead. I am one of only three Jopall left alive. I slump, hollowed by shock, against a lichen-covered rock with the others of my hive as the Skinners lock down the perimeter and take the spoils.

'What do you want?' Pig asks, and I turn.

He is sawing the head off an ork corpse with a serrated knife.

'What?'

'An ear? A tooth? You earned it.'

My gut tosses in revulsion. 'Skin ichor is leaking from the sawed incision he is working and forms a stinking slick on the water's surface.

'Don't make a mistake now, Ondy Scalber.' It is Deadhead. His voice is low.

'A mistake?'

'Pig's offering you a trophy. Can't remember the last time Pig did that for skinbait. It's an honour. Don't refuse it.'

'A tooth then,' says I, turning back to see the butchery.

'Yeah,' agrees Deadhead. 'He had a good eye back there. Saw them first.'

Pig nods, snorts, and digs his blade in.

'A good eye? Then that's what he'll get. A good eye for Good Eye!' Pig and Deadhead laugh.

Pig hands me the trophy. It dangles like a pendant on its long rope of blood-black optic nerve.

I can't refuse. I take it, tie it to my dog-tags. It thumps against my chest like a rubber ball at every move I make. As soon as Pig is gone, I'll lose it.

The Skinners build what they call warning shrines. Ork skulls and limbs spiked on posts or nailed to trunks. The idea is the 'skins will now shun this area because it stinks of murder and defeat. But the Skinners wire up the remnants to grenades anyway, in case the 'skins decide to recover their dead.

It's what Keyser calls a win-win situation.

Keyser. I see him across the clearing as the Skinners raise the ork heads on display all around us. He is bent over the eviscerated body of Captain Lorit, who is cruelly still alive. Toaster says Keyser is giving the captain last rites. I see the sudden twist of Keyser's hand. That wasn't last rites as we know it.

The nest is close. We move in, forming small groups. I find myself with Pig, Toaster, and two other Skinners called Slipknot and Buck.

In the glade ahead, swathed in vapour, rises a great, ghostly tree. I sense it is not one tree but several that have become wrapped around each other over time. Hundreds of metres tall and thousands of years old, the great, entwined trunks are lifted clear of the water by a vast raft of winding roots. Birds flitter in the upper canopy. Beetles crawl and gnaw on the exposed roots.

We enter the root system, finding a tunnel half-filled with rank water. The roots coil and interlock above our stooped heads, reminding me of the interlocking arch vaults of the glorious Ecclesiarchy chapel back home on Jopall.

Toaster leads the way. We can smell the leaking promethium of his blackened flamer.

Buck shows me how to take a strip of field dressing and soak it in the swamp water to make a breath mask. Already, the pungent smoke of fires deliberately lit by the scouts on the far side of the nest is creeping back to us.

I breathe through wet gauze.

They're on us a moment later. Toaster scours the tunnel with his flamer, but they're pouring out of side turnings we didn't even see. I'm killing them even as I realise these are youngsters, small ork spawn no taller than my waist, weeping and shrieking as they run from the smoke.

Children. That's what we'd call them.

I don't care any more. Slipknot and I push down a side-vent, clawing our way through the tangles of black roots, and engage fierce 'skin youths, who jab at us with short spears and broken blades.

No match for las fire.

'This way, Good Eye!' I hear Slipknot shout.

Then I'm into a larger root cavity, with Buck and Slipknot on my heels. We can still hear the rasp of Toaster's flamer nearby, and smell the burning promethium.

Feral orks are all around us now, many full-grown and massive. Some have guns. Slipknot is blown apart by a bolt round. His left hand slaps against my shoulder as it is blown clear of his carcass.

I kill the ork with the bolter. Then Buck and I pepper the cavity with random automatic fire. Green blood splats and sprays in the close air.

An ork is right on top of me, howling, raising a blade in a meaty paw bigger then my head. My gun is out. I fumble. It sees the eye bouncing across my chest and it seems to make it pause. I need no further urging. I slam the bayonet up into its jutting chin so the blade-end punches out through the back of its skull. Its huge jaws, spasming shut as it dies, bite the end off my lasgun.

I take up its blade in my right hand, holding my autopistol in my left. With the blade I dash out 'skin brains. With the pistol I wound and cripple and kill. I am plastered with 'skin blood now, as feral as the things I slay, murderous, wanton, out of my mind.

Jopall seems a long, long way away. Further than ever before.

And I know now I can't go back there.

Not now.

Not after this.

Toaster comes in behind us and yells for us to drop. Buck does, and I pull my head down as the flamer wash gusts like a sun's heat over our heads, incinerating the rest of the chamber.

We're all laughing as we clamber out of the nest. Golder and Spaff, the remaining Indentured Squadrons, look as me as if I have run mad. I know how I must look to them, singed and filthy and covered in 'skin blood that is baked like treacle. I don't care. I don't care what they think. I don't care for anything any more.

Keyser is fighting the boss. Driven out by the smoke and carrying a ragged stomach wound, the massive 'skin has found himself cornered in a sap-pool east of the nest. Keyser confronts him. We all group around to watch. No one interferes. We just watch and whoop and chant.

Like orks.

The 'skin boss is one hundred kilos heavier than Keyser, and massively muscled, with molars like daggers and tusks like bayonets. It wears a turtle-shell breast plate, and carries a hooked bill on one paw and a gutting knife in the other. Its torn belly oozes foul-smelling ichor, making the thing crouch.

Keyser, lank and lean in tattered camo-fatigues and webbing, his skin white with paint, has only a shear-knife. They circle and jab. We stand around the clearing, clapping and cheering, chanting 'Key-ser! Key-ser!' like animals. The boss circles in, sidestepping Keyser's blade and taking a decent cut of meat from Keyser's left thigh with its bill. In return, Keyser swings and kicks the monster square in its wounded abdomen, throwing it back into the water in a spray of slime.

The boss rises to its feet awkwardly. Keyser is now limping from the ragged slice in the meat of his thigh, a slice that has flapped the skin open to show pink meat and gleaming white bone.

Another swing with the bill, an evasive deflection from Keyser's knife. How can he go on with a wound that bad, I wonder?

But he does. Keyser splashes through the churning, foamy water and rips his blade along the boss' forearm, causing it to drop its bill.

Then Keyser swings in counter-clockwise and buries his blade up to the hilt in the boss' throat.

Gurgling and aspirating mists of blood, the boss falls on its back, surging water across the clearing under its vast bulk. And dies.

We chant Keyser's name so loud that leaves shake loose and drop from the canopy.

Ondy Scalber is dead. He died somewhere and somewhen in the glades of Armageddon's vicious jungles.

I only barely remember him now. He was a good sort, I suppose.

What I am become now, only time will tell. I hate it, yet I love it too. It is a way of life and of death that appeals to me in its simplicity. To hunt, to kill, to be a better hunter and better killer than the brutes we stalk. To be Good Eye.

One day, perhaps, I'll remember Jopall and the life I had there. Perhaps. I may wake screaming in the night, dreaming of it. I may not.

The Green waits for me. There I will do my work, in the Emperor's name. There I will find my glory.

WULFEN

CHRIS WRAIGHT

His smell makes my nostrils pucker. Somehow, even amid all the grime and misery of this place, I can still detect his stink, like a clot of sweaty blood that won't dislodge.

'Name,' I say again, wondering if he is capable of answering me.

He stares back, looking through me, slumped against the walls of Cell 7897, his limbs slack and his palms upturned.

I stare back at him, forcing myself to go through the prescribed procedure. Coteaz will want details of all of this. I do not wish to disappoint Coteaz; no sane woman would.

He is painfully thin. His cheeks are cadaverously sunken, his uniform hangs loosely about him. I can see a griddle pattern of ribs under his torn flak jacket. A hastily stitched regiment badge hangs from his chest. It bears the words 'Creed's Blade'.

All the other subjects have the same badges on their uniforms. I find the name ridiculous. Everything about these people is ridiculous. They were brave but stupid.

Perhaps there is little difference.

'Tell me your name.'

The cell is just like all the rest: metal walls running with corrosion, lit up by a single dirty lumen bar. It is dank, overheated, thick with the accumulated verdigris of human misery.

I wonder for how many centuries it has been in use. I wonder how many men and women have found themselves here, locked deep inside Coteaz's fortress-moon without hope of release or recovery. None of them, I notice, took the time to scrawl their names on the wall or leave marks indicating their presence. Perhaps they would have done so if they had been incarcerated in some other kind of institution, one where a hope, however small, remained that they would see sunlight again.

But this is Coteaz's place. They do not need to be told that to know that their lives are over. Only a very few are brought into the sunless chambers of the Inquisitor Lord; those who are damned, or have witnessed damnation, or who know too much, or who do not know enough.

'You can still serve. Even now. Give me your name. That will be a start.'

I know his name. His name is Mattias Morbach. I know that he was once a sergeant in the 345th Cadian Armoured, and that he had a wife and family on Ulthor before it was destroyed. I know that he joined up with the Creed's Blade regiment soon after that. Perhaps he was driven by grief; he does not seem to me to have the wide-eyed idealism of some of the others I have seen.

I know all the things I am asking him to tell me, but information, at this stage, is not important. I wish him to start with the simple things, and then perhaps we will be able to move on to those things that are less simple. So many of those poor souls brought here can no longer talk at all. I wonder if he is one of them.

I crouch before him. My soft leather boots crease. I feel my fur-lined cloak settle over my shoulders and the holster of my bolt pistol pinch at my armoured waist. I am warm, and I am beginning to sweat. Briefly I consider removing my cloak, but it would diminish my presence and I am reluctant to lose the trappings of authority.

I am Alisa Damietta, inquisitor of the holy Ordo Malleus. I have standards to maintain.

'I know you have suffered. Tell me your name. You can still serve. We are not wolves, we are here to help you.'

Then he looks at me. I wonder what I said to unlock his attention. His eyes swim into focus, which is obviously painful for him. For the first time he seems to realise where he is.

'Morbach,' he mumbles. 'Sergeant.'

'Good,' I say. 'That is a start. Let us build on it.'

He keeps talking. I am pleasantly surprised. None of the others got further than giving me their name. I listen. He tells me how he joined up with Creed's Blade, what their hopes were, how they planned for the attack. I am moderately interested in this and ensure the words are recorded for further analysis. Perhaps someone in authority on what remains of Cadia can be implicated for the fiasco. It always helps to have someone to blame.

'Good,' I say. My voice does not do soft cadences easily; I have to work to keep it encouraging. 'Now tell me what happened when you got there.'

He doesn't reply at once. The stink of fear returns; an animal response.

'Do you mean...?' he begins.

'Yes,' I say calmly. 'Tell me what happened on Voidsoul.'

The world's name makes him shiver. Despite the uncomfortable ambient heat he seems incapable of getting warm.

But he starts to talk, and he keeps talking. Perhaps he needs to. I record all these words and listen carefully as they are stored.

'We could see it from space before we landed,' he says. 'Red, like a scab on the void. Saw things moving across it. Thought they were clouds. Storm clouds. Remember thinking the descent will be tough. That was my main concern: might not make it down, miss out on the fighting.'

He gives a strange half-smile, a wry one, and his lips twist awkwardly. I see that he is breathing more heavily. His pupils start to dilate and a thin gloss of sweat forms on his forehead.

'But we did. Somehow, we got down. Carriers discharged early. Landers shot down, too fast, far too fast. Everyone on edge. Knew something was wrong – air in the crew chamber suffocating. Everything vibrating, coming apart. Heard screaming. From *outside*. Checked my weapon, and my hands were shaking. Served for twenty years. Seen plenty of bad things. Hands never shook before.'

I watch him carefully. I note the red rims around his eyes and the twitching of his dry fingers. I see saliva at the corners of his mouth. I see his pupils dart back and forth.

He is there now. He is back on Voidsoul with his foolish brothers.

'Made planetfall. Doors opened. Holy Throne, I don't... I don't have the words.'

He thinks, he remembers. His brow creases into withered folds.

'The sky. Like... boiling blood. Everything stank. Hot metal and smoke. Couldn't hear anything, not on the comm, not from anything. Screaming just made you want to cover your ears and cower. The air was screaming. Understand? The *air* was screaming.'

I begin to make preparations. I have seen men lose themselves in testimony such as this. I don't want to kill him unless I have to, so must be careful. For all that, I feel a vestige of pity for him. No human should witness what he has witnessed.

'Some couldn't get up – just wept in their harnesses, rocking like children. I got up, though. Started to break out. We ran down the ramps, trying battle-cries, trying to see where the standards were raised. Saw landers explode as they came down, hundreds of them, flaming. Saw the sky blister, like... boils. Like boils bursting.'

He shudders. He sweats.

'*They* came,' he says, and gaunt horror fills his face. 'Swarms, thousands, over the red earth, flickering, shrieking. Saw them rip through whole battalions, carving them up. Like slabs of meat, gorging on blood, gulping it, gargling into it. Striding, trailing smog and guts, grinning, tearing. Red horns, teeth like black needles, and their eyes... The *eyes*...'

I sense the time has passed; he is falling into apoplexy. I should stop this, but I wish to learn more.

Let me be candid: I wish I could have seen what he has seen, if only for a second. The neverborn are my life's study, but I have never been to one of their worlds. How could I? They would devour one of my kind in the space of a heartbeat. But part of me, a forbidden part that condemns me, wishes to glimpse what terrible places spawn the creatures of our nightmares. I will no doubt be punished for that yearning one day, but still it remains.

So I let him speak.

'We tried to ascend a ridge, one running up from where our lander had come down. Somehow a command group had reached the summit. They'd got a banner up. Remember running towards it, tripping over rocks as sharp as knives, hearing my comrades being cut apart. Took seconds, just a few seconds, and so many had already died. Knew I was next. Emperor damn me, but I *wanted* to die! Shaking so hard I couldn't carry my weapon. Wanted to vomit but my body wouldn't let me. They followed us. So *fast!*'

He gets more agitated. I withdraw, ready to prepare a sedative. This is interesting, and I resolve to petition Coteaz for more time with this one.

I don't know how I miss his movement. He looks so near to death – he should be incapable of anything but an exhausted torpor – but he suddenly bursts up from the floor. His eyes are raging, splayed wide in terror and desperation. He does not see me; he sees the creatures of Voidsoul. For a moment, I am exposed.

He goes for my face, fingernails raking. I jerk back, feeling his skin-and-bone frame clatter against my gilt-edged breastplate. He screams at me, and his dehydrated spittle sticks against my cheeks.

I twist around, striking him on the shoulder with my closed fist. He crumples instantly, and something snaps under his skin. I follow up quickly, smoothly, drawing my pistol and cracking the grip across his temple.

He falls, out cold, scrawny limbs akimbo on the metal. Spots of blood mark his soiled uniform and drip onto the pressed-mesh floor. I am tempted to hit him again, just to discharge the shame I am already feeling, but I do not.

It is then that I see something on his neck, something I had missed before.

I stoop over him again, noting his trembling breaths and twitching fingers. Something is embedded in his flesh just below his shoulder-blade. The rough fabric of his jacket has come open, exposing grey, bone-stretched skin underneath. An angry weal disfigures it, raised and tight to the touch.

I probe gently, pressing gloved fingers on either side of the wound. The skin breaks and a foul swell of pus emerges. It is followed by a thin object, smooth like a pine-needle but triangular in shape, slightly curved and tapered, as long as my finger from knuckle to tip.

I withdraw it carefully. It has the look of a talon or a claw. Knowing where he has been, my first instinct is to destroy it, but something holds me back. I do not sense any corruption in it, and my sense for such things is usually good.

So I take it. I stow it in a capsule at my belt and pull away from the twisted body of Mattias Morbach. I regret that I allowed matters to get out of hand. He is scheduled for destruction; if I had more time, I might discover something of value.

I pull myself upright and dust myself down. A residual trace of mortal stink lingers on my fine apparel, a hazard of such dreary work. I turn, depressing the rune on my glove's lining that will open the doors and allow me to leave the cell.

I am calm. The momentary exertion did not seriously trouble me. I have certainly experienced more taxing episodes when confined alone with a prisoner.

As I walk into the corridor outside, however, my belt feels heavy at my waist. This troubles me. I do not know why.

I walk quickly, heading up from the cell levels to the laboratoria. I go past dozens of locked doors, each one cut from unburnished metal and marked with a single number. The numbers are not in order: I pass 568, then 3458, then 998. Some numbers are missing entirely. Coteaz has his reasons for such a scheme. I do not know what it is, but then he is privy to esoteric knowledge that I am not.

The air remains humid. I hear the groans of the incarcerated. From lower down I hear the echoes of screams. Perhaps they are the result of prisoners' nightmares, or perhaps the excruciation chambers are in use. Such sounds have been a part of my life since I arrived here five years ago; I barely notice them now.

I climb stone-cut stairs. Parchment scrolls hang from the walls, flaky with age. Each one has a benediction inscribed in High Gothic. The ink is brown. It is old blood.

At times I wonder if such theatricality is necessary, but Coteaz is one for the grand gesture.

'I do nothing that is not needful,' he once told me, his stern eyes shadowed by feathered ice-white eyebrows. 'Nothing.'

And though I remain unsure about that, I trust him. I trust his knowledge, his commitment, his iron will. He inspires me as much as he scares me, which is, I suspect, exactly how he likes it.

I reach the level where the chirurgeons practise their trade. I pass through brightly lit chambers, each one lined with white tiles and harbouring arcane machinery. I see rows of coloured vials and racks of scalpels. I see half-dissected cadavers and strapped-down live subjects, their eyes bulging and fearful.

I keep walking until I find Chirurgeon-General Oskar Kieem. His apron is streaked with blood and his hands are pink from recently removed latex. He sits at his pedestal desk tapping on a dataslate. He does not look pleased to see me.

'Damietta,' he acknowledges, dipping his bald head.

I take the talon and show it to him. His eyebrow does not raise; he has no eyebrows. He has no hair of any kind.

'What is this?' he asks.

'Embedded in a subject,' I say. My voice is severe. Kieem is a proud man, and needs to be reminded who is in charge. 'Why was it not detected during incoming quarantine?'

Kieem looks at it carefully. He tries to hide it, but I can see he is embarrassed. The wrinkled skin at his collar flushes a pale pink.

'I do not know,' he says. 'We have had so many bodies to process. Perhaps–'

I do not let him finish.

'Sloppy,' I say. 'I should report it.'

His flush grows.

'Of course,' he says.

'Give me your expert judgement,' I say, offering him a way out. 'Is it tainted? Something I should worry about?'

He turns it over in the palm of his hand. Then he reaches down to a lead-lined drawer and takes out what looks like an array of spyglasses held together by a cage of metal. The brass rim has esoteric devices hammered into it, and I recognise wards against corruption engraved in the lenses. He adjusts dials and slides switches before looking at the talon through it. A soft green light bleeds out across his flesh. The machine hums. It smells of ammonia.

He studies it for some time before turning the device off. He hands the talon back to me.

'I see nothing untoward,' he says.

'Then from an animal.'

'Perhaps. If so, I do not know what kind. Beasts are not my speciality.'

I put the talon back in its capsule. I am relieved to find that it possesses no corrupt essence, but the mystery of its presence still remains.

'I will make enquiries,' I say, turning away from him.

'And will you…' he begins. 'Will you report the failure?'

I do not answer. I keep walking, going back the way I came, leaving Kieem wondering. It will be useful to me to have him guessing for a while.

But he does not, in truth, matter much. My next appointment will be of more consequence.

'No,' says Coteaz.

I do not dare ask again, but I hesitate, just for moment, before acquiescing. That is rebellion enough.

In that minuscule pause, I look at his features as if for the first time. I see the scarred bald pate, the tanned skin as tough as flak-mesh, the immense shoulders with their ruffled, furred pelt standing proud. His armour is polished gold and his livery is blood-red. Even without it he would be broad-set and intimidating; within his timeworn plate he looks scarcely less imposing than an Angel of the Adeptus Astartes.

When he looks at me, it is as if he scrutinises me naked. I have many gifts and do not cow easily, but I cannot shake that belittling sensation. Of all his many powers, that is perhaps the most lethal and insidious: the capacity to make the mighty feel like children.

'By your will, lord,' I say, bowing my head.

Inquisitor Lord Torquemada Coteaz, High Protector of the Formosa Sector and Scourge of the Daemonic and Unclean, continues to look at me harshly.

'You wish to object?' he asks.

I do not. I wish for nothing but to escape his dominating presence. But I persist for a little while longer. I have been told I am a stubborn soul.

'None of the others talked like he has,' I say. 'If I had a little more time, I might discover more.'

Coteaz does not look impressed. He places his heavy gauntlets together with a dull clink. Those hands have ended the lives of thousands. He moves them like a blacksmith might move his hands – heavily, deliberately, in the knowledge that they are the tools of his sacred craft.

'Discover more, Inquisitor Damietta?' he asks. 'This is what we know of these fools. They formed themselves into an army called, fancifully, Creed's Blade. They launched a suicide mission to the daemon world E678, which they call, fancifully, Voidsoul. Nearly all of them died. The few that survived are now mad or mute. Those who retain the use of their tongues rant only of their nightmares.'

As he speaks, he continues to stare at me with his dark eyes. I wonder exactly what horrors those eyes have seen.

'We know that a daemon world is a world of nightmares,' he says. 'We do not need to be told it again in every detail.'

I swallow. There is little point in trying to hide my nerves.

'Then what is the purpose of interrogating them?' I ask.

Coteaz's expression does not change. He does not smile, he does not frown. I have rarely seen his stony visage express anything other than imperious disdain.

'One of them, one day, might tell us something we do not know,' he says. 'This one has not. He is broken. His usefulness is over.'

He towers over me. He keeps his killer's hands clasped.

'He will be annihilated, just as scheduled,' he orders. 'Now go. Sleep. Your next shift starts at dawn.'

This time I do not hesitate. He has indulged me more than I might have expected; I must not press my luck.

'Yes, lord,' I say, bowing in defeat.

I have never disobeyed him before, but this night I do so twice.

The first transgression is one of bodily weakness: I cannot sleep. I writhe in my bunk, feeling the sheets twist around me like fetters. It is too hot. The air is too still, too moist.

I open my eyes and push myself up. My vest is damp and clammy. In the darkness of my cell I see visions of another world. I see the vistas described to me by Morbach. I see a horizon of boiling blood, and brass-coloured plates of stone coating a core of angry magma. I see the sky screaming and men dying, hundreds at a time.

'Lumen,' I say, and the narrow chamber flickers into light.

I swing down from my bunk. I stumble to the wall-mounted ewer and splash water on my face. I dress, donning jodhpurs, a stiff tunic, boots and my cloak. I take my pistol. I do not take my armour – that would take an age to assemble, and I already feel time is pressing down on me.

I glance at the chrono above my bunk. It tells me that in four hours Morbach will be dead. As I watch the runes count down, I make the decision to disobey Coteaz for the second time.

The corridors outside are deserted and echoing. It is the deep of night, and the fortress interior is like a city of stacked tombs. I hurry along, feeling furtive and hunted. I have no need to feel this: I am an inquisitor with full licence to roam where I will.

But I cannot fool myself. I am doing this because a compulsion has been awakened in me. I am indulging that most base and trivial of sins: curiosity.

I reach Cell 7897. Morbach is lying where I left him, tangled and supine on the floor. I close the door behind me and crouch over him. His smell assails me again; it has got worse with time and confinement.

I withdraw a vial of combination adrenaline and locquazine from the casket array at my belt and load it into a syringe. I push the needle into Morbach's withered arm, depress the plunger and wait for the results.

He awakens moments later, disorientated and shivering. I stay close, looming over him. I want him to be as scared of me as he is of his dreams.

'Finish what you were saying,' I order.

I see the confusion in his addled face, but he will not resist for long. The chem-mix already fizzing in his bloodstream will bring him to lucidity quickly. If he talked before, he will do so again.

'Quickly,' I say, feeding the word with a resonant threat-harmonic. 'Speak quickly.'

He stares at me. He cannot tell where he is. Only when he

starts speaking do I see that he is back on Voidsoul again. I doubt that he will ever truly leave.

'Up on the ridge,' he rasps. 'They were coming up after us.'

'Good,' I say. 'Keep talking.'

And the words spill out.

'Dying, all of us dying. Fired my lasgun, aiming at something in the sea of teeth and horns. Don't think I hit anything. Could we even hurt them? Don't know. Didn't see one fall. It had all been a mistake, a hellish mistake.'

His eyes swivel, as if scanning for targets. I watch him carefully. If he attacks me again, I will be prepared.

'Saw one come for me. It bounded up the slope, bodies still in its claws. It saw me. It pounced. I could do nothing. Transfixed. It moved like men do in dreams – flickering, shifting, jerking. That was it. I was dead.'

Despite myself, I smile.

'You were not dead,' I say. 'What happened?'

'Don't know,' he says.

Then he smiles too. This time it is not wry; it is wistful. His face is transformed by it. He might almost pass for human again.

'Don't know what they were,' he says. 'One got me, grabbing my shoulder. Pain was terrible. Hurled away, right through the air as if I weighed nothing. Landed hard, nearly blacking out. Remember blood down the inside of my helm visor. Armour torn open.'

His smile lingers.

'It had thrown me clear,' he says.

'What had?'

Morbach looks at me, his eyes drawing into focus.

'One of the beasts,' he says.

'Beasts?'

'In the armour of men. Massive, grey, howling. They were

unstoppable. Brutal as the creatures that swarmed around us. They charged through the blood and smoke as if born to it. The monsters screamed back at them, but the beasts did not hesitate. The beasts could hurt them. They did hurt them. They made them *yowl*.'

He chuckles at the memory.

'What were they?' I ask again, pressing him. I remember the talon. I remember old myths, rumours, legends. I begin to wonder.

For a moment Morbach does not answer. He is lost in some reverie, a rare recollection of defiance amid a bloodsoaked swathe of shudder-cold memories.

'Saw one of them clearly,' he says, musingly. 'The one who threw me? Maybe. Stood straighter than the others, like a man, but far greater. He carried an axe that glowed with blue fire. His beard was as grey as ash, long hair matted. He looked at me, just for a second. Eyes were mournful. Never seen a face so grim. So noble.'

Morbach's smile fades.

'Then he was gone, stalking off, his old cloak rippling in the wind.' He looks down at his hands. They are still trembling. 'Those of us still alive, a pitiful tally, we boarded the few landers that still remained. Remember clambering into the crew bay. My shoulder was agonising and inflamed, but I didn't care. We got out. Limped back home. The rest you know.'

I am fascinated. Coteaz was wrong: this is something new. None of the others have given coherent accounts of what happened on Voidsoul. I see the conviction of truth in Morbach's eyes, and wonder what else we can learn from him.

I struggle to contain my excitement. We have so few weapons against the daemonic. Since the ravaging of the Gate we are hard pressed. If allies exist, capable of cutting down the neverborn on their own cursed worlds, then we must learn more of them.

I get up.

'Try to remember everything,' I say. 'Every detail: any symbols on their armour, any words they spoke. This is important. Your soul may yet be saved. I will return soon. While I am gone, try to remember.'

He looks at me strangely, confidently.

'Do not fear for my soul,' he says.

I slip out of the cell, taking care to lock the door as I leave. The space outside is empty and hung with shadows. I hasten down the corridor towards the stairway. I reach the spiral shaft and pick up the pace, taking the steps two at a time. I ascend one level, then another. As I climb, I activate the comms-stud at my collar.

'A message for the Lord Inquisitor,' I say, hurrying.

A servitor replies.

'State nature of message.'

I curse. Coteaz is always busy, but time is short and I know he will be difficult to persuade.

'Priority summons from Inquisitor Damietta. This will not–'

The lights blow.

Everything plummets into darkness. For a moment I am lost in shock. Then I regret the fact I do not have my armour-helm. I have no dark-vision and little protection. I draw my pistol and crouch low, listening.

I try to re-establish a comm-link, and get nothing but static. From far below I hear muffled bangs, like krak grenades going off.

My heart starts to race. I click the safety off and begin to move, creeping back down the stairs. I listen carefully, trying to make sense of what is happening. I hear movements from the levels below – doors slamming, more distant crashes, the echo of boot-falls. I try to gauge numbers, positions.

Then alert klaxons begin to sound. Emergency lighting flickers on, limning the corridors in blood-red. I spit another curse – my concentration broken – and start to move again.

I reach the corridor just above the level containing Morbach's cell. It extends away from me, occluded despite the floor-level glow. Rows of locked doors line each side, intact and monolithic. The stairwell down is at the far end, a hundred metres distant. I barely make out its open aperture; just a black void amid the shadows.

I pad down the corridor. No noise emerges from any of the cells as I pass by; their inmates have barely enough life left in them to breathe, and if they have heard the disturbances then they will do nothing more than huddle against the far walls, eyes open and breath shallow.

I hear more noises from below – something like coarse snuffling, or maybe growling, breathy and hot. The hairs on the back of my arms rise. I smell cordite. I smell… other things; musty, bestial things.

I reach the spiral stairwell and edge downwards, keeping my pistol pointing ahead of me two-handed, going silently. My heart is thumping.

I reach the base. I am in a circular antechamber at the head of the cell corridor, less than ten metres in diameter. It is darker here, almost pitch black – something has happened to the emergency lumens. I can just make out the outline of the blast doors I need to pass through. They have been broken open and hang at angles from the frame. They are thick, those doors. Their edges are jagged, as if something has bitten into them.

I hesitate. For some reason, my nerves betray me. This shames me – I have seen combat on a dozen worlds against many foul creatures – but still I feel the cold touch of fear snaking down my spine.

It is then that I realise that I am not alone.

I turn, slowly, and see two points of light in the dark. They stare back at me, liquid and luminous. A vice of horror seizes my stomach.

I fire once, twice. My aim is not good – I am panicked. Two shells explode out and detonate in flashes of white against the far side of the chamber. In those two freeze-frames, stark and jagged with jolting movement, I glimpse fragmentary aspects of what lurks there.

I see something huge, far bigger than me. I see armour pieces glinting, curved and lined with brass. I see a shaggy jowl, dripping with loops of saliva. I see yellow teeth pared back in a snarl, and ragged flails of pelts and leather. I see golden eyes, rimmed black and sunk into a bestial, hirsute face. I feel the rush of air as it leaps across me, veering effortlessly through my shots and bounding clear. Its stink overwhelms me, pungent and musky, before it is gone.

I shrink back, my arms shaking. It broke through the blast doors, shouldering the remains aside and crashing free.

Swallowing my fear down, I go after it. I clamber through the door-wreckage and out into the corridor beyond.

The space is silent. The aroma remains, cloying and potent, but I see no sign of its owner.

I edge forwards, sweeping the pistol muzzle gingerly. My heartbeat thuds heavily in my ears.

I reach Cell 7897. I already know what I will find. The doors are broken. The interior is deserted. No blood, no sign of struggle. Morbach is gone.

I look at the shattered doorway. It has been built to withstand immense impacts, but it has been ripped apart. I can see gouge marks on the steel, deep like stonemason's grooves. I run my finger lightly along those marks. They come in fours, running parallel.

I remember Morbach's last strange, confident look.

Do not fear for my soul.

I lower my weapon.

From deep down, buried in the heart of the fortress' dungeons, I hear more noises – echoing, damp growls, hammer-blows, sporadic gunfire.

I make no move. I would not be fast enough. They have got what they came for. They are leaving now.

When Coteaz arrives I am still standing there, staring at the floor of Morbach's cell. He is in full armour, as imposing as ever. The electric nimbus of his thunder hammer lights up the dark places, glossing them with a blush of gold.

He is furious. His face is tight with it. This is *his* place, ringed by hexagrammatic wards and layer upon layer of sentry walls. He had thought it inviolate. Even now, even after all that has taken place on Cadia, he still trusted in stone and metal to keep the bad dreams out.

'What did you see?' he demands.

I feel no fear of him this time. I am still unsettled by what I witnessed; beside that, Coteaz's fury feels little more than mortal petulance.

'I do not know,' I say, truthfully.

He clenches a fist in frustration.

'How can this *be?*' he hisses, pacing around the cell.

He is as impatient as he is angry. He has nothing to fight. He has been humiliated, but he has no target to take his choler out on.

He turns to me again. He looks suspicious. I return his gaze equably.

'All of those retrieved from Voidsoul,' he says. 'All of them. Gone. Their cells empty, no trace remaining. None of the others touched. How did they do it? Our grid has not been compromised.'

I have no answers. All I can see is the animal face in the dark – something like human, but so changed. I shudder to recall it.

As I think of something to say, we both freeze. A new noise has broken out, far away, beyond the perimeter of the fortress walls, audible even over the drone of the klaxons.

I listen, and it makes my blood run colder. Even Coteaz is stilled. I see his gauntlets grip the hammer-shaft more tightly.

They are howling out there. Out on the dark surface of the fortress-moon, under the hard, unmediated light of the stars, they are *howling*.

Coteaz scowls to hear it. The sound smacks of deviancy. If he could destroy those beasts, he would. I am sure he has already dispatched kill-teams to hunt them down, each one moving fast and armed to the teeth with forbidden weapons. I am equally sure that none of them will find anything but echoes.

I release the capsule at my belt and the talon falls into my palm. I look at it again, dull in the light of Coteaz's metallic nimbus.

It is long, gnarled, old-looking. An animal's, perhaps. Or maybe a man's, his body changed by ancient arts of gene-sorcery, then tempered in the fires of daemon worlds. That is possible too.

I remember what Morbach said.

Stood straighter than the others, like a man, but far greater. He carried an axe that glowed with blue fire. His beard was as grey as ash, long hair matted. He looked at me, just for a second. Eyes were mournful. Never seen a face so grim. So noble.

'So what were they?' demands Coteaz.

I shake my head.

'I do not think we will ever know,' I say.

That is almost certainly not true. Archives will be scoured, leads hunted down. Coteaz is thorough. In time, he will at least have a name to pin on the creatures that broke into his interrogation chambers and took his subjects from him.

But I care little for that. As I listen to the last of the howls dying out and fading into silence, a new thought occurs to me.

They came for the ones who had witnessed them. They came for those who knew of their existence and had evidence that such half-breed things walked among men. No citadel of the Inquisition could keep them out.

I clutch the talon in my palm. I feel it dig into my softer flesh.

I have been told too much. I know too much. The after-echoes of the howls still linger, eerie and ephemeral.

Do not fear for my soul.

I let my curiosity get the better of me. I followed leads I should not have followed. I thought I was doing the hunting; perhaps that was a mistake.

They were unstoppable.

They came for him. They came for all of them.

And so I wonder then, remembering Morbach's unexpected confidence, surrounded by claw-marks and emptiness, when they will come for me.

THE GLORIOUS TOMB

GUY HALEY

There has been a time of nothing. How long, I do not know. I know nothing when I sleep. There are no dreams, no sensation.

My first indication that my slumber is done is that I am cold and in pain. Praise be to the Emperor, for the pain and cold tell me that I live, that soon I will serve Him again from beyond the doors of death. Praise be! *Invictus Potens* is active, my glorious tomb awakens!

The cold will be fleeting. The pain is with me always.

A blinking cursor appears in my mind's eye. It is all I can see. *Invictus Potens'* eyes are inactive, and my own have not seen anything for five hundred years.

Words scroll across my implanted viewplate.

Cogitators alpha, beta, gamma, active. Life support systems awakened. He that giveth life, holdeth life. Let His grip be firm. Logos memorandum operational. Blessed are the recollections of the past, for in them are the seeds of tomorrow's victories.

Invictus Potens has a mind of his own, a bestial thing that meshes with mine. The logos awakens along with the logic engines that house his spirit. It will record my mental state along with his. My thoughts. These thoughts.

Initiate testing sequence.

There is a pause.

Testing sequence initiated. Engaging engine. Fuel pumps active. Ignition sequence starting... Three... Two... One...

A shudder rumbles through me, a sense of growing heat. *Invictus Potens'* joints move, motive fibre bundles tighten, pistons push against gravity. He stands tall. I feel the Dreadnought's movements as if they are my own, but the sensations are unreal, as if my flesh were numb.

I have little flesh remaining.

Engine test successful. Praise the Omnissiah! Engaging systems array. Engaging weapons links.

Invictus Potens' full systems array comes online in a blaze of coloured text, runes and informational dialogues that fill my sensorium. The date and time appears at the top left, chrono stilled at the moment my last sleep commenced. Targeting reticules paste themselves over the blackness. Ammo counts, all at zero, power levels, shell integrity, temperature, lubrication levels, fuel levels, elevation, air pressure, air mix, nutrient levels, amniotic status, biological component status, and more. They glow green against the black. His systems are hale. Beyond this, I still cannot see.

Remote activation sequence coupling requested. Guard the key, for the key is the gate. Remote activation sequence coupling accepted. Forge pass coding recognised. Identity coding AA/LIF/5538 Dreadnought Chassis 'Invictus Potens'. Remote systems control granted.

I sense an intrusion from outside, a questing, electric presence that observes and notes. It infiltrates *Invictus Potens'* body. His weapons mounts activate and deactivate under this intruder's control. I watch the power feed graphs flicker up and down. These are phantom sensations. My tomb will be limbless, not yet fitted with weaponry for whatever role I have been woken for. The pain grows. I– *Argh!*

Biotic linkage error. Logos Memorandum interrupt. Reinitiating.

This is not a phantom sensation. It is growing, as it always does. It will reach a crescendo that is not quite enough to consume me, and thereafter become tolerable. The climb to that plateau is the worst part, and is not yet done. I grit what is left of my teeth. The muscles in my jaw are wasted. All of them are. My body is broken. *Invictus Potens* is my might, his strength replaces my own. His power uplifts me, that I might serve still. Praise be.

Weapon links functional. Weapon mounts functional. Weapon interface functional. Weapon power couplings functional. Praise the Omnissiah! Engaging auto-senses.

My vision activates, my hearing, my voice. *Invictus Potens'* augurs flare bright, whiting my sensorium out. I would blink, if I could, but I can do nothing but endure the glare until the view stabilises. It duly does. Grainy and imperfect, distorted as if viewed through a fish's eye. My sepulchre has been moved from my crusade's strike cruiser, the *Majesty*. I see the Mausoleum of the *Eternal Crusader* instead, flagship of our order.

I am free of the sepulchre's restraints. The oil bath has been drained, the blast screen lowered into the floor, but I am still within the alcove. Not time yet, then, for me to march to war. This is an initial activation, as is standard. I remember everything and nothing. Only my thoughts are my own, only the moment.

A Techmarine and an Apothecary stand before me, clad in their battleplate. Chanting forge-serfs are close by, and thralls attend them. A Chaplain in robes strides the room shouting praises to the Emperor. At the edges of my sight, bent around me by the *Invictus'* wide-angle augur distortion, I see the stone of my grave, stained yellow by preservative oils.

'*Invictus Potens*! Awake!' declaims the Techmarine as he flicks scented lubricants at me. The Techmarines of the Black Templars follow the rites of the Omnissiah-Emperor punctiliously. I do not recognise him.

'I am awake,' *Invictus Potens* says. I have never been able to think of it as my voice, so deep and harsh: a machine's voice, not a man's.

'Praise be! Praise be! Praise the Ominissiah, who art the Emperor of Man in the form of most holy machine. Praise the melding of the flesh and the steel. Praise the Golden Throne, that which embodies this melding. Praise *Invictus Potens*, a hallowed reflection of our Lord,' the Techmarine says, his forge-thralls chanting with them.

'Praise be,' says the Apothecary, more quietly. The Techmarine looks at my casing, whereas the Apothecary stares deep into the distorting eye of *Invictus*, as if he would see me behind the machine's plating.

'All systems operate within holy parameters. *Invictus Potens* is functioning without the taint of malfunction,' states the Techmarine.

The Apothecary leans in to examine some device plugged into *Invictus'* front. 'Biologics read healthy. How are you, Brother Adelard?'

He speaks into the Dreadnought's ear, hidden behind the glacis. He addresses me directly, not the machine-man melding I have become, and so uses my old name. I appreciate his attempts to make me welcome, but what is in a name? *Invictus Potens* is my third. It is a label, nothing more.

'Pain,' I say. I hear the strain in *Invictus'* voice. The pain has yet to reach its maximum level, I know this although there is no gauge to measure it. The Apothecary nods and tweaks something. Warmth pulses through my wizened remains.

'Better,' *Invictus Potens* grates. The Apothecary places his hand briefly upon my sarcophagus in sympathy. His gesture is wasted. I feel nothing that is not directly relevant to the prosecution of war.

I think I recognise the Apothecary.

'What are my orders, Brother Hengist?' I say.

'What are my orders, Brother Hengist?' *Invictus* says for me.

I am wrong.

'I am Clovis. Brother-Apothecary Hengist was my master.' He hesitates. 'He died seventy-three years ago.' I have nothing to say to that. I have no memory of Hengist having a novitiate. 'I understand your error. I inherited his blessed wargear when he fell, praise be,' he says. 'The *Eternal Crusader* is en route to the Armageddon sector. An ork invasion, a large one. Many of our brothers have gathered. Do not rouse yourself overly, you will sleep again soon.'

I see activity behind him. Another Dreadnought – an Ironclad – is being exposed. Flashing lights over his sepulchre indicate his oil bath has drained. His sarcophagus door, marked *Cantus Maxim Gloria*, is sliding down. Incense curls around his grave. He is truly ancient, an Old One. This information is presented to me, not recalled.

'How long?' I say.

The Techmarine adjusts his bulky equipment. A new line scrolls across my vision.

Time check. Internal chronograph reset. Resetting.

The date blinks out on my display chronometer. When it returns, it is running again.

760998.M41.

Nine-nine-eight.

I have slept for 89 years.

Reset complete. Praise the Lord of Man, praise the Lord of Machines. Praise the binary of the twain.

'Eighty-nine years?' *Invictus* speaks.

'I am sorry,' Brother Clovis says. 'There was deterioration in your nervous system, a viral infection. It has been arrested, but it took time, and Marshal Ricard was unwilling to risk you until you were well.'

Marshal Ricard? I remember a Ricard. He was a novitiate, a boy.

'You awaken me now?'

'We are waking you all,' says Clovis.

Invictus Potens' engine deactivates. The power bleeds from his systems. The light is receding. I have many questions, but his voice is robbed from me. The clamps of the sepulchre reach out and grasp the shell of my tomb.

Testing complete. Testing complete.

Blessed are arms of iron, blessed are feet of steel.

'Blessed is he who impels them, though his own limbs be shorn from his body,' say the forge-thralls, following the same cant as *Invictus*' systems.

Initiating mid-term temporary shutdown.

Blackness returns, crowding out the world. My vision overlay blinks out, the strength goes from the muscle bundles. *Invictus Potens* sags on his legs.

All that I have left is the pain. That never leaves me. Even as I slip into the dreamless sleep it is there. It is there now.

There is a mighty clamour on the embarkation deck. Squads run to their drop pods. I see Brusc, for a moment, my last neophyte, leading a Crusader squad. It is he, I am sure of it. I do not remember how long he has been a Sword Brother, but I recognise his battleplate. Then he is gone.

Prayer, hymns and oaths vie with the noise of machines. Men kneel before Chaplains for the blessings of the Emperor. Ash crosses are smeared upon their brows, oath papers affixed to their armour by serfs with hissing seal stamps.

There is focus here, amid the clanging and the shouts, but an observer would see only disorder. Once each blessing is undertaken, the squad, brothers and neophytes mixed, leaps up with votive cries and jogs to the drop pods, another squad taking its place for prayer.

The last few of the pods sway in loading claws tracking across the ceiling, dragging them out of their armoured storage hangars. Chains wider than *Invictus Potens'* shoulders rattle as the pods are lowered into position over their launch tubes. The noise is deafening. Auto-worshippers recite endless prayers from metal mouths. Thunderhawk engines whine up and down, and tanks grumble into position. Loading claws bang. Sirens, klaxons, machines, servitors, brothers... All the holy tumult of war's preparation.

Apothecary Hengist–

Error.

Apothecary *Clovis* leads me to my drop pod. My feet are heavy on the deck. Brother and serf alike bow their heads and clasp swords reversed in front of them as I stride past. I am a Chapter Ancient, a living relic. In the honour of my entombing, they see an echo of the Emperor Himself. It is an analogy I am not worthy of. I do not deserve such veneration.

The drop pod is freshly painted, bedecked with seals that will soon burn away. *Invictus'* name plate is attached to the front.

The *Eternal Crusader* shakes, under the tread of armoured feet, under the fury of ork bombardment, under the pressure of our zeal. This is a full combat drop. An armada of ork vessels assail our flagship outside. We go about our business without fear. The *Eternal Crusader* is strong and our faith is stronger still. The Emperor protects His son's sons. Praise be.

I enter my pod. As the ramps rise, one of our lay preachers shouts out our battle cry: 'No pity! No remorse! No fear!' He, like all the serfs, is armed and armoured. The lowliest of them are capable warriors. Such is our way. There is no room for weakness. Any who can bear arms are expected to do so, no matter their station.

It is silent in the pod. I wait. If it were not for my chronometer, I would not know how long. Time has lost its meaning, like so much else. I do not sleep outside of my hibernation. But I meditate, upon my purpose, upon the Emperor's will, upon the Endless Crusade, and I give thanks that I am still a part of it.

Praise be.

A chime, generated directly in my mind by the sacred technologies of my glorious tomb, announces the setting of the mission chrono. A second time count appears beneath my chronometer. It blinks red three times, counts down to zero, turns green and begins running forward. It is this alone that alerts me to my imminent drop.

A slight shift in my mass centre. I am moving into the drop chute. There is a burst of noise from the escape thrusters. I feel heavy, my flesh body moves in my amniotic fluid, and for a moment I feel with my old skin. The pain intensifies as I shift.

Only for a moment.

Acceleration is constant. I am falling through the atmosphere. They woke us all, Brother Clovis told me. An unusual move. Across Armageddon, seven of my dead brothers are marching to war again. Three crusades have been established. War wracks the entire system and a good part of this sector. The ork invasion here is of a staggering scale.

I am impatient to join the fight. I have slept too long.

The drop is short, and ends with terrible force. Again, my body moves within the fluids that protect it. I recall similar drops from my other life, when I was a man of flesh and blood. Then the blow of landing jarred every bone in my body. Now I am protected from the worst of it, numbed to it. I am distant from every sensation, and move as if in a dream. Only the pain is constant, curled around me in my tomb, intimately embracing my shattered body.

The doors blow outwards. Pale light falls across *Invictus*' metal hull. Ahead of me is an ugly ork fortress, an asteroid landed directly on the surface of the world. The land here is dry but not the driest – sub-savannah, low thorny trees and grey grass, all parched. A lush landscape by Armageddon's standards. All is caked with ash. The Season of Fire has recently drawn to a close. The weather is calming, not that you would guess it. The Season of Shadows has begun.

It is my task to aid in the rock's destruction. A worthy task. Battle rages already. I stride into it with great joy in my heart. Praise be!

'Praise be!' roars *Invictus Potens*.

Drop pods fall from the sky all around me, igniting the scrubby vegetation with their braking jets. I am one of the first, the spearhead of the Ash Wastes Crusade second group! Praise be! Fifty-six battle-brothers, forty-nine neophytes. Various armour assets are being landed further out, under Thunderhawk air support. All this and other information scrolls along the edges of my sensorium. Bright flashes and war-lightning show through the ash-tainted sky: the Void Crusade embattled in orbit. As above, so below.

Cantus Maxim Gloria is with me, emerging from his own drop pod sixty-three metres to my right. He is already firing, mass-reactive shells flaring as they accelerate away from the storm bolter slung under his arm.

I never knew him as a brother. What his name was is a mystery to me. He is and always will be *Cantus Maxim Gloria*, and that is how the other brothers see me. Not as Sword Brother Adelard, once-Marshal, but as *Invictus Potens*.

Am I *Invictus*? Or am I still Adelard? I no longer know who I am. It does not matter. Only the will of the Emperor is important. His will is that I serve. Praise be.

I seek targets of my own as I stride towards *Cantus Maxim Gloria*. Boxes and circles blink around the rock, highlighting potential threats, mission priorities and points of strategic interest. I determine a mob of screaming xenos, coming at us quickly, to be of the most immediate threat. *Invictus* continues to walk towards *Cantus*, but I pivot his torso and my sarcophagus ninety degrees to draw a line upon the aliens. By will alone, I discharge my storm bolter. The recoil of it, so slight on the great arm of my glorious tomb, feels sublime. War is the greatest act of worship, and I perform it gladly for our Lord.

Several orks are destroyed. The rest scatter for cover.

More drop pods are coming in to land. Fifteen are on the field. It seems all have made it down. Doors blow open and Black Templars emerge, covered by the storm bolters and deathwind launchers of their insertion craft. Controlled by machine-spirits, these switch back and forth with mechanical swiftness and precision, felling orks as my brothers form up for the assault.

The rock is seventy-nine point four metres at its highest point, an alien cliff-face dropped on the landscape like a pebble tossed by a careless giant. Steel doors and shutters cover its apertures. They slide back and the wide muzzles of ork guns are pushed out. Orks pour down from ramps and ladders, orks scream atop the battlements along its craggy top. I am surprised at how untouched the landscape appears around it. No scorching of the vegetation, no impact crater. A delicate descent.

Orks are remarkable creatures, a survivor race. I have fought them in swamps, forests, deserts, hives, snow, the sea and the void. They infest them all equally. Their success makes them all the more despicable. They are brutish, violent, inimical to all order and impervious to sense. I respect them and I hate them. I kill all the enemies of man with satisfaction, but I particularly enjoy killing orks. Praise be.

'We go forwards,' says *Cantus*. I let him advance ahead of me, to absorb the fire raining down on us from the walls of the rock. Six Centurions fall in behind us. We are the breaching party. Our brothers lay down suppressive fire where they can. It is not our preferred way of combat and they will be envious of our advance.

As we approach, I kill many orks with my storm bolter, but do not use my assault cannon, not yet. Its ammunition counter stands at full, a healthy dark green. Thirty thousand rounds are in my hoppers. A goodly number, but I will receive no more until the battle is over. 'The Emperor rewards with victory he who counts his ammunition', I recall a Chaplain saying. Which one, I cannot remember. I have known many.

We approach the gateway. *Cantus Maxim Gloria*'s seismic hammer rises and comes alive.

I think back to the briefing. Three crusades, all bearing fresh names for the campaign – Helsreach, left behind by Helbrecht some months ago under Reclusiarch Grimaldus, the freshly instituted Ash Wastes under Marshal Ricard and Marshal Amalrich. Lastly, the Void Crusade, under High Marshal Helbrecht himself. We have arrived late to this war. We must pay for that with the blood of the foe.

I had never met Helbrecht before yesterday. I have the logos memorandum replay part of his speech.

'A victory is required. Morale demands it. Too many have died in this system already. The orks believe their fortresses inviolable, but worse, the warriors of the Imperium come to think of them that way also. The Salamanders enjoy some early success, but we too shall prove the case to be contrary. Let the orks taste the wrath of the Black

Templars,' he said. *'We shall not leave all the glory to the Salamanders! Let strike the true believers, the hammer of the Emperor. The sons of Dorn!'*

I hear he is a man of great temper and exceptional skill at arms. He seems worthy of his position.

Cantus Maxim Gloria approaches the door to the rock, wide and high. The orks build roughly, and this door is no exception. But it is strong.

'I will provide ingress,' he booms. 'Support me.'

His mighty seismic hammer sets to work, jerking forward, reeling back, bashing at the door relentlessly. The attached meltagun scours into the metal. Centurions join him, their siege drills chewing holes the size of plates, twists of swarf falling around their feet. I imagine the stink of hot metal. Bullets, missiles and many rocks bounce from our armour. I slay where I can, not a great tally here. The angles are poor.

A bright lance beam hits one of the Centurions, cutting downward through his neck into his body. My brother inside is killed, his Centurion suit locking his corpse in place. I have *Invictus* step backwards, tilting his torso back. I put myself at risk doing so, but this outrage must be avenged. *Invictus*' sophisticated targeting systems pick out the one responsible, a burly ork hefting some incomprehensible energy weapon on a jutting bastion above. For the first time that day, I let the assault cannon speak. The barrels whine and pick up speed. It is operating at optimum efficiency. The rites have been performed diligently.

A stream of bullets spark from the rock, sending gravel pattering down onto the breaching party. The orks above are driven back, and the assault from above peters out. I cannot see if I have slain the burly gunner. *Invictus*' readings are inconclusive.

The doors burst inwards with a resounding boom, one ripped so roughly from its housing that it forces out a small avalanche of rock. *Cantus* rips at the remains with his power fist. Then we are inside.

From that moment on, my assault cannon is not silent.

We wade through a sea of howling green faces, into a labyrinth of roughly hewn rock and abominable machines. These mechanisms the Centurions destroy. None can stand before us – our armour is proof against the crude axes and firearms of the orks. *Cantus* and I smash them down with impunity. We are surrounded, but that is of no consequence. Our mission goal is close.

Pain is my companion. The pain is constant, all encompassing. Death's legacy, a reminder that I no longer live, my gift from the Emperor and one I willingly share with these orks. A plasma burst from a xenos weapon ended my last actions as a Space Marine. I remember the heat of it, my flesh burning under my armour – agony, agony, agony searing out my eyes. They never told me, once I had been entombed, how much of me was left. We prayed, we celebrated, but we did not speak of my injuries. I have determined, after five centuries in this armour, that very little of my body survived. One arm. My upper torso. Most of my head. Perhaps my face still sits on my skull. Perhaps not.

The pain I feel now is nothing to the pain I felt then. But it is with me, always. I let it fuel my anger, I bless the bolts of our gun with it, it launches each blow of *Invictus Potens'* fist, lends its fury to the spinning barrels of the assault cannon. This weapon, such a weapon! It clears corridors of greenskins in an eyeblink, leaving their remains to slide from the walls.

Warning. Ammunition at fifty per cent.

I check the ammunition counter. It is now orange. Fourteen thousand three hundred and sixty-one rounds left, but I cannot afford to slow down. There are thousands of orks here. I blow them to pieces, crush them underfoot, smash them down. Skulls crack in my giant's hand. So many of them die, die, die, but always there are more.

'We near the mission point,' says *Cantus*. 'Stand ready.'

We burst through another armoured door, into a large cavity at the heart of the fortress.

'Here,' he says, striding forwards. He is authoritative. I wonder who he was when he lived. A marshal perhaps? A castellan? He may have been a simple brother. Death changes a man.

The Centurions are behind us, walking backwards to cover our vulnerable rear plating. The systems array informs me that there are four of them left; where the other fell I did not see. There are many doors here. All of them are opening. Hundreds of orks swarm within.

'Activating teleport beacon,' says *Cantus*. The module mag-locked to his rear armour begins to blink with unhurried blue light. I carry one also, as do the Centurions. Multiple redundancy. We activate them all. It is a signal. Outside, the remainder of the Ash Wastes Crusade will be readying themselves, singing the *Pugno Gloriosa Mundi*, ready to rush into the rock.

There are over nine hundred orks in the chamber, according to *Invictus*' best estimate. Many are of the larger kind, leaders and specialists. I highlight these and commit their positions to *Invictus*' targeting memory.

'Stand firm,' I say.

The orks stand, staring at us, roaring at us, making their crude threat displays, but make no move against us, until one, a huge beast, moves out from the crowd and bellows a long challenge. It is taken up by the others, and they charge.

My assault cannon speaks until it has run out of words. Thereafter I use its red-hot barrels to brand orks with the mark of death. It is a holy mark, but no absolution comes with it, only annihilation.

A group of orks armed with large explosive charges and crude missiles come shoving through the crowd. I raise *Invictus'* storm bolter, but that too is empty. Red mars the green of my systems array – no ammo, overheating, dropping fuel.

They charge towards *Cantus Maxim Gloria*. I interpose myself to save him, and doom myself.

They are all over my tomb, slapping charges to its limbs. One swings its strange rocket hammer at me, but I catch him, engulfing head and shoulders in *Invictus'* fist, rendering them into a pulp.

There is a dim blue glow coming from the centre of the room. Greasy smoke smears the air. Shapes form. Marshal Ricard and Sword Brothers in Terminator armour step out from the light. Our mission is a success. But it is too late for me.

There is an explosion on *Invictus'* lower portions, then another. The ground rushes up at me as he falls. My tomb's pain arrests me, but it is feeble compared to my own, and is quickly over.

Warning. Warning. Warning. Systems compromised. Await aid. Fortitude is the ultimate fortress.

There follows a long list of damaged machinery. Blinking red text and runes. All I see beyond them is the gritty floor. I do not read it. I do not need to read it. There is another explosion, this time upon *Invictus'* back. Shortly after, the systems array blinks and goes out, never to come again. I lose my connection with *Invictus* entirely.

I am left in the dark with my pain.

My fluid is pouring out through the crack in my sarcophagus. *Invictus* is sorely injured, but my brothers will slaughter every ork that stands between they and he, even if the greenskins are a million in number. *Invictus* will fight again. I, however, will not.

I pray.

I realise that I can still hear the sounds of battle, the hymns of my brothers, the triple bark of bolt rounds being expelled, igniting, exploding. I smile, or attempt to. I hear with my own ears for the first time in five centuries – the final time.

I do not know what to expect next. It strikes me as amusing that I actually expect something more, that I assume the procession of events cannot end. That is why humanity is so indomitable. Even dying, we do not stop. Perhaps, as a race, we die even now, and my situation is analogous in miniature to the situation of every man, woman and child of our species: awaiting the next event, when there is only death.

I will never know if this is the case or not. I have faith that mankind will prevail. If I have no faith, what do I have? Defeat. I have faith. Even as I die I know victory.

These are my thoughts: What happens to us when we die? Does the Emperor wait for me, whole in spirit as He no longer is in life, to call me to His side and sit with Him at the table? Will it simply end? There is no golden light, no sense of impending doom, no terrifying sensation. No comfort either.

The last of the fluid has gone, exposing my skin to the air. I am aware now, of how little of me there is left, trapped in this glorious tomb. Things tug at my flesh, the pipes and cables of *Invictus*' interface. A terrible chill grips me. I struggle with the urge to breathe, but I have no lungs. The oxygen levels in my blood are dipping dangerously low. My skin crawls as my remaining genetic gifts, the Emperor's holy boon that made me into a Space Marine – broken things now – struggle to keep me alive. Too late, too late. The final journey approaches.

Consciousness recedes. I have felt little emotion since the day I was entombed. Pride, zeal, courage, honour – all come back to me as I die, and I am grateful to feel them again. The day I was chosen to become a Black Templar. My elevation to Sword Brother. My days as a marshal. The battle on Vellinus, the reaving of the Cemetery Worlds, the misguided Passion of The False Saint Cleon, the hunting of the Ork Wyrd. All ended in blood and death. Brusc, Oberon, Danifer, Theilred, Chardin… So many faces I have known, all going into the black. A million deaths by my hand. If not all were righteous, most were. I can ask for no more than that. Was it not blessed Artemisia who said 'Better a thousand good men die than one traitor go free'?

Older memories, long neglected, resurface. Golden light, a man's laughter. My father, perhaps. A rare moment of peace on my benighted homeworld. He pushes me on a swing, a rope on a tree branch over the only safe water for kilometres. I am shrieking with fright at how high and fast he is pushing me. He pushes harder.

'Be brave, Kellon!' he shouts. 'Be brave!' I shriek louder, a boy's squeals. He reminds me of how brave I am when the gentar reptiles come. I am already inured to death, already a warrior, but it does not prevent my shrill cries, a little fear, but mostly pleasure. He mocks me fondly for it. 'I have been brave for all my days!' I shout in my boy's voice. 'I have known no fear!' But he is a memory and cannot hear.

I close my eyes, I listen to that laughter. Four years after this I had no father, and no home, but that is yet to come. Such pleasure: simple, potent, and pure. So different to the holy joys of battle, so different to the raptures of worship. There is no aim to it, no reason – it simply is. I wonder what my life would have been had I not trekked to the keep, if I had not undertaken the trial. I think this, only for an instant, Lord, but I think it. Forgive me this last sin, O Emperor.

The air of my youth is warm but I am cold. A shadow comes, dimming the sun. My father does not notice. I try to get his attention. Still he does not hear, trapped as he is in the past. It is fitting, perhaps, for the past is all I have. The final curtain is drawing over my life. I have fought well, have I not, O Master of Mankind? My toil is over, and I go gladly to my reward.

Despite my faith, I am afraid I will not be heard.

But praise be! Thanks to the Emperor, he hears me! He hears me! There comes a last blessing. The cold recedes. I am warm. I am free. I turn to tell the fading vision of my past, calling out in joy to the shadows in the thickening dark.

'The pain is gone,' I cry. 'The pain is gone!'

++ Appended Black Templars Forge note, 987721/3/2 AA/LIF/5538 Dreadnought Chassis '*Invictus Potens*' internal datalogue. Brother Adelard Logos Memorandum records cease. '*Invictus Potens*' recovered. ++

++ Praise be. ++

PACKIN' HEAT

MIKE BROOKS

What do I do about a problem like Nizkwik?

This had been the question going round Snaggi Littletoof's head for days, but the answer still eluded him. He *should* have been grotboss by now, lauded and celebrated as the greatest gretchin to have ever lived, and leading his own Waaagh! in a glorious crusade against humies, bugeyes, and anyone that wanted to stop him from getting his claws on their stuff. Unfortunately the orks over whom he should be ruling had ignored the will of the gods, and after a particularly traumatic journey through some interdimensional portals he'd ended up here, on a world mainly consisting of grass and dust and mountains, and right back down the pecking order in a completely different Waaagh! The TekWaaagh!

And subservient to Nizkwik.

'Oi, Snaggi!' Nizkwik hollered. 'Bring dat oil squig over 'ere!'

Snaggi grimaced, but picked the rotund little creature up and crossed the floor of the big boss' bunker to place it in the hand of Nizkwik as he sat, eyes crossed with concentration, in front of the big boss' third-favourite slugga.

Nizkwik was another grot. He was the grot's grot. If you took all the grots in the galaxy, ground them down to their component atoms, and then made the single grottiest grot you could from what you had, it would look like Nizkwik. He had everything you'd expect in a grot: the dagger-like nose, the ragged batwing ears, the long clawed fingers, the pale green skin, and the tattered clothing in the colours of the orks he served: yellow and black in this case, since the TekWaaagh! was dominated by Bad Moons. On the face of it, there was nothing to distinguish Nizkwik from the veritable hordes of grots that existed throughout the galaxy.

Snaggi, however, knew better.

Nizkwik was the personal grot of Ufthak Blackhawk: the big boss in charge of this part of the TekWaaagh!, and an ork that was not only massive but utterly fearsome. Snaggi didn't trust Ufthak, not one bit. He was too smart for an ork, too smart by half, with a nasty habit of following facts through to a logical conclusion. An ork that smart was bad news for everyone. Or at least, bad news for Snaggi, which was basically the same thing. After all, how was Snaggi supposed to have another stab at fulfilling his gods-given destiny and becoming grotboss if an ork like Ufthak was hanging around ready to stamp on him? It was zoggin' unfair, is what it was.

Nizkwik was the key, Snaggi was sure. The other grot had somehow managed to inveigle his way into Ufthak's surroundings, and had become if not actively welcome, at least tolerated in the sense that Ufthak yelled at him to do things rather than get lost. In Snaggi's experience, that was as close to an expression of trust as orks got when it came to grots. Nizkwik must have some special understanding of orkish nature in order to manage this, and Snaggi needed it.

However, Nizkwik must also have his own plans, since no grot got close to an ork unless he had to. A grot's natural instinct was to do as little as possible, nick stuff, and throttle anything smaller that annoyed him, while an ork's natural instinct was to make grots do everything for them except fighting. That wasn't to say they didn't make grots fight as well, just that the orks wanted what they considered the most fun for themselves, which meant using grots as living shields for the dull stuff like getting shot at. It was surely one of the gods' greatest jokes, Snaggi had previously reflected, that orks and grots were almost always in close proximity to each other.

Snaggi's preferred place was well away from an ork's eye, either doing something unimportant that no ork bothered to check up on or, preferably, plotting his own ascension to glory while a group of other grots convinced of his genius ran around for him and they all awaited the perfect moment to overthrow their masters. He had decided to make an exception here, simply because he had to find out what Nizkwik was up to. What was his plan? Why did it involve being so close to Ufthak? And how did the deceitful little git manage to never give himself away?

'Dere we go,' Nizkwik said with every indication of happiness, squeezing the oil squig onto the slugga. He worked the weapon's action, ensuring the oil was evenly distributed and the moving parts flowed smoothly past each other, then placed it carefully back. Snaggi watched the whole procedure closely, but saw no sign anything was amiss. The oil was genuine squig oil rather than some corrosive substance, and no miniature explosive had been planted to make the slugga explode if Ufthak fired it. To all appearances, Nizkwik was genuinely servicing the big boss' weapons when Ufthak wasn't even around and telling him to do it.

The fiendish complexity of it! Snaggi considered himself a strategic mastermind, but this long game was currently beyond his comprehension. He would have to stay on his guard, because Nizkwik surely had exactly the same doubts about why Snaggi was here. They were two trampla squigs circling each other – not yet at the stage of snorting and pawing at the ground prior to charging, but definitely eyeing each other up and working out their rival's intentions.

Snaggi was concerned that he was at a disadvantage. Nizkwik had been around the TekWaaagh! longer, so this was essentially his home turf. He knew the important orks and what would enrage them, and he knew the hidden strata of grot society; indeed, he sat somewhere near the top, based simply on his status as 'Ufthak's grot'. If Nizkwik decided that Snaggi was a problem or a threat, then Snaggi was likely to become squig food after he got blamed for nicking Da Boffin's hammer-wrench, or Dok Drozfang's favourite scalpel, even if he'd been nowhere near either ork at the time.

Perhaps, Snaggi thought, it was time to come clean, rather than wait for Nizkwik to start hostilities when he wasn't looking. Nonetheless, this was going to take subtlety.

'So,' he said conspiratorially, sitting down on the floor next to Nizkwik. 'Wot's da plan?'

Nizkwik looked at him, his brow wrinkling in confusion. 'Da plan?'

'Yeah,' Snaggi prompted. 'Ya know. For da boss.' He waggled his eyebrows knowingly.

'For da... Oh. *Ohhh.*' Realisation dawned on Nizkwik's features, closely followed by suspicion. 'How'd yoo know about da plan?'

Snaggi suppressed a thrill of excitement that his genius insight had, once again, been accurate. 'Well, sort of obvious yoo're gonna have a plan, innit?' he said, then realised how that sounded and hastily back-tracked. 'I mean, not obvious to *everyone,* of course not to *everyone,* but to anuvver grot wot's hangin' around and has da same sort of brain...' He tapped the side of his nose. 'Yoo can trust me. Promise.'

Nizkwik's eyes narrowed. 'Promise?'

'Promise,' Snaggi said, making his own face as open and honest as possible. He didn't mention anything about how trusting him only extended so far as him not instantly revealing that plan to Ufthak, and should in no way be interpreted as trusting him not to, for example, quite literally stab Nizkwik in the back once he'd gleaned every useful scrap of information he could from the other grot.

'Well, alright den!' Nizkwik said with satisfaction. 'Wiv two of us, we can get dis done! Come wiv me!' He got to his feet and trotted out of the bunker without a backward glance. Snaggi hurried up and followed him, grinning as he went, eager not to let this new-found trust expire through tardiness.

Finally, a breakthrough!

Nizkwik led the way with the casual aplomb of someone who had long ago learned which squig pens were too ramshackle to venture near in case the occupants got excited at the sight of a grot and burst loose to try to eat you, which areas of open ground you only ventured into if you wanted to get mashed flat by the speed freeks as they engaged in their near-incessant races, and which piles of junk were prone to explode without warning as a mekboy tested his latest invention. Snaggi kept up, storing all this information away for future use and wondering what exactly they were after. Were they stealing a particularly powerful weapon from a mekboy's workshop to vaporise Ufthak when he returned, in order to then take command of the Waaagh! through force of arms? Were they going to nick experimental gubbinz from a painboy which they would clamp to Ufthak's skull when he was asleep, and somehow control his brain and therefore his behaviour? Were they going to stab someone?

Apparently not. They passed through the riotous core of the camp, through the bustling markets where teef were traded for guns and ammo, fungus beer and fried squig legs, new boots, and armour with only one previous owner who sold it cos he got somefing better, definitely not because he died – ignore da hole in da back of it, dat's just for flexibility so yer arms don't get stuck when yoo're swingin' yer choppa, right?

Then they snuck through where the bulk of the orks camped down, which was in many respects a lot more dangerous. Orks in the markets were busy making or selling wares, or buying and testing those wares. A grot might find himself suddenly used as target practice to test the accuracy of a slugga, but other than getting kicked for being in the way, being victimised by an ork in those surroundings was a relatively rare occurrence: orks only tended to turn on grots when they literally had nothing better to do.

Out where the orks camped, they *didn't* have anything better to do. Any ork who hadn't found an actual enemy to get stuck into was mooching around, waiting either for the nob to decide zog this, they were going out to try to find something to fight; or for the distant sound of dakka to be carried in on the breeze, at which point they would take up their weapons and pile off in that direction as fast as possible. A pair of grots would make a suitable, if short-lived diversion for any number of the brutes currently kicking their heels.

'Wot are we doin' here?' Snaggi hissed as they weaved their way through the maze of ramshackle huts, crude tents, and rough shelters thrown together from bits of wreckage.

'Gotta get to da uvver side,' Nizkwik said. 'C'mon, dis way!' He picked up his pace, little legs flashing back and forth, and Snaggi had to break into a run to keep up with him.

He thought they'd been discovered when a nearby rumble of ork voices rose into a roar, and he had a sudden mental image of being chased and shot at until the sheer volume of fire overcame even the orks' natural lack of accuracy, but then they crept past the back half of a trukk and he saw a big crowd of orks standing in a circle, far too close for comfort, but all fixated on something in the middle of them.

'Dis is da best way,' Nizkwik whispered, with some satisfaction. 'Sneak past 'em while dey're busy!'

Snaggi paused for a moment in morbid fascination, as the snarling, snorting shape of a smasha squig ran straight at an ork. Instead of scrambling out of the way, the ork charged it with his own head lowered: there was a sickening crunch on impact and then, to Snaggi's shock, the squig toppled sideways with its eyes rolled back and tongue lolling out, while the ork staggered around in a triumphant circle; obviously woozy, but still on his feet.

'Dat's just Mogrot,' Nizkwik said dismissively. 'He won a head-buttin' contest wiv a wall, once.'

Snaggi started to become suspicious when they made it past the last few shelters, and were hurrying across scrubby grass and dusty soil towards the low hills that lay just beyond. However, Nizkwik wasn't reaching for his blasta, and Snaggi couldn't think that the other grot had set up some sort of ambush with any third party. Strange though it might seem, he had to assume there was a genuine purpose to them coming all the way out here. The best thing to do was to be patient and wait for it to become clear.

'Woss goin' on?' he said, grabbing Nizkwik's arm. 'Where're we goin'?'

'Up dere!' Nizkwik said, pointing ahead of them. Halfway up the nearest hillside was a dark hole – a cave? Or, Snaggi thought as he squinted up at it, an entrance. There looked to be stones around it, which suggested that someone had thought it was important enough to prop open and mark.

'Wossat?' he asked.

'I'll show ya!' Nizkwik replied happily, and scurried off again. Snaggi followed him, wondering exactly when the other grot was going to drop his brainless act. Surely at some point soon they would be able to have a conversation about the nature of Nizkwik's plan, and how he intended to seize control?

The climb up the side of the hill was exhausting, but grots were naturally fit and resilient, mainly because any grot that wasn't could expect to be flattened in short order in the hustle and bustle of an ork camp. When they reached the entrance, Snaggi realised that it had caved in only a few feet back from the outside, leaving a pile of rock and earth that blocked access.

'Dis is a speshul place for da skrawniez wot lived 'ere before da Waaagh! came,' Nizkwik said, beaming with glee. 'Dey were sort of Snakebite skrawniez, rode around on dere versions of squigs an' not many of 'em had da usual skrawnie weapons, but some of 'em had da good stuff, like da nobz an' dat. I heard Da Boffin tell da boss dat dere was probably some fancy skrawnie weapons in dis hill, since dey fought really hard to keep us out of it an' pulled da roof down at da end, but da boss said he couldn't be bovvered to go diggin' when dere woz still plenty of skrawniez to scrag out 'ere, and den he hauled Da Boffin off to do somefing else, but I *remembered*.'

Snaggi felt a grin of his own creep across his face. Skrawniez were annoying gits, all flippy and zippy so you thought they weren't going to do anything, then *surprise*, they'd shot you full of their whizzer-discs and you were in seventeen pieces on the floor. Skrawnie weapons were *weird*, but they often hit harder than they looked like they should, *and* – and this was important – they tended to be a lot lighter than ork weapons. That was important: a good shoota weighed as much as a grot. This made stealing a good weapon from an ork almost impossible, which so far as Snaggi was concerned was just another example of the galaxy's shameless conspiracy against him.

Skrawnie weapons, on the other hand... Snaggi reckoned he could lift one, *easy*. If he could lift it then he could shoot it, and if he could shoot it then suddenly the balance of power between him and the orks had shifted.

'So, how do we get in?' he asked eagerly. In answer, Nizkwik pointed to a small, dark hole at about waist height in the tumbled blockage, where a large stone had become wedged over a couple of others as it fell, leaving a gap beneath.

'Froo dere,' Nizkwik said. 'Dat's a start, anyway. Ain't dis *excitin'*?'

'Excitin',' Snaggi muttered, eyeing the hole. 'Yeah.' He thought for a second about how much he would enjoy vaporising or eviscerating any orks that got in his way with the treasures that could lie on the other side of this obstacle, and the sheer power he would feel as a result. His ascension to grotboss would be unquestioned! And of course, once he had his hands on whatever lay inside, there was no reason why Nizkwik should make it out again.

'Yeah!' he said with more enthusiasm, heading for the hole. Snaggi Littletoof had been shoved into worse and smaller places than this before now, and for considerably less potential reward. Now he was doing it on *his* terms.

'Come to Snaggi,' he hissed, clawing his way forward into the darkness.

Darkness. That was the problem.

It was as dark as the inside of a squig, which Snaggi supposed he should have guessed beforehand, but he pressed on and wriggled his way forwards by touch, silently cursing Nizkwik all the way. Why couldn't the git have *told* him they were going underground? Well, there was no way he was going to give the other grot the satisfaction of backing out again and wailing about being unable to see. Claustrophobia was not something you suffered from as a grot, or at least not for long; orks would shove grots into any small space to find out why something was broken or to try to fix it, and if you panicked and came back out without having done the job then the ork would probably feed you to a squig. As a result, the only grots that tended to survive were the ones who had no problem with small spaces, if not actively sought them out as somewhere orks couldn't reach you.

Snaggi froze as a new thought struck him. What if Nizkwik was even now preparing to bring down the unstable rocks? What if he had identified Snaggi as a rival and a threat, and was seeking to either crush him or trap him here? Being comfortable in small spaces was all very well, but that was assuming there was a way out again. It was a cunning plan – Snaggi could tell, because he'd just thought of it – and utterly deniable. Snaggi could just hear Nizkwik's artfully innocent voice now, explaining things to Ufthak: 'I told 'im not to go in, boss, but 'e wouldn't listen!'

Snaggi told himself he was being ridiculous. Nizkwik wouldn't have to explain things to Ufthak, mainly because the big boss wouldn't care enough to ask.

Well, if Snaggi's pride wouldn't let him reverse out, and staying in place and waiting for Nizkwik to collapse the entrance on him wasn't a good idea – which it definitely wasn't – then the only thing for it was to press on as quickly as possible and get out before his treacherous companion could complete his dastardly deed. Snaggi huffed and wriggled, squirmed and crawled, until finally his groping hands found not just a narrow aperture ahead of him surrounded by more rock and earth, but an actual opening too. He pulled himself through eagerly, his little pot belly scraping over the last stone, and flopped onto a hard, flat rock surface: presumably the floor of the cave which had been blocked off. The air was warm in here, far warmer than outside, and smelled sour.

His head came up as he realised that there was light emerging from the hole out of which he'd just exited, and he sat up just in time to see Nizkwik's head appear. The git had a lamp strapped to his forehead!

'Where'd ya get dat?!' Snaggi asked, outraged.

'Dis?' Nizkwik looked up towards his forehead, where Snaggi's finger was pointing. 'Nicked it off a mek ages ago. Fort yoo'd have one. Here ya go!' He pulled a similar lamp-and-strap combination out of his belt pouch and handed it over.

Snaggi took it without a word, his inherent distrust at Nizkwik not giving it to him at the start not exactly mollified by this act of generosity, more balanced out by a different sort of distrust at it being handed over so casually now. Still, being able to see with both hands free was definitely an advantage.

'Right,' Nizkwik said, emerging fully from the hole. 'Let's get da goods!' He drew his blasta and Snaggi imitated him, partly because he had no intention of letting another grot be armed next to him without having the means to defend himself, and partly because a nasty thought had just occurred to him.

'Nizkwik,' he said. 'Y'know when da skrawniez pulled da tunnel down… Were any of 'em *inside* at da time? Like, trappin' 'emselves inside wiv da loot? Waitin' to slice us into tiny pieces, is wot I'm gettin' at.'

'Dunno!' Nizkwik said cheerily. 'I fort dey all stayed outside an' got stomped by da ladz, but I could be wrong! Now come on!' he said, forging ahead and brandishing his blasta.

Snaggi hesitated for a moment, trapped in an agony of indecision. On the one hand, the sensible thing to do was to back away, squeeze through the hole, quietly return to the camp at a casual saunter, and let Nizkwik get dismembered by whatever terrifying guardian had been left in here. On the *other* hand, Snaggi was damned if he was going to let Nizkwik get any potential glory for himself, let alone any appealingly powerful skrawnie weapons. Being a grotboss came with responsibilities, damn it, and one of those responsibilities was not letting another grot have anything better than you did.

'Fine,' he muttered, slinking along in Nizkwik's wake. 'Yoo go first.'

The cave tunnel into which they had emerged ran for a short way further, turning a couple of corners as it did so. As they rounded the first corner Snaggi realised that there was a dim red light from ahead, sufficient to render the tunnel as textured shadow in his vision rather than simple blackness wherever his lamp beam failed to reach.

Then they rounded the second corner, and his trepidatious inner musings about the light's origin disappeared in a wash of awe.

They had emerged into a much wider cavern, the floor of which dropped away from the stone walkway that ran around the edge, and on which they were now standing. Both grots stopped for a moment and stared about them, the beams of their headlamps skittering off into the red-lit gloom. Snaggi's eyes found shaped rock walls into which had been carved fantastically detailed friezes depicting warriors and combat. He shuddered involuntarily as his eyes lit upon the telltale smooth lines and pointed helmets of skrawnie armour, and their slender weapons, distinguishable even when rendered in two-dimensional images. Ranged against them – and dying – were an assortment of foes, many of which Snaggi could recognise from his own heroic adventures around the galaxy in the service of Gork and Mork. There were the heavy-shouldered, pointy-nosed shapes of beakies – real proper beakies like all the boyz said used to show up for fights, not the new-fangled version with flat faces – and their weedy little regular humie mates; the four-armed, many-toothed bugeyes and their various weird beasties; even a few short, thickset shapes with prominent beards which Snaggi took a moment to place.

'Wow,' he said. 'I ain't seen a stunti in *ages.*'

'Dese gits really liked makin' rock look like somefing else, innit?' Nizkwik commented, staring around. 'How bored d'ya have to be to look at a rock an' fink, "Y'know wot dis needs? A picture of me an' all me mates on it!"?'

Snaggi took a tentative step towards the edge, wary both of treacherous footing and the potentially treacherous grot next to him, and looked down. The strange, sour smell he'd already been detecting rose up and smacked him in the nostrils, along with a great rush of heat. Eyes watering, he squinted downwards into the red glow and saw, through heat haze that made the air shiver and shake, a pool of molten rock. Most of the surface was a thick crust of black, but it was shot through with cracks and veins of liquid fire, and as he watched, a portion of it went *glooop* and bubbled upwards, bursting with a wet slowness that revealed a fiery, furiously intense cherry red beneath.

'Urk,' he muttered, backing away hastily. Still, they were here, and there was no other option except to go back, so he began to make his way cautiously along the rock path that ran around the wall to the right.

'Yoo'd fink dere'd be a rail or somefing,' Nizkwik said uneasily, pressed up behind him a little too close for Snaggi's comfort.

'Skrawnie place, innit?' Snaggi pointed out. 'If ya try an' stab 'em, da gits'll jump up an' balance on da blade edge. Dey don't need a rail to stop 'em fallin' anywhere.' Not that rails were a prominent feature in much ork engineering either, but that was less because orks had an innate sense of superb balance, and more because watching other orks fall off things was funny.

They edged forwards, and downwards, because the path was starting to dip. Snaggi was a little unnerved by that, but although it was hard to see in the fire-tinted darkness, there looked to be an opening off into the stone wall on the right well before the path ran on down to the level of the molten rock pool. He began to pick up his pace a little bit, eager to get into a side chamber and away from the source of the sulphurous stink, and realising that once you'd become accustomed to the idea of burning death awaiting you below, the path itself wasn't that narrow. It didn't show any signs of weapons, though.

Another grot – a grot less blessed with intelligence – might have made some comment of that nature to Nizkwik. They might have highlighted how their expectations were not being met, or even uttered dire imprecations for what might happen if this state of affairs did not change. Snaggi, of course, was far too wily to do such a thing. If he was going to engage in vicious, bloody betrayal – no, that was a negative attitude: *when* he was going to engage in vicious, bloody betrayal – he would do so without having given any warning of his intentions beforehand, in order to ensure maximum effectiveness with minimum risk.

'So,' he said brightly. 'Got any idea where we might find da loot?'

'Try dat cave up ahead,' Nizkwik replied excitedly. 'Dat looks like da sort of place ya might find somefing good!'

Snaggi had, of course, already thought just such a thing, only he'd done so in far less pathetic language. He was somewhat taken aback by the lack of any sign of betrayal so far, but Snaggi wasn't going to demand to know Nizkwik's true plans when there was a pool of molten rock so nearby. Let him have his fun, and think Snaggi was still taken in. That just meant that when Nizkwik attempted his own inevitable betrayal, he'd have no idea that Snaggi was ready.

The heat got more intense the lower they went – which just went to show that Mek Zagblutz had been wrong about his claims that heat rose, but what could you expect from an ork? – and Snaggi's skin was starting to feel a little tender by the time the cave entrance loomed up. He ducked into it gratefully and advanced into the darkness, almost as glad to be moving away from the molten rock as he was to be heading towards something that might actually make this journey worthwhile.

And there it was, ahead of them.

The cave led to a chamber, far smaller than the one behind them, but still many times Snaggi's height and a goodly distance from wall to wall. It was illuminated by the faintest light from cut crystals set in sconces, and whoever had carved the walls outside had really let themselves go in here. Coiling plants and leafy vines so realistic that Snaggi almost expected them to sway in a non-existent breeze reached up towards the depiction of a sun that occupied the ceiling, and trailed between archways that contained wondrously detailed statues.

'Argh!'

Nizkwik yelped suddenly, and Snaggi whirled around with his blasta levelled, only to find the other grot on his backside on the floor and chuckling ruefully.

'Gave me a shock, it did,' Nizkwik said, pointing. Snaggi peered, then gave a start of his own: lurking half-hidden behind the carved creepers was a monstrous reptilian shape, so artfully rendered that it looked exactly like a predator waiting to spring.

'Pull yerself togevva,' he snapped, not wishing to admit how startled he'd been. 'Look. *Look!*'

There was a plinth in the middle of the room, the sides of

which were decorated with more reptiles: long, sinuous shapes covered with thousands of individually carved scales and with flames erupting from their mouths, and so interwoven that every space between two of them appeared to be occupied by yet another. However, it was not the artwork that had grabbed Snaggi's attention, but what rested on the plinth's flat top.

It was a gun. It was a *skrawnie* gun. It was smooth and largely matt-black, with a cylindrical canister set on the underside just in front of the firing mechanism, and a roughly conical, fire-red barrel, which narrowed to something that looked like a nozzle. It was beautiful and deadly and glorious, and Snaggi wanted to hold it and fire it more than he had ever wanted anything in the galaxy.

'Ooooooh,' Nizkwik said, getting up with his eyes wide. 'Wot d'ya fink it does?'

'Dere's all dese pictures of fingies breathin' fire, an' it's in a cave next to a pool of melty rock,' Snaggi pointed out, 'so I reckon it's one of dere fancy burnas.' He shoved his blasta into his belt and flexed his fingers avariciously as he reached out with both his hands. This wasn't something you just *grabbed.* He wanted to make it a *moment* – something that divided his life between the before, when he didn't have the burna, and after, when he did have the burna and everyone who'd wronged him was going to be *sorry.*

'Snaggi?'

He gritted his teeth in frustration. Nizkwik was definitely going to be first on the sorry list. '*Wot?*'

'Did dat statue just… move?'

Snaggi looked around. The statue in question was of a skrawnie warrior, complete with blank-eyed helm, but in somewhat different armour to what Snaggi had seen before. It was less form-fitted, more obvious plates with soft cloth between, and a cloak of actual fur that looked far too primitive for most skrawniez. This must be a representation of one of the beast snagga-types Nizkwik had mentioned, the backwater skrawniez who lived on this world and were in the process of being exterminated by the TekWaaagh! It was so lifelike that in the dim light, the stone it was carved from almost seemed to possess actual colour.

'Nah,' he said, staring at it. 'It's just yer imagi-*zoggin' 'eck!'*

The skrawnie...

...moved.

It lurched forwards, bringing a long blade up in its left hand. Snaggi made an abortive grab for the burna, then jerked backwards as the blade came down where his wrists had been a moment before. The edge bit into the stone, and the skrawnie took a moment to heave the blade out again, giving Nizkwik a chance to empty his blasta in its direction with an ongoing scream that appeared to be in defiance of the notion of concepts like breathing and airflow.

The wall behind the skrawnie popped and puffed with dust and chips of stone as the slugs struck home, but as Nizkwik's blasta ran dry and his scream finally tailed off, the skrawnie itself remained unhurt. It looked down at itself in apparent disbelief, then its head snapped back up and it finally pulled its sword free again.

'Arrgh! It's a ghost, it's a ghost!' Nizkwik wailed, back-pedalling until he came up against the wall behind him.

'Nah, ya just can't shoot!' Snaggi snarled, hauling his own blasta out of his belt. The skrawnie stepped forwards again, blade swinging menacingly, but Snaggi had seen real skrawnie warriors in action and although this one wasn't a ghost, it was certainly only a pale shadow of its kin. It was slow and clumsy in comparison, and where its first thrust should have spitted him like a roasted squig, he was able to dodge aside from it and fire two shots.

The first one struck the skrawnie in the chest, and the force of the impact stopped it in its tracks. The second took it in the right knee, and blew the joint out in a spray of blood and bone. The skrawnie collapsed with a grunt of pain, and Snaggi put his next shot right between where its eyes presumably were under its helmet.

The shot knocked it onto its back, the strange substance skrawniez used as armour cracked and split, and the parts of the helmet fell away to reveal a face that even Snaggi recognised as old. The hair was white and lank, the cheeks were sunken and lined, the eyes milky and struggling to focus. How long had it been standing here, guarding that weapon, waiting for an intruder or, perhaps, one of its own kind to show up and take it to use in battle?

Snaggi didn't know, and realised he didn't care. The only thing standing between him and his destiny was at the end of his gun, and he was about to–

'Outta da way, Snaggi! I'm gonna toast 'im!'

Snaggi looked around in horror, but sure enough Nizkwik had hauled the burna – *Snaggi's burna!* – off the plinth and was fumbling it around to aim it at the skrawnie.

Snaggi saw red. Absolute fury washed through him, fury mixed with envy at Nizkwik being the first grot to ever get their hands on that beautiful death machine, and also mixed with trepidation, because he *was* standing directly in front of the gun and Nizkwik's finger *was* slipping closer to the firing stud, and Snaggi *wasn't* sure that the other grot was going to have either the ability or inclination to stop it...

'Oh, zog,' Snaggi said, and dived to one side.

On the floor, the skrawnie laughed: a harsh, broken sound flecked with pain and malice. Snaggi had just enough time to wonder what that was about, and then Nizkwik fired the burna and Snaggi's eyeballs fused to the back of his skull.

Or at least, that was what it felt like. The weapon's beam was a lance of acetylene fire, even harsher than normal in this gloom, which scored a line across Snaggi's vision so bright and lingering that for a moment he struggled to tell whether his eyes were open or not. When he began to make out details again, the skrawnie was mostly gone. Its legs were still there, although the upper edges of the remaining fabric were on fire. The lower half of its torso was a blackened ruin, which flaked away into ash round about the chest area, and everything above that was just… gone. Unless you counted the black smear on the floor, or the fine particles that now laced the air.

'*Wow!*' Nizkwik said happily, grinning from ear to ear. 'Dis is *amazing!*'

'Dat's *mine,*' Snaggi growled, but he growled it very quietly, because it was unwise to show aggression in front of a grot who could vaporise you with a twitch of his finger. Then he blinked. 'Er, are me eyes still messed up, or is dat glowin'?'

Lines of cold light had descended from the top of the plinth, and were now spreading across the floor. Snaggi scrambled out of the way of one of them, which ran on and into the wall.

Something above them creaked. Snaggi looked at the now-empty plinth, at the gun in Nizkwik's arms, thought back to the skrawnie laughing in the face of its impending death, and put things together faster than a mekboy on fungus drops.

'Leg it!' he yelled, getting to his feet and bolting for the tunnel that would take them back to the main cavern.

'I'm right behind ya!' Nizkwik said encouragingly as Snaggi shot past him. There was an almost overwhelming urge to turn, to insist that Nizkwik go first and then shoot him in the back, steal the burna and leave him here, but even Snaggi's greed took orders from his self-preservation. He ran on as fast as he could, relieved to hear Nizkwik's feet pattering on the stone behind him. At least the git was bringing himself along so Snaggi could slit his throat and get the weapon off him later.

He slowed and cut hard left at the main cavern, pounding up the rock path as fast as his feet could carry him. The cold light was keeping pace, spreading out and running in angular lines through the carved friezes, casting new shadows over the sculpted figures as it went. Snaggi yelped in terror as a large piece of the cavern ceiling plummeted into the fire lake and disappeared with a glutinous splash that sent tiny red-hot particles of molten rock arcing up into the air and down around him on the path.

'Keep runnin'! Keep runnin'!' Nizkwik wailed from behind him.

'Whaddya fink I'm doin'?' Snaggi bellowed, hopping and leaping over sizzling blobs. Why did the skrawniez have to be so greedy that they'd set their cave to collapse if someone took their stupid gun without doing some sort of stupid ritual or whatever was required, when they weren't even *using* the zogging thing?

The tunnel by which they'd entered was coming up now. Another bit of ceiling rock dropped, this one only missing the path by the width of a starved snotling, and Snaggi ran on while looking upwards, hoping against hope that he wouldn't see a large bit of darkness suddenly growing in his vision, too big to avoid. Then he looked down again, panicking about tripping over something and falling headlong into the fire lake. Look up, look down, look up, look down, running all the while...

Tunnel! He clattered desperately into it, well aware that he was doomed if the ceiling started coming down in here too, but what was his alternative? He took the bends at speed, bouncing off the walls, and dived head first at the gap in the rockfall that led to the outside world. It was easier now he had a headlamp to let him see what he was doing, and he squirmed back out far more quickly than he'd made it through to begin with. He hauled himself up, ready to run on and get fully clear of the hill…

And stopped. He could see daylight now, and the threat of entombment and crushing felt considerably less. Maybe if he pulled his blasta out and waited, he could get Nizkwik as soon as he poked his ugly little head out of that hole, then get the burna and run. Yes, that was a good plan, the sort of kunnin' plan that was worthy of a grotboss. He eased his blasta free.

The barrel of the burna emerged first, pointed straight at his face. Snaggi hurriedly shoved his blasta away so that by the time Nizkwik's head emerged he was standing there innocent as you liked, without any sign of betrayal.

'Fanks for waitin'!' Nizkwik said cheerfully, extricating himself from the hole while, somehow, the barrel of the burna never quite wavered far enough away from Snaggi for him to risk going for his own weapon again. Then the other grot pulled out a piece of fur: the remnants of the skrawnie's cloak.

'Wossat for?' Snaggi asked, bewildered.

'Kunnin', eh?' Nizkwik said with a grin. He wrapped it around the burna. 'I fort da orks would be less likely to try to steal da gun from us on da way back froo da camp if dey couldn't see it!'

'Good finkin', good finkin',' Snaggi said, nodding. The blasted barrel was still a bit too close to him for comfort. 'Ya sure ya don't want me to carry it for a bit? Yoo had to get it out of dere, after all. Must be heavy.'

'Nah, it's fine,' Nizkwik said, beaming. 'Honest, I'm good. Yoo go on an' check da route back to da boss' bunker. I'll be right behind ya!'

'Right behind me. Yeah.' With few other options available, and unwilling to stay in place any longer in case this part of the hill *did* decide to collapse, Snaggi turned and led the way out while fighting the uncomfortable feeling that he'd been outwitted.

The trip back through the camp was nerve-wracking, but successful. The sun was setting, and although an ork camp was never a silent and peaceful place, a fair percentage of its inhabitants worked on the basis that going to sleep would make the next battle arrive sooner. Snaggi and Nizkwik made it through without being shot, stamped on, or harassed over the nature of the fur-wrapped bundle in Nizkwik's arms, and found Ufthak's bunker just as empty as when they'd left it some time earlier.

'Da boss must still be out huntin' skrawniez,' Nizkwik said knowledgeably. 'Dere's only a few left. We'll just have to wait for 'im.' He pointed. 'You hide in dat corner, an' I'll hide in dis one, an' den when da boss comes back...' He stroked the burna lovingly, and grinned wildly. 'Surprise time!'

Snaggi nodded, and retreated to where he had been directed. This was fine. He could still turn this to his advantage. The important thing was that Ufthak died; after that, Snaggi could slit Nizkwik's throat while the git was celebrating and claim the glory for himself!

They waited, and waited, as the sky outside darkened from blue down to black. Snaggi was just starting to think that the big boss had rumbled their scheme and was too savvy to come back into his bunker when the door opened and the massive shape of Ufthak Blackhawk strode in.

He was immense, a giant in black and yellow, one hand casually clutching the Snazzhammer, a weapon easily as tall as a humie and probably heavier. He threw it into a corner with a clatter and a grunt, and Snaggi nearly jumped at the noise. What was Nizkwik waiting for? Ufthak was going to notice them at any second, and then–

'Surprise!'

Nizkwik jumped out, gleefully brandishing the burna. Ufthak whirled around shockingly fast for something approximately the size and weight of a Killa Kan, and glowered furiously at the grot.

'Wot da zoggin' hell d'ya fink yoo're playin' at?' he thundered.

Go on! Snaggi silently urged Nizkwik. *Do it! Roast 'im, before he realises somefing's up!*

'We got ya a present, boss!' Nizkwik said happily, and he

held

the

burna

out.

Snaggi's jaw dropped, as a sucker punch of dismay, betrayal, consternation and utter fury socked him in the face. What was…? Why was…? This *wasn't fair!*

'Wot's dis?' Ufthak growled, snatching the burna from Nizkwik and peering at it. The weapon looked tiny in his massive hand.

'It's a burna, boss!' Nizkwik gushed. 'It's a skrawnie gun wot shoots *really hot* stuff dat burns gits right up!'

Ufthak grunted. Then, without apparent effort, he closed his fist and crushed the burna.

'Do I look like I want a zoggin' *skrawnie gun?*' he bellowed. 'Bloody unreliable trash, is wot dat is!' He ripped the canister off the ruined weapon and threw it at Nizkwik, hitting the grot in the chest and knocking him over. 'Dat's the fuel fingy, take it to Da Boffin an' see if he can make somefing useful wiv it. Now *get out!'* He suddenly noticed Snaggi, and his huge head whipped around to skewer him to the wall with a glare. 'An' wot are *yoo* doin' here?'

Through the sweeping despair and the tattered ruins of his ambitions, Snaggi managed to point a finger at Nizkwik. 'It was his idea!'

He lunged forward, grabbed the other grot, and towed him out of the bunker by the scruff of his neck. Ufthak slammed the door behind them, and Snaggi whirled around to press Nizkwik up against the wall.

'Wot,' he hissed, 'da *zog*, was dat?!'

Nizkwik's eyes were wide with shock. 'Wot was wot?'

The realisation hit Snaggi like a hammer. He'd been wrong. He'd been *so* wrong. He'd assumed that Nizkwik had got close to Ufthak because he was cunning, because he was scheming: because, essentially, he was like Snaggi. He couldn't have been further from the truth.

Nizkwik wasn't *pretending* to be a clueless, servile grot with the intelligence of a concussed squig; *he was exactly that.* Snaggi had grossly overestimated him, and in so doing had lost the one shot he had at taking the big boss down and seizing his destiny.

'Dis is wot I get,' he said to the galaxy in general. 'Dis is wot I get for assumin' anyone else could be even half as brilliant as me! Why am I cursed wiv greatness? *Why?*'

'Er, wot?' Nizkwik asked.

Snaggi couldn't bring himself to answer. He just turned and walked away, back out into the darkness.

Some time later, in amongst the ongoing noise and bustle that forever permeated an ork camp, the careful listener might have heard the sound of weeping, interspersed with the dull, rhythmic noise of a grot repeatedly driving his own skull into a sheet of metal out of sheer frustration.

ROAD RAGE

MIKE BROOKS

The first indication Ufthak Blackhawk had that something was up was when Nizkwik sailed past him at head height.

'Someone to see ya, boss!' the grot wailed, before it collided with a pile of scrap in the corner. Ufthak straightened up from where he had been prodding at his shokk rifle – cautiously, because he wanted to keep all his limbs attached – and turned to face the cave mouth.

Caves. That was part of the problem. Ufthak's arm of the Tekwaaagh! had landed on this planet in search of interesting gubbinz with which they could make things explode, and had found very little. There weren't even any impressive, tall buildings: not that the Tekwaaagh! tended to leave much standing in its wake, but tall buildings were useful to take a look around and see what you wanted to stomp flat next. The low, sprawling temple complexes they had seen from orbit turned out to be annoyingly sparse on interesting tek or shiny loot, and somewhat overpopulated with useless frescos and surprisingly lethal traps. Ufthak had resorted to using a cave as his bunker, and newly minted big boss or not, it was hardly the sort of impressive surroundings that would convince the boyz of his right to command.

Especially not, it seemed, the group of orks doing their best to block out the light from the cave mouth. Other species in the galaxy might assume that orks were always threatening, and to be fair, so far as most other species in the galaxy were concerned, that was an accurate assumption. The only reason an ork didn't want to scrag or blow someone up was if something else was currently a more interesting target.

Ufthak, being an ork himself, was more attuned to the niceties of orkish behaviour and body language. He was a big boss now, after all, one step down from Da Meklord himself. Da Meklord was the warlord of the Tekwaaagh! and possibly the greatest teknikal mind the orks had ever produced: at least, that was what he said, and no one seemed very interested in contradicting him. Ufthak now had a goodly chunk of Da Biggest Big Mek's authority, and most orks knew better than to give him any lip lest he remove said lips for them, possibly along with their head.

Judging from the puffed chests, squared shoulders and bared fangs currently between him and the outside world, this group of orks were in the minority.

'Wotcha want?' Ufthak asked lazily. None of them were close to him in size, which surely meant they weren't going to be foolish enough to challenge him to a fight. It was not always true that the biggest ork would win scraps over rank, but it was as near a certainty as made no difference. That was why any ork boss worth his name would keep an eye on whether any of his underlings were bulking up as their metabolisms went into overdrive to prepare them for a leadership challenge, and dish out a remedial beating before the upstart got, quite literally, too big for his boots.

'Wot do we want? Oh ho,' said the ork at the front, with a hollow laugh. Ufthak frowned. Sarcasm was a concept he had only recently discovered himself – since the bigger an ork got, the smarter he got – and he did not appreciate it being used in his presence when he was not quite sure of its target.

'Dat's wot I said,' he declared, folding his arms and glowering. 'Get on wiv it.'

'Why? Are ya busy?' the head ork sneered at him. He wore the yellow and black of a Bad Moon, but the zag-stripes and the goggles on his forehead marked him out as a Speed Freek. ''Cos *we* ain't busy, an' dat's da problem!'

Ufthak shrugged. 'Yeah, we killed all da skrawniez an' dere big monsta-fings. Anuvver win for da boyz ain't good enuff?'

'Dat weren't a win!' the other ork declared hotly. 'Dat was barely even a fight!'

The problem was, he had a point. Pointy-eared skrawniez rarely offered a decent fight in any case: the gits hit you and ran away again, possibly doing backflips at the same time, which was somehow more infuriating than an enemy who ran away without fighting at all. However, at least they could make it interesting, if razor-sharp slicey-discs that took your arm straight off, or screaming at you until your spine froze, counted as 'interesting'.

The skrawniez on this planet, however, hadn't had any of that fancy stuff. They'd mainly had simple guns, a lot of pointy sticks, and giant, scaly monsters, some of which were larger than even the biggest squiggoths Ufthak had ever seen. It had been a bit of a challenge at first, because your basic shoota wasn't even going to dent one of those behemoths, but if there was one thing the Tekwaaagh! wasn't short of, it was dakka. As Ufthak had observed, in a fight between dakka and monster, the monsters came off worse.

With their monsters blown up, out, and generally about, the skrawniez hadn't stood a chance. There were probably still a few hiding out here and there, but the fighting had finished fairly quickly. That might have suited other species in the galaxy, who had a notion that you should be fighting for a *reason,* or that winning a fight should get you something in particular, but orks didn't hold with that nonsense. The point of fighting was *to have a fight.* Winning was more of a bonus, providing it didn't happen too quickly.

'Da gitz here was weedy,' Ufthak said. 'It happens. Da next ones'll be better.'

'We don't believe ya,' the frontmost ork said bluntly. 'Ya wouldn't know a good fight if it walked up an' slapped ya!'

Ufthak laughed despite himself. 'Ha! Dat's a good'un! D'ya know who yer talkin' to, my lad? I'm Ufthak Blackhawk! Ufthak Gargantsmasha! I took down one of da humie Gargants wiv nuffin' but me hammer an' a squig!' He pointed to where the Snazzhammer was resting in the corner, next to the large, red mound of sleeping flesh that was Princess the squig. Admittedly, Nizkwik the grot had been there as well, but it hadn't been much help. And yes, Mogrot Redtoof had been with Ufthak too, but Mogrot wasn't here right now, and what he didn't know wouldn't hurt him: which in Mogrot's case meant he was probably pretty much invulnerable to anything the galaxy could throw at him.

'Not just a hammer an' a squig, was it?' the ork said nastily. 'Nah, ya had a dragsta too, didn't ya? A shokkjump dragsta! Or are ya forgettin' dat part?'

Ufthak blinked, nonplussed. 'Is dere a reason yer so bovvered about da dragsta?'

The ork's eyes went so wide Ufthak thought they might pop out of their own accord.

'It was my zoggin' dragsta, ya git!'

Ufthak tilted his head to one side and examined the furious Speed Freek. He vaguely remembered clobbering another ork with the Snazzhammer and stealing the shokkjump dragsta he and Mogrot had then used to jump through the Gargant's force field, but he'd never really thought about it past that. Another ork had something that Ufthak wanted, so he'd taken it. That was how ork society worked.

'Oi, Nizkwik!' he bellowed, and was rewarded with a clattering noise as the grot managed to extricate itself from its landing site, where it had remained until now in order to avoid drawing any more unwelcome attention.

'Yes, boss?' Nizkwik puffed, hurrying up.

Ufthak pointed at the Speed Freek. 'D'ya know dat ork?'

Nizkwik squinted, then nodded. 'Yes, boss, dat's Riptoof.'

'Did I nick his dragsta?'

Nizkwik, whose job it had been to shoot the shokk rifle on that very same dragsta prior to Ufthak ripping it off and using it as his personal weapon, and who had stuck around with Ufthak ever since rather than go back to its former boss, nodded again. 'Yes, boss. An' a great bit of nickin' it was too,' it added loyally.

Ufthak sighed, and glared at Riptoof. 'So I nicked ya dragsta, used it ta help kill a Gargant, an' wot? Now ya fink ya gonna start trouble wiv me over it?'

'Not over dat,' Riptoof replied, although Ufthak reckoned he was lying. 'I'm just da one wot's got da gutz ta come talk to ya. Da boyz ain't happy. Da Meklord never should've made ya big boss. Y'ain't found us a proppa fight. Ya ain't got *respekt.*'

Ufthak looked meaningfully at the Snazzhammer. 'How about I knock yer head in? Would dat get ya respekt?'

'Dere's only one fing Speed Freeks respekt,' Riptoof retorted, 'an' dat's speed! Yoo an' me, head-ter-head! Me new ride against da dragsta wot ya nicked!'

'I ain't got da dragsta no more,' Ufthak told him. 'It sorta fell off da Gargant an' smashed. I fink,' he added, 'I was a bit busy killin' da Gargant.'

'Ain't my problem,' Riptoof sneered. 'If ya want da boyz to follow yer orders, yoo'll be ready to race when da sun comes up tomorrow.'

There were a few enthusiastic 'Yeah!'s and 'You tell 'im!'s from the other Speed Freeks, and then the whole posse turned around and left again.

Ufthak considered it. On the one hand, he could go after them and dish out a beating. Orks understood and respected violence. That should reinforce his right to be in charge.

On the other hand, the Kult of Speed made up a sizeable portion of the force under Ufthak's command, and Speed Freeks were a bit, well, weird. Just knocking some heads together might look, to them, as though Ufthak was scared of taking up the challenge, and that would never do. Besides which, somewhere in the back of Ufthak's brain was the notion that he had no intention of stopping at big boss. Da Meklord might have an accident one day, or if no convenient accidents occurred, one might have to be arranged; possibly involving a shokk rifle and the Snazzhammer. Accidents could look very deliberate, sometimes. And if, one way or the other, Da Meklord found himself headin' off to see Gork and Mork before Ufthak did, it would be very useful if a lot of the Tekwaaagh! was already inclined to follow Ufthak's orders.

And for that, he needed respekt.

'Nizkwik,' he said. 'Go an' find Da Boffin.'

Some orks might not trust a mekboy who'd replaced his own legs with a gyro-stabilised monowheel, which just showed how lacking in imagination those orks were. Granted, you might not want Da Boffin to improve *you,* but he zoomed around on a single wheel and never fell over, which was a pretty good indication his teknologikal know-wots were up there with the best.

'Wot's it yer after?' Da Boffin asked, buzzing alongside Ufthak as they walked under clear skies and three moons. 'Straight-line speed? Cornerin'?'

'Best have some of each,' Ufthak said. 'Riptoof didn't say wot da race is gonna be, an' if I show up in somefing dat's great at one, he'll probably change it to somefing else. Fink he's a bit kunnin' like dat.'

'An' ya need it by sunrise,' Da Boffin mused.

'Dat's right.'

The mek did the universal sucking-in-of-breath of an expert in his field giving bad news to one less well educated. 'Gonna be a tall order.'

'Ya know I'm good for da teef.'

'Ain't teef dat's da problem, it's da time,' Da Boffin said. 'All da teef in the galaxy can't buy time.'

'Ain't sure about dat,' Ufthak said. 'Some of dose tinhead gitz seem to be able to make time speed up for dem, or slow down for us, or somefing like dat.'

Da Boffin's eyes gleamed in the moonlight. *'Really?'*

'Yeah, seen it,' Ufthak confirmed. 'Didn't do 'em much good against da weirdboyz, but it was a fancy trick while it lasted. Fink you was fixin' a Gargant at dat point.'

Da Boffin scribbled something on a piece of squig hide. 'Well, dat ain't gonna help us, 'cos I ain't got somefing wot can do dat. Yet,' he added. 'So it's just gonna be wot me an' da spannerz can get togevva by mornin'.'

Ufthak nodded. There was no point offering further bribes, let alone threats. Da Boffin would take this as a challenge, and would do his best to make sure that any vehicle Ufthak drove was as good as possible so that the glory of Ufthak's win would reflect on him. Besides, insofar as any ork trusted any other ork, Ufthak trusted Da Boffin. He and the painboy Dok Drozfang – who had attached Ufthak's intact head to his old boss' intact body, thereby giving Ufthak a head (ha ha) start up the ranks of the Tekwaaagh! – had been around Ufthak since the beginning of his rise to power, and knew a good thing when they saw it.

'Is it just gonna be yoo?' Da Boffin asked.

Ufthak had given some thought to this. 'Nah. Gonna have Mogrot ridin' wiv me.'

Mogrot Redtoof was the only other ork Ufthak might say he trusted, combining as he did the combat skills of an enraged smasha squig with the intelligence of a concussed snotling. Mogrot was just bright enough to know he had no hope of coming up with decent plans himself, but was willing to fight pretty much anything he was pointed at and strong enough to have a decent shot at killing it, which made him the perfect second-in-command.

'Dat's extra weight,' Da Boffin warned.

'Let me worry about dat,' Ufthak said confidently. 'Mogrot's worf his weight in... Well, he's worf his weight, an' let's leave it at dat.'

The next day dawned with a brooding mass of rain clouds on the horizon, blowing in from the west towards the Waaagh!'s campsite, pressed up against a labyrinth of limestone ridges and ravines. To the south, the land spread out a little: the rock formations became more isolated, and were separated by large expanses of scrubby grassland on which the skrawniez' massive monsters had grazed.

Riptoof was not alone at the improvised starting line, drawn up by the simple expedient of dragging a big stick through the dirt. A whole bevy of Speed Freeks had decided that if there was a race going down then they wanted in on it, and a motley collection of vehicles on two or more wheels were waiting and revving their engines when Ufthak wandered up.

'Ain't ya forgotten somefing?' Riptoof hollered. Ufthak studied the Speed Freek's new vehicle for a moment before answering. It wasn't a shokkjump dragsta – shokka tek wasn't common, after all – but it had a similar sort of build: low-slung and sleek, although with enough clearance to cope with rough ground, and shiny chrome pipes jutting out at all angles.

Flashy, and fast-looking. Well, Ufthak had expected nothing less.

'Me ride's just comin' now,' Ufthak told Riptoof.

'I said "when da sun comes up",' Riptoof said warningly, pointing to where the top of the local star had already edged above the horizon and was casting long, stretched shadows across the ground. 'Yer late.'

Ufthak shrugged. 'If ya fink ya need to leave now in order to beat me, go ahead.'

He'd pitched his voice to carry over the rumble of idling engines, and the assembled Speed Freeks laughed at his bravado. Even Riptoof gave Ufthak a grin, although it was even teef whether he was genuinely amused by the joke, or just thought Ufthak was so overconfident that his victory was assured. He didn't take Ufthak up on the offer, though. The Kult of Speed wouldn't have much respect for a Speed Freek who took a head start to win a race.

As for dirty tricks once the race was underway... Well, that was all fair game. But that was why Ufthak was bringing Mogrot along.

A new roar made itself heard above the general din, and Ufthak stepped back as Da Boffin's latest creation grumbled its way to the starting line with Mogrot Redtoof behind the wheel. The various orks who had gathered to watch clapped and hooted in appreciation, and the Speed Freeks on the line – at least, those who were not already sweating with the effort of not careering off towards the horizon – gave it a once-over as they tried to work out what they were up against.

It was, to all intents and purposes, a trukk, mainly because that was all Da Boffin had been able to scrounge up at short notice. However, to consider it just a trukk was to consider the Snazzhammer just a hammer: broadly accurate, but lacking an appreciation of nuance that could make the difference between victory and defeat, or indeed life and death. It had chunked-up wheels, on the basis of Da Boffin's logic that 'big wheelz means dey don't have to turn so quick to move you da same distance', which went beyond Ufthak's understanding of mathematics but which he was prepared to take at face value, particularly if the alternative was trying to work it out himself. The engine had been replaced with something far larger and more powerful, and the extra weight at the front end was counterbalanced by a pair of jet engines bolted onto the back 'for when yer goin' straight for a while'. Ufthak wasn't sure where Da Boffin had got them from, or indeed whether a fly boy had woken up this morning to find his prized fighta-bomma missing a few critical parts, but that wasn't important. What was important was winning this race, and Da Boffin had built Ufthak something probably twice as heavy as anything else competing, but with enough muscle to shift a small mountain.

'Move over,' Ufthak grunted to Mogrot, who obliged. It was a bit of a tight squeeze for Ufthak to fit behind the wheel, since he was a lot larger than most orks, but he managed it just as an ork with a slugga and a grot holding a black-and-white flag both climbed onto a solitary rock next to the starting line.

'Alright, listen up!' the ork bellowed. 'Dis is da course for da race!'

Ufthak revved his engine, and it responded with a sound like a war god's coughing fit. He grinned, and looked down the line to where Riptoof sat stony-faced behind the wheel of his own vehicle.

'Yooz gotta go out dat way, past da big bit of rock wot looks like a big bit of rock,' the ork announced, pointing south. 'Ya swing right, past da skrawniez' place we burned a few days back, den into da gullies. Find yer way froo 'em, an' da first one back to camp is da winner!'

Ufthak nodded. That sounded simple enough.

'Ready?'

The grot raised its flag. Two dozen orks hovered their boots over go-pedals, or gripped handlebars.

'STEADY!'

The grot beamed, anticipating its moment of glory, as the ork readied his slugga to fire the starting gun. One biker, unable to take the strain any longer, accelerated away in a spray of dirt. From the looks of it, he wasn't even trying to follow the loosely described course of the race, but simply succumbing to the Speed Freeks' incessant desire to change *there* into *here.*

'GO!'

The flag dropped, mainly because the ork had pulled the trigger on his slugga and shot the grot in the head. The little green body slumped forwards, but no one noticed: partly because it was a grot, and partly because two dozen or so vehicles had slammed pedals, thrust levers or handlebar throttles as far down, up or around as they could go.

The trukk jolted beneath Ufthak, and lurched away with enough power for him to think for a moment that the old stitch scars on his neck were going to rip loose and his head would come clean off. He managed to get his body under control after a moment, just as the trukk hit the first sizeable bump. It jarred into the air, which was a testament to how fast they were already going, given how much it weighed.

'Arrrgh!'

'Shneerrrrrk!'

Ufthak had expected a bunch of different noises out of the trukk, but neither of those shrieks fitted the bill. He stole a look over his shoulder, and saw the small, green-skinned form of Nizkwik and the substantially larger, red-skinned shape of Princess thudding back down onto the trukk's flatbed, which would normally be occupied by a mob of boyz ready to leap out and clobber someone. He looked sideways at Mogrot, who had the roll cage in a death grip, and was either grinning manically or losing the battle between his lips and the headwind.

'Wot da zog are dey doin' here?' Ufthak yelled.

'Princess goes everywhere with ya, don't it?' Mogrot managed. 'An' I fort da grot could, y'know, make sure stuff don't fall off. Or make it fall off, if we need to lose some weight.'

Ufthak glanced backwards again. Nizkwik was indeed clutching a blowtorch. He groaned.

'Yoo!' he bellowed at the terrified grot. 'Don't touch *nuffin'* unless I tells ya to, got it?' He risked taking one hand off the wheel to point at Mogrot. 'An' if yoo gets me squig killed...'

He didn't finish the sentence. As well as the Snazzhammer, his fancy beakie-made armour and his shokk rifle, Ufthak had got quite attached to Princess the squig. It was always cheerful, never asked annoying questions, and had already eaten three of Mogrot's hands, which served the dual purpose of keeping Ufthak amused and keeping Dok Drozfang in work transplanting new ones on from 'donors'. Conquering the galaxy just wouldn't be the same if Ufthak didn't have Princess on hand to eat any enemies he'd got bored of.

He forced his attention back to the race. Some of the field

had already dropped back or away, plagued by engine trouble, unexpected sabotage, or a lack of sufficient attention span to remember that there was an actual course to follow. However, there were a good dozen vehicles still in the running, one of which was Riptoof's dragsta. The Speed Freek was in the lead, in fact, but three warbikes were hard on his tail, and a wartrike was keeping pace with them. They'd all had the advantage of acceleration over Ufthak's trukk, but the massive, snarling engine was starting to muscle its way back up the field now.

'Use da rokkits! Use da rokkits!' Mogrot yelled excitedly, but Ufthak shook his head.

'Not yet. Might need 'em later, an' we're gonna be turnin' soon…'

Sure enough, the rock spire was looming up, easily as big as a Gargant, the eastern side lit by the slanting rays of the early morning sun, and the west still wreathed in darkness. Ufthak watched the line of its shadow getting closer and closer, judging when he was going to have to put the trukk into a skid to take the corner with the least loss of momentum…

A shape appeared on his right, roaring up alongside him. Some git was trying to overtake! Ufthak cast a quick glance at it – a boosta-blasta, complete with burna exhausts – and instantly decided that he was having none of this.

At the speed they were going, small movements had big consequences. Ufthak surreptitiously steered a little to the right, forcing the boosta-blasta a little closer to the rock if it wanted to keep clear of him, then swerved just enough to clip it. The size difference between the two vehicles meant the smaller buggy never had a chance: it careened out of control and went straight into an outcrop, exploding in a shower of parts and flames.

'Dat's wot I'm talkin' about!' Ufthak yelled in glee, and threw the trukk into the turn. Riptoof was still ahead of him, but the dragsta's straight-line speed did not translate into being good at cornering. The trike wasn't doing well either, lacking either the stable base of four wheels, or the ability of the bikers to put their knees down. Ufthak's trukk, heavy as it was, at least managed to maintain a reasonable amount of traction on the ground, although it came at the expense of some ferocious sideways G-forces which sent Nizkwik and Princess tumbling into the flatbed's side plates.

Ufthak grinned, and jammed the go-pedal down again. The trukk's wheels dug into the dirt and it powered out of the skid, cutting into Riptoof's lead.

'Right,' Mogrot puffed, 'now we go past da skrawniez' place, an'...'

He tailed off, a confused expression spreading over his face. Which, admittedly, was not an unusual occurrence, but this time there was a good reason for it.

'Boss... Were dey dere before?'

Ufthak took a moment to realise what Mogrot was on about. Then, as the burned wreckage of the skrawniez' camp began to disgorge shape after fast-moving shape, he realised what the potential problem was.

Spikiez.

Skrawniez were skrawniez, and they wore all sorts of different colours, presumably to mark out their clans. However, spikiez were a bit different: 'droo-kar-ee' instead of 'ale-dar-ee', or whatever silly names skrawniez called themselves. Spikiez tended to be pointier, and liked hooks, and hung out with weird, stitched-together creatures which the most experimental painboy might scratch his head at, and used poisons that could make even an ork feel a bit unwell. They loved raiding as much as Freebooterz did, too, although their favourite loot tended to be alive rather than shiny. They still crumpled if you actually managed to hit one, but their amour had a tendency to get caught on your choppa afterwards.

'Nah, dat's new,' Ufthak said, eyeing the approaching swarm. One of their big floaty trukks that often carried a bunch of their boyz, a smaller floaty thing with a big gun, a few zoomy floaty-bikes, and five of those gits what zipped around standing on rokkit packs and thought they were the squiggoth's knees.

'Are we gonna scrag 'em?' Mogrot asked eagerly, producing his slugga and choppa from somewhere.

'I got a race to win,' Ufthak said dubiously, refocusing on Riptoof's dragsta. Of course Mogrot would get distracted, but an ork who wanted to be warboss some day needed to be able to think long term. Win the race, get the Speed Freeks onside, *then* deal with the spikiez: that was the kind of detailed plan that would take Ufthak to the top.

Of course, spikiez basically never did what you wanted them to, and it looked like that state of affairs was going to continue.

'Dey're comin' right for us!' Mogrot announced gleefully, as the dark, sharp shapes began to converge on the race like shards of shadow. 'Looks like dey want a fight!'

Ufthak eyed their nets and hooked chains. 'Wonder if we ruined dere fun when we scragged all da local skrawniez?' Other species might be baffled by the complicated politics that covered the alliances and enmities between various sorts of skrawniez, but it seemed simple enough to Ufthak. He was an ork, and he'd happily fight other orks if there was no one else around. Presumably skrawniez and spikiez were the same.

The spikiez' vehicles closed in, and Ufthak braced himself for the inevitable hail of poisoned pointy bits. However, instead of opening fire, the skimmers weaved their way into and amongst the bikes, buggies and trakks. The largest one veered in front of him, and he looked up to see pale, sharp-featured faces leering down at him.

Then it accelerated away, accompanied by derisive hand gestures.

Ufthak's eyes went wide with rage. Spikiez shooting at him? Fine, it was better than being bored. Spikiez shoving barbs and hooks into him? Whatever, he did the same to them if he got the chance, although the Snazzhammer was not what you might call a precision instrument. But spikiez butting into a race and *showing off*? Not even shooting, like the orks were no threat?

This was intolerable.

He snatched his shokk rifle up one-handed, and took aim – which was against his usual instincts, but he was so offended that he didn't care. Trusting Gork and Mork to sort out who did and did not get hit was all very well most of the time, but this was a zogging insult.

The rifle whined for a moment as its shokk-generator powered up, then the lower right rear side of the spikiez' vehicle disappeared in an angry flash of light. Presumably that did something to their floaty-motors, or possibly the aerodynamics, because the whole thing began to list off to the side.

'Dat's right!' Ufthak yelled at them, as their jeerings were replaced by expressions of chagrin. 'Dis is wot ya get when ya mess wiv us!'

'Boss!'

That was Nizkwik's shout, and the urgency in the grot's voice made Ufthak duck instinctively: just in time, because a blade as long as his forearm slashed through where his neck had been, and buried itself into the seat back.

'Mogrot, take da wheel!' Ufthak bellowed, and made a grab for the pointy-eared git who had swung the blade in question.

The spiky tried to get its weapon free, but the sharp edge was well and truly stuck, and the floating plank-thing it was standing on might have been excellent for zipping around, but didn't give much of a solid base from which to tug loose an embedded blade. It hesitated for a moment too long, unwilling to abandon its weapon, and Ufthak's fist clamped around its throat.

The spiky hissed and lashed out, but although Ufthak wasn't wearing his beakie armour (too much weight, and he hadn't been planning on a proper scrap), it would take more than a thrashing pointy-ear to give him trouble. He clenched his fist until he felt the delicate vertebrae snap, then released his hold. The spiky collapsed bonelessly, and tumbled off its floaty-plank. However, its mates were still around, and they bore down on Ufthak out of the sky like vengeance made flesh.

That suited Ufthak just fine. He grabbed his weapons and clambered through the trukk's roll cage onto the flatbed, leaving Mogrot in charge of the driving. Ignoring a fight in favour of a race was a fine plan, but not when the gits wanted to make it *personal.*

Combat had been joined in earnest all around, now: the boyz were having none of the spikiez' attempts to show off, and the spikiez had decided that trying to race against orks without attempting to kill them at the same time was a one-way ticket to getting stomped. Dakkaguns roared, and spiky-rifles spat. Pointy-eared warriors in even pointier armour did backflips off their floating trukk to land perfectly on engine blocks and riddle Speed Freeks with envenomed splinters, or fall backwards to go under the wheels with shattered faceplates from a well-aimed wrench.

And four more screaming flying plank-riders bore down on Ufthak.

One of them stitched a line of white-hot pain across his chest with the weapons of its ride, but Ufthak was used to pain. The spiky in question clearly thought it had already made its kill, because it swooped down with a shout of fierce joy to try to take his head off with a single blow, and instead got swatted out of the air by the Snazzhammer. The next one discovered that even an ork found it hard to miss at point-blank range, and collapsed with most of its torso missing as the shokk rifle bored a warp tunnel straight through it. The third pivoted in mid-air, causing Ufthak to miss his first swing at it, and drew back its blade.

'Shneerrrrrk!'

The last plank-rider, swooping in on its own attack run, found its board's momentum suddenly arrested by the jaws and sizeable weight of Princess jumping up to bite it. The rider's own momentum suffered no such arrest, and it was instead catapulted forward to collide with its companion just before the blow landed. Ufthak barked a laugh, then mashed both their heads with the Snazzhammer before they could sort themselves out.

'Wow, look at dis!' Nizkwik shouted, vaulting onto the skyboard Princess had hold of, and pressing things apparently at random.

'Oi!' Ufthak shouted. 'Get off–'

'AAAAaaaahhh…!'

The skyboard's motors went to full, and the entire thing took off again to corkscrew through the air with a new cargo of one terrified grot, and a squig determined not to let go of something which was apparently still putting up a fight.

'Zoggin' grots,' Ufthak groaned. 'You bring me squig back right dis minute!' he bellowed at the sky.

Nizkwik, unsurprisingly, did not immediately return. However, something did heave into view: the mid-sized spikiez skimmer Ufthak had seen before. One of the masked warriors on the back pointed its big gun at him, and Ufthak braced himself. Without his armour, this was *definitely* going to sting…

The big gun did not open fire. Instead, the gunner was dealt a swift blow around the head, and a new shape vaulted into the air. It performed a deft front flip and landed effortlessly on the rear of the trukk's flatbed, despite the distance between the two vehicles and the speed at which they were both travelling.

A tall, many-pointed helm, topped with a crest of dark, flowing hair. A long crystalline blade with an ugly, sneering face worked into the hilt, and a pistol glowing with a darkness that seemed to suck light into itself. Various hooks and chains, and the flayed faces of several different species serving as decoration on its many-plated armour: including, Ufthak noticed, at least three orks.

'Da Spikiest of da Spikiez,' he muttered. 'Alright den, my lad, let's see if ya can take a hit.'

He raised the shokk rifle, and fired.

The spiky *wasn't there.*

The shokk rifle's reality-chewing blast crackled through where it had been a moment before, and took out the engine of a squig-buggy bringing up the race's rear. The spiky itself had flowed away with astonishing speed, and was now vaulting off the trukk's side with its blade aimed at Ufthak's head.

Ufthak backhanded it out of the air with the fist gripping the Snazzhammer, and the Spikiest Spiky clattered onto the flatbed with, Ufthak liked to imagine, a startled expression behind its obscuring faceplate. However, when he brought the hammer-head down to crush its skull it raised its blade and glanced the blow just far enough off to one side, and vaulted up to its feet before he could try again.

When it attacked this time, it didn't try to be showy.

Ufthak instantly knew that he was in for the fight of his life, so he dropped the shokk rifle and wielded the Snazzhammer in both hands. Mork damn it, but the thing was quick! Its blade flashed out almost faster than he could see, and only instincts and reflexes allowed him to block its strikes. He jerked aside from the muzzle of its pistol and heard a *crump* as one of the trukk's side panels disintegrated, then landed a blow in the midsection with the haft of the Snazzhammer and knocked it back a step, but when he activated the weapon's power field and swung the axe head at it, the spiky ducked under the blow. Ufthak's swing took out a grab rail, and he felt ice-sharp pain as his enemy's blade pierced his ribs.

He kicked out, felt his boot connect with something solid, and spun the Snazzhammer as he turned. There was a *clang* as the weapon's head knocked the crystalline blade from the spiky's grip, and Ufthak reached out to grab it by the throat to hold it still for long enough to mash its head in.

The thing about spikiez was that they *always* had another blade somewhere, and this one came up fast enough and sharp enough to take Ufthak's grabbin' hand off halfway down the forearm.

'Argh!' Ufthak yelled, recoiling involuntarily. 'Dat was me favourite ha–'

The spiky raised its blaster, levelling it directly at his face.

And Princess fell out of the sky, with the happy squealing noise of a squig that could see lunch in its immediate future. The spiky's reflexes might have been up to dodging Ufthak's gunfire, but it was not prepared for a ballistic squig which must have weighed as much as it did. Princess took its arm off at the shoulder with one bite, gun and all, leaving nothing but a ragged wound gouting dark blood.

'Whoo!' Nizkwik yelled, zooming overhead. 'Gobbo to da rescue!'

The spiky staggered. Ufthak drew back the Snazzhammer, ready to finish the job...

...and the spiky turned and leaped, recovering its balance and poise immediately despite now lacking an arm. It landed for a moment on top of the trukk's roll cage, before vaulting through the air back to its transport.

'Coward!' Ufthak bellowed at it, but his insults fell on deaf ears. The Spikiest Spiky's skimmer accelerated away, swerving into the first of the gullies.

The gullies. They were getting close to the end of the race.

'Follow dat...' Ufthak yelled at Mogrot, pointing with the Snazzhammer at the skimmer, but found himself lacking in terminology. 'Wotever it is, just follow it!'

'Yoo got it, boss!' Mogrot shouted. He might excel in combat, but Mogrot Redtoof was just as happy driving something really fast.

Ufthak took a quick look around while he waited for his arm to stop bleeding. The attrition of combat had taken its toll, and there were only a handful of vehicles left now: one of the warbikes, a megatrakk scrapjet, Ufthak's trukk and, still out in front, Riptoof's dragsta. For the spikiez, the plank-riders were all dead, and their floaty-bikes had bought it as well, one way or another. The skimmer-trukk was still going, although it was a bit wobbly, and their boss' smaller transport was pulling away ahead. The spikiez might not have even wanted to be a part of the race any longer, but they were now walled in by the sides of the ravine, so they had little choice.

The sides of the ravine...

Ufthak scanned the upcoming terrain, searching for something that would enable him to enact the plan that had just flashed up in his mind. It was only a matter of seconds before he found it: a spur of rock jutting upwards and inwards. He took a moment to judge distances, angles and speed, his brain making connections that it never bothered with when it came to aiming gunfire, and came to his conclusion.

This was going to work. Either that, or it would fail spectacularly, which was nearly as good.

'Steer for dat!' he yelled, pointing at the spur. Mogrot obeyed, without irritating questions like 'Wot's da plan?' or 'Ain't we gonna crash?' Ufthak waited one more second, then used the butt of the Snazzhammer to hit the big red button Da Boffin had installed on the dashboard.

Now the rokkits on the back fired, roaring into life and propelling the trukk forward with ludicrous acceleration. Ufthak only just managed to hook the stump of his arm around a bar to prevent himself from being knocked off his feet entirely; Mogrot, flattened in his seat with his arms outstretched holding the wheel in a death grip, just made a wordless noise of jubilation.

They hit the spur of rock.

They went *up* the spur of rock.

They flew *off* the spur of rock, and the tremendous thrust granted to them by Da Boffin's rokkits powered even the trukk's impressive bulk into the air, in an almost-graceful forward arc.

However, what went up almost always came down again. In this instance the trukk came down right on top of the Spikiest of Spikiez' transport, which, although it was jinking around to evade fire from a pair of dakkaguns, was in no way prepared for a ton or so of high-velocity ork machinery to drop onto it from out of the zogging sky.

CRUNCH.

The jolt was tremendous, but the trukk's wheels hadn't stopped turning, and the rokkits hadn't stopped roaring: they were off and away, leaving nothing behind them except what had once been a sleek spikiez skimmer but which was now a pile of wreckage, if a pile could be flat. Ufthak stole a look back and saw the one-armed shape of the spikiez' boss, with a thick tyre track right through where its chest had been.

'Try dodgin' dat, ya git,' Ufthak growled in satisfaction. If the spiky could get up from that, then so far as Ufthak was concerned, it deserved to walk away. 'Mogrot! Shift yerself!'

Mogrot obligingly shuffled back into his original seat, and Ufthak dropped back behind the wheel. He only had the one hand now, of course, which made steering a bit trickier, but it was worth the effort for the expression on Riptoof's face as the rokkit-propelled trukk powered past him down the home stretch. Ufthak waved cheerily with his stump, then wrenched on the wheel and brought the trukk around just in time to avoid a rocky demise on the gully wall. One final turn, and the beginnings of the camp were looming up, with a crowd of orks eagerly awaiting the participants, and a finishing line consisting of some unlucky grots chained together.

The rokkits began to sputter and die. Ufthak didn't look back. It wouldn't do any good. He just had to hope he had enough of a lead…

Whump!

The trukk's front bumper smashed into the finishing line, sending blood and small limbs flying, and prompting a massive cheer from the assembled orks. The cheer only rose in volume when the spikiez' skimmer-trukk, apparently unable or unwilling to change direction, zoomed into the camp hot on the tail of Ufthak and Riptoof, and was immediately deluged in eager orks piling aboard it looking for a fight.

'UFT-HAK!'

'UFT-HAK!'

'UFT-HAK!'

Ufthak grinned as the trukk rolled to a halt. Riptoof looked like a squig that hadn't been fed for a week, but that particular Speed Freek's opinion was meaningless now: the rest of the camp had seen Ufthak win the race to which he'd been challenged, and he'd brought back a quick scrap for them as a bonus.

'Mogrot,' Ufthak said contentedly. 'I fink fings are lookin' up.'

Mogrot obediently tilted his head skywards.

'Not like dat.' Ufthak sighed. 'I meant–'

'No, boss, yer right!'

Ufthak frowned, then imitated his second-in-command. For a moment he could see nothing other than the incoming thunderheads, still rolling in from the west. Then he saw them: three sleek, dark shapes, diving out of the sky towards the camp.

Flyers. Spikiez flyers, no less.

A wide grin spread across Ufthak's face.

'Gitz incomin'!' he roared, standing up on the trukk's seat. 'Get da traktor kannons fired up! Mogrot! Get me armour! Nizkwik! Get *off* dat zoggin' fing, an' tell Dok Drozfang to find me a new hand! Everyone else...'

He pointed at the sky, and every ork face followed his gesture.

'*Waaaagh!*'

MAD DOK

NATE CROWLEY

I

Ghazghkull Mag Uruk Thraka, the Prophet of Gork and Mork, who left worlds ablaze in his boot prints, was dead.

There wasn't much arguing with that, since his body was hanging in a hundred pieces, on a rusty scaffold as high as a Stompa's chin. But that was all right, as far as Dok Grotsnik was concerned. In fact, he reckoned the human Blackmane had done him a bit of a favour, by removing Ghazghkull's head. He'd been asking the boss for permission to remove it himself for years, after all, saying that the best way to fix all his wonky bits would be to just… *switch him off* for a bit, and get 'em all done at once.

But since Ghazghkull's counter-offer had always been that he should do the same thing to Grotsnik (without the fixing or the putting back together afterwards, mind), the dok had come to terms with the fact it probably wouldn't ever happen.

But then along had come Blackmane and his mob of beakies – chop, clang, whirr, splat, *thud* – and here Grotsnik had found himself, with a blank canvas to work on at last. Letting the corners of a rare grin begin to work across his staple-puckered face, the dok looked up at the jungle of chains which bore the bits of the Prophet, and flexed his talons in anticipation of the work ahead.

They were good hands, these new ones: extra-nimble ones from his private stash, which he'd grafted on fresh that morning. And while they were still a bit fuzzy under the talons from barrel-mould, and itchy where his blood was still finding its way through the dead bits, Grotsnik knew they were ready to work wonders.

And what wonders they would work. He had big plans for the rebuilding of the boss. Plans so big, in fact, that he couldn't see the whole of 'em at once, just bits here and there. Still, the dok was sure inspiration would show him the way, once he'd started cutting. That was how it had always been, during his truly great works.

It was certainly how it had been on the night of his *greatest* work, all those years ago: the night when he'd first operated on the ork who would go on to become Ghazghkull Thraka. Under the leaky patchwork of that squighide tent, with just that bucket of third-rate tools to work with, Grotsnik had forced the whole galaxy to reconsider what an ork was capable of.

And now? Well. Now he was going to do it again. But bigger. And better. And with *much* fancier kit.

Inside the ferrocrete dome he'd claimed as his lab, deep down under the big human *kafeedral* where the boss had been felled, was enough weird machinery to bring *anything* back to life. Stacks of generators ringed the edge of the vault, exposed coils alive with sizzling blue discharge sparks, while banks of pumps and bioreaktors chugged and hissed and gurgled with every fluid the dok had been able to get his hands on. That was just the start of it: Grotsnik had spent years hoarding machines that looked like they might do interesting things if you attached living things to 'em, and at last he had an excuse to get the whole lot out to play with. And so, every few minutes, a new pile of crates appeared with a bang and a sizzle of dirty yellow light, as they were *telly-ported* down from the belly of his medikal frigate in orbit.

Then there was all the meat-bits. A row of cages held packs upon packs of all the painboy's staple squig breeds, from bulbous transfusion squigs to saggy-faced skinlender-squigs, as well as a few mobs of hysterical, shrieking snotlings. Beneath them, a second, worse row of cages held a load of captured beakies, with their eyes and jaws and hands taken off so they couldn't cause trouble. Grotsnik wasn't certain what he'd actually do with 'em, since their blood was about as much use as piss in an emergency. But at the very least, they'd give him something to drill holes in while he was thinking.

And there, of course – well, *everywhere* – was Ghazghkull.

With all the bits of the boss suspended around the dome, Grotsnik was reminded of one of those *horrereys* the human meks made, in service to their pointless obsession with how fast stuff spun round in space. The bits of armoured gristle were like brooding green planets, he reckoned, orbiting the massive slab in the middle of the dome, where Ghazghkull's head sat looking way angrier than anything dead should've been able to.

The dok hobbled over to the slab then, until his torso was level with the dark green cliff of Ghazghkull's face. He admired the yellowed jags of his tusks, reflected in the glassy surface of the Prophet's good eye. Then he poked the eye, just because he could. The head retained its bloodied scowl of fury, but nothing happened.

The boss could be as angry as he liked, Grotsnik figured, letting his grin stretch into a great, giddy leer as realisation dawned. Because right now, the boss was dead. More than that though, he was a patient. And patients *never* got a say in what happened during surgery. *Medikal effix*, the humans called that. It was one of their rare good ideas.

Grotsnik ran a talon over the web of rope-thick scars covering the patient's hide, and as he saw how many had been left by his own blades, he snarled with pride. This was *his* monster. And how well he had done, under the circumstances. Every bolt he'd hammered into the boss over the years, every bloodpipe he'd stapled to another bloodpipe, he'd had to get permission for, from Ghazghkull himself. He'd had to cheat and sneak his way to every creative flourish. And still, he'd created a masterpiece.

Naturally, all the underbosses would've said the boss was the work of Gork and Mork. But Grotsnik had never seen either of 'em show up with a spanner. Ghazghkull might have been the *design* of the gods, sure. The dok would give them that. But Ghazghkull was *Grotsnik's* work. All Gork and Mork had ever contributed to their Prophet, for all their holy clamour and barging, had been a beakie-forged bolter shell to the skull. The dok had been left to figure out the rest, and he'd done *mirikals.* But it had all just been practice, for the work in front of him now. And in the hours to come, he was finally going to show Gork, and his big idiot twin, just how much room he had found to improve on their work.

What new feats might the boss go on to rack up, Grotsnik dared to wonder, now that his creator was free to flex his art muscles without constraint? How many more planets would he swallow up with war, and make fit for orks to thrive on? The dok looked up past the scaffold to the dome of masonry above, and pictured the stars beyond it turning green one by one. A whole galaxy, claimed for orks by Ghazghkull... and by Grotsnik too, if you thought about it properly.

The dok thought about it very properly, until he found it was too big a thought to keep inside his brain. So, since he was grinning anyway, he vented it all in a big, mad roar of a laugh, which filled the dome just as thoroughly as his authority. At last, if only for a little while, his genius was free to burn out of control. *No gods, no warlords: just Grotsnik.*

That wasn't a bad note to get started on, the dok thought. So he fished his oldest scalpel from his belt – the tool he'd made the first cut with, the night Ghazghkull was created – and leaned in to begin the operation.

II

Just as Grotsnik's blade was about to meet flesh, something heavy and wet smacked into the flagstones next to him. A spatter of small, viscous gobbets followed, coating the left-hand side of his body, and as they began to slither down the grooves of his knobbly musculature, his grin shrivelled into a mean, crooked grimace.

'It was that one what dropped it,' a voice squawked down, from the top of the scaffold. But Grotsnik's immediate interest was in what had been dropped. He looked to the floor where, just as he had expected from the sound of the splat, Ghazghkull's heart lay in several ragged pieces.

It was going to have been Ghazghkull's heart, anyway.

Alongside the bits of the Prophet's original body hung around the dome, there were a lot of bits from other orks too. Some, Grotsnik had been saving for years, putting them on ice whenever he'd found himself operating on a patient too thick to notice the lack of a few ribs or a kidney. Others, to the dok's amazement, had been donated, as word of Ghazghkull's fall had spread across the trenches of Krongar.

This had been the route by which he had acquired the heart. A titanic but simple-minded Goff known as *Got-So-Angry-He-Tried-To-Fight-Himself*, had come to Grotsnik's lab just days before, ducking under the lintel with an expression that made

Grotsnik instinctively reach for his chain-scalpel. He had presumed the giant had come to hurry the work, via traditional Goff motivational methods. Instead, the hulk had simply prised a broad slab of armour from the centre of his chest, before reaching into the shell-wound which the carapace had covered, and tearing free his heart with a rubbery snap. *For the boss,* he had mumbled as he had handed Grotsnik the organ, before slumping to his knees and passing out.

It had been a first-rate heart, Grotsnik thought, as he watched its ruptured mass quivering on the stone – the kind of organ he'd once have sold half his tools to acquire. Now it was just more meat for the squigs, however, and he supposed he'd have to modify the fuel pump off a truck instead. But before Grotsnik could even register the disappointment he felt, it had transmuted itself into anger, and his gaze had snapped to the gantries high above, scanning them for the likely culprit.

He did not have to look long. Awaiting his gaze were a cluster of grots in stained overalls, all frantically jabbing fingers of mute accusation at each other. Behind them, the winch which had been conveying the heart towards its socket swung to and fro forlornly.

Grotsnik found he did not care which of the snivelling things had dropped the organ. He wanted, very much, to shoot the lot of 'em, if only to dodge the tedium of listening to them blame each other. And any other day, he would have done just that. Indeed, his hand was already reaching for the slugga at his hip to do some killing. But a muted boom from beyond the dome above, and a trickle of dust from its apex, checked his arm before he could level the weapon's sights. Because this was not any other day.

Ghazghkull might have fallen, but the battle wasn't over. Up there, beyond the dome, hundreds of thousands of orks were still fighting a vicious defence against Blackmane's Space Wolves. The beakies' boss had been thoroughly gutted in the process of getting Ghazghkull's head off, but rather than calling it evens and moving on, his lads had reacted by getting really, *really* upset.

The orks weren't winning.

Privately, Grotsnik had even started to wonder if the orks were *losing*. Ghazghkull's forces had, by now, been driven entirely into the crypts beneath the kafeedral. They were trapped there. And with every day that went by, they were being driven deeper and deeper, to the makeshift command bunker and the dok's lab at its centre. Even if it felt ungodsly to think about it, Grotsnik knew that if that load of grey-armoured nutters pushed all the way down before he could get the boss up and running again, they'd be done for.

'Mightn't even have that long,' Grotsnik muttered to himself through his tusks, as he glanced at the heavy blast doors sealing his laboratory off from the rest of the bunker. When he'd set the place up, he had hoped the doors would give him a bit of quiet to fill with the noise of his own work, but he'd soon been disabused of that notion. From the tunnels outside came a constant, discordant racket of bickering and roaring, which grew louder by the hour as more orks were forced down here, and as they got closer and closer to breaking Ghazghkull's Big Rule, by coming to blows.

From the sounds of the current bout of hollering, *Finds-Bullets-He-Has-Not-Lost*, the Deathskull lieutenant who was meant to be in charge while the boss was 'recovering', was moments away from unleashing his fists on Urzog, the Goff chieftain who considered himself to occupy the exact same role.

The idea of being nominally in charge – like the idea of not fighting whenever you felt like it – was a Ghazghkull thing. Usually, if a boss got so much as mildly brainshot, that was that: he'd be done for, and the next biggest orks would slug it out for the job. It was a testament to the Prophet, Grotsnik supposed grudgingly, that the underbosses were waiting at all for him to recover.

But they wouldn't wait forever. One way or another, whether by angry humans or angrier orks, this miserable little burrow of theirs was going to get torn apart. Unless, of course, Ghazghkull came back to will it otherwise.

There was too much work to be done, Grotsnik knew, for him to afford a few shot grots. It was a pure case of what he knew as *straight-line-thinking,* and it made him *miserable.* He hated it, more than anything, when he was forced to reason himself out of what he knew was the *right* thing to do. It felt... alien. Made him think of all the bones he'd had cracked in his youth, all the blades he'd taken, for being *unorky.*

His habit of straight-line-thinking was why they'd called him *Mad* Dok Grotsnik, back on Urk, and it was why they'd treated him like second-hand squig turds. But eventually, as he'd grown older and nastier, he'd developed a knack for this weird, ungodsly cunning. He'd learned to use it to his own advantage, and soon, the cracked bones had started to belong to other orks.

'Who you gurner shoot then?' asked one of the grots on the scaffold, breaking the dismal fog that had settled on Grotsnik's brain, and prompting him to scowl upwards again.

'None of yer,' growled the dok, finding a new ceiling for his already extraordinary hatred of grots, and he drove all thoughts of the burst heart from his mind. 'Too much work to do. But if I were any of you – and thank Mork I ain't, you rotten, degenerate gits – I'd set to getting a new zoggin' heart for the boss fixed up, from anything in the Big Pump Store.'

Grotsnik turned then, with only the quiet splintering of a clenched tusk giving away how much fury he'd made himself swallow, and began stalking back over towards Ghazghkull's head. He'd just got to wondering why he couldn't hear the anxious, moist rustling of a pack of grots getting to work, when the question came.

III

'Is there any real point to it though, boss?'

'You *what?*' Grotsnik said, in a voice like a knife-tip glinting in the dark, and stood stock still.

'Well... is there any point in working, now?' repeated the voice. It was reedy and nasal, just south of a full sneer – and worst of all, without a trace of terror in it. Grotsnik spun round to its source, baring his fangs and narrowing his good eye, only to find... another grot. It wasn't as if he'd ever bothered giving his orderlies proper names, given how long they tended to last, but he'd always thought of this one as Drippa, thanks to the thin strand of mucus which seemed perpetually suspended from its gristled promontory of a nose.

'You're going to have to *explain your reasoning* there, Drippa,' replied Grotsnik, not doing much to stop his hand reaching for the slugga again.

'This place is done for sooner or later,' said the grot, clamping a miserable twist of fungus trimmings between its fangs, and lighting the tip with a sparky-stick. It took a vicious little wheeze, shrugged, and spoke its next words through a thin cloud of rancid brown smoke. 'And we all know you're a miracle-doer, 'cos you tell us all the time and all. But... well. Look at 'im, boss.'

With only a waggle of its broken-and-reset jaw, Drippa dipped the tip of its smoke-stick towards the mute immensity of the dismantled Prophet, and grimaced uncertainly.

'Even if we had a whole year to work,' said the grot, 'you honestly reckon the boss is coming back from *that?*'

The dok wanted to roar that he *very much did reckon that.* But when he did, he found that his jaw had fallen open in shock, so he just made a noise like something dying from a massive and sudden blow to the abdomen.

The shock hadn't come from the way Drippa had spoken to him, since basic disrespect from his minions had long been no surprise to the dok. Just as other orks had always looked down on him, grots had never treated him with the same rightful, undiluted terror as they did other orks, no matter how many acts of extreme violence he conducted either in front of them or upon them. It was like they saw him as nothing more than an especially big, strong, nasty grot.

But for all Grotsnik hated that, he was at least used to it. No: the thing which had struck Grotsnik like a mortar barrel across the brow was the fact that Drippa – disrespectfully or not – had made a good point.

Every grot came out of its hole knowing straight-line-thinking. It was natural to them, which was a big part of why it was such a shameful trait for an ork to exhibit. And in that one little question – 'Is there any real point?' – Drippa had demonstrated just why proper orks held such common contempt for reason. Because too much straight-line-thinking, if you weren't careful, could lead to the unorkiest thing of all. It was a concept so wrong, Grotsnik only knew it as a human word: *dowt.*

And now, to his horror, his brain was awash with it. As his eye flickered over the scattered armour plates, muscle chunks and limb ends that currently made up Ghazghkull Thraka, Warlord of Warlords and Prophet of the Gods, more and more dowt rushed in through it. It was a flood, and the boulder of rage which had been growing in his mind sank down into it, dissolving into nothing. Then, as he carried on staring, slack-jawed, at the suddenly impossible scale of the task, Drippa carried on.

'S'just not gurner happen, dok. Beakies are at our door, bosses at each other's throats, and the big boss is in bits. S'no blood in him. No...' The grot flailed its arms, as if groping for words big enough to describe what it was thinking. 'No *Green* in 'im.'

Grotsnik found a spark of rage at that, even in the murk of the dowt. Because even though he considered the gods idiots, that was *blasfermy,* that was. The Great Green was bigger than gods. It was bigger than every ork and grot and snot and squig stacked together, and nobody but the Prophet had a say in what did and didn't have the Green in it. Grotsnik didn't respect much beyond his own abilities, but he respected that.

'Zoggin' *wretch!*' he barked, lunging a pace forwards and prompting Drippa to skitter three back. 'Who do you reckon you are, then, to be the sayer of that?' With his heart thudding, and the seams on his wrists splitting as his hands clenched into killing-claws, Grotsnik felt a reassuring surge of orkiness, and pressed on without questioning it. With every step he took towards Drippa, the shadow of his confidence swelled. Indeed, by the time he gripped the creature by the throat and lifted it, spluttering, into the air, Ghazghkull's resurrection felt like a near certainty.

'You don't know *nothing,* bin-git!' hissed the dok, snatching the tattered roll-up from Drippa's teeth with his spare hand, and taking a vicious drag of his own, before discarding it. 'You think this is beyond *Grotsnik,* do yer? Think you've seen the extent of what he can do, in the clawful of stinking, cringing years you've spent in the world? Have you forgotten, *grot,* that I've brought the boss back from the Great Green once? Never woulda *been* a Ghazghkull to begin with, if it weren't for me bringing him back to life, back in that tent on Urk.'

Drippa's thin lips writhed over its rotten fangs, as it wrestled to draw enough breath to speak. When it did, Grotsnik couldn't believe what he was hearing.

'It… wasn't you though... was it?' gargled Drippa. 'You just… killed him, operating. Was... *Makari* what brought him back to life.'

The only reason Drippa didn't die then, is because Grotsnik was too distracted hating someone else. Makari. The grot who had dragged bodies for him back on Urk. Or rather, the thing that grot had become, out in Grotsnik's corpse-yard, as they had tried to prise the adamantium plate from the skull of the dok's freshest failure. Because while Makari had been the grottiest grot who had ever skulked out of a hole, they'd also been… something else.

Grotsnik didn't know what that was. Makari had always insisted they were just the Prophet's banner-waver. But the dok knew better. He knew Makari had been granted visions by Ghazghkull. Visions and secrets, and some weird, unknowable connection with Ghazghkull that should've been Grotsnik's. That little scrap of gristle had always stood between Grotsnik and his creation. And while he couldn't prove it, he swore Makari *talked* to Ghazghkull – nudging him here and there, and always keeping Grotsnik from seizing the control which he knew would have made the Prophet unstoppable.

The banner-waver had died at the same time as Ghazghkull, in the scrap with Blackmane up top. But that didn't do much to reassure Grotsnik. Makari had died plenty of times before now. The dok had even killed them himself, once. But the little turd-scrap *came back,* every time – even though everyone knew grots were too rubbish to live more than once. Grotsnik couldn't figure it out in the slightest. And if there was one thing he hated more than grots, it was puzzles he couldn't think his way through.

'Makari's dead,' barked Grotsnik, throwing Drippa into a bank of sparking capacitors, 'and so's their name. They was a thief, is all they was. Got that? It was *me* what brought Ghazghkull back, and that... chancer just happened to be standing in the right place when it happened.'

'If you say so, boss,' croaked Drippa, wincing as it tried to sit upright. Grotsnik lurched towards the little ingrate, intent on giving it a further pasting. But as he did, he became aware of the dozens of watery, beady little eyes fixed on him. The only thing grots enjoyed more than watching their own rise up against their masters was watching them get beat back down, and it seemed that Grotsnik's entire horde of orderlies had gathered to watch the show.

The dok's fists itched, and not just because they'd recently been someone else's. He knew it was right for Drippa to die. But he also knew – somehow – that this was the moment that everything yet to come hinged on. There was another lesson he could teach here, besides the ever-reliable lesson of fists, that might save Ghazghkull, the battle and the whole of the Waaagh! He didn't know how. He didn't even know what the lesson was. But the dok trusted his brain well enough to know it wouldn't have piped up for nothing.

There'd be something there, if he just started talking. *If.* And that was what it came down to, he supposed. Would he be a proper ork and beat Drippa to mush? Or would he be Mad Dok Grotsnik?

'Listen up, you puddles of squig-pus!' shouted Mad Dok Grotsnik, glaring all around him at the grots assembled in the shadow of Ghazghkull's lifeless bonce. 'You're going to work yourselves to squigmeat, every last one of you. You know why? *'Cos I says so*. Something's only impossible, you see, if Grotsnik ain't done it yet. And since the boss *is* coming back – and it's gonna be me who brings him – then *this ain't impossible.* Got that?'

There was a faint flicker in the dark, as a swarm of grots looked at each other in frantic incomprehension. But it didn't matter, because this time, not even Drippa was stupid enough to speak up.

'But before we get to work,' added Grotsnik, as his mind finally worked out what the masterplan was, 'I'm going to tell you a story. It's not one I've ever told anyone. It's not something anyone ever saw, besides one other ork. And it's why you're going to work your snot-green arses off, once I'm done. Because guess what? There was another time Ghazghkull died, after the first. And that time, there was no Makari to get in the way. I brought him back, all by myself. *And this is how it happened.*'

IV

It happened not long after the boss invaded Armygeddon for the second time. We were down under the ocean, sneakin' up on Tempestora Hive in a great big fleet of *submersibbles.* And of course, I know yous lot weren't even spores back then. But you know what I'm talking about, don't yer? I've seen the little scrawlings you do in places you think I won't see, in glyphs you think I can't read. You pass down your little... *histreys,* and so you know what happened well enough. At least, you think you do.

Oh – and before any of you gits tries to say otherwise... those submersibbles? My idea. Oh yeah, I know very well everyone says it was Orghamek. But who do you think grew all of Orghamek's brains, eh? And who got 'em to play nicely together? Yeah, that's right. Grotsnik. So anything he invented counts as my idea, 'cos of *intallectual propatee.*

Still, it's not all bad that I don't get the credit for the subs, 'cos they weren't exactly our best work of the war. They did their job and didn't sink, sure. Two-thirds did, anyway. But I swear by Gork's bloodied boot-nails, you've no zoggin' idea what it was like on board those things.

We'd welded 'em together from scrapped human tankers in the wastes up north, bulked up with armour plate that the void-boys cut off the hulls of the kroozers in orbit, then dropped straight down through atmosphere. It was tough stuff, all right. But it was leaky as a Blood Axe cipher – in the end, we gave up trying to weld all the bullet holes shut, and just packed 'em with scrap metal and squig resin.

Then there was the heat. You've not got the know-wots to understand this, but spaceship metal's meant to work best surrounded by loads of… nothing, yeah? Put it under the sea – 'specially a boiling hot, sludgy sea like Armygeddon's – then stick one of Nazdreg's mega-reaktors in the arse end, and you've basically made yerself a moving kiln full of thousands and thousands of orks. We was boiling alive in those things – up to our knees in soupy bilge slime wherever we went, blistered all over from the reaktor leaks, and only eating tins of whatever humans we'd managed to round up and render down during the rush to get the Mork-snicked things built.

That's not even starting on the squigs, neither. See, thanks to a snarl-up with the first landings, half the Goff Dread-mobs the boss had ordered for the Big Boat Attack, ended up halfway across the planet, wonderin' where the sea was. And what did we get instead? A whole karrier full of Beastsnagga warbands, complete with their stamping, farting, biting squigs. Worse still, 'cos the boss' sub was the biggest, it ended up with the biggest squigs. So we had this giant barn filling a full third of the hull, packed with tank-sized turd factories. Let's just say it didn't help with the smell, right?

Anyway. I'm only telling yous all this, so you can get an idea how... *worked up* we all was, after what felt like forever chugging along at the bottom of that 'orrible sea. You think you've seen orks spoiling for a fight? Not till you've seen 'em packed inside a hot tin for days on end, you haven't.

It was that bad, even Ghazghkull weren't above it. Dunno whether it was the heat, or the radiation, or the poison I'd been injecting in his neck because I wanted to see how mad he'd go, but his headaches had been getting worse and worse the whole time. It'd got to the point where he wasn't getting any words at all from the gods during 'em, they were just roaring right into his brain, making him thrash so hard he left dents in the walls. Gork's grin, though – it got so bad I even laid off the poison in the end, just in case he thrashed so hard he made a hole and sank us.

Before we left, the Prophet had stood up on the battlements of the flagship's peekin'-spire, and he'd sworn to every ork there that he'd personally lead the charge, once we'd crossed the ocean and beached at Hive Tempestora. The cheer was so zoggin' loud, after he said that, I wondered if they'd hear us in the bleedin' hive itself, all the way across the sludge.

But when, at long last, the day of the landings arrived, I went up to Ghazghkull's throne-chamber to check on him, and found him in the rottenest state I ever saw. He was twitching, and snarling, and he couldn't seem to go three squeezes of a timer-squig without his whole body going rigid and shaking like a Deff Dread's drill arm. It was like nothing I'd seen before. I'd definitely gone too hard with the poison, but there was something more than that, too. Like something had grabbed him by the head, and wouldn't let go.

Now, I've never been one to *under-esty-mate* my own work. Especially a piece of work so killy as Ghazghkull. I knew what kind of punishment the boss could take, 'cos I'd dished enough of it out to his brain, and even taken proper notes. But it looked like here, at last, was the limit. One look at the boss that day told me all I needed to know. He was, in my medikal opinion, *proper busted,* and there was no way he was gonna be leading any charges at all, unless they was charges face first into the sea.

Naturally, I had a plan. I reckoned I could loosen some of the pressure in Ghazghkull's skull. Knew I could, in fact, 'cos I always left a few screws overtightened in there, just in case I ever needed an excuse to get in his head for a bit. He'd need a full overhaul of his headmeat, soon enough. But I figured a quick tune-up, finished in time for the boss to give his big pre-fight speech, would be enough to get him through the day. So I told Ghazghkull that I needed to operate.

Didn't go down well. Lucky for me, he was in such a state that the punch only clipped me, cracking my left arm, and then burying itself two tusklengths into the steel of the chamber wall. Still, I knew I couldn't let that put me off. I *needed* to get inside that skull. 'Cos if I didn't, and Ghazghkull went ahead and led the invasion anyway, it wouldn't take the underbosses three kidney-beats to realise their Prophet was cooked in the head.

Well... desperate times, yeah? What can you do? Well, this is what *I* did. After a quick breather to steady myself, I told the boss he was being an idiot, and that he needed the op done there and then.

The second punch didn't miss me. Or at least, it wouldn't have done. But Ghazghkull never finished it. He launched himself towards me, all full of murder, then stopped dead halfway with his face gone slack, and fell to the deck like a sack of anvils and steak.

Seeing him lying there, not even twitching... Well, it was almost like I couldn't see him at all. My eyes was taking him in, all right, but my brain wasn't having any of it. Dropping flat for no reason? That just... didn't happen to Ghazghkull.

But there he was, dropped flat. Don't think I could quite grasp what'd happened, to be honest. Same way you lot would lose the plot if, oh I dunno, I *paid you,* or something.

'Cos of what a mindbuster it was, it was a good long while before I worked up the nerve even to go over and poke the boss. And for all my surgical know-wots, poking was all I could think to do, for a while. Eventually though, I heaved the boss' face off the floor, and wished I hadn't. There was blood pouring from his nose, his ears and the corner of his good eye, and even leakin' out from the edge of his metal skullplate. Now, as an expert in bleeding, that told me all I needed to know. The Prophet'd got so angry, on top of the state his head was in anyway, that some part of his brain had just… burst.

That was just… that. Burst brain. And if he hadn't been dead when he'd hit the floor, he definitely was by the time I'd worked out what was going on.

The boss was dead. And wouldn't you know it, at *just that moment,* the shouting-boxes roared into life all down the inside of the sub, and started blarin' out a message from the lookouts up top in the peekin'-spire. They'd seen the target, hadn't they? Just visible through the smog on the horizon, lurking like a git-nest in a marsh, was Hive Tempestora itself.

And that meant that, in the time it'd take you to refill any of those lymph tanks over there, the whole fleet of subs would be ploughing up out of the water, beaching 'emselves on the slag-drifts of the shore, and grinding over any human defences like soil-gits under a boot. When that happened, every ork, on every sub on the fleet, would be waiting in the holds chanting the great war chant, ready to follow the Prophet into battle. Even before that, now that the hive had been sighted, they'd be expecting the boss to show up down in the musterin' chambers, to give his big pump-up speech.

Only... his brain had burst.

There wasn't even time to panic. I knew, right then, I needed to snatch up every moment of time I could possibly get my gristly hands on, to have a hope of *resussertatin* the Prophet before we hit the beaches. That meant someone needed to cover for the boss down below, playing for as much time as possible. And I knew just the someone.

That's not good, Biter had said, when they'd climbed up through the hatch into the throne-chamber, and clapped eyes on the stone-dead Ghazghkull. Typical Biter.

They're all zoggin' weird, the Blood Axes are. But Biter – or Taktikus, as they'd called themself back then – was something else. They'd just become the chief Blood Axe *genrul* on Army-geddon, after shanking their predecessor during a raid behind human lines, and they was probably the weirdest ork I've ever come across. Actually *likes being around humans*. Fought with 'em once, they says. Still betrayed 'em in the end, mind. But they're a creepy git however you look at it.

Unfortunately, they're a clever git and all. And in that moment, they was the only ork on that rotten boat who I reckoned had a chance of seeing Ghazghkull dead, and not completely losing their mind. So in that moment, they was the most precious thing in the world to me. Straight-line-thinking, yeah? Anyway, once they'd got a grip on the situation, I sent them down to where the speech was due to be held, and told them to think up some zoggin' good reasons for the boss not being there.

So that was one problem dealt with, at least. Later, I found out exactly what Biter had done to keep the troops busy, and I will grudgingly admit it was a *masterpiece* of a lie. They'd said Ghazghkull had left the sub to fight a sea monster, because he'd got too annoyed with being cooped up below decks. They'd even had mines detonated just outside the hull, so it sounded like there was a fight going on out in the sludge. Bought me a lot of time, Biter did, with that little ruse.

Not enough time, though. Working like a grot trying to wall up a gap in a gnasher-squig pen, I'd opened up the whole of Ghazghkull's bonce, and laid it out in bits on the floor of his throne-chamber, all the while hoping nobody walked in on me. It was a miserable situation for brain surgery to begin with, what with the dim red emergency lights, and the stench of the squigs and all. But it got worse, fast.

When the subs at the front of the fleet burst through the defensive perimeter of the human sea wall, the hive's defenders scrambled their bombers, and started filling the sea around us with depth charges. They launched too late to actually cause much damage, mind, since the subs were wrapped up in spaceship metal after all. Think they only managed to sink a couple of dozen boats, if I remember right. But the rocking of the hull, and the constant zoggin' concussion waves from the blasts, really tested my detail work. For almost every bloodpipe I managed to close up in the boss' knotted great ball of a brain, it seemed another got tore open when an explosion knocked my hand.

Still, what I lack in precision, I've always made up for in speed. I was makin' progress. And as we passed under the bombardment, I got every rupture in the Prophet's brain closed up. I even charged it with a few gobfuls of my own genius blood, so it'd have enough juice in it to think with, once I got his hearts started.

And I swear, for all that I hate both of the gits, thank Gork and Mork I managed to get his skull bolted together, with just an instant to spare, before our keel hit the beach.

'Cos when I say beach, I'd be better off saying junkyard. Weren't a grain of sand to be found there – just piles upon piles of smashed-up human machinery, eaten through with rust, and with all the gaps filled in with jagged chunks of slag from the foundries upcoast. The sound of it, as jags and snags tore through the sub's belly like squiggoth claws, made it feel like being stuck in the inside of a dakkajet turbine.

As the sub ploughed all the way out of the water and started grinding along under its own weight, I thought we was going to be shook to pieces. And if I hadn't had the massive dead weight of Ghazghkull to cling onto, I would've been smashed to splinters against the walls. It was a grim old ride, that. Sometimes, you know, I wonder how many more mobs might've made it out onto the beaches, if we'd thought to put handholds in the troop bays.

I couldn't believe how long we kept on skidding. But then, I s'pose a ship the size of a small city, sat on a nuclear turbine going at full blast for days, is gonna build up a bit of momentum, isn't it? Still, gravity's such a hard old brute that even ork hardware can't outlast it. In the end we came to a long, rattling halt, and after one last massive groan of metal, and a crack of the central girders for good measure, there was silence.

Gork knows how many of the other subs got shredded to bits on the way out of the sea, or broke in two once they had to take their own weight, but I could see the little red lights on the wall of the boss' throne-chamber pinging green as the survivors reported landfall, and it looked like it was probably more than half of 'em.

Not bad, I know. Weren't gonna last, though. Already, the silence'd been broken by the drone of the human bombers, as they wheeled back round out at sea to take another run at us. And this time, we were sitting targets, with no sludge to hide under.

I heard the rattle and crack of the flak turrets on the sub's tail opening up, but then they stopped again, one by one – no doubt as the gunners took slaps across their heads from their bosses. Why? *'Cos Ghazghkull had said he'd start the attack*. That was how it had to go; so far as every last ork in the fleet saw it, that was how the gods were going to give us our win. And if that meant losing a few more subs, while the boss chose the perfect moment to strike? Well, that was just the way things went.

All well and good, only the boss' heart wouldn't start. I'd tried squishing it with my hands. I'd tried getting the spare one going first. I'd tried sticking the sparky end of a sliced-through cable into the middle of it. I'll be honest, I'd even tried battering it with a wrench, just in case. But the zoggin' thing just sat there between the boss' ribs, cold and rubbery, refusing even to twitch.

The bombs were falling now, of course. But I had to keep trying. So, with my making-things-bigger goggles on and a glow-squig between my teeth, I pushed my head right inside the Prophet's chest for a proper look. At least it was a break from the smell of squig turds.

I don't really know what I expected to find in there. But as it turned out, I was in luck. The problem was stupidly simple, actually. Shining my light through the walls of the boss' main bloodpipes, I saw the biggest one coming out of his heart was all blocked up. I spent a good while squinting at it, trying to work out what it might have been, when I remembered I'd injected him with molten plastek a few days previously. Supposedly, it'd been a cure for the rashes on his neck – which I'd also caused, with a swab dipped in used reaktor coolant – but really it'd just been a bit of spite on my part. For a moment there, I almost regretted having done it.

Especially when something started cutting its way through the wall.

As soon as I managed to pull my head out of the boss, I saw sparks flying, and I knew that the fierce, white-orange square drawing itself slowly across the inner hull could only mean one thing. We'd taken so long to invade the beaches, *that the zoggin' humans were invadin' us.*

Before that moment, I'd been coming up with a dead elegant plan for clearing the boss' bloodpipes. But that had to go down the drops sharpish: this was no time for fancy surgery. Knowing I'd have to go with my gut, I stopped any sort of straight-line-thinking, and solved the problem like any good ork.

That'll do, I thought, spotting a skinny, jagged little banner-pole sticking up from Ghazghkull's shoulder armour. Twisting it off with a neat little snap, I peered back into the boss' open chest, poked my tongue between my tusks to make my aim better, and jabbed him right in the *ventrikular arteree* with the sharp end.

Two things happened at once, then. There was a big, gurgling pop from Ghazghkull's heart as it unclogged itself and started beating, and a massive hollow clang from behind me, as the cut section of hull fell through. The whole chamber filled with smoke, and I had to use my rivetgun blind to close the incision, accidentally putting two bolts through my hand in the process. But I closed it, and as I swept the worst of the muck from the seal, I could feel the thud of the boss' heart through the skin.

Which was just as well. Because standing in the hole in the wall were three massive beakies. I'd spent so long in that miserable, dim red light that they were just black outlines against a wall of blinding white. But there's no mistaking a beaky when you see one – those big pretend shoulders, that tiny little head, those big ridiculous boots: they're all a dead giveaway. Still, it wasn't the most welcome sight in the world, right then.

I was squinting down the barrel of one of their chunky guns, I remember, trying to remember how good beakies could see through smoke, when I heard it. The best sound I'd ever heard in my life, even though it was just five words.

'Move out the way, Grotsnik.'

V

'Now obviously,' said Grotsnik, his stitch-riven chest puffed out with pride, 'there was a lot of fighting still to come, after that. But as far as I'm concerned? *That* was the moment we won the invasion of Tempestora Hive.'

'Yeah,' said Drippa, its face entirely motionless, earning it a scowl from the dok. 'Great story, boss. Just got one question, though.'

'Oh, did I miss something?' hissed Grotsnik, nostrils flaring, as he towered over his nonplussed audience.

'Just one thing, yeah... the pole.'

'What pole?'

'The one you fixed the boss' heart with. You said it was a banner, right?'

'I... think you... yeah.' The dok snorted, taken aback. 'What's that got to do with anything?'

'Do you remember what was... on the banner, at all? Like, a picture or sumfink?'

'Uh?' grunted the dok, his long, scarred face crunching up in bafflement. But then, as some mean little detail fell into place, deep within the algal folds of his own mind, realisation set in. His lone red eye, furrowed into a smouldering volcanic crack with concentration, flared suddenly in shock, and his mouth gaped in wordless exaggeration, as what had seemed such a trivial detail at the time swelled to monumental importance.

'Was it that banner?' asked Drippa, a mean strand of mucus swaying across its sharp little grin, as it extended a claw towards the mountainous shape of Ghazghkull's torso in the gloom.

There, screwed into a socket high up on the boss' fortress of a shoulder, and glinting weakly where endless bullet-strikes had hammered and holed it, was indeed a tattered metal banner. And on its lumpy surface, copied faithfully from the copy of a hundred previous copies, was the design that had first been daubed in the Prophet's own blood, back in the yard behind Grotsnik's own medical tent.

Makari? Makari? Makari?

The name echoed in Grotsnik's head, like a drumbeat, coming from every direction at once. *Is this it?* he thought to himself, as the full misery of the truth continued seeping through his skull like ice water. *Am I finally, properly, going mad?*

But Grotsnik was not going mad. Or if he was, it had nothing to do with the name he could hear being shouted, over and over again. Because the name, he heard now, was being repeated in the same, unmistakable voice whose bellows and barks had underscored Grotsnik's work for some time now. It was Bullets, somewhere outside the laboratory's door. And there was, in fact, a drumbeat underlying it. Something like a drumbeat, anyway: a wet, thudding crack, just a moment or two after each repetition of that hated name.

Makari? Crack! Makari? Crack! Makari? Crack!

Despite the many, many other thoughts clamouring for space in Grotsnik's mind, then, he could never ignore the evidence of somebody else getting know-wots wrong, and he clicked his tusks in contempt.

'The zoggin' *moron,*' he muttered. 'He's trying to find them, isn't he? Trying to find a new Makari. Goin' along a line of grots, I'll bet, and braining 'em when they don't respond.' The dok shook his head mournfully, and absent-mindedly gathered a spanner from his belt. 'Doesn't he have the wits to realise it was always the boss' *touch,* brought the little bin-git back, not just the name?'

'We've still got the Prophet's old hands…' said Drippa, nodding conspiratorially towards a hopper at the back of the dome, stacked with hunks of leathery green flesh. 'Wonder if they'd still work?'

Grotsnik the ork opened his mouth to roar abuse, with fangs bared and talons arched. But Mad Dok Grotsnik said nothing, because he was doing *straight-line-thinking*. The grot, for all its attitude, was correct. There was one factor that had been common to both incidents of Ghazghkull's resurrection, it turned out. And yet, it was absent from this attempt. For all that he hated Makari, he knew that – as a scientist, if not as an ork – it was his duty to suffer them once more.

He took a long look down at Drippa the grot, and narrowed his eye. Was there a similarity there? No. But it didn't matter: the little sods looked different every time. But the attitude? The spiteful, smug piety? Oh, yes; on that front, Drippa was more than halfway there already. It'd make a perfect test subject.

Drippa had been about to say something, but didn't get the chance before the ork's arm swooped down and picked it up bodily by its ragged, greasy ear.

'Congratulations, Drippa,' announced Mad Dok Grotsnik, a smirk of triumph finding a foothold on his face again at last. 'You're about to pioneer an entirely new field of research with me. I suggest you start thinking godly thoughts.'

He turned, then, to the rest of the lab's grot workers, who had been beginning to disperse in disappointment, now that it looked like further violence was unlikely.

'And you lot?' boomed the dok, his eye gleaming with reflections of arc lightning from the capacitors. 'Fetch the boss' old hand, and pulley armature three. We're going to do a little experiment.'

'How's that gonna help?' screeched a miserable specimen at

the back of the crowd, with a feeble shrug. 'Bringing the Prophet back's still impossible.'

'Foolish grot,' grinned Grotsnik, turning his wild gaze to the ceiling once more, and the green stars which shone, concealed, behind it. 'Something's only impossible, you know, if the Great Green ain't willed it yet.'

BLOOD RITE

RACHEL HARRISON

ONE

BROTHERS

The Sanguine Tear, now...

The company standard is dappled with blood. To Thaneod Darrago, the pattern of it looks like a starfield painted in negative. Some of the blood is old. Very old. Some is new, and belongs to his brothers, both lost and living. It is the blood of Sanguinius. Angels' blood. The same as Darrago's own. As he smooths the standard flat with care, he catches the scent of it. It is rich and familiar, a contrast to the cool, recycled air of his quarters aboard the Blood Angels strike cruiser *Sanguine Tear*. Like the rest of the ship, Darrago's quarters are clad in iron and gold, but unlike the grand halls and the decorated, ornate bridge, they are spare. Darrago's work station takes up most of the space. It is a smooth marble surface on which the company standard lies under lumens that are warm and yellow like sunlight. Stylised skulls set into the walls watch him from blank eye sockets as he lays out his tools. Needles made from fine steel. Golden thread, carefully woven by Chapter thralls at the Arx Angelicum. They are fine things. Delicate things.

'In blood are we made,' Darrago says, as he sets about his work.

The fine steel needle is as familiar to him as his weapons and wielded just as easily in his badly scarred hand. The standard is his to bear. His to carry, to mend and to care for. His to stitch with new glories, in golden thread. It is scarred, as he and his brothers are scarred. It has been mended one thousand times, by one hundred hands, but Darrago knows well enough that it is impossible to ever truly reverse damage once it has been done. You can overstitch it. Strengthen weak areas and restore faded glories. You can even conceal damage, if you so wish.

But you cannot undo it.

'Company Ancient.'

Darrago looks up at the words. The speaker is one that he expected, though that does nothing to lessen the cold weight that accompanies his presence, and the questions that Darrago knows he will ask.

'Well met,' Darrago says. It is hard to mean the words because there is only one thing that calls this particular brother of his.

Blood.

His brother approaches. He is clad not in robes, but in full battleplate. It growls in the silence like a caged thing. He remains standing, though there is space to sit, because he is not the type to rest.

'You know why I am here,' his brother says.

Darrago nods. 'Because of Luminata,' he says. 'The shrine of Sanguis Gloria.'

'And the chalice,' his brother says, looking down at the standard. 'A new glory for your banner.'

'Not a glory,' Darrago says, and he goes back to his work.

'What, then?'

Darrago keeps his eyes on the shape of the chalice as he re-makes it in thread.

'A memorial,' he says. 'Something to commemorate.'

There is a pause, during which Darrago can hear the low

rumble of the *Sanguine Tear* as she plies the warp, and the beat of his hearts, quickened by memory.

'The chalice held at Sanguis Gloria was said to be an immaculate vessel,' his brother says. 'It was said that our father himself gave it to the people of Luminata as a show of faith.'

'I know the stories,' Darrago says. 'We all know the stories.'

'Yet corruption was drawn to the chalice,' his brother says. 'Evil sought it out, to use it against us. To twist the immaculate and make violence of it.'

Darrago stops his work. 'I saw what was done on Luminata,' he says. 'I saw the chalice taken by traitors. I saw the shrine afire. I saw the storm they meant to make, and what it took to stop it.'

His brother is silent for a moment. His dark eyes do not flicker. Do not blink. Darrago knows that the stillness is momentary. That his brother can be swift and violent.

Merciless.

'And what did it take to stop it?' his brother asks.

Darrago's eyes fall to the half-made chalice. He remembers Donato, bowed.

Sanyctus, screaming.

'Great sacrifice,' Darrago says. 'And angels' blood.'

The Sanguine Tear, then...

The shrine of Sanguis Gloria stands astride the pilgrims' city below. An angel, carved from the white face of the tallest mountain on Luminata, it wears the cloud layer for a crown, and casts long shadows with its wings. Long enough for thousands of pilgrims to stand in and sing their hymns. They move as the shadows move with the sun, but they never stop their singing. It carries upwards on coursing winds. A constant chorus. Standing in the shadow of Sanguis Gloria and being surrounded by the roar of the pilgrims' song is a memory that Thaneod Darrago holds on to. One that reminds him of all of the ways that mortal hearts can be good.

Which is especially important when they fail.

He watches through the eyes of his brothers on the ground and in the shrine, through a dozen pict-feed links broadcast directly onto his helm's display from the Blood Angels fighting on Luminata. He sees the sky twist and burn around the shrine of Sanguis Gloria. Clawed clouds, and lightning earthing in reverse, reaching up to strike at the sky. He sees bodies fall from the platform built into the shrine's summit to join the others that lie broken at the foot of it, where the pilgrims once sang.

A pool of blood grows around them like another long shadow. Darrago sees cultists wrapped in bloodstained bandages torn apart by bolter fire, dying for those that twisted them and turned them against the Emperor. Lastly, Darrago sees warriors clad in crimson and silver that burn with witchlight and wickedness. Heretic Astartes.

Word Bearers.

Darrago's hearts thunder at the sight of them. The marks they wear. The darkness that follows them. Darrago has a great capacity for hatred. Of the alien. Of the mutant. But no hatred burns as fiercely for him as that he holds for the heretic. For those who turned their backs on their brothers and embraced Chaos.

The feed flickers and distorts. Over the roars and battle cries of his brothers, somehow Darrago catches the sound of whispers. The words are reversed, just like the lightning. Demented, hollow echoes that sound like gasping breaths. He grits his teeth and shuts it out, then winds his fingers tight around the standard he carries and takes his place alongside his First Company brothers on the teleportation dais, because the time has come for the Archangels to join battle. Each of them has a particular space on the dais amidst the warding words set in gold. Those words are ancient, much older than the *Tear* herself. Darrago can see where they have been flash frozen by repeat teleportations, leaving micro fractures running through the gold. Too many to count. Eleven of his brothers stand on the dais around him, clad in scarlet and gold. Command falls to Larracus Donato. The captain is a veteran amongst veterans, his mastery of battle-craft rarely matched. If Donato is the Archangels' tactical mind, Darrago is their soul. The company standard is not the only thing to fall under his care. He watches over his brothers, too.

Darrago looks to Radst Phaello first, and the four members of his squad. Sanguinius' blood runs in every one of them, but

Sergeant Phaello is the one who most resembles the graven images of their father. The Angel, serene. That composure of his carries over into battle, where Phaello is deliberate and measured. The other four veterans are sworn to the giant, Diordis Victorno. Like Phaello, he is fair and pale. Where Phaello is serene, though, Victorno is fierce like the radstorms of Baal. He favours the thunder hammer and the heart of a fight, as do those who fight with him. They are the Archangels' wrath. Darrago knows that to be particularly true of one of his brothers. The one he has known for the longest time, and whom he watches with the most care.

Adiccio Sanyctus.

He stands beside Victorno now, curling and uncurling his hands in their lightning claw gauntlets. He goes without his helm, and his one remaining eye is furious and dark.

'Adiccio,' Darrago says, using his given name because he knows it will cut through, like it did on Kalatar.

Sanyctus looks at him. Of all of Darrago's brothers, he is one of the most scarred. He has been mended nearly as many times as the company standard, but with nowhere near the artistry.

'Thaneod,' he says. 'We must go. Now.'

Darrago has never known Sanyctus to be patient, but with every battle, the urgency in him grows. It becomes more vicious and desperate.

Darker.

'The lesson,' Darrago says. 'Do you remember?'

It takes a moment, but then his brother blinks. There is a flicker in the snarl of scar tissue that is all that remains of Sanyctus' right eye as the lid tries to close.

'I remember,' he says.

Sanyctus stops curling his hands inside his gauntlets. He lifts his helm and locks it in place, and his scars and his fury are hidden behind a beautifully artificed mask of red ceramite.

'Tur Zalak and his coven have taken the Crown.' Captain Donato's voice carries easily, without needing to be raised. The seals affixed to his Terminator plate catch gently in the recycled air as the vox-spoiled sound of war echoes in Darrago's ears. The pict-feed shown to him is a frozen, flickering image of the shrine of Sanguis Gloria, seen from the air. The angel's eyes are dark hollows that billow black smoke. Dark stains run down the shrine's marble face like tears. 'The storm is their doing. They have used it to blind our Librarius and blunt our aerial assaults.' Donato's voice is cold. 'The Word Bearers intend to despoil the shrine of Sanguis Gloria, and Luminata with it.'

He pauses. His face is set, but Darrago sees the fury in the captain's eyes.

'It is not just the Crown that the heretics have taken,' Donato says. 'They have also taken the chalice.'

'The bastards will burn,' Victorno says. He slams the haft of his thunder hammer on the dais. 'Every one of them.'

Donato nods. 'We will restore the shrine of Sanguis Gloria, and we will recover the chalice. None shall stand against us.'

Darrago answers alongside his brothers.

'None shall survive our wrath!' they roar together.

'In Sanguinius' name,' Donato says.

The words conjure the pilgrims' song once more in Darrago's mind. The glory he felt at the sound of it. At standing in the shadow of great wings, on a world on which his father is said to have set foot. Then the teleportarium lights turn white and the storm surrounds him.

The Sanguine Tear, now...

'The chalice. You said before that you know the stories.'

Darrago nods. He has abandoned his work on the company standard. It seems in poor taste to do it in the face of these questions. In the face of this particular brother.

'Do you believe them?' his brother asks.

Darrago exhales slowly. He sets to winding the golden thread he has been using back onto the spool. It catches the lumen light and glitters. The spool is made from carved bone that has been polished so smooth it could be mistaken for something made, and not something grown.

'I served on Luminata long ago. Before the Archangels, when I was of the battle companies. I spent one month at the shrine as part of the standing guard,' he says. 'As one of the ten who always remain to watch over the chalice and the shrine built in our father's name.'

'Remained.' There is no change in his brother's face, but his choice of words is cold and deliberate.

'Remained,' Darrago says, with a nod. 'I looked upon the chalice once in that time.'

'And what did you feel?' his brother asks.

Darrago thinks about it. It had seemed small and delicate, made from thin-spun gold. The face of the chalice was without blemishes or the tarnish of age. It was a small and delicate thing, yes, but a perfect thing too.

'I felt pride,' he says. 'Awe.'

'Then you believe that it was indeed crafted by the primarch's hand?'

Darrago shrugs. He puts the wound spool back into the heavy wooden box it came from, nestling it among rolls of crimson silk.

'That I do not know. You asked what I felt, and that is my answer.'

'There are those among us who would have taken the chalice from Luminata if they could have,' his brother says. 'That would have sooner seen it cared for at the Arx Angelicum, with the other Chapter relics. Who considered mortal hearts much too weak to trust with such a thing.'

'It is true that there is weakness to be found in mortal hearts,' Darrago says. He thinks of those who shed their faith and devoted themselves to Tur Zalak and his lies. Who turned on each other and against those sent to save them. But then Darrago thinks too of those who sang at the foot of Sanguis Gloria when he first set foot on that world, all those years ago. Of the roar of the song. The way it carried on the wind and rang from the marble.

'But there is strength in mortal hearts, too. Perhaps that is what our father saw, if the stories are to be believed.'

'Perhaps,' his brother allows, and for the first time there is a small change in his face.

A moment of understanding.

'And what of the second time you saw the chalice?' his brother asks. 'What did you feel then?'

Darrago remembers reaching the Crown on the day of the

battle. Or night. By then it had become so dark that it was hard to tell the difference. He remembers the chalice, small and delicate. Surrounded by balefire and warpstuff and the whispers of heretics. It was a point of light in the darkness that flickered and failed as he looked upon it. He remembers seeing his brothers fall around him. Seeing them succumb to the storm.

'I felt despair,' he says, because he cannot lie. He will not. 'It was blackening as I looked at it. Becoming spoiled.'

'Flawed.'

The word is cold, and heavy. Deliberate, just like all of his brother's words.

Darrago nods. 'Yes,' he says.

The Shrine of Sanguis Gloria, then...

Teleportation is both instant and endless. A barrage of noise and of nothingness. This time, though, something influences the jump. Something great and dark that brings with it the sound of whispers played in reverse. He sees his brothers, lost and living. He sees the heart of the storm. The ritual site. The Dark Apostle, Tur Zalak. His eyes are shadowed pools and his smile is one made of needle teeth. Last of all, Darrago sees the chalice, said to have been given by Sanguinius to the people of Luminata. It fills with blood until it spills over the sides. The smell of it is strong. Rich and familiar.

Angels' blood.

Then the endless instant is over, and Darrago opens his eyes.

He has fallen to one knee. The rough stone floor around him is cracked and slicked with hoarfrost. Darrago still holds tight to the company standard, keeping it aloft despite almost falling himself. The thin coating of ice that has spread across his armour shatters and flakes off as he stands and takes in where he is. He raises his storm bolter and points it into the half-dark.

'This is not the Crown,' he says.

The chamber is a vast ossuary, built from and decorated with the timeworn bones of the dead. According to Darrago's helm display, it lies over a kilometre down from the Crown. Warm, dry air hits him, carrying with it the scent of old parchments and older bones. Dust and grit falls from the arched ceiling far above, ringing against Darrago's armour as the shrine tremors around him. Just like during the jump, the sound of whispers surrounds him. Nonsense words, spoken in reverse. Dozens of shadows move between the streams of dust. Fast, erratic shadows, clad in shifts and linen bindings and masks made of bloodstained sackcloth. They carry glittering, hooked blades.

Cultists.

'Blood,' they hiss, and it sounds just like the storm that Darrago fell through to get here. 'Blood for the Blessed.'

They come for him, leaping and running, moving with misfiring twitches of their limbs. Darrago plants the standard, splitting the stone underfoot even further.

'Not mine,' he roars, and he fires on them with his storm bolter. 'Not today.'

Muzzle flashes light the ossuary. Two of the cultists are ripped from their feet. Ripped asunder by the explosive rounds. Darrago catches the scent of their blood in the air. It is old. Sour. Corrupt. It makes his canine teeth ache up into his head.

A third cultist collides with him bodily. That glittering knife she carries scores a deep line across his armour though it should be able to do nothing of the kind. Not to Terminator plate. Smoke rolls from the blade and the gouge it leaves. The sackcloth mask the cultist wears is torn open at the mouth. Darrago can see the way she grins with filed teeth as she tries to go for his throat with that smoking blade.

'Blood,' she says, again. 'Blood for the Blessed.'

Darrago backhands her. The blow knocks her clear off her feet and collapses her chest with a wet crunch. She lands amongst the dead and goes still. Darrago turns to face the other cultists to find that Victorno's squad have joined the fray.

To find that he cannot see Donato, or Phaello, or any one of his squad.

'The others,' Darrago says, over the vox. 'Where are they?'

'I cannot raise them,' Victorno answers as he knocks a cultist aside on the face of his storm shield. 'The vox is fouled, just as the damned teleportation was. Auspex too. It was something in the storm.'

Something in the storm. Darrago remembers Zalak's needle-teeth grin and he snarls.

'The Dark Apostle,' he says. 'This is his doing.'

'Then we will make him answer for it.'

Victorno's thunder hammer connects with one of the cultists and the flare of light prints on Darrago's vision. The sound echoes in his ears. The impact of the power weapon shatters the cultist completely. Victorno roars, already moving. Not fast and erratic like the cultists, but unstoppable. Maeklus fires on the heretics with his flamer, lighting the ossuary with purifying flame. The promethium clings and steals the cultists' screams but they do not stop. Darrago puts them down with bolt rounds. Ebellius catches one leaping at him in mid-air and closes his power fist around the cultist's body with a snap of ozone and of bones.

'This is just like Corolis,' Ebellius says. His voice is loud and booming. 'Just like the caves. The heretic militia, and their damnation engines. There must have been sixty of them. Not a bolt shell left, but I had the launcher.' He rolls his gauntlet into a fist and thumps it against his chestplate. The cyclone launcher mounted on his shoulder clicks and grinds in sympathy. 'I emptied the missile rack,' he says. 'Caught them in the collapse. I was the only one to walk out–'

'Through the dust,' Maeklus says, interrupting him. 'We know. If you plan to collapse this place too, then please catch me in it. I would rather be buried than listen to another of your old boasts.'

His voice is not loud, or booming. It is a seldom-used rasp. Maeklus rarely has much to say, but if anyone can draw him, it is Ebellius. To one outside the Archangels, it might seem that they antagonise one another, but Darrago has known them both long enough to know better.

It is just a kind of balance.

'Look at them run,' Ebellius says, ignoring Maeklus. 'I said it was just like Corolis!'

But Darrago can see what they are doing. They aren't running. They are redirecting. Moving like the tide to crowd around Sanyctus.

The cultists scrabble at his armour plates and try to pull him to his knees, even as he cuts them down with his lightning claws. They are targeting his armour joints to destabilise him. Trying to maim him and pull him to his knees, all the while screaming those same words, over and over.

Blood for the Blessed.

Darrago kills his way through to Sanyctus, reaching him only as the last of the cultists falls to his brother's claws.

'Adiccio,' Darrago says.

Sanyctus takes a breath. Darrago can see it in the fractional movement of his armoured shoulders.

'Arthemio,' Sanyctus says, and there is not just anger in his voice then, but grief too. 'He is gone.'

And Darrago sees. The fifth member of Victorno's squad, Arthemio, is lying amongst the dead, surrounded by those timeworn bones. His armour is still glittering with ice from teleportation.

'I saw him fall. Before the heretics swarmed us,' Sanyctus says.

'He did not say a word. I saw him and he saw me, and then he just fell. It must have been the teleport.'

'Something in the storm,' Darrago says, absently.

He has lost many brothers in service to the Throne. It is always painful, but it is more so when the death is quiet. When it is the kind that cannot be fought or answered.

Darrago bows his head.

'May the Angel watch over him,' he says.

'We must go.'

The words belong to Victorno. The sergeant's armour is chipped and scored and the heavy head of his thunder hammer is blackened from the power field's activation. From the slaughter. Ebellius and Maeklus stand beside him. Darrago knows that there is grief in them too, just as he knows how they will cope with it. Ebellius will make jests that he does not mean. Maeklus will say nothing, until they return to the *Tear*.

'The mission still stands,' Victorno says. 'We make for the Crown before they can complete the rite. Before the storm breaks.'

Darrago nods. Sanyctus is still looking down at Arthemio. Darrago puts his hand to his shoulder guard to draw him away.

'Aye,' Sanyctus says. 'Before it breaks.'

Not far from the first of the ossuaries, Darrago and his brothers find those amongst the shrine's mortal defenders who did not defect. Darrago remembers the Militia Gloria from the thirty days he spent at the shrine. Everywhere in the Imperium has a standing army, especially if it is deemed sacred, and Sanguis Gloria is no different. They are pilgrims too, of a kind – those who chose to stay and take up arms to defend the shrine, rather than returning to their far-flung homes.

The bodies of the Militia Gloria surround Darrago as he treads the memorial hall alongside his brothers, crunching broken glass underfoot. The dead are not clean and timeworn as they were in the ossuary. These deaths were messy. There is very little white and gold left to their uniforms. Everything is blackened and reddened. Shell casings and discarded powercells lie everywhere.

'They fought bravely,' Victorno says. 'Desperately.'

Darrago looks around and nods. The Militia Gloria are not the only dead. The cultists and converted were bled here too. Their linen-wrapped bodies lie alongside the militia. Their jagged knives and their scavenged guns. With the mess that has been made of them, the two factions are almost indistinguishable. He curls his hand tighter around the banner pole.

'They were devoted,' he says.

The memorial hall is one of the main thoroughfares into the shrine proper. It is clad with plasterwork murals on both sides that depict the Passing of the Chalice. The murals show hundreds of mortals clad in white with their hands outstretched as the primarch Sanguinius holds out the chalice to them. Sanguinius himself is rendered entirely in gold leaf and rubies. He catches so much light that his shape becomes unclear. Hard to look at.

'They meant to hold them here.' Maeklus is at the head of the group, as always. The heavy flamer he carries makes him a pathfinder. A clearer of ways. He stands before an archway which was once a doorway. It was once barricaded, too, but now splintered wood is all that remains of either. Blast marks pock the stonework and plaster, and dust is still spiralling in the air. That is where most of the militia lie. Darrago notices that even in death, they are still gripping their lasguns tightly.

'Devoted,' Sanyctus says, looking too. 'You are right about that.'

Darrago can hear gunfire echoing from the way ahead. The shrine carries and bends the noise.

'We keep moving,' Victorno says. 'Succeed where they could not.'

Victorno takes another step towards what is left of the door that the militia tried to hold, and there is a noise. Movement amongst the dead. Then a bright light and a *crack* of air. Las fire splashes harmlessly across the face of Victorno's raised shield.

'No further!'

The voice belongs to one of the Militia Gloria. She pushes herself upright against the wall and holds her lasgun pointed at them in shaking hands. Her white and gold uniform is blackened and spattered with blood, but Darrago sees the mark of rank on her. Shrine-sergeant. He sees, too, the marks that the enemy left on her.

A deep wound bisects the shrine-sergeant's face, from her jawline to her shaved scalp, marring the faith-tattoos there. Speaking opens the cut afresh, sending beads of blood into the creases in her skin. The woman's heart rate is elevated and thready, her breathing shallow.

Victorno lowers his shield.

'Enough,' he says. 'We are not the enemy.'

The shrine-sergeant blinks. Her pupils are dark and dilated.

'We do not have time for this,' Maeklus says.

His words come over the vox so that the mortal cannot hear them. They are not callous or cruel. Maeklus is neither. He is being logical, as always. Victorno only sends one word in reply.

'Wait.'

'You say that you are not the enemy,' the shrine-sergeant says. Her words collide and run together. 'Neither were they, either. Not to begin with. But they became enemies all the same.'

It is Sanyctus who takes another step forwards then. The shrine-sergeant snaps her rifle over to him, but she does not fire.

'No further,' she says, again.

Sanyctus moves slowly. Carefully. He unlocks his helm and lifts it free to reveal his face.

'If she shoots, she could have your other eye,' Ebellius says, over the vox.

Sanyctus does not acknowledge Ebellius' words, but Victorno does. He fixes his eye-lenses on Ebellius, who nods.

'Merely an observation, brother-sergeant,' he says, in his smiling voice.

'We mean you no harm, shrine-sergeant.' Sanyctus modulates his voice to speak to the mortal, softening it. 'We were sent here to save this place. We are Blood Angels.'

She blinks again, then looks at each of them in turn. Her eyes fix on Darrago last of all and the company standard he carries, and then her face falls as she realises what she is looking at, and what that means.

'Blood Angels,' she moans. 'I fired upon *angels*.'

The shrine-sergeant lowers her rifle.

'Forgive me, lords,' she says, and she goes to one knee amongst the dead. 'I have failed. In defence of the shrine. In deference.'

'No,' Victorno cuts her off. 'There is no forgiveness due. No failure either. Not yet. Not while you live.'

'What can I do?' she asks.

'You have a choice,' Victorno says. 'You can allow your injuries to claim you, or you can fight.'

The shrine-sergeant glances down at the lasgun in her hands. The weapon is clean and well-maintained. An aquila has been carefully hand-painted onto the stock. It is fine work. When she looks back at them, her eyes are still dark and dilated, but they are clearer now.

'That is not a choice,' she says. 'I swore to protect this place. The chalice. I will fight.'

'There is fire in this one,' Ebellius says.

Victorno puts down his thunder hammer, head first. The

sound of it on the stone is like a tolling bell. He puts out his gauntleted hand to the shrine-sergeant.

'Then stand,' he says.

She reaches out and takes hold of his hand and he pulls her to her feet. She is still shaking when he lets her go, but her face is set and she keeps her balance.

'What is your name, shrine-sergeant?' Darrago asks.

'Orako,' she says. 'Talina Orako.'

In answer, the Blood Angels name themselves in turn. Darrago sees Orako mouthing the shapes of their names with a kind of reverence that he has seen many times in mortals. It is a reverence that has always made him feel vaguely uncomfortable.

'Know this, Talina Orako,' Victorno says. 'We will not slow for you. We cannot protect you. We will take you as far as we can to allow you to rejoin what remains of your militia, but we can take you no further. Our path leads us to the Crown, and it will be bloody.'

Orako puts one hand to the icon pinned to her uniform. The golden chalice.

'Yes, lord,' she says. 'Thank you.'

'There is no need to thank us,' Victorno says, and this time Darrago can hear the smile in his voice. 'Nor to call any one of us "lord". Names and ranks will do.'

Victorno has always been the same. He has no patience for graces. Deeds are his only concern.

Orako blinks again. She nods, slowly.

'Yes, brother-sergeant,' she says.

They follow Orako through the shrine. It is a labyrinth of arch-roofed corridors that twist and divide, leading to other ossuaries. To cathedrals and prayer chambers. To the unadorned billets of the Militia Gloria, and the spare halls used by the pilgrims.

Those in particular are filthy and worn. Sheaves of prayer paper scud across the floor as the Terminators pass through, pulled into eddies by the static cling of their weapons' power fields.

'This is the swiftest path,' Orako says, sweeping her lasgun side to side. 'It will take us to the central spine, and the lifter platforms that lead to the Crown.'

Darrago knows that keeping pace with them taxes the shrine-sergeant. He can hear it in the beat of her mortal heart. He knows that it is more than just the pace that taxes her, though. More even than her injuries. It is the whispering, too. The ever-present words spoken in reverse that carry on the cool air. Despite what Darrago is, those whispers pull at his edges and set him ill at ease. He watches the way Orako's fingers tap a nervous rhythm on her lasgun's stock and listens to the quick and thready beat of her mortal heart, and wonders how much of it she can endure.

How much of it they should allow her to endure.

'Your militia,' Darrago says. 'Where are they?'

Orako frowns. Her pace falters, as if thinking and moving are a struggle to do at once.

'The Climb,' she says. 'They were evacuating pilgrims and innocents down through the Spinal Climb.'

Darrago has seen the Climb before. It is narrow and twisting and runs up from the shrine's feet to its crown. Much too narrow for power armour, never mind Terminator plate. For a moment, he cannot help thinking of the pilgrims and the innocents pushing their way down that spinal stairway. They will be afraid. Their hearts will be loud.

Like prey-animals running.

Darrago shakes his head, hard. He shakes the thought clear, too. The vile thought.

'And you know this from the vox?' Victorno asks. 'You have communications?'

Orako shakes her head.

'The shrine-general sent a runner,' she says, then she stops walking completely. 'He sent Luriet, because of his quick feet.' Her face twitches and she sniffs. 'He was quick, but not enough. They cut him to ribbons. The traitors. The Devoted.'

Orako blinks. Her heart rate is quicker still. To Darrago it sounds like drums.

'The things they did,' she whispers. 'The things I saw.'

Victorno is watching her carefully, his helmed head slightly tilted. Darrago can read that look and knows what the sergeant is thinking. What Orako's fate will be if she has seen Tur Zalak, or one of the creatures summoned by his rites. Mortals cannot be allowed to know of such things.

'What did you see?' Victorno asks, his voice deliberately level.

Orako's tapping on the gun stock stops and she looks at him.

'Violence,' she says. 'Such violence.'

Then she shakes her head too. That same quick shake.

'Forgive my distraction,' she says, and the barest smile flickers on her face. 'This day has been wearing.'

Ebellius laughs at that. It is not as loud as usual, as if he has tempered it to keep from startling her.

'A truth if I ever heard one,' he says.

Together, they press on through the pilgrim halls, past crumpled sheets and rolled blankets and over stone worn smooth by thousands upon thousands of bare feet. There are picts and inked drawings pinned to the walls around them. Hundreds of faces look out at Darrago, watching with frozen eyes. Some picts are new. Some are yellowed by time, tattered and frayed. They are pinned over and on top of one another and they ruffle and turn in the cold air that blows through the shrine.

'The picts,' Darrago asks. 'Why are they pinned here?'

'They are the devoted dead,' Orako says. 'Those who died on

their path to the shrine, or on the Climb itself. Those who live pin the images here as a memorial. To commemorate them.'

'What claims them?' Sanyctus asks. He has set his helm back in place now, so the question is accompanied by the snarl of external vox. 'Why are there so many dead?'

Orako glances at him briefly.

'Many things claim them. Starvation. Thirst. Exhaustion. There are no provisions made for those who make the Climb. Faith will take them to the summit. To the chalice.'

'Have you ever made the Climb?' Sanyctus asks.

Orako nods. She is back to tapping that insistent rhythm on the stock of her gun, a nervous action.

'Yes,' she says. 'I was a pilgrim once. I travelled for thirty-six days to get here. Ship to port, to ship again. It took another week to get into the city. Another three days to make the Climb.'

'And then you chose to stay.'

'After I had seen the chalice, I couldn't bring myself to leave. It was beautiful.'

It had been beautiful to Darrago, too. Not just the chalice, but the crowds of pilgrims. Those hymns, sung loud. But it was not just beauty he saw, nor faith. He thinks too of the highest ranking members of the priesthood, borne aloft on clockwork walkers, or carried on palanquins by the faithful.

'When last I served here, I saw the divide between the pilgrims and the priests,' Darrago says. 'Between the poor and the privileged.'

He remembers the fat those priests had carried. The heavy cloth of their robes and the thick chains of gold they slung around their necks. The wine they drank and the food they wasted.

'The divide grows wider every year,' Orako says. 'Recently, peace has been hard to maintain. Even before the storm began, there were problems. Acts of cruelty.'

'Among the pilgrims?' Darrago asks.

Orako shakes her head.

'No,' she says, softly. 'I should have seen it. Should have realised what was happening. But then the storm came, and everything changed.'

'With quick work, we can yet salvage this place,' Darrago says.

'Damage like this, though,' Orako says. 'Can it ever truly be undone?'

Darrago takes a moment to answer. He will not lie to the shrine-sergeant, so he chooses his words carefully. He thinks of overstitching tears in cloth. Drawing ragged edges together.

'We can restore it,' he says.

Orako shakes her head. She takes a ragged breath.

'I do not understand how those who turned could do it. How they could defile this place, after giving everything just to see it.'

'Weakness.'

The single word comes from Maeklus. Orako looks to him, as if she is expecting him to elaborate.

'You will have to forgive my brother, shrine-sergeant,' Ebellius says. 'His words are few, and rarely comforting.'

'Better that than a talkative fool,' Maeklus replies, flatly.

Orako looks from one to the other. Darrago can tell by the expression on her face that she cannot tell the humour for what it is.

'He speaks in jest, of course,' Ebellius says, and he laughs.

'Of course,' Maeklus says, just as flatly as before.

'Quiet, the both of you,' Victorno says, and he stops in place.

Darrago realises why when the vox hisses live in his ears.

'Archangels.' The voice belongs to Captain Donato. *'Do you live?'*

'Most of us,' Victorno answers. 'We lost Arthemio. The failings of the teleport took him from us.'

There is a snarl that isn't just vox. It is Donato, too.

'Alfeo and Vytali fell the same way,' Donato says. *'Lost to the storm.'*

Darrago remembers the moment of translation. The smile of Tur Zalak and the dark shape that brought with it whispers played in reverse. Whispers that he can still hear.

'To something *in* the storm,' he says, over the squad channel.

'Aye, brother,' Donato says. Gunfire undercuts his words. *'There is a prayer hall at the centre of the shrine. The Angel's Heart. Make for it, and we will regroup with you. From there we will push up together and retake the Crown.'*

'Aye, brother-captain,' Victorno says.

The vox-link severs with another hiss. Darrago realises that Orako is looking blankly at them.

'What is happening?' she asks.

'A change of plan,' Victorno says. 'The Heart first, then the Crown. We must reunite with the brothers that we have left.'

Orako's eyes widen. 'Then you have taken losses too?'

She makes it sound unthinkable. Darrago remembers what it is that mortals see when they look at the Adeptus Astartes. He remembers his first service on this world, where the pilgrims bowed before him and would press their hands to the stone in the wake of his passing, as if he were holy to them too, just like Sanguis Gloria.

'We lost three of our own,' he says.

The breath Orako takes makes her shoulders fall. She puts her hand to that icon pinned to her robes again.

'I am sorry,' she says.

Darrago thinks about those words. Death is expected for him and his brothers. It is why they are made, to deal it to their enemies and to endure until they too succumb to it. That does not mean that he does not mourn, or grieve, or that he does not appreciate the sentiment behind the shrine-sergeant's words, simple as they may be.

'Thank you, Talina Orako,' he says.

When the cultists come for them, those reverse whispers seem to grow louder. Darrago can hear them even over the sound of las fire, and bolt shell detonations. He can hear it over the growl of armour, and the splintering of stone. Over the cultists' own bellowed words.

Blood. Blood for the Blessed.

A thousand dead pilgrims watch in frozen silence from the walls as Darrago fires his storm bolter into the press, sending cultists reeling. In the staccato light of muzzle flare, he catches a clear glimpse of one who has cut away a good deal of his own skin so that his teeth are always bared. Like the woman in the ossuary, the cultist's teeth are filed to points in what feels like a poor mimicry of Darrago's own pointed canines. The cultist's jaws hinge wide in a wordless, slurring scream that is cut short as one of Darrago's bolt rounds hits him, centre-mass.

Beside Darrago, Sanyctus cuts through the crowd. Orako is at his side as she has been since they found her in the memorial hallway. She fires her lasgun in bursts, catching those who are not cut down by Sanyctus' claws. Ahead, Maeklus makes fires of the traitors, while Ebellius clears the space around him with his power fist, setting the air crackling with the displacement field. Victorno pushes a wedge into the crowd with the face of his shield, breaking bones and crushing the fallen underfoot.

'Push through,' Victorno shouts, over the noise. 'Do not let them slow us.'

'The launcher is always an option, brother-sergeant,' Ebellius says. 'Just give the word. I could have the lot of them dead in an instant.'

'Didn't you learn a thing from Corolis?' Maeklus asks.

'Of course I did,' Ebellius says, with a laugh. 'It was very effective.'

'No launcher,' Victorno growls. 'Not until I allow it.'

There is a rasp from Ebellius' external vox that Darrago knows to be a sigh.

'Aye, brother-sergeant,' he says.

So they keep pushing forwards through the dead. Watched *by* the dead. Darrago holds tight to the standard, keeping it raised even as the crowd of cultists pushes and pulls like a tide and the floor underfoot becomes slick with blood.

Blood, the cultists say, as one. Blood for the Blessed.

Two cultists part the crowd. They are big, gene-bulked men with replacement arms of functional steel, as if they might once have been labourers. Both of them carry toothed industrial vibro-blades that are made to cut stone. Matching, ragged wounds mar the cultists' faces where they have excised their loyalty tattoos. One of them lunges for Darrago. The vibro-blade skids and scrapes across his vambrace with a burst of sparks. He raises his storm bolter and fires again, putting two smoking craters in the cultist's chest. The cultist bellows like an animal, dropping his weapon on the stone. Ebellius puts the wounded cultist down for good with his power fist. The other cultist goes for Orako. The shrine-sergeant fires her lasgun until the cultist is too close to fire on. She ducks under the blade, but it snags her and makes her cry out.

'Blood!' the cultist roars.

Darrago turns to aid Orako, and sees Sanyctus do the same, but the shrine-sergeant is already moving. She gets inside the cultist's reach and drives the butt of her rifle into his face. Once. Twice. Blood sprays over her and the cultist falls onto his back, his nerveless fingers still gunning the vibro-blade. Orako drops onto his chest and keeps hitting until Darrago can hear the rifle impacting against the stone floor. As the rest of the cultists fall to bolter and blade, he approaches her.

'Shrine-sergeant,' he says.

She doesn't look up. Her strikes have become weak and clumsy. Her head lolls and her shoulders heave with breathing.

'Talina.' It is Sanyctus who speaks her given name. It seems to bring Orako back to herself. She finally stops and looks up. Her face is dashed with dark blood.

'Angels,' she says, and she frowns, before looking back down at what is left of the cultist she killed. 'Oh,' Orako says. 'Oh, no.'

She staggers to her feet and lets her rifle hang by the strap. The stock and body are dented and misshapen from where she used it like a club. She wipes her hand over her face, smearing the blood. Darrago is struck by a memory then, of a distant world, long ago. A memory that he shakes clear before it can sink its teeth in.

'I wanted to make them stop,' Orako is saying. 'That's all.'

'You have,' Sanyctus says. 'We have.'

'Not the cultists,' she says.

'Then what?' Darrago asks.

She looks at him. She is shaking again, though this time it is adrenal and violent. Instinctual.

'The whispers,' she says. 'They are torture.'

'She is breaking.'

Again, Maeklus' words come over the vox, and again they are not meant to be cruel. He stands and watches her, his eyes narrowed above his breather mask.

Sanyctus shakes his head. The movement is sharp and jagged.

'No,' he says, over the same link. 'She isn't. She won't.'

Those words, and the desperation with which Sanyctus says them, grieve Darrago. He remembers a different conversation between himself and Captain Donato. One that made him feel that same desperation, though he tried his best to hide it.

He will not break, he had told Donato. I swear it.

'Talina,' Sanyctus says to Orako. 'The whispers will only hurt you if you let them. Hold close to your name. To your oaths. To yourself.'

Darrago recognises the words easily, because they are not so different to the words he used with Sanyctus on Kalatar. He wonders if it is a deliberate choice.

With all of them watching, Orako straightens herself.

'Talina Orako,' she says, absently. 'Sworn to protect the shrine of Sanguis Gloria. Once a daughter, then an orphan. A trader, then a pilgrim. Last of all a soldier.' She looks down at the body once more. 'But always a loyal servant of the God-Emperor of Mankind.'

'Good,' Sanyctus says. 'Hold to that.'

Orako nods. She bows her head, one closed fist to the icon of the chalice pinned to her uniform.

'See?' Sanyctus says, over the vox-link. 'She will not break.'

Maeklus merely shrugs and turns away. Victorno lowers his hammer fractionally.

'I hope that you are right,' Victorno says. 'Because you know what must be done if you are not.'

Darrago sees Sanyctus clench his fists inside those clawed gauntlets he wears as he watches Orako set off towards the next hallway.

'I know,' he says.

The Sanguine Tear, now...

'That violence you saw in the mortal. You believed the rite was the cause.'

Darrago thinks about that for a moment. He looks down at his hands. They are the hands of a killer, made blunt and heavy by his ascension and criss-crossed with scars from everything that has come since.

'I believe there is violence in every soul,' Darrago says. 'The rite just drew it out. Fed it and fuelled it.'

'Just for the mortals?'

Darrago knows the question isn't really a question. That his brother knows the answer, and wants to hear it spoken aloud.

'We have more than our fair share of violence in our souls,' Darrago says. 'You know that better than most.'

'I do.' Darrago's brother says nothing else. He just waits. That kind of studied, deliberate silence is in itself an art. In some ways it is no different than Darrago's own needlework, or Captain Donato's weaponcraft. It all takes patience and skill. Darrago listens to the ship humming and the ceaseless exhalation of the ventilation systems, and he knows that he cannot outlast that silence. That he must speak, and do so honestly.

'The rite drew out the Thirst, too,' Darrago says. 'I felt it keenly. Each moment was a test.'

'And what of the Rage?'

The word sets a fire in Darrago's blood. Rage. The Thirst is hard enough to speak of. It is a constant pressure. A shadow companion that hangs at all of their backs like darkened wings. The Rage, though. That is *other*.

'Had I felt that keenly, we would not be having this conversation,' Darrago says.

'And what of your brothers?'

The words are like a physical blow.

'What of them?' Darrago replies, struggling not to snarl.

'Before you even set foot on Luminata, you were watchful of Adiccio Sanyctus. Is that not true?'

Another question that is not truly a question.

'I watch over all of my brothers,' Darrago says. 'That is part of what it means to be Company Ancient.'

His brother does not frown, and his temper shows no signs of breaking. Darrago knows that is studied and deliberate too.

'But Sanyctus more than any other,' he says.

Darrago thinks of standing in the teleportarium. He thinks of the days and weeks before that. The *years*.

'Yes. Because he asked it of me, long ago, and I could never refuse a friend. Especially not one to whom I owe so much.'

'For what?'

'Deaths he spared me from,' Darrago says. 'A dozen, or more. The first was during the Torix campaign, before I bore this banner. Before I was granted the honour of Terminator plate. Adiccio walked through fire to find me, when the pyrostorms breached the citadel. We felled the last of the Torix witches together.'

'I know the story,' Darrago's brother says. 'I have seen the memorial scrolls.'

'Torix was just the first,' Darrago says. 'He has always put his brothers' lives before his own. He has always fiercely defended those who cannot defend themselves. Mortals, especially. He is selfless.'

'Self-sacrificing,' his brother says.

Sacrificing.

The word stirs Darrago's blood.

'Sacrifice is our father's legacy,' he says. 'It is no sin.'

'No, not a sin,' his brother says, evenly. 'But darkness can often be found in brothers who seek death so desperately.'

Darrago shakes his head. His blood is more than stirring now.

'You twist my words,' he says.

'No,' his brother says, patiently. 'I seek the truth. That is my duty, just as yours is to tend that banner, and to counsel your brothers. Duty is not spiteful, or malicious. Nor is the truth, though it may feel as if it is when it concerns a friend. I know that you feel that you owe Sanyctus. Perhaps you even wish to protect him, but you cannot. We may hide aspects of what we are from those outside the Chapter, but we must never hide from one another. That way lies darkness.'

Darrago exhales a slow breath. Some of his anger bleeds away again in the face of his brother's own unbroken temper.

'I know.'

Darrago starts putting the silver needles he uses back into the box alongside the spool of thread. He pushes them back into the needle cushion one at a time, exactly back where they came from.

'You were more watchful of Sanyctus than the other Archangels.'

'Yes.'

'And why was that?'

Darrago thinks of the years before. Of Torix and Solace and

Perdicia and every other battle. Of standing on the teleportation dais on the *Sanguine Tear* and seeing the distance in Sanyctus' face.

'Because I could not let him fight his curses alone,' he says.

The Shrine of Sanguis Gloria, then…

Darrago knows that close to the shrine's summit, the hallways and prayer halls are grand. When last he saw them, the level of artistry had reminded him of the Arx Angelicum. Of the home that he was given. Those upper hallways have high, arched ceilings and delicate gilding inlaid into the walls. The marble underfoot is pristine and veined with crimson stria. This hallway, though, is far from the shrine's summit, from the Crown. It is not grand, nor gilded. It is the pilgrimsway, built for those who come to Luminata with nothing but their souls to offer. It is wide like a roadway, made for dozens to walk side by side. Bare and functional and made of cold, old stone. Candles burn in wall niches, scenting the air with heady perfume. Red wax runs from them in long, slow trails. Everywhere Darrago sees graven images of his father carved from plaster and stone. Sanguinius is wrought a hundred times, in all of his aspects. The Angel, serene. The Angel, triumphant.

The Angel, wrathful.

Darrago throws out his arm and slams one of the cultists against the wall of the corridor. Both the man and the stone break under the impact of it. The man's robes were white and gold once like Orako's, sewn with the symbol of Sanguis Gloria – a chalice with feathered wings. Now they are dark with dirt and the deaths of others.

'You cannot defeat us,' the cultist says. His words are wet and rasping. 'We are *devoted*. We will take blood. Blood–'

'Enough,' Darrago says, and he cuts the blasphemy short by breaking the cultist's neck.

The man grins wide even as he dies. Darrago releases him in disgust and the body slides down to lie broken at his feet. Blood paints its way down the wall, black and filthy with corruption.

Another long, slow trail.

Even through his helm's filters, the smell of that blood hits Darrago hard with every breath that he takes. It stirs the primal part of him that never truly sleeps, that thirsts for blood and revels in the scent and the spill of it. The same part of him that imagined the panicked heartbeats of the pilgrims and thought of people as prey. The caged, vicious animal at his core. It is a curse he carries, as all of his brothers do. One of two: Thirst, and Rage. Darrago has been fighting his twin curses every day since his ascension to the Chapter. Keeping them contained is a matter of will and of strength, so he takes another breath and squeezes his eyes closed for an instant, thinking of a handful of old words that have always served him well.

In this, we are angels.

Darrago opens his eyes.

His brothers are pushing up the pilgrimsway, leaving a trail of the dead. Torn by claws. Crushed by hammer blows. Broken and mangled and sundered. He hears hoarse shouts. The flat bangs of bolter fire and the crack of power fields as they go about their duty. Because that is what this is. Duty. They swore an oath to liberate the shrine. To take back the chalice. They can only go forwards, never back. There is no retreat. No respite. He must go forwards. He must endure.

So Darrago pushes on, too. Through the Devoted and their blades. The enemy are swollen by their new allegiances, made fast and strong and deadly. They grin and whisper and sigh as Darrago tears and crushes and breaks. Jagged edges score his battleplate and snag the soft joints. Bloodied hands trail down his faceplate. He breathes in, and the smell hits him again. It hurts more than any of the physical blows ever could. Darrago sees the others in stuttering glimpses.

Then he catches sight of another figure, and he freezes.

The primarch Sanguinius looks down at them, hands outstretched. His face is mournful. Tears glitter on his cheeks. Darrago finds he cannot catch a breath at all.

'Father,' he manages to say, though the word threatens to clot in his mouth.

Those tears catch the light as if they are moving. They are cut gemstones. Sanguinius' skin is marble. His eyes are painted in gold leaf. It is another statue, but it does not feel that way to Darrago. He looks around again, and now he sees more than just glimpses. The pilgrimsway has become a slaughterhouse. It is like a channel cut for blood to flow through. His brothers are painted red on red, still tearing and crushing. Still breaking. Darrago's purpose is violence. His duty is death. But he knows the difference between duty and darkness. He knows the pull of the Flaw when he sees it, but never has he seen it afflict so many, so completely.

'Violence,' Talina Orako says. 'Such violence.'

They are the same words as before, but Orako is not looking at the cultists. She stands at the heart of the storm and the darkness and looks at Darrago and his brothers now, with that same horror in her eyes.

As Darrago watches, she opens her hand and drops the blade she carries. It hits the floor with a clang like a struck bell, and

Sanyctus turns to face her at the sound. He snarls. His claws are lit and hissing. Darrago sees Orako's eyes widen and he smells her fear, even through his helm's filters.

'Adiccio,' he says, urgently.

Sanyctus' hands curl inside their gauntlets and the claws deactivate and go dull. Darrago hears him take a ragged breath.

'Do not be afraid,' Sanyctus says, but his voice isn't so well modulated this time. 'We mean you no harm. We are Angels.'

Darrago catches the way Orako's eyes flicker to the wreckage at their feet. He remembers again what it is that mortals see when they look upon the Adeptus Astartes. Angels, in more than name. But that is not the whole of the epithet that he has heard uttered on so many worlds since his ascension.

'Angels of Death,' Orako whispers.

The climbward approach of the pilgrimsway is once again pinned with the dead. Dozens of blank and staring eyes follow them as they approach the spinal climb, but this time they are not picts or drawings. They are bodies. Hundreds and hundreds of bodies.

Darrago looks to the walls as he follows his brothers through the pilgrimsway. The bodies are pinned there like prey caught by a butcherbird, as if they have been mounted on thorns to make feeding easier. The arms of the dead are wound with linens torn to resemble wings. The false feathers move in the stale air. Darrago sees pilgrims and priests. Thralls and retainers.

'No.'

The word comes from Orako. He has heard her murmur it infrequently the deeper they go. The more they see. Now, though, she hisses it and Darrago sees why. Pinned amongst the dead are those dressed in marble-white, with the icon of the golden chalice pinned to their tunics.

The Militia Gloria.

Orako goes to the closest of them and puts out her hand. She stops just short of touching those once-white robes.

'They are gone,' she says. 'My brothers and sisters.'

Darrago sees her hand close into a fist hard enough to make the knuckles turn pale.

'They have been bled.' Sanyctus has stopped. His voice is a hollow echo. Darrago stops too and looks at the closest of the sacrifices. A priest, by his robes. Darrago puts out his hand and turns the man's head and sees the mess of his throat.

A mess made by teeth.

Darrago pulls his hand away.

'They drank from them,' he says, and his voice is hollow too.

Unbidden, a memory wells up from the depths of his mind. One that he has tried for the longest time to forget. The day that he succumbed for an instant to the Red Thirst. It presses at Darrago in every waking moment, but especially now, in this place. Especially with all of the blood spilt and with that hateful whispering that never stops. Darrago's fangs ache at the thought of it, and his hearts do too.

'This is blasphemy,' Orako says.

'Blasphemy.'

The word is a ragged gasp. An exhalation. It comes from Darrago's left, from the sacrifice that is hanging closest to Victorno. This one is not dead. Not a priest either, but one of the shrine militia. He is breathing quickly now that he has awoken. Darrago can hear the thready movement of his mortal heart.

'Sahbal,' Orako says. 'Oh, Throne. *Sahbal*.'

She goes straight to him. The militiaman's eyes open and a wide, rapturous smile spreads over his face at the sight of Darrago and his brothers.

'Angels,' he slurs. 'You brought angels.'

Orako sets about trying to free Sahbal, but she cannot do

it alone. The iron spikes pinning him in place are driven too deep into the stone.

'We have to get him down,' she says, and she looks at Victorno. 'Please, brother-sergeant.'

Victorno nods. He slings his hammer and Ebellius maglocks his storm bolter. Each of them takes hold of one of the metal spikes pinning Sahbal to the wall.

'Deep breath, now,' Orako says to Sahbal.

The militiaman's eyes go wide, and then he screams as the Blood Angels pull the spikes free. Victorno takes his weight and lowers him to the ground. Sahbal has been bled, too, like the others. Just not enough to kill. When Victorno lets Sahbal go, he falls to his hands and knees and Orako crouches in front of him.

'What happened?'

Sahbal looks at her. His eyes are wide and dark and the pupils are fixed.

'The storm came,' he says. 'It brought the truth with it.'

Orako frowns. 'What are you talking about?'

'All this time standing in the Angel's shadow,' Sahbal says. 'Looking up. I didn't understand.'

'This is delirium,' Maeklus says. 'He is dying.'

'No,' Orako says. 'He is not going to die. He is going to be fine.' She puts her hands on either side of Sahbal's face. 'We are getting you out of here. Get on your feet.'

'I cannot leave,' Sahbal says. 'None of us can leave. We swore ourselves to the Angel.'

'Make him leave, or leave him,' Victorno says. 'Whatever your choice, make it quickly.'

'You cannot stay,' Orako says to Sahbal. 'There is violence here, Sahbal. Violence and darkness, and if you stay, then it will take you too.'

Sahbal blinks slowly. He allows Orako to drag him to his feet. The movement is awkward and stilted.

'Violence,' Sahbal says. 'And darkness. Yes. But those things were here before the storm. They are just plain to see now. That is the truth, brought by the storm. By the true angels.'

Beside Darrago, Sanyctus' claws flicker live.

'He is not what he appears to be,' Sanyctus says.

Orako shakes her head, and moves to block Sahbal with her own body.

'You would kill him as if he is an enemy. He is not. It is this place, making us see enemies where there are none. The whispers mean to make monsters of us.' She pauses and looks at her own hands. Takes a breath. 'I feel it, worse with every moment, and I think that you feel it too.'

A heavy silence falls at Orako's words. She looks ashamed to have said them, but she does not move aside. Darrago feels shame then too, because he knows that there is truth in what she says. That they should be above such things, but they are not. He puts his hand on Sanyctus' shoulder guard to pull him back.

'I would kill this creature because he is an enemy,' Sanyctus says, shrugging him free. 'Can you not see it? Can none of you see it? He is one of them. The Devoted.'

'Devoted,' Sahbal says absently, and he looks to Sanyctus with those wide, dark eyes. 'Of course I am devoted.'

And then Sahbal collapses back against the wall. His limbs thrash. Orako turns to hold him still as he seizes and his eyes roll back.

'Sahbal!' she shouts.

'The truth,' Sahbal says, through his gritted teeth. 'You will see.'

And then, before Darrago or any one of his brothers can act, Sahbal moves with preternatural speed, taking Orako's blade from her belt and burying it in her chest. She cries out and staggers backwards, her bloodied hands wrapped around the blade's hilt. Victorno catches her as she falls. As the militiaman's bones break and reshape. They grow longer and bend back on themselves. His jaws distend and the once-militiaman laughs in many voices like the song of a tuneless choir. Sanyctus roars and charges, and buries his crackling claws in the creature's chest. Sahbal screams again, this time in that terrible, multiple voice, and a pressure wave rolls out from the two of them like the detonation of a frag missile. It is enough to knock Darrago reeling, and tear thread and cloth from the company standard. Sanyctus is thrown backwards with a pained yell. The once-militiaman grows and swells and becomes something horned and blackened that laughs all the while without needing to breathe. Wings unfold from its back and snap wide, trailing smoke. As one, Darrago and his brothers fire on the once-militiaman, wreathing it in fire and tearing welts from its smoking flesh with bolt rounds, but still it laughs. Still it stands.

Then it moves.

Darrago sees his brothers disarmed and sent reeling. Hears them bellow and breathe ragged over the vox connection. Their heart rates waver in his helm's display even as the once-militiaman comes for him and tears his storm bolter from his grasp as he fires it. It slams him against the wall of the pilgrimsway and Darrago feels his ancient, inviolable armour creak and break. Something breaks inside him too and he grunts in pain, the sound of his own pulse filling his ears as he falls to one knee. The creature turns away from him and snaps its wings, propelling itself at Sanyctus. It pins him to the floor with a clawed hand as Darrago tries to get to his feet.

'And you,' the once-militiaman says to Sanyctus, through distended and dislocated jaws. The laughter undercuts every one of its words. ***'You will be the last and the greatest sacrifice. Blood for the Blessed.'***

Darrago hears his brother roar in defiance and sees the flare of light from Sanyctus' claws as he plunges them once again into the creature's chest. It howls, and it sounds like singing. Darrago finds his weapon, raises it and fires. The shells tear holes in the creature that was once Sahbal. Darrago keeps firing on it, bellowing old words dredged up from memories he cannot quite grasp. The creature relinquishes its grip on Sanyctus and is forced backwards, still howling. It tries to use its shadowed wings to protect itself, but even that does not last, because Darrago's brothers are back on their feet. As one, they surround it. They fire at it and strike it with blade and hammer and claw, snapping bones and shredding its wings to smoke. Crushing its jaws, and breaking its chest open to the air. Only then does it finally stop its infernal laughing, allowing the pilgrimsway to fall silent save for the creak of weapons cooling and that whispering that never ceases.

That, and the sound of Talina Orako dying.

The shrine-sergeant is propped against the wall of the pilgrimsway. As Darrago watches she lowers her lasgun and it falls to the floor with a clatter. The barrel glows from repeat firing at the thing that Sahbal became. Orako is shaking uncontrollably now. Blood runs from her nose, and her eyes are wild with fear. Sanyctus approaches her. He goes to one knee and removes his helmet again.

'They made a monster of him,' Orako stutters, through her teeth. 'Such a monster. Wings and teeth and those eyes. Those terrible *eyes*.'

'It is a choice,' Sanyctus says. 'Always a choice. Do you understand?'

'He let the whispers hurt him,' Orako murmurs.

Sanyctus nods.

'I did what you said,' Orako says. 'Held close to my name. My oaths. Myself.' She exhales, and that is a stutter, too. 'I am dying, aren't I?'

'Yes,' Sanyctus says.

Orako's head rocks forwards in a nod.

'But I didn't give in, though it would have been easy to. So easy. I think perhaps I can be proud of that.'

Sanyctus blinks. Darrago sees the scar tissue on his face flicker.

'Yes, you can,' he says, softly.

Orako shifts, and blood wells from the wound in her chest.

'I am Talina Orako,' she says. 'Once a daughter. Now an orphan. Once a trader. Now a soldier.' She lifts her hand and holds it out. In her palm glitters the symbol of the golden chalice. Sanyctus holds out his own massive, clawed hand and allows the icon to fall into it.

'But always a loyal servant of the God-Emperor of Mankind,' Sanyctus says.

Orako smiles at the sound of her own words given back to her, then she shudders and her eyes become flat and fixed. Sanyctus closes his gauntlet around the icon and gets to his feet.

'To the Heart, then,' he says, still looking down at his closed hand.

Victorno nods. 'To the Heart.'

'After the daemon's words?' Maeklus says. 'Do not be a fool.'

Darrago can see where the creature's clawed hand pressed into Sanyctus' chestplate, leaving a mark that looks almost like a bruise. He thinks of what he saw in the moment of transit. Of the chalice spilling over with angels' blood.

'The last and greatest sacrifice,' he says, slowly. 'The blood they want is yours.'

'Let them try and take it,' Sanyctus says, a snarl twisting his face.

'Think clearly, Sanyctus,' Maeklus says. 'We cannot take you with us.'

'Well, we cannot leave him behind,' Ebellius says. For once, he is serious. 'We are few enough as it is. We need his blades.'

Maeklus shakes his head. 'If they were to capture him–'

Ebellius snorts a laugh. 'Let them try, like Sanyctus says. They will soon see what happens when they do.'

'This is not something to take lightly, brother,' Maeklus says.

Ebellius flinches as if Maeklus has struck him. 'I know that. You know that I do.'

'Stop.' Darrago does not raise his voice, or clash the standard pole on the stone. He just speaks clearly and evenly, and they fall quiet. 'It is not your decision what we do – any of you. Nor is it mine.'

He looks to Victorno. The sergeant is still looking at Talina Orako's unmoving form, resting one hand on the haft of his thunder hammer. Victorno shakes his head.

'There is no way out other than victory. No extraction. We will not give them what they seek, because Sanyctus will not fall. None of us will fall.'

Victorno looks up from the shrine-sergeant's body and hefts his thunder hammer.

'The only thing that we will give to the Devoted and to Tur Zalak and his coven is death.'

The Sanguine Tear, now...

'The Devoted fed upon the faithful.' There is a change in the face of Darrago's brother then. The shadowed hollows of his eyes seem to grow darker. 'It is a perversion of our own rites,' he says.

Darrago thinks about that. About drinking from the Red Grail all of those years ago when he had but a mortal heart. He cannot remember it clearly, but he remembers the dreams that followed during the Angel's slumber. Dreams of feathered wings and a voice like choirsong. Dreams of warmth, but not the warmth of a rad-desert, or a blazing sun. It was a golden kind of warmth, a pure kind. Drinking from the Grail is what granted him and every one of his brothers ascension. It is a sacred rite. Pure, like the warmth from the dream. What he saw in the shrine does not conjure images of that rite, but images that he would sooner forget.

'They tore out their throats,' Darrago says, absently. 'Like animals.'

He feels a change in himself as he speaks the word *animals*. He thinks of the lone watch-station of Solace, so long ago now. Of catching his own reflection in fire-lit steel and glimpsing an animal there, baring bloody fangs.

Darrago blinks and lets out a breath.

'It was not so much a perversion of our rites, as a reflection of our failures. Something meant to expose us, not only to ourselves, but to those who had built Sanguis Gloria in our father's image. To those who consider us angels.'

He thinks of Orako's words as she stood against them.

The whispers mean to make monsters of us.

I think that you feel it too.

'You feel sorrow over the mortal's death.' There is no judgement in the way his brother says those words, just a cold curiosity.

'All deaths are sorrowful in one way or another,' Darrago says. 'It means a life cut short. One less loyal soul to fight and live and defy everything set against us. We are few, in a vast galaxy.'

'Mortals live short lives, Thaneod. They die easily, in great numbers. That is why we are made. To fight where they cannot. To stand where they fall. To endure what breaks them.'

Darrago nods. 'But Orako did not break,' he says. 'She endured the whispers. She endured her once-brother turning into something dark and hateful that she could not hope to understand. Despite all of that, she kept to her name and her oaths, and died without losing herself.'

'That is what truly concerns you,' Darrago's brother says. 'There is a part of you that seeks a noble death. That dreads watching a brother become something dark and hateful. This isn't about the mortal, not really. It is about the Flaw and the pull of it. It is about the fact that she saw a glimpse of it in the five of you, and that makes you feel ashamed.'

Insight is another of his brother's masteries. He uses it as deftly as he does a blade and with just as much certainty.

Darrago shakes his head. 'There is already so much for them to fear,' he says. 'Xenos. Traitors. The lost and the damned. They should not need to fear us, too.'

'There are few things in this galaxy that are assured. Death is one. War is another. For mortals, fear is just as certain. I said it before. It is why we are made.'

'To endure what they fear until the day that we become it ourselves,' Darrago says, before he can stop himself. 'Tell me, brother, what does that make us?'

His brother, as always, does not look away when he answers.

'Angels,' he says.

The Shrine of Sanguis Gloria, then...

'How did you know?' Darrago asks. 'You knew before Sahbal turned what had become of him.'

Sanyctus blinks. That scar tissue flickers. The damage looks deep in the half-light of the pilgrimsway as they keep moving towards the Angel's Heart.

'It made me think of Perdicia,' Sanyctus says.

Darrago remembers every battle. It is one of the gifts that comes from ascension, though where battles like Perdicia are concerned, remembering sometimes feels more akin to a curse.

'The cult of masks,' Darrago says, softly.

He remembers what the cult had done. What his brothers did, too, to make it right. He remembers standing beside Sanyctus to protect a cathedral full of innocents who had taken sanctuary from the sins of their neighbours. He remembers in the aftermath, how the families had come to thank them. They had pressed their hands to Darrago's armour as if in reverence and he had not known what to do, or what to say. He remembers Sanyctus dropping to one knee as the innocents took to their prayers, taking the time to speak good words for their lost.

'A cruel day,' Sanyctus says. In the moments between battles, he sounds more as Darrago remembers him to, more like his old friend, who spoke with the people of Perdicia. 'Every ninth mortal in the city tier crowned with molten silver in the name of something false.'

'I remember,' Darrago says, and he can smell the silver and the burning. 'But I do not see what that has to do with what became of Sahbal.'

'They gave themselves up to it willingly on Perdicia,' Sanyctus says. 'I could see the choice on them. In their eyes. They all had the same look. The same madness.'

Darrago thinks of the once-pilgrim and his wide, dark eyes. The intensity of them. He thinks of the cultist he killed earlier and the words he spoke.

'Devotion,' Darrago says. 'That is what you saw in them. A devotion to darkness.'

Sanyctus nods. 'They chose the easy path,' he says. 'They chose to give in, instead of fighting it. I saw the same madness in Sahbal.'

'The pilgrims and the priests chose to follow heretics,' Darrago says. The idea is unthinkable to him. His mind fights it. 'They chose Zalak and his coven.'

'Out of weakness or fear,' Sanyctus says. 'Perhaps they did not fully understand the choice that they were making, or what they were truly becoming, but they made the choice nonetheless. They still had to answer for it.'

He looks at Darrago. For a moment, he almost looks serene beneath the blood and the ashes and all of his scars, then he takes his helm and locks it back in place. Darrago just sees himself reflected in the jade eye-lenses.

'As we all will, in the end,' Sanyctus says.

The approach to the Heart is filled with candles. Thousands of them, still lit and flickering, two or three times Darrago's own height. New ones have been affixed over the old ones, and over time they have melted and combined to create grand, twisted stalagmites of wax crowned with those tiny flames. Flames that endure despite the sawing breaths of dry, stale air that push and pull through the shrine. Despite the candlekeepers who lie dead at the feet of each of the red wax monoliths. They burn on heedless as the Archangels tread through puddles of softened wax, leaving heavy, pressed footprints behind them. There are other footprints in the wax, too, crossing over one another as if made in panic. Most of them were made by boots or soft shoes. Some by bare feet, that look misshapen and distorted.

'They should have gone out,' Maeklus says.

He is looking up at one of the candles. It is so large that the candlekeepers have carved hand and foot holds into the face of it in order to reach the top and tend the flames.

'There is something to be said for light that can endure in a place this dark,' Victorno says.

Maeklus frowns. 'They should have gone out,' he says, again.

Sanyctus stops moving. 'Quiet,' he says, the combat-edge made by adrenaline turning his voice sharp. 'Do you hear that?'

Darrago listens. He hears the burn of candles. The drip of wax. The snarl of his own Terminator plate.

The whispers in reverse, growing louder.

'Ready yourselves,' Victorno bellows.

At his words, every candle in the corridor roars to new life. The flames grow to reach the ceiling, then as one they blow out. Everything but the pilot light on Maeklus' flamer. Darrago's eye-lenses adjust instantly to compensate for the darkness, and to reveal spiked, horned shadows peeling away from the walls, wielding jagged blades. The daemons' eyes glow balefire red and Darrago's world becomes a handful of instances, lit by gunfire. The daemons are only part-born, not truly corporeal, and they flicker like the candles did, disappearing and reappearing and trailing smoke. They roar like working engines without needing to take a breath, a constant assault of noise. Where they are hit by bolt shells, or by power weapons, the daemons discorporate and burst, scattering ashes. But there are many. One of their jagged blades strikes Darrago's armour at the waist and goes through. It goes through him, too. He roars in pain, coughing blood onto the inside of his faceplate. Darrago fires his storm bolter until the daemon's balefire eyes gutter out. Beside him, Ebellius shatters marble and daemonstuff alike with his power fist. Victorno's hammer lights the corridor with every strike. Sanyctus' claws cut and rend as the daemons shift and swarm and move on him as one. They seek his blood, too, just like the Devoted.

'Adiccio!' Darrago shouts, as he loses sight of his brother.

'Burn them!' Sanyctus roars.

'Aye,' Maeklus says, and he turns his heavy flamer onto the daemon-tide.

The corridor ahead of Darrago lights, hot white and red. The flames roll over the daemons, and over Sanyctus too. For a moment, he is lost to it. Consumed by it. But Terminator armour is built to withstand the worst of punishments.

And so are those who wear it.

The flames go out and the daemons are dust, but Sanyctus remains. Fire clings to his armour, burning his oath seals away. Wax runs over and off the plates. They are blackened by ashes now too, save for those red wax trails. Sanyctus' eye-lenses have cracked with the heat of it. He tears his helm free and locks it to his belt. He is breathing deeply and raggedly.

Maeklus does not speak. He just approaches Sanyctus and thumps his closed fist against his shoulder. Sanyctus nods in answer.

'Blinded all over again, brother,' Ebellius says. 'There is such a thing as wanting too much for glory.'

Ebellius laughs, because Ebellius always laughs, especially when things are dire. Sanyctus doesn't join in. His one good eye is dark and furious. The firelight reflects in it.

'Glory,' Sanyctus says. 'No. Not glory.'

Then he turns away and moves off up the corridor, and for a moment to Darrago the red wax trails on his brother's armour look just like saltires.

Red on black.

The closer they get to the Angel's Heart, the darker it becomes. There are no more candles. No more pennants or banners. No more murals or gilded glories. They have all been torn away and replaced with eight-pointed stars and inverted chalices and those same words that the cultists keep saying.

Blood for the Blessed.

It is painted in great, angry strokes that flake and smear and smell like iron. It is dizzying, that smell.

Overwhelming.

Darrago crushes devotionals underfoot just as he crushes the cultists holding the cloisters of the pilgrimsway. The heretics. The once-priests that have painted red trails down their faces and the fronts of their robes. He breaks their bones with his gauntleted fist. His breathing is loud and ragged inside his helm. Beside him his brothers fight and break and kill too. They are unstoppable.

Blood.

The word echoes for Darrago as the cultists roar it at him.

Blood.

But then he breaks and he kills until all of the cultists are dead, but still the roar does not stop.

Because the roar is his own.

Darrago stops. Staggers. He plants the company standard to keep from falling. His limbs tremor and his fangs ache up into his head. He blinks. Sees his brothers kill in what seems like half-time. The cultists still do not scream, but some of them laugh as they die. The golden thread sewn into the company standard catches Darrago's eye. The glories, and the lessons learned.

'In this,' he shouts, through the pain and the darkness and the want to give into the roar. 'We are angels!'

His words echo back at him from his helm's emitters and off the walls of the pilgrimsway as his brothers falter and stop their snarling. Their shaking.

All save for one.

'Sanyctus!' Victorno shouts.

Sanyctus has left a trail of the dead and a thick slick of that black blood. It takes much of Darrago's strength not to let it unsteady him. Overwhelm him.

'Adiccio,' Darrago says, between breaths.

At the sound of his name, Sanyctus turns. His one good eye is wild. A thick stripe of blood paints its way down his chin and the front of his Terminator plate. He drops the cultist that he is holding in his gauntlet and his lightning claws snap live. He lunges for Darrago, and Victorno blocks it with his storm shield. The power fields clash together with a boom of pressure.

'The lesson!' Darrago shouts. 'Adiccio!'

Sanyctus finally falters. Finally stops.

'The lesson,' he slurs through his teeth. 'I remember.'

Victorno pushes Sanyctus back and lowers the shield slowly. Sanyctus looks down at the marble floor. At the bodies and the blood.

'This place,' he says, and his voice is less slurred. More like his own. 'We mean to save it. To make it clean. Yet there is already so much ruin.'

'We will save it. We are the only ones who can.' The pause Victorno makes is deliberate. Weighted. 'We are the only ones strong enough.'

After a long moment, Sanyctus nods slowly. 'The Heart, then the Crown,' he says. 'Then it is done.'

Darrago is unsure in that moment whether Sanyctus is talking about the task that lies ahead, or about himself. He does not get the chance to ask because his brother turns away and the five of them set to moving along the pilgrimsway. Into the darkness and towards the Heart. This time Maeklus leads, with Ebellius walking beside Sanyctus. Victorno stays at Darrago's side.

'He barely saw you, this time,' Victorno says, over a private vox link. 'It is getting worse with every fight.'

Darrago shakes his head. 'It is just this place,' he says. 'That is all.'

'This place is vile,' Victorno says. 'That is true. It presses at the edges of my mind. Feeds the curses we carry. But he meant to fight you, Thaneod. He meant to kill you. That is more than a moment of weakness. That is failure.'

Darrago lets out a slow breath. 'The words brought him back,' he says. 'It is not failure yet.'

'The lesson,' Victorno says. 'Remember the lesson. Why does it bring him back? What does it mean?'

Darrago tightens his grip on the company standard.

'The lesson comes from Kalatar,' he says. 'From the war with the orks.'

Victorno grunts. 'Those that took his eye,' he says. 'Damn near took my head. I remember. But what is the lesson?'

Darrago watches Sanyctus, keeping half an eye on his brother's vital signs. The heartbeat monitor is more steady now, but it is always a pace quicker than the others.

'We fought furiously on Kalatar,' Darrago says. 'But Adiccio most of all. When the battle turned, he would not fall back. He meant to kill their warlord in vengeance for the death and destruction they had wrought on that world, but he got cut off from the rest of us. I lost sight of him amongst the hordes and I only found him again by the trail of greenskin dead. There was not a glimmer of gold left on his plate for the blood and the damage. I thought that he could be dead too, he was so still.'

Darrago shakes his head. It makes the servos in his armour whine.

'I called out his name, and he moved. He looked at me with the eye left to him and put his hand to the ruin of the one that he'd lost and told me that was the price for his failure. That his rage truly had blinded him. Then he asked me to remember it. To never let him forget the lesson.'

'And when he cannot be reminded?' Victorno asks. 'When the words no longer work?'

Darrago feels a pull of grief on his hearts, just as when he saw Arthemio lying amongst the timeworn dead.

'You know the answer to that question, Dio,' Darrago says. 'We all know the price for that kind of failure.'

The Sanguine Tear, now…

'Then you had considered the fact he might fail? That the Flaw might claim him?'

Darrago has set about folding the banner now, leaving his work half done. He will return to it later, when his head is not so clouded and he is not so troubled. When the questions are done, and judgement passed.

'It would be ignorant not to,' Darrago says. 'There is an inevitability to it. It is a decline that cannot be denied. The path leads only downwards. It is what you do on that path that you can control. How surely you can slow the descent.'

Darrago's brother nods. 'Meditation. Training. Craft or creation. Mantras, like your own.' He pauses. 'In this, we are angels.'

When the mantra is spoken by Darrago's brother, the inflection is different. More sombre.

'Those words remind me what I am,' Darrago says. 'What I should be.'

'And where do they come from?'

Darrago finishes folding the banner. He pushes out the last of the creases.

'Adiccio,' he says. 'He spoke those words to me on Solace, long ago.'

The memory of that day comes back to him now, as it does often, and he catches the chill that comes from shame. Darrago pushes it aside with effort and tries not to think of that blissful blindness and the euphoria that came with the taste of blood. That is why those words became a mantra, because they ease the pain of that memory and keep him from making any more like it.

'It is another thing I owe him for,' Darrago says. 'More so than the deaths denied, in truth.'

Solace was the moment that truly bound the two of them together. A singular instance of terrible vulnerability, the likes of which Darrago had never known before that day, and has not known again since, thanks to that handful of words given to him by a brother.

'It would have been ignorant not to consider the Flaw, or how it circled my brother,' Darrago says. 'But that does not mean that I doubted Adiccio, or that I believed he would fail. He has always been selfless, as I said, but he has always been strong too. Capable of arresting that descent, no matter the pull of it. He always returns to us.'

'And after the chalice? Was that truly Adiccio Sanyctus who returned to you then?'

Darrago thinks about it a moment. About golden fire and the screams of warp-sent horrors. About the look in Sanyctus' remaining eye, beatific.

'Yes,' he says. 'I believe it was.'

The Shrine of Sanguis Gloria, then...

The Angel's Heart was once a hall of worship, grand and arched. There are smooth furrows in the marble floor from the passing of hundreds of thousands of pilgrims. From where they have knelt to speak the words of worship carved into the floor before another representation of Darrago's father. This one is three times Darrago's size and made from gold. It is sculpted with a beneficent smile and a hand outstretched as if it means to offer something.

Instead, the offerings have been made before it.

The bodies of pilgrims and priests have been dragged and moved and heaped to make that same eight-pointed mark on the floor at the foot of the statue. It burns, that mark, with blue fire that dazzles Darrago even through his helm's lenses. In the centre of the circle, surrounded by the dead and the fire, are five kneeling figures, clad in crimson armour trimmed with silver. They are chanting unwords. The same unwords that carry on the cold air as whispers.

'Heretics.'

The five Word Bearers stop their chanting and get to their feet. They trail smoke as they turn as one, their armour plates swelling and shifting as curves of bone push through the ceramite. They grow horns and claws and jutting spines, their eye-lenses glowing balefire red.

'Warp-kin,' Victorno snarls.

Darrago and his brothers fire on the possessed Word Bearers without hesitation, but the shells burn up when they hit the ritual circle, burst by tongues of blue flame.

The first of them laughs, in a twinned, asynchronous voice.

'Hail, angels,' he says. ***'Come to make an offering, have you?'***

He turns his head with a creak of ceramite and metal, and looks to Sanyctus. The five balefire lenses set into his helm flicker.

'And such an offering it is, too,' he says. ***'This fractured angel, with violence boiling his blood.'***

Sanyctus roars at the Word Bearer. His claws light and he takes a step forwards.

'Wait,' Darrago says, because he can guess what will happen should Sanyctus try and cross that burning circle. 'Adiccio.'

'I will show you violence,' Sanyctus bellows at them. 'I will show you blood.'

The Word Bearer laughs again, and his four brothers echo it.

'Perfect,' he says. 'Just as the Blessed said.'

There is another creak of ceramite, and with a rolling cloud of smoke, leathery wings unfold from the traitors' backs, casting long shadows in the light from the witchfire.

'Such a shame,' says the Word Bearer, with his five golden eyes flickering. 'For you to think yourselves angels, but never to know how it truly feels to fly.'

His next word is an echoing chain of syllables that sends Darrago blind for an instant and makes his ears ring. The witch-fire circle rolls out as the Word Bearers snap their wings and leap into the air. Darrago moves with his brothers to shield

Sanyctus, taking the brunt of the tide of witchfire across his armour. The standard is caught in it too, making the glories wrought in golden thread catch and smoulder. Darrago feels the fire as if he is not wearing armour at all. It scorches his skin, and stings his eyes and his throat as he tries to breathe.

Through the blindness and the pain, he barely manages to raise his storm bolter and fire at the Word Bearer that comes to kill him, claws outstretched. This one has no eye-lenses at all. His faceplate has shaped itself to resemble nothing but teeth. The traitor's armour shifts to catch the detonations from the bolt shells and deflect them in the instant before he lands heavily, trying to knock Darrago to his knees. He punches his jagged claws through Darrago's armour at the shoulder and the chest. The pain of it sets Darrago's nerves alight and makes his vision dazzle. He cannot cry out, because with the claw buried in his chest he cannot breathe, but Darrago does not fall, because he is made to stay standing. He is made to endure and defy. He moves despite the bleeding and the pain and his empty, breathless lungs, firing his storm bolter at point-blank range up into the Word Bearer's body.

The traitor goes reeling and his claws come clear. That hurts twice as badly. Darrago's armour systems blare warnings in his ears. The Word Bearer snaps his wings to regain his balance, but Darrago will not let him fly again. He punches the standard pole through one of the traitor's wings and pins him to the ground with it. The Word Bearer twists and pulls and the wing tears and begins to reshape, but he is not quick enough this time. Darrago empties the rest of the storm bolter's magazine into the traitor's head and chest until the ceramite cracks and the bones beneath it shatter and the heretic falls with a crash of armour plates, bleeding black all over the floor.

Darrago pulls the standard free and he turns to see his brothers fighting furiously to keep the Word Bearers from taking Sanyctus. Ebellius shatters the frozen, grinning helm of one of them with a blow from his power fist. Maeklus has set one of them afire, but the Word Bearer keeps his feet, fighting even as he burns. Victorno uses his storm shield to push the one with the five golden eyes onto his back foot.

'Every drop of blood spilt is just another offering,' the Word Bearer says. ***'The rite has already begun!'***

He turns Victorno's hammer strike aside with his gauntlet, though such a thing should not be possible. It sets Victorno off-balance, opening his guard. Then the Word Bearer lashes out with his other clawed hand, shattering Victorno's faceplate and sending his blood across the marble floor. The sergeant staggers and slurs an old Baalite curse. Darrago's bolter is empty, so he charges instead, but he is slow from his wounds and the way the witchfire burned him.

So Sanyctus gets there first.

Sanyctus hits the Word Bearer with all of his weight, burying both of his lightning claws in the traitor's chest.

'Perfect,' says the Word Bearer. 'Such a perfect, violent thing.'

He steps back and free of Sanyctus' claws with a welter of black blood and smoke. The traitor answers with his own claws. One strike opens Sanyctus' face to the bone. The other buckles his chest plate and drives him to his knees.

'No!' Darrago shouts.

The Word Bearer's mask tilts towards him, and the warped ceramite splits like a smile.

'Blood,' he says. ***'For the Blessed.'***

Then there is a roar, and the Word Bearer's smiling mask is pulverised by a spear of bright light fired from behind Darrago. The Word Bearer staggers backwards and lets go of Sanyctus, his faceplate trying to reshape through the colossal damage. Darrago looks back to see Captain Donato haloed by light as he charges into the fray. Phaello is with him, and the two shield-brothers that remain of his squad, Ivaro and Lurani.

'No,' Donato bellows. 'The only blood spilt here will be yours.'

TWO

WEAPONS

The Sanguine Tear, now...

Larracus Donato has never found much respite in rest, so when he is not called to battle, he trains. He chooses to do so without his Terminator plate. Without his power fist or his storm bolter. Instead, he wears the kind of roughweave training clothes an aspirant might wear. That too is because it allows him respite, from the weight of the armour and what it means to wear it, but there is another reason for Donato's choice.

Because there is value in remembering what you once were.

So Donato trains alone in the lower decks of the *Sanguine Tear*, under white-hot lumens that remind him of home and make the wooden boards underfoot warm. He trains with a simple, short-bladed sword that he cast for himself. The combat servitors outnumber him three to one. They are armed with their own jagged blades and set to draw blood, because there is no respite in an easy fight either. Donato turns aside from the erratic motion of the first, and puts the momentum of that movement into severing the second servitor's arm at the shoulder. His follow-up strike sends it reeling and broken and sprays oil across the training hall floor.

Donato's hearts beat steadily in his chest. His mind is clear, and the fury far away. This fight is to him as painting or poetry is to his brothers. It is about artistry. About technical skill, and perfect execution. The third servitor lunges for him with its heavy, augmented limbs. Donato ducks under the strike and punches his sword through the servitor's nervous centre. It spasms and falls aside. As he moves to finish the fight, the heavy doors to the training hall open and an armoured figure enters. One of Donato's brothers, but one he rarely has cause to speak with. One he feels no joy at the sight of. His brother waits in silence outside the training circle. There is no ending the fight other than by victory, so Donato despatches the last of the servitors quickly. That last one manages to cut him before it falls, snagging him across the arm with the jagged blade it carries.

'Damn,' Donato says, and he puts his hand to the wound.

It is not severe. Donato barely feels the cut itself, and it certainly will not scar, but his hearts are not steady now. The fury is not so distant. To some degree, it is because of the blood; even spilling his own sets the curse he carries singing. But Donato is practised at ignoring that song. The true cause for his unrest is that Donato knows that he could have won without injury, but he let the presence of his silent, watchful brother unsettle him.

'I would speak with you, brother-captain,' his brother says.

'Then speak,' Donato says, as he crosses the hall and takes up a cloth with which to clean the oil from his training sword. Normally thralls would already be clearing the circle, but there are none present. The questions that this brother asks are only for those of the Chapter to hear. 'Know that if you mean to ask about Luminata, I fear there is little more I can add,' Donato says. 'I have already made my report. I have already spoken with Lord Commander Dante.'

His brother has crossed the hall too. If the mention of Dante's name gives him pause, he does not show it. Nothing ever shows on his face in moments like these.

'I have read your report,' his brother says. 'It told me much, but not everything.'

Donato catches his own reflection in the blade of the training sword. Just like the wound he took from the servitor, the scars that he earned on Luminata are already fading.

'Then what do you want me to tell you?' he asks.

'I want you to tell me about Adiccio Sanyctus,' his brother says.

That does stoke the fury in Donato's blood. He waits for it to pass before he speaks again, because he must be calm in the face of his brother's questions.

'You want me to tell you of Sanyctus,' he says. 'I will tell you. He has given much in the name of our father. In the name of the Throne, and of the Emperor. I saw him save Victorno's life when we fought at the foot of the Stone Saint. He felled the ork tyrant of Kalatar. Stood against a tyranid horde alone at the Shieldworlds' edge, to allow the Astra Militarum to regroup and emerge victorious. To spare the lives of mortals and lend them strength.'

'Those stories too, I know,' his brother says. 'Glories are not why I am here.'

Donato shakes his head. 'No, they are not,' he says, coldly.

His brother does not remark on his words, or the tone of them, though he would have the right to.

'I want you to tell me what truly happened at Sanguis Gloria,' his brother says. 'I want to know what became of Adiccio Sanyctus.'

The Shrine of Sanguis Gloria, then...

Donato watches as Maeklus sets light to the circle of offerings and the bodies burn all over again, this time gold and red, and not unnatural blue. His helm filters out the smoke, but not the scent of it. Funeral pyres. Donato lets the last outside transmission he received after teleportation play back again.

There will be no reinforcements, it says. What forces remain on the surface work to clear the pilgrims' city of traitors, and of innocents. This task is left to your Archangels, brother. If the shrine cannot be saved, then it must fall, and our enemies with it.

'They sought to take Sanyctus.'

Donato turns from the fire at the words. Darrago's armour is split and battered and splattered with black blood. The Company Ancient is breathing with a rasp that suggests the slow reknitting of a punctured lung. He has removed his helm and locked it to his waist, exposing a face made up of blunt angles and old scars. The aquila brand burned into Darrago's flesh is stark but his eyes, as always, are contemplative. The Company Ancient is a warrior, as they all are, but over time he has become the conscience of every one of the Archangels, including Donato.

'Just Sanyctus,' Donato says.

Darrago nods. 'The one with the golden eyes called him perfect,' he says, absently. 'A perfect, violent thing.'

Donato thinks about that. About Kalatar, and the Shieldworlds' edge, and every battle before this, and he cannot find a lie in those words.

'We will not let them take him,' Donato says. 'I do not intend to lose another brother.'

Darrago shakes his head. His eyes are more than contemplative now. They look sorrowful.

'Nor do I,' he says.

'Spare an eye for him, Thaneod,' Donato says. 'Just as we spoke about.'

'Always,' Darrago says, with a nod. 'The traitor said something else. He called Sanyctus the last sacrifice. For the Blessed.'

The Blessed.

Donato snarls at the name. At the twisted suggestion of it.

'The name that Tur Zalak has given himself,' he says. 'He thinks himself a priest. Thinks himself enlightened. He is no more than a heretic. A mad dog, serving false gods. His death is long overdue.'

'We will serve it here,' Darrago says. 'For our lost.'

Donato puts a hand on his brother's shoulder.

'For all of the lost,' he says, because he does not just want to kill Zalak for those lost here. For Arthemio and Alfeo and Vytali. He wants to kill Tur Zalak for what he did on Perdicia. For the cult of masks, and for the knotted scar across his chest that Zalak gave him that still aches, though it has no right to. He wants to kill Zalak for every one of his sins, from the Great Heresy until now, but most of all Donato wants to kill him to clear the stain on his honour. On Perdicia, Donato failed, but he will not fail again. Not here, under the sight of his father.

'We go now,' he tells Darrago. 'And we end it.'

The Sanguine Tear, now...

Donato chooses to continue the questioning in his own chambers, rather than the training hall. It is a large chamber as befits his rank. Weapon racks line the walls, hung with instruments of war. Swords and spears. Axes and knives. Donato walks to the empty space and racks the sword he trained with alongside the others.

'All of these weapons were made by your hand?' his brother asks.

'Every one,' Donato says.

It is another act that quiets the song in his blood. Another deliberate act that requires technical skill and perfect execution. He never uses them in battle, only in training, when he is trying to find peace.

'The broken ones,' his brother says. 'You keep those too.'

Donato turns and looks to the west wall. Every weapon hanging there is damaged. Blades are snapped or dulled. Splintered and cracked.

'They are all lessons,' Donato says. He crosses to the west wall and puts his hand to one of the splintered blades. 'This one was tempered in a weak flame.' He moves his hand to the next. An axe, with a bowed edge and a crack in the face of it. 'This one was quenched too soon. It makes the blade weak.'

Donato puts his hand to the last of the swords. The most recent. It would have been a longsword, and a beautiful one, but it shattered halfway up its length the first time he used it in training. He remembers that the splinters cut him.

'There was something in the steel of this one,' he says. 'It could never have done anything but break.' He drops his hand away. 'To discard them would be to forget them,' Donato says. 'And I do not make a habit of forgetting my failures.'

'Nor your enemies.'

Donato looks to his watchful brother. 'You speak of Tur Zalak,' he says.

'You had faced him before,' his brother says.

Donato nods. He can feel the thrum of the *Sanguine Tear* through the floor of his chambers. It rattles the blades on the walls minutely. They sing a shrill, barely audible song.

'On Perdicia,' he says. 'Fifty years ago.'

'You were sent to kill him, and to save the world from damnation.'

'Yes.'

'Perdicia was saved, but you failed to kill Zalak.'

Donato's hand goes to his chest. It is an unconscious action. A bad habit. The old, knotted scar there aches as if it is made fresh. It always does, when he thinks of Perdicia.

'I fought him alone,' Donato says. 'In a place that was sacred to Perdicia's people, but that Zalak and his traitors had desecrated in the name of his false gods.'

'The Temple of the Emperor Ascended,' his brother says.

Donato nods again, remembering. The temple was a ruin. Smoking, cracked and slicked with molten silver. Every surface was a shattered, warped mirror.

'I had him,' Donato says. 'I had shattered one of his legs and broken his arm. Taken his staff from him. He was doing little more than crawling away from me.'

'And then?'

Donato frowns. 'I could have fired on him to finish it,' he says. 'But instead I meant to crush him. To break him, as he had broken Perdicia, and her people.' He shakes his head. 'I was arrogant. Blinded by pride. I left myself open, and he struck me when I thought him already defeated.'

That old scar aches again. The damage runs deep. Zalak had cut Donato to the hearts and escaped, leaving him to bleed all over the mirrored floor of the profaned temple. Even in that moment, as he had been close to death, the smell of the blood had set the curse singing.

'And in the shrine?' his brother asks. 'Did your pride blind you then, too?'

'Blind me to what?' Donato asks, coldly.

His brother tilts his head, minutely. For the first time in a long time, Donato feels how it must feel to be prey.

'Failure of a different kind,' his brother says.

The Shrine of Sanguis Gloria, then...

In the corner of Donato's helm display, there is a red line tracking warp activity. It has been climbing since they entered the shrine. The closer they get to the summit, the steeper the line. The darker the path. The heavier the pressure of the storm that Zalak makes at the Crown. Donato feels it press against his mind as he advances up the marble steps, with his brothers in tow. Gunfire rains down on them from above from emplacements manned by cultists. It rings against his armour like rain on steel.

On either side of Donato, blood runs down the walls, collecting on the steps until the pools grow too wide and it spills over to the next and the next. The stink of it surrounds him. Suffuses him. It sets the curse he carries singing more loudly than it ever has as he keeps pushing up the steep climb. It takes every ounce of Donato's will to ignore the song of the curse. He thinks of training. Of deliberate, controlled movements, and the steadying of his hearts.

He thinks of the message.

This task is left to your Archangels, brother.

'Do not falter,' he roars. *'Archangels!'*

They answer him in kind. Some over the vox, and some aloud.

All of their voices are ragged with the strain of ignoring the song, but there is one that Donato barely recognises. One that sounds nearly animal.

Sanyctus.

His armour is blackened and burned. Cracked and trailing smoke from where it has turned aside the gunfire. He is snarling. Showing his fangs.

The Archangels hit the top of the marble stairway, and hit the cultists too. The mounted guns are smashed aside. Bolter fire thunders in the half-dark. But the cultists are not alone. There are creatures with them that have been called by the storm. Great, flayed hounds with jaws full of jagged teeth. They howl at the sight of the Terminators, and to Donato that too is another terrible, atonal song. One of the flesh-hounds leaps for him, and he fires on it with his combi-melta. The beam is searing white, an instant of light in the darkness. It punches through the daemon's form and discorporates it before it can collide with him. The ashes that are left of it scatter across his armour, and then they too disappear.

'Push through!' Donato yells.

And his Archangels obey. Donato sees it in flashes, by the light of gunfire and by the roar of Maeklus' heavy flamer

Phaello, choosing his targets. Not wasting a single round.

Ivaro and Lurani with their storm-shields locked and braced.

Victorno, crushing the skull of a flesh-hound to ashes.

Ebellius turning aside the beast that come for Maeklus with a roar that is both joy and anger.

Darrago, holding the company standard high. The only gold in the darkness.

Sanyctus, swift for one clad in Terminator plate. The kind of speed that comes from angels' blood. That comes from the song that Donato has spent decades ignoring. In the flashes of bolter fire, Donato sees Sanyctus tear cultists asunder with his claws.

Sees him break them against the marble and grow the pools of blood on the floor. As the fight drains away like the blood does over the edges of the steps, he sees Sanyctus fall to his knees with a crash of armour plates. There are furrows carved into the stone wall from where he put out his claws to try and keep from falling.

Donato goes to his side as the last of the cultists dies, and the last of the flesh-hounds are sent howling back to the warp.

'Brother,' he says. 'Can you stand?'

Sanyctus raises his head. Drool strings his teeth when he opens his mouth to speak.

'Can you hear it, brother-captain?' he slurs.

Donato can hear many things. The hum of armour and power weapons. The thunder of his hearts. Those damned ever-present whispers. The song in his blood. Before he can say anything, Sanyctus turns his head and looks at him sidelong.

'He watches us,' he says, in a voice made of broken edges. 'Our father sees. He calls for us.'

Donato has served for centuries, he has seen and heard and endured terrible things, but in that moment he feels the claws of unease cut deep. He remembers hearing words like those before, long ago. A different world. A different brother.

He remembers what he had to do.

'Our father,' he says. 'You hear our father?'

Sanyctus blinks. He looks away from Donato and down at the marble floor, and the mess that is left of their enemies.

'I fell,' he grunts, and he sounds more like himself. 'When did I fall?'

Donato moves his finger from the trigger of his gun. He maglocks it to his armour and puts out his hand.

'You haven't,' he says, and he pulls Sanyctus to his feet, with the unspoken end of that sentence echoing in his head.

Not yet.

The Sanguine Tear, now...

'Could you have killed him in that moment?' The question cuts Donato's retelling short. The silence that falls is heavy. 'Could you have made that choice?'

Donato looks at his brother and wonders if the question is really to do with what happened in the shrine, or if it is to do with this particular brother's own duty.

'I did not have to,' Donato says.

'That is not an answer.'

Donato has to think of training then. He has to steady his hearts.

'In the event of a true failure, and without one of the Chaplaincy present, dealing with that failure falls to the officer of rank. It would have fallen to me.'

His brother tilts his head again in that same way as before. 'That is still not an answer, brother-captain.'

Donato thinks of the moment in the shrine. Of Sanyctus' words.

Our father sees.

He thinks of a scream that becomes a roar. Of an angel, becoming animal.

'Yes,' Donato says, with certainty. 'I could have made that choice. I could have killed him, if I had to. When a soul is truly lost, death is a mercy.'

'A mercy,' his brother says. 'For them, or for us?'

That roar echoes in Donato's head again.

'Both,' he says.

The Shrine of Sanguis Gloria, then…

Their path upwards brings the Archangels to another ossuary. This one is above the heartline of the shrine, so it is built for the rich and the powerful. The consecrated bodies of the dead are set into the walls and ceilings and the tall, spiral columns. The bones are coated with gold leaf, studded with gemstones and laser-etched with prayers and hymnals. Far above, slaved cherubim still circle lazily on old commands, scattering handfuls of silk shreds made to look like feathers. But the rich and powerful dead are not the only dead in the ossuary. It is the site of another slaughter. Of another rite, but this time the sacrifices are not pilgrims or priests.

They are angels.

'The keepers of the chalice,' Darrago says.

The Company Ancient has taken a knee to turn one of the dead. The body is shattered and broken. There are tectonic cracks in the ceramite and the plasteel is twisted and misshapen as if by heat. There is not much of the face left to recognise, but the mark of the keepers still remains. It is a loop of white silk tied around the Blood Angel's vambrace, sewn with the icon of the golden chalice. Donato knows that Darrago wore it at one time, long ago, as he did.

But it is not the only mark that the keepers of the chalice bear.

On the throat of the shattered and broken body that was once one of their brothers, there are marks made by teeth.

'Something drank from them,' Donato growls.

Darrago gets back to his feet.

'Just like the other sacrifices,' he says.

The false feathers fall against Donato's armour, brushing over the plates with a sound like whispers.

Just like the other sacrifices, the whispers say.

The words echo from all around them. From every curling scrap of silk and every set of frozen, gold-leafed jaws. The words are harmonised, almost choral. Donato reacts instinctively. He raises his combi-weapon and points it, though there is no target to see. No threats highlighted in his helm's display.

'Show yourself!' he bellows.

Myself?

The words dizzy him, even through his helm, and he feels his nose start to bleed.

I would rather show you yourself, the whispers say.

The ossuary around Donato runs like wet paint and sloughs away. In its place grow spires and arches and panels of stained glass. They push up around him and enclose him. Donato's hand goes to his chest, to that aching, old scar. The wind howls around him, bringing with it the smell of fire.

Perdicia.

It is always Perdicia.

Around him, his brothers fight against Zalak's traitors. A clash of arterial red, and bruised crimson. Donato sees Ebellius and Maeklus, fighting side by side. One breaks, the other burns. He sees Darrago, planting the banner pole and standing defiant as the wind pulls at the cloth. He sees Victorno leading the charge. Phaello, sending one of the Word Bearers reeling with a well-placed shot. Lurani and Ivaro, with their shields locked. He sees Sanyctus by the flash of his claws as he cuts down another of the traitors.

Last of all, Donato sees Tur Zalak, standing at the head of the hall with his arms outstretched. Darkness coils around him like smoke. He grins, showing needle teeth.

Donato roars at the sight of him and charges forwards. His tread sends cracks through the floor underfoot, and it begins to give way. Donato's world turns and he loses sight of Zalak. His brothers cry out around him as the floor collapses, and together they all fall through cavernous darkness until Donato loses sight of them too.

He lands like a comet striking earth. More shattered marble. He should be shattered, too, from that height, but he is not. Dust rains down on him from above and it too sounds like whispers against his Terminator plate. Perdicia is gone, as is the Temple of the Emperor Ascended. He is back in the shrine of Sanguis Gloria, with the old wound in his chest aching so much that it is almost blinding. Donato puts his hand to it again, and finds it comes away bloody. His battleplate is split, the way it was on Perdicia. Struck by a traitor's blade.

'You are a fool, Angel.'

The words are familiar, because Donato has heard them before. He knows the voice. It is carefully pitched and controlled. Each word enunciated.

The voice of a traitor.

Tur Zalak stands under the fall of dust. It glitters on his warped, battle-scarred armour like ice. The Dark Apostle's face is what enrages Donato the most. Aside from those needle teeth of his, Zalak looks much as he might have before he turned. His eyes are painted with charcoal ash, golden markings tattooed beneath them.

He does not look like the monster that he is.

'I will kill you,' Donato says, with certainty. 'You will fail here, as you did on Perdicia.'

Zalak smiles. 'You might consider Perdicia a failure,' he says. 'But I do not. Had I completed the rite there, the reward would have been paltry in comparison to what I will be given in trade for all of this. For Sanguis Gloria, and the chalice. For true angels' blood.'

Donato tries to get to his feet. To kill Zalak. To break him, as he should have on Perdicia. The action makes him bleed all over the marble and himself. Makes the curse in his blood sing.

'That is far enough,' Zalak says.

Another figure stirs in the darkness beside the Dark Apostle. It is a woman dressed in ragged robes marked with pointed sigils. She is so thin that she looks as though she was built from bones deemed too poor for the ossuary. She sticks close to Zalak like a second shadow and looks out at Donato through her tangled fall of blonde hair.

You will listen, she says, in a voice that sounds like whispers. Like feathers made from silk, brushing over his armour. That voice locks Donato's limbs and holds him still. The psyker giggles and Donato sees pointed, bloody teeth, made for tearing.

'*You,*' he growls. 'You bled my brothers.'

Donato struggles against the binding the psyker has placed on him. His limbs burn and his armour creaks with the stress of it.

Zalak just smiles. 'Visia here did not bleed your brothers,' he says. 'They did it to one another, after they fed upon the Militia Gloria, and the priesthood.'

'Lies,' Donato says, struggling to such a degree that his vision dazzles. Even his bionic eye crazes with static.

'You should have seen it, Larracus,' Zalak says, as if he has any right to name Donato like a friend would. 'You Blood Angels are thought of as perfect, but I can tell you that you are never more so than when you stop fighting what makes you strong.'

'Lies,' Donato says again, as his vision flickers.

Zalak sighs. 'Show him,' he says to the psyker he called Visia.

He sees it in violent, swift glimpses. Donato is struck by the smell of blood and by the taste of it, as if he himself has done the tearing. His jaw locks, crashing his teeth together.

'See,' Zalak says, as the visions fade and the taste of blood with it. 'Perfect, just as I said.'

Donato manages to shake his head. Everything he was shown felt real. It felt true. He has seen enough to know that it is not impossible, too.

But still, he refuses to give in.

'Release me,' he says to the psyker. 'Do so now and I will make your death swift. It will be a mercy.'

The psyker retreats behind Zalak, her bony, thin hands pressed against his vambrace. She hisses at Donato and the pressure on his limbs increases.

'A mercy,' Zalak says, unconcerned. 'That is what you said to me on Perdicia, when you thought yourself victorious.' He tilts his head. 'You said that death was a mercy that I did not deserve.'

Zalak draws a dagger from his belt. It is jagged and crooked as if it was grown and not made. The blade is black, but it glitters like the void when he starts tapping it against the palm of his gauntlet. It is coldly familiar – the same dagger that Zalak buried in Donato's heart. Donato tries to shout defiance at the sight of it, but he finds he cannot even do that, now. The psyker has silenced him.

She giggles again, as if she can hear his thoughts.

'But death is not a mercy,' Zalak says. 'Death is a means to an end. It is payment.' Zalak stops tapping the blade. 'You think me indiscriminate,' he says. 'A monster.' He smiles. 'Perhaps that is true. I have done monstrous things, certainly. But I have done them gladly, knowing what I will gain in return. I have dedicated my monstrous acts to gods who love me for them. But you, Larracus Donato. You and your brothers. You hide what you are. You fight it. You call yourselves Blood Angels and clad yourselves in gold and red until the moment that you can no longer pretend to be something that you are not. That is why you think that death is a mercy. Because you would rather be dead than accept the truth.'

Zalak's smile widens.

'That you are the true monsters.'

He steps back and the psyker makes a shape in the air with her spindly hands. Donato sees his Archangels this time, in violent, swift glimpses, just like before. He sees Ebellius turn on Maeklus and shatter his helm and the face underneath. The two of them burn as they kill one another. He sees Darrago struck down by Victorno, before Phaello fires on him and kills him in turn. Lurani and Ivaro tear each other apart like animals. He sees Sanyctus by the flash of his claws as he cuts Phaello's throat, before falling to his knees. Sanyctus looks right at Donato then and speaks.

'He calls for us,' Sanyctus says.

Zalak walks over to Sanyctus. He doesn't react. Donato cannot even cry out to him.

'I thought it was your blood I needed, Larracus. That you would be the one to stand on the knife's edge of control under the Angel's eyes. That you would be the perfect sacrifice. It would have had such symmetry. Blood for blood, after Perdicia and how you wounded me. But it was never you.'

He pulls Sanyctus' head back to expose his throat.

'It was always Sanyctus,' he says, and he opens Sanyctus' throat with the dagger.

Donato roars then, despite the psyker's control. He moves, though he can barely breathe for the pressure. Donato gets to his feet as drool strings his teeth and blood bursts from his nose. A tear paints its way down his face at the sight of his brothers, lost, and he lunges for Zalak. Donato means to break him. To utterly destroy him. The blow never lands, because Zalak discorporates and blows away like smoke.

But the psyker does not.

Visia hisses again. She raises her hands and lashes out at Donato with panicked, invisible force, but he will not be stopped again. He will not be silenced. With the psyker weighing his limbs and cracking his battleplate open with telekinetic force, he manages to raise his combi-melta and fire.

The beam catches her full in the chest and obliterates her. In the micro-seconds before she realises that she is dead, the psyker whispers for a final time.

It was always Sanyctus, she says, as the darkness steals away and Donato finds himself standing once more in the ossuary amongst the dead. Amongst his Archangels, who are just as still.

'Brothers,' he says, and his voice echoes from the old bones.

For an instant, not one of them moves or speaks, and Donato's heart aches just as keenly as it did in the dream, but then they stir and move and stand again and Donato realises that the dream was a lie. Maeklus' faceplate is intact. Ebellius is not burned. Darrago is not broken, and Phaello did not have to fire on Victorno. Lurani and Ivaro did not tear one another apart, and Sanyctus did not turn his claws on his brothers. His throat is not cut. They are not lost.

Not yet.

The Sanguine Tear, now...

'Why do you think that Zalak considered Sanyctus the perfect sacrifice?'

'Attempting to understand Zalak is madness,' Donato says. 'There is nothing that can be learned from the minds of heretics.'

'I am not asking you to understand him. I am asking you to speculate, brother-captain. To draw a conclusion from observation.' His brother tilts his head. 'I know that you pride yourself on seeing every eventuality. Every outcome and the path that leads to it. So tell me what you saw. Speculate.'

Donato feels as though he is training, then. As if his brother has just disarmed him. He can almost hear the clatter a blade makes when it drops. He exhales a slow breath.

'I believe that Zalak thought Sanyctus the closest to breaking,' he says. 'The most affected by the shrine, and by the rite. The closest to succumbing to the Flaw.'

'And was he?'

If Donato felt disarmed before, now he feels as though he is being held at sword-point.

'I told you before, if he had been, I would have dealt with it.'

'Then why do you suppose Zalak showed you those things. Why did he tell you his intent?'

The question puts Donato on the back foot. He is being outmanoeuvred.

'In an attempt to break me,' Donato says. 'To make me weak. An easy kill.'

'To make you afraid.'

Donato looks at his brother flatly. 'Fear is lost to us. You know that. I will not say that it does not trouble me, but I feel no fear.'

His brother shrugs. It is a slight, spare movement. Everything he does is economical, until the moment his wrath is required and he stops being caged.

'Semantics, brother-captain,' he says. 'The idea of succumbing to the Flaw unsettles you.'

'It unsettles all of us,' Donato says. 'That, I can be sure of.'

His brother blinks. Donato thinks it might be the first time he has done so since the questioning began.

'But you did not see yourself succumb to it,' he says. 'You saw your Archangels fail, one after another. You saw them murder each other, and then be murdered in turn.'

Donato's hearts thunder at the memory of it. 'Yes.'

'Then what troubles you most is the idea that they might fall, and that you might see it.'

Donato thinks of the dream. Of a different world. A different brother.

'Yes,' he says, again.

His brother nods. 'It is an ugly thing,' he says. 'No matter how often you see it.'

Donato finds himself at a loss at the words and the honesty in them.

'Ugly as it might be, though, we cannot turn away from it. To do so would be more of a failure than falling.' That trace of honesty is gone now. Donato's brother is back to being inscrutable.

Back to judging.

'I do not plan on turning away,' Donato says. 'Not from this, or from anything else.'

The Shrine of Sanguis Gloria, then…

'The dream you were shown. It was of Perdicia, wasn't it?'

Phaello's words are softly spoken, even though the vox-channel he is using to speak to Donato is private. The two of them tread up from the Heart side by side. This path is lined with arched windows through which Donato can see the storm outside and the constant flares of lightning. Rain runs upwards on the stained glass, like tears being shed in reverse.

Donato nods. 'It is always Perdicia.'

The two of them have spoken of it before, because Donato has had no other dreams since that day. On the rare occasions he truly sleeps, that particular failure is always waiting for him.

'I saw it too,' Phaello says. 'Though it was changed. Zalak twisted it, and had you die before I could reach you.'

Phaello had been the one to find Donato half-dead in the Temple of the Emperor Ascended and to call the teleport that saved his life. That is why Donato told him of the dreams, something that even Darrago does not know.

'I will kill him here,' Donato says. 'As I should have then. He will pay for the dream. For Perdicia. For everything he has done.'

'May I speak plainly, brother-captain?' Phaello asks.

Donato looks at him, knowing that Phaello's words will set his temper afire, whether they are meant to or not. He knows, too, that is why he must listen to them.

'Always,' he says.

Phaello nods. 'I have seen you do great things,' he says. 'Marshal armies. Command a company-wide assault with ease. I have seen you oversee teleport strikes and orbital assaults and turn the tides of dozens of wars. You did those things because you have always been able to see the battle in its entirety, even from the ground. You always see everything. The whole battle, and not just the pieces that make it up.'

'You asked to speak plainly, Radst, so do it. Get to your point.'

Phaello's face is hidden behind his helm, but Donato hears the concern in his voice clearly enough.

'I do not think that in this you are capable of seeing everything. I think that you are driven to kill Zalak, and nothing else. That you are letting revenge decide things for you.'

Donato has always asked for honesty from his brothers, but it does not mean that Phaello's words do not stoke his temper. Especially because, at his heart, he knows them to be true.

'Zalak means to take Sanyctus from us and use him to complete his rite,' Phaello says. 'If he does that, we fail. The shrine falls. The chalice is lost. We are acting according to the enemy's design and being moved like pieces in a game.'

'What would you have me do?' Donato asks. 'Turn back? Leave Sanyctus behind? Neither of those things are an option, brother. Nor can we await Zalak. His armies are endless, and we are all that is left. Our only option is to go forward.'

'I know. I am not suggesting retreat. I am just telling you what it is that I see.'

'Because you think I cannot,' Donato says.

Phaello pauses, as if he is loath to speak his next words.

'Can you, brother-captain?' Phaello asks.

Donato hears the rain and the thunder and the whispers. The old wound in his chest aches furiously. The red line in his helm's display climbs. He blinks, and sees Zalak's grinning face, as he has every time since they left the Heart. He remembers how they ended up facing one another alone on Perdicia. He had planned the battle so carefully. Considered every eventuality. Acted reactively and rationally. He had ordered his brothers to evacuate the innocents, or to hold critical locations. To fight elsewhere, because he had considered himself sufficient to defeat Zalak. He had thought it a precise application of force.

And he had been wrong.

Donato exhales a long, slow breath.

'Fifty years have passed since Perdicia and my failure. I was short-sighted that day. Arrogant. I am not the same as I was then. None of us are.'

'That is a truth,' Phaello says. 'But the failure is not yours alone to bear. Everything we do, we do together. That is the way of a brotherhood.'

Donato nods. He knows that Phaello speaks the truth. That that is the strength of the Adeptus Astartes, but it does not change the way he feels when he thinks of Perdicia. It does not change the ache of that knotted scar.

'I appreciate your counsel, brother,' Donato says. 'But today will not end as that day did. I will not allow it.'

Outside, the clouds bloom with light. They are twisted and bloated, almost appearing like great, mocking faces. A second later, thunder booms, and the shrine tremors around them. Donato holds tight to his weapons.

'This time, it will be different,' he says. 'This time, I will not fail.'

* * *

Zalak's storm has found its way inside the shrine. Violet lightning crackles over the marble and arcs to Donato's Terminator plate as they push for the lifter platform that will take them up to the Crown. Boiling clouds hang in the vaulted space. Thunder booms, and rain falls inside, rain that is black and thick and paints trails across everything it touches. With the storm come creatures, not half-formed things like they fought in the lower levels, but creatures that are whole and strong and buoyed by the storm. Donato's helm display is nearly solid crimson with threats.

'We are running out of time, brother-captain,' Phaello says. 'We need to reach the Crown.'

His voice is calm, as it always is, but Donato knows Phaello to be troubled all the same. He feels it too, because of the rite Zalak is conducting and because there will come a point when the shrine and the world itself are beyond repair. Beyond saving. Something that broken cannot be made perfect again.

He thinks of the message.

If the shrine cannot be saved, then it must fall.

The daemons move for him, bringing with them a cloud of perfumed, choking smoke. They trail it with their every movement, shedding flakes of ash that glitter like broken glass. One of them smiles, exposing pointed, even teeth, and strikes at Donato with its massive, clawed hand. He turns it aside with his power fist and fires his combi-bolter into the daemon's head and chest. It discorporates, blowing that glittering ash across his armour, where it scores and chips the paint. Thunder peals. Ahead, through the melee, the rain and the shadows, he sees Sanyctus cut through another of the daemons with a strangled yell that echoes louder than the thunderclap of the creature's death. He is already moving for his next target. His heart rate is a jagged line in Donato's helm display.

'You are right,' Donato says to Phaello. 'We are running out of time.'

Ivaro and Lurani move in step with Sanyctus, using their shields to turn aside the daemons resolving from smoke all around them. The creatures are grey-skinned and black-eyed with maws of pointed teeth and cutting claws in the place of their hands. When Donato takes his next breath, he catches the scent of dried flowers and gravedirt, even through his helm's filters. He fires on them. Takes glancing blows from those claws across his shoulders. Ahead, Maeklus' flamer lights the chamber. The vox is fouled with atonal, contented humming as the daemons move and twist and cut, almost too quickly to see.

Quick enough to slip through Ivaro's guard.

'*Brother!*' Lurani shouts.

Donato hears Ivaro take a breath over the vox, but his words are stolen from him as one of the daemon's hooked claws severs his shield arm at the elbow. His shield falls with a crash and Ivaro cries out, but that sound too is stolen as the daemon's other claw severs his spine. The creature opens its maw and sings a twisted dirge as Ivaro falls to his knees.

'No!' Lurani roars.

He turns and slams his storm shield into the daemon, shattering it with the force of the blow, before finishing it with a strike from his thunder hammer. He holds guard over Ivaro with his shield raised and his shoulders set.

'Keep moving!' Phaello orders him.

Lurani rasps a breath over the vox. 'I will not abandon him.'

Around him, the daemons laugh in their splintered voices.

Such pain, they sing, and they lunge for him.

Lurani braces, but they never reach him, because Phaello does not allow it. Donato has never known another soul as keen-eyed as Phaello. As clear-headed. One of the daemons goes over backwards, a smoking hole made of its chest. Another is spun by his second shot. Its head disappears in a burst of glittering ashes. A third is discorporated mid leap as Phaello's rounds punch through it. Two more end on Sanyctus' claws. The smell of flowers and death is cloying and choking. Underneath that are the whispers in reverse. Ever-present. Dizzying.

Donato turns aside another strike and the daemon he is facing hums through its pointed teeth. That same contented noise. It goes to cut him like Ivaro was cut, but Donato saw how it was done. He catches hold of the claw and snaps it before firing his own bolter into the daemon's body until it too bursts and disappears, taking the humming sound with it. It is replaced by another sound. The urgent ring of Ivaro's life signs as they falter.

'Keep going,' Ivaro slurs. 'Before they return.'

Lurani shakes his head. 'I cannot,' he says, as Donato and Phaello reach them. 'Not without you.' Lurani has locked his thunder hammer to his armour and he has his hand outstretched. 'Get up,' he says, though he must know that Ivaro cannot.

'Can't,' Ivaro says. 'Nothing works. Not my legs, nor my arms.'

The damage is bad. Too bad for a sus-an coma, going by the vitals in Donato's helm display. It is only the false muscle structure of Ivaro's armour keeping him upright.

That, and his stubbornness.

'Go. Finish it.' Ivaro smiles, showing bloody teeth. 'Archangels.'

Then Ivaro's head lolls, and the flatline alarm rings in Donato's ears. Lurani's hand drops to his side.

'Archangels,' he says, to his dead shield-brother.

The lifter platform hangs on massive links of chain, slung around cogwheels ten times Donato's own height. The way up is lit by flashes of lightning. Wind howls down from the summit, far above, rattling those chain links together. It carries with it that ceaseless whispering and slick black rain that puddles on the platform and spills over the edges. The lever to start the mechanism is so outscaled and heavy that it takes both Victorno and Darrago to engage it. Donato remembers the priests using gene-bulked, augmented servitors to do it when he last stood here.

'Why haven't they cut the chains?' Phaello asks. He looks up into the darkness with his storm bolter raised as the lifter starts to grind slowly upwards. The sound is tectonic.

Sanyctus stands at his side, flexing his fingers absently inside his lightning claw gauntlets. He looks up into the dark, too. His one good eye is narrowed. 'Because of me,' he says. 'All of this is because of me.'

'No,' Donato says. 'All of this is because of Zalak.'

Sanyctus shakes his head. 'They seek my blood,' he says. 'That is why they have not cut the chains. That is why they have not collapsed the levels and buried us.'

'Then I suppose I should be thanking you,' Ebellius says. 'Being buried once in a lifetime is quite enough.'

Sanyctus glares at him. 'We are playing into their hands. Moving according to Zalak's plan. He means to thin our numbers, to weaken us until I am all that is left.' He takes a breath that sounds painful. 'Maeklus was right. I should have been left behind.'

'We leave none behind,' Darrago says. 'You know that.'

The Company Ancient is watching over Sanyctus as he always is. Darrago puts out a hand to lay it on his shoulder guard, but Sanyctus shrugs him free.

'I am a danger,' he says, and his words are jagged. They run together in the way of delirium. 'Do not tell me different. I see the way you look at me. As if I am an animal. As if I am already lost.'

'Addicio,' Darrago begins.

'No,' Sanyctus snarls. 'Do not lie to me. Arthemio is dead.

Alfeo and Vytali. Ivaro. They are all dead, and I am still standing. It is not *right.*'

Victorno slams the haft of his thunder hammer on the deck of the lifter. He takes a step towards Sanyctus. 'That is enough,' Victorno says, warningly. 'I won't have those words. Not from you.'

Sancytus shakes his head. The movement is almost spasmodic. He is shaking as if he is going into shock. 'It. Is not. Right.'

There is a moment shorter than the space between heartbeats where Donato glimpses the dream again. Feels the pain he felt at seeing his brothers murder one another.

'Enough,' Donato bellows, over the whispering that has grown so loud now. Louder than the movement of the lifter platform or the peal of thunder. Louder than his hearts, drumming in his ears. 'We all know what it is to be Angels. What it takes, and how it tests us. What it means to fail those tests.'

He looks to his Archangels in their burned and battered Terminator plate. Each with hundreds of glories to their name, and scars enough to match the stories.

'But we are more than just angels,' Donato says. 'We are brothers. We are blood. We face every task and every test together.'

His words silence his brothers and break the moment of confrontation. Phaello looks to him and nods, but Donato is distracted. He realises he can no longer hear the whispers. Not because they have stopped, but because they are being drowned out. Smothered, by a roar from above. Donato looks up as a vortex of warpfire opens above them at the summit of the lifter channel. The rain is replaced by motes of flame that fall and stick and cling to the lifter platform as the spiral of fire descends. In the tumult, Donato sees yawning maws and leering eyes, all aflame.

'Brace!' he yells, as the warpfire vortex surrounds them.

Creatures resolve from the fire. Carry it with them. Spew it from their wide-open jaws. It trails from their eyes. The heat stings Donato's own eyes and steals the air from his lungs, even through his helm. The temperature readout in his helm's display skyrockets as he tears one of the creatures from the storm and slams it onto the lifter deck. The warpfire catches and clings to the ceramite. Donato can hear his armour groan with the heat as he crushes the creature into dust. Beside him, Darrago roars. He fires on the daemons in an effort to keep the banner he carries from catching. Power fields flare as thunder hammers strike and power fists snap closed. Bolt rounds detonate. The vortex shifts and changes and moves, trying to separate the Archangels. Trying to cut Sanyctus off from the rest of them.

'Together,' Donato bellows, again.

And they move as one, weapons turned outwards, as the fire closes in. It is agony – breathless, boiling agony – but not one of the Archangels falls. Not one of them breaks the line. They stand together. Send the daemons back to the warp, together. The lifter chains creak in the heat as the summit draws near.

'Ebellius,' Donato shouts. 'Deal with the vortex!'

Above them, the source of the warpfire yawns like a maw. It is a rift from which more of the creatures spill and claw their way.

'With pleasure, brother-captain,' Ebellius says, and even now, in this apocalypse, Donato can hear the smile in his words.

Ebellius moves out with Victorno on one side, Lurani on the other. They use their shields and their bodies to keep the daemons from him. Ebellius slams his closed fist against his chestplate, an old affectation that makes a sound like a war drum. The missile launcher mounted on his shoulders tracks up as far as it can before locking and firing. The boom of displaced air rolls the fire and smoke back for just long enough for Donato to catch sight of the missiles detonating above them.

The rift screams and begins to collapse. Fire rains down around them. To Donato, half-blinded by pain, it looks like stars falling to earth. The daemons around him burn out as they reach for him and then blow away like smoke.

In the aftermath, he hears the clicking and creaking of armour as it cools, and the thunder of the lifter as it grinds to a halt at the summit of the shrine. The path to the Crown is crowded by mist and dappled with flickering light. The whispers are so very loud now. The red line that tracks warp activity is sheer. Donato's helm display registers a whole host of new threats. He hears bolter fire. Sees muzzle flare.

Donato steps off the lifter platform to face their enemies and his Archangels follow him, trailing ash and smoke from the edges of their armour plates. They are burned and battered. Chipped and scored. Laced with new scars.

But they are still standing.

'This is it,' Donato bellows, as gunfire cracks against his armour.

'The end,' Sanyctus rasps from beside him, his voice burned raw.

The Sanguine Tear, now...

'You knew that Zalak wanted Sanyctus' blood. That he thought him the closest to breaking, and the final sacrifice required for the rite to be complete.'

Donato nods. He is still looking at those broken blades of his. At the jagged edges.

'You knew that if you were to fail, that Sanguis Gloria would be lost, and Luminata with it. Millions of lives. Millions of *souls*.'

'Such are the odds we face,' Donato says. 'Every battle, every campaign. We are always the ones left standing on the blade's edge between annihilation and salvation. That is what it means to wear the armour we wear. To be Blood Angels.'

'That is true, but this battle was more than that for you, captain. You say you had no choice but to go onwards. To make the climb and face Zalak in the Crown.'

'There was no extraction,' Donato says, reaching out to the longsword that could have done nothing but break. 'No retreat. Of that I was certain.'

'Even if there had been, would you have accepted that as a choice?'

Donato is quiet for a moment as he puts his fingertips to the broken blade. It cuts him easily, and he pulls his hand away again.

'No,' he says. 'I do not think that I would have.'

'Because you believed that you could keep Sanyctus from death. From the Flaw and the chalice and becoming Zalak's sacrifice, by standing together. You believed that you would not fail a second time.'

Donato turns his hand and watches the blood paint a thin line down his fingers. By the time it reaches his palm, the cut has already started to clot and knit back together.

'I believed that I had learned from my failure,' he says. 'That I would be able to save my brother, and the shrine into the bargain. I believed that I could make right everything that had been broken or changed. That I would stand once again in the Angel's Crown and look upon the chalice as I had all of those years before.'

The blood settles into the creases of Donato's palm like molten steel running into a mould.

'But I was wrong,' he says.

The Shrine of Sanguis Gloria, then...

Donato has set foot in the Angel's Crown once before. He remembers how it looked on that day, all of those years ago. A white marble chamber far above the clouds, lit by pale sunlight streaming through the Angel's eyes. He remembers how it had been dappled with colour from the glassaic. How he had walked through shards of coloured light to approach the stasis field in which the chalice was held. Donato remembers priests murmuring blessings constantly around him as he stood before the chalice. All that he had been able to think about was how perfect a thing it was. He had seen no marks made from casting. No tarnishing or flaking of the gold.

No flaws.

Not like today. The Crown is dark and violent. It is not light that streams through the Angel's eyes, but smoke that billows out of them as if it burns from the inside. The floor is dappled with coloured light, but this time it is violet and crimson and makes the shapes of screaming faces where it hits the marble. In the centre of the Crown, the dead have been dragged into a pile. Their arms are all spread like wings and their blood has been painted to make a jagged, uneven star on the floor. Cultists kneel around the sacrifice circle, clad in strips of linen. Sixteen of them. They put their hands flat down in the blood and then press it to their chests and faces and throats in jagged, marionette movements. The stasis field is broken, but the chalice still floats in space at the heart of the darkness, at the heart of the rite. It is turning black as Donato looks at it.

'It hurts.' Sanyctus' voice over the vox is a slur. 'The chalice hurts.'

Donato struggles to tear his eyes away from that perfectly made vessel. Ruined now. Around it stand eight figures clad in crimson and steel, whose armour is decorated with horns and jagged edges and scraps of tanned skin. They are the ones to murmur now, to utter profane blessings as the darkness twists to a point above their heads.

Donato registers all of this in seconds, despite the pressure of the rite and the roar of the whispers, so loud now. His mind turns, assessing the threat even as his spirit sets fire at the sight of what they have done.

'Traitors!' Donato bellows. The word tears its way free from his throat. His voice has a near-animal edge. Donato feels as though his vision has narrowed to a singular, specific point as one of those figures clad in crimson and steel turns. One who wields a staff of bones, and whose skin is painted with golden cuneiform.

The figure drops into a neat, mocking half-bow and smiles with needle teeth.

'Ah, brother-captain,' Tur Zalak says, in his deliberate, sonorous voice. 'It is good to see you.'

'Do not speak that word,' Donato snarls. 'You have no right to speak of brothers.'

Zalak steps down from the dais. A pressure wave precedes him that breaks against Donato's armour like an ocean tide. Donato's limbs tremor. He wants to charge Zalak more than anything.

He wants to destroy him. To shatter his bones and break open his skull.

To spill his blood.

Blood.

Donato shakes his head, hard.

'The chalice,' he voxes to his squad. 'It is the locus of power. We must destroy it.' It hurts to say it, to suggest the destruction of such a thing. But better that, than allow it to become something twisted. 'We stand together, for that is how we are strongest. We go forward, and we finish it. Kill the traitors. Destroy the chalice. End the rite.'

'Together!'

The answer comes from every one of his brothers. It echoes in Donato's ears.

'I promised you death,' Donato says, to Zalak. 'I have come to deliver it.'

Zalak tilts his head. His dark eyes flicker with amusement as his traitor brethren step down off the dais too. They grow wings which flicker and distort and change. The darkness grows, and the pressure with it. Donato feels blood run from his nose. He barely tastes it. His blood is already singing.

Zalak laughs, and it is twinned and echoing. 'Death?' he asks. 'No. Not death.'

Zalak raises his other hand, the one holding the jagged dagger that cut Donato so badly on Perdicia. That scar aches again now, sending fire along his nerves. Zalak holds the dagger in a loose grip, pointing it towards Sanyctus. Donato is dimly aware of the sound Sanyctus makes in response. Of the snap of his lightning claws as they go live.

'What you have delivered is the last sacrifice,' Zalak says. 'The greatest sacrifice.'

Donato's vision is so tunnelled that all he sees is Zalak's hateful, traitor's grin.

'A perfect, violent thing,' Zalak says.

And then he crashes that staff of bones on the marble floor, the murmur reaches a crescendo, and a jagged star of balefire rolls out from Zalak. It is crimson and violet and yet more black than the empty void. The balefire quests for spaces in the Archangels' formation and tries to push them apart and build walls of flame between them. But Larracus Donato and his Archangels are made to endure. Made to withstand. They stay on their feet and they stay together, just as he ordered. As one, they push forwards through the fire, towards the chalice. Donato's armour creaks and splits across the surface layers. His cloak is turned into tatters and his helm's eye-lenses splinter. Donato views the world through fractured sight as Zalak and his daemon-possessed Word Bearers come to meet them.

Donato raises his combi-melta and fires. One of the Word Bearers is torn asunder by the scorching beam of light. He sheds smoke as he crashes unceremoniously to the floor of the Crown. Beside him Victorno and Lurani raise their shields and block another of the traitors from reaching Sanyctus. Power fields scream and flare and then Phaello and Ebellius both fire their storm bolters on the traitor, shredding his wings. The Word Bearer's shifting mask splits, becoming toothed jaws that open wide as he bellows in pain. Darrago remains with Sanyctus. At his side, as always. Donato thunders his power fist into another of the Word Bearers and breaks his tainted form open to the bone. Curved claws close around Donato's vambrace in answer. The ceramite bends. Buckles. The bones in Donato's forearm buckle too. Integrity alarms blare in his ears as he lands another blow with his power fist. This time, the Word Bearer is more than broken. He is obliterated.

Zalak is upon them now. The balefire parts for him and coils in his wake. Donato fires on the Dark Apostle. The combi-melta beam is white against all of that darkness. It dazzles Donato's flesh-and-blood eye, and his bionic adjusts to compensate. The melta fires true as it always has. Donato knows that he will not fail, not this time. He will kill Zalak now, just as he should have all of those years ago. He will make the Dark Apostle pay for Perdicia. For every death.

For every sin.

But then the balefire coils around Zalak in defence, swallowing up the melta-fire, drinking it like sand drinks rainwater. Donato doesn't have time to fire again, because Zalak is not weighed down by the darkness. He is buoyed by it. Elevated. Almost too quick to catch.

Almost.

Donato raises one arm in time to turn aside a strike from Zalak's jagged knife. He drives the weight of his combi-bolter into the Dark Apostle's face, breaking bone and sending dark, sour-smelling blood into the air. Zalak tries to break Donato in return, but Donato catches the staff of bones in his power fist before the blow can land. The power fields snarl, and for a moment in time, the two of them face one another. The angel, and the monster.

'You could have defeated me,' Zalak says, through his broken teeth. 'Had you just let go. Had you just given into the gifts of your blood.'

'You know nothing of my blood, or my gifts,' Donato says, as the staff of bones begins to splinter in his power fist's grip. 'And you *are* defeated. You just do not know it yet. *Archangels!*' Donato roars.

Phaello and Ebellius weather the cutting claws and bolter-fire of the possessed Word Bearers to move in perfect concert with one another. They fire their storm bolters on Zalak while Donato has him locked in place. The impacts blow craters in the Dark Apostle's armour and the flesh beneath it, scattering his blood across the marble and across Donato's own battleplate. Zalak's guard fails and his staff drops away, breaking the deadlock. Donato does not give him an opportunity to recover. He crashes his power fist into the Dark Apostle's chest. Once. Twice. Even warp-touched and elevated by darkness, it is too much for Zalak to withstand. He falls to his knees with his armour buckled and smoking, looking up at Donato as he bellows and raises his fist to strike again. To kill Zalak, as he should have on Perdicia.

For all of the lost.

For his failure.

But then in the instant between heartbeats, when time itself seems frozen, Zalak smiles and speaks a string of hideous unwords in his heretic tongue.

Donato is pushed backwards. He goes momentarily blind. Deaf. His mouth fills with blood and the animal part of him that he so carefully controls surfaces, furious. But he cannot move. Cannot act. The animal is caged, and so is he. Donato's limbs lock and his fingers go numb. He drops his storm bolter and falls to his knees as his armour's sensors chime and wail in distress. Donato looks down to see that his armour is broken open, and that he is too, along that old, aching scar. He cannot breathe. Cannot stand. He can do nothing but watch as daemons resolve from the balefire at Zalak's command and roll across his Archangels like a hateful tide. As one of the possessed Word Bearers, a monstrosity of horns and teeth with one lidless eye, buries its bladed hand in Lurani's chest. Donato hears Lurani gasp over the vox as his shield falls, and his hammer with it. Lurani's last act is to take the traitor's head in his hands and crush it, even as his hearts fail. With Lurani's death, their line is broken. Ebellius is pulled to his knees by red-skinned daemons wreathed in balefire. Maeklus roars and wades into the fire to save him. Victorno's shield is cracked like glass. Phaello is disarmed and sent reeling. Darrago's armour is splintered. He has to use the standard to keep himself upright. Sanyctus cuts and cuts at daemons and at the Word Bearers alike but the noose is closing around him.

No, Donato tries to say, but he can no more speak than he can move.

Zalak manages to get back to his feet by leaning heavily on his staff of bones. Black blood scatters as he limps forwards. His chest rattles with every breath. Despite that, Zalak smiles.

'Old wounds, brother-captain,' he says, haltingly. He has that jagged knife in his hand. 'They never quite heal, do they?'

Donato tries to move. To act. To speak. But it is just like the ossuary and the dream he was given.

'I know what it is that you dread,' Zalak says. 'You dread seeing your brothers torn apart. Seeing them die. Seeing them fail and change.' Zalak's smile broadens. 'I could kill you now,' he says. 'But I rather think that death is a mercy that you do not deserve.'

Donato's fury is caged inside the prison of his body. He can do nothing but twitch and struggle to breathe as Zalak turns away to make for the dais. To make for Sanyctus.

'Now, Larracus Donato,' the Dark Apostle says. 'You will see the true value of angels' blood.'

THREE

ANGELS

The Sanguine Tear, now...

Adiccio Sanyctus is badly burned. Arms. Hands. Throat and chest. His face, too, he thinks, from the way it feels. Those burns open anew when he shifts his weight and when he moves his manacled hands. That is where the burning is the most severe. As if from contact. The adamantium manacles are cold against the bubbled, ruined skin of his wrists. It looks like candlewax put to heat and left to run. Left to set itself again as it cools. It should be agony to be burned like that, but Sanyctus feels no pain at all. Not even when the wounds open again. He is just numb. Distant.

Calm.

Sanyctus takes in the cell that surrounds him. For that is where he finds himself standing. In a cell. It is dark and shadowed, lit only by the grey light coming through the narrow, horizontal slit in the door. The walls are plain, decorated not with marble or gold or paint, but with marks made by hands, or something like them. It smells like cold iron. He is unarmoured, instead wearing roughweave as an aspirant would. The manacles he wears are thick binders, made to hold back those who are strong. Who cannot hold themselves back. They are scored and scuffed just like the cell is.

A memory comes back to Sanyctus then, just a splinter of one, of him offering out his hands, and allowing the manacles to be closed around his wrists. The others were there, too. The Archangels. His brothers. His captain.

It had been Donato who closed the manacles.

Sanyctus blinks. The old scar still tries to mimic his good eye, even after all this time. He is not sure that is the sort of thing that can be unlearned. It is instinctual. He uncurls his closed hands. One is empty, but in the other there is something he recognises. A small icon, wrought in gold. A chalice, with feathered wings. He has been holding onto it so tightly that it has made an impression in the skin like a bruise.

Another splinter of memory hits him. A woman's face, cut deeply and bleeding. The mortal's head is shaved and marked with a faith-tattoo.

Violence, she says. Such violence.

Sanyctus waits to recognise her. But the woman's name will not come, and neither will the rest of the memory. All he has are the words and the look of shock and awe on her face.

That, and the instinctive knowledge that whoever she is, the woman in his memory is dead.

Sanyctus curls his hands and it makes the chain link on the manacles click together, and the burns open up on the backs of his hands.

He let them close the manacles. He wanted the chains. The cell.

The quiet.

So he sits in the quiet for what feels like hours as what happened returns to him slowly, like a dream remembered on waking. Luminata. The shrine of Sanguis Gloria. The lost. Arthemio. Ivaro. Alfeo, Vytali. Lurani. His brothers.

And the mortal, Talina Orako.

Sanyctus remembers the way she looked at him in the moments before life abandoned her. The words she spoke.

But I didn't give in, though it would have been easy to. So easy.

I think perhaps I can be proud of that.

And he wonders if he can feel the same.

Sanyctus is drawn from his thoughts as the bolt holding his cell closed slides free and the door opens. The smell of incense smoke steals inside in the moments before his visitor steps over the threshold. It is one of his brothers. One Sanyctus knew to expect from the moment he saw the manacles and the markings on the inside of the cell door. His brother is clad in crimson armour that is sculpted to resemble raw muscle. It is intended to look as though it is laid bare. A truth. His pale face is unhelmed, framed by a fall of tangled dark hair. His eyes are darker. Reflective, like glass. He stops before Sanyctus and draws the weapon of his office, putting the head of it to the stone with a heavy thud. The curved edge of the executioner's axe catches what little light there is.

'Do you know why I am here, Adiccio Sanyctus?' asks Astorath the Grim.

And Sanyctus realises that he does know why. It is a memory that should unsettle him, but doesn't. Just like Astorath's presence should, but also doesn't.

'Because I asked to speak with you, High Chaplain,' Sanyctus says. 'Because I wished to submit myself for judgement after the events of the battle for Sanguis Gloria.'

Astorath nods. It is an economical action. He does not wear his shadow-black wings here, but he looks no less like a dark reflection of their father for it. One gauntleted hand rests easily on the pommel of that axe he bears.

'Then speak, Adiccio Sanyctus,' he says. 'And I will judge.'

The Shrine of Sanguis Gloria, then...

Sanyctus is dimly aware of the battle around him. Of his brothers, falling. Failing. Bleeding. Trying to protect him. Some part of him recognises the moment Lurani flatlines and the sight of Donato going to his knees. Recognises Darrago's urgent voice.

'Adiccio,' he says. 'Wait.'

Sanyctus can hardly look away from the chalice. It is turning so black. Bruised and rotting. There is barely any gold left to see.

Closer, it says.

'Let me go, Than,' he says. 'I need to go.'

'No,' Darrago says. 'Don't be a fool. Remember the lesson.'

Sanyctus shakes his head, and his vision smears with the movement. The only thing that stays sharp is the chalice. Darrago's words make no sense. He does not remember. He cannot find the want to try either because of that *voice*. It is beautiful. Mellifluous. It makes Sanyctus think of the slow spill of molten gold. Of choir song. But the voice is in pain too. Such pain that it makes Sanyctus' fangs ache. Makes his hearts ache. A tear paints its way from his good eye. He has been able to hear it since the teleport. With every step it has grown louder. With every kill, more insistent.

Closer, the chalice says.

And Sanyctus pushes forwards. He breaks the line, leaving Darrago behind.

'Adiccio!' he keeps shouting. 'No! Stop!'

Sanyctus sees Darrago try to follow, to stop him, but the Company Ancient is halted by shadowed, horned daemons that resolve from the marble and the storm. They claw at Darrago's armour and sing twisted joy. Sanyctus wants to help his brother, but he can't. He cannot stop. He must reach the chalice. He turns away, cutting down the possessed Word Bearers with strength that comes from pain and rage and grief. He cuts through the Devoted cultists who remain. Spills their blood. It hangs in the air before being drawn into the growing rift and swallowed, with a sound like laughter. The rift screams and yawns and opens wide. Tectonic fractures run through the shrine, splitting the floor underfoot and sending cracks up the walls. What glassaic is left blows inwards in glittering clouds, cutting Sanyctus' face and clattering against his armour.

And the chalice's pleading word becomes a song-like scream.

Sanyctus' limbs tremor inside his armour as he climbs the stairs to the dais. Mortar dust coats him like a shroud, and chunks of stone clatter down on either side of him. The rift grows and grows, and his vision tunnels to a needle's eye. All that he can see is the chalice. The dark, pulsing striae twisting through what is left of the gold. Flaws, made by darkness.

Adiccio, the chalice says.

Sanyctus puts out his hand. The rite and the rift splinter the claws and the gauntlet. Shatter his armour clean away. He feels the agony the chalice feels, but he doesn't stop. He pushes through the pain and the darkness, dimly aware that Tur Zalak is with him on the dais. The Dark Apostle is laughing. Saying something Sanyctus cannot quite catch.

Something about sacrifices.

Sanyctus feels a blade press against his throat, but he will not stop now. Not even if it means death. So he reaches out with the last of his strength, and he takes hold of the chalice.

And loses the shrine to darkness.

When Sanyctus' sight returns to him, he finds himself walking up a steep desert dune, holding the chalice of Sanguis Gloria in one hand. The gold is blackened and twisted, and the gemstones have splintered like poorly made glass. He is unarmed. Unarmoured. Clad in a simple tunic and trousers made of roughweave fabric. The sun hangs ahead, a bright white disc that heats the dunes around him. The sand burns the soles of his bare feet with every step. It is treacherous. Sliding and shifting as he climbs. He puts out his free hand to keep from falling, and that burns too.

Sanyctus looks back over his shoulder. The bottom of the dune is lost to darkness. The wind howls down there. It sounds almost animal. It would be easier to stop. To give up. To turn around and let the sand take him back to the valley below, into the cold darkness.

Sanyctus blinks and curls his burned-raw hand into a fist, then he struggles back to his feet and continues upwards.

He has to reach the top of the dune.

He has to follow the other footprints.

They are larger than his own. Evenly spaced and unbroken, as if the sand did not have the heart to break beneath the climber. On either side of the set of footprints there are shallow furrows from something trailing and catching the sand.

Adiccio.

Sanyctus looks up to the top of the dune, where the sun sits. It is too bright to look upon for long. Dazzling. It prompts a tear from his good eye that falls and hits the sand where it is swallowed up straight away.

Closer.

Sanyctus starts to run as best he can up the face of the dune. The sand slides and pulls and tries to trip him, but he puts his feet into those other prints and finds the safe path. The only path that leads to the summit. He reaches the top with his hearts beating loud in his chest and his skin burned from the sand, and he falls to his knees. It is not because of the pain, or the exertion. It is because of the figure waiting for him. Tall and glorious and rendered in light.

'Father,' Sanyctus manages to say.

The figure takes a step closer, and the bright light dims just enough for Sanyctus to glimpse feathered wings, and soulful eyes. A patient, proud smile.

My son.

Sanyctus cannot bear those words, or that smile. He glances down at the chalice of Sanguis Gloria, blackened and broken.

'I have failed you,' Sanyctus says, and those words hurt more than any injury he has ever received. 'I could not stop them. The chalice is damaged. Too far gone to be saved.'

Adiccio.

Sanyctus looks up at the sound of his name.

The chalice is merely an object. A beautiful one, surely, but just an object nonetheless. It is not my legacy. Neither is Sanguis Gloria. Legacies are not made of gold, nor stone. Not thread nor script. Shrines may fall, and icons may be lost, but my legacy remains in you, Adiccio. You and every one of your brothers. My Blood Angels.

Sanyctus thinks of everything he is. Everything that he has done. He smells blood and tastes it, and his limbs start to shake.

'Your legacy,' he says, and he feels hollow. 'I want that to be true, but I think that it cannot be. I think that I am damaged too. Just like the chalice. Too far gone to be saved.'

His father looks down at him. A tear paints its way from the primarch's eye. It falls and hits the dune, where it becomes another grain of sand. This close, they glitter like precious stones.

No, he says. *You are not. You chose to fight the pull of the sand. The call of the darkness. You chose to tread the steeper, more difficult path towards the light. The Flaw might tempt you and test you, but in those moments of being tested you will find strength. The will to deny it. You are made to fight, my son. To endure. You are strong.*

And with his father's words washing over him, Sanyctus feels strong. Nothing hurts anymore. Not his burned skin, nor his injuries. Not his head, nor his hearts.

'I will not fail you, father,' he says.

Sanguinius puts out his hand.

I know, he says.

Sanyctus glances once more at the chalice in his hand. The twisted form of it. Then he reaches up and takes hold of his father's hand, and the world goes white.

Sanyctus takes a breath as though breaking the surface of water. He tastes blood, smoke and spoiling.

Molten gold.

The chalice is in his hand. The gold flows like water, coating his arm and searing the skin. Lightning arcs from the chalice to his battleplate. To the dais around him. Above him, the gateway to all the hells of man's imagination screams. That blade is still at his throat, as if no time has passed at all, but it must have, because Sanyctus doesn't feel pain. He feels strong, just as he did at the summit of that dune.

'The last and greatest sacrifice,' Tur Zalak hisses.

Sanyctus blinks. 'No,' he says. 'Not a sacrifice. I am my father's legacy.'

And with that, he tears the chalice free from the storm and crushes it in his hand. The storm screams and lightning arcs wildly. Golden fire travels up Sanyctus' arms and across his body, despite his armour. It scorches his face. It burns Zalak, too, shattering the black dagger in his hand. Zalak screams like the storm does, his skin afire. Sanyctus endures it, because that is what he is made to do.

Because he is strong.

He turns and lights the claws he has left and cuts the Dark Apostle deeply. Deep enough to damage both of the traitor's hearts. Zalak staggers backwards down the steps. He coughs up black blood and smoke.

'A perfect thing,' Zalak slurs, with his eyes fixed and dilated. 'A perfect, violent thing.'

And then there is the boom of a bolt shell detonation, and Zalak's grin disappears in a burst of blood. He falls, dead. Donato is standing, despite the terrible wound in his chest. Smoke spirals from the muzzle of his storm bolter.

'I said that I would do it,' he manages to say, to the still form of Zalak. 'I told you I would kill you.'

With Zalak's death, the storm completely destabilises. That yawning rift screams and roars and sings and starts to draw back in. The Dark Apostle's body is drawn up into it. Taken gladly by clawed hands and remora-mouths. Daemons are stretched and pulled and torn apart as they too are taken back by the rift. Another tectonic rumble shakes the shrine, and the floor underfoot splits further. Columns of stone collapse around Sanyctus as he staggers down from the dais towards his brothers.

'Adiccio.'

For a moment, Sanyctus thinks himself back on the dune under the bright white sun, but of course the voice is Darrago's. His old friend still lives, though his armour is shattered and burned and broken. Phaello and Victorno are standing, too. Ebellius and Maeklus.

'It is done,' Sanyctus says.

He takes a step forward and falls to one knee. Puts out his burned, unarmoured hand to catch himself. It doesn't hurt. None of it hurts. His brothers pull him back to his feet and help take his weight. He dimly hears Donato contacting the *Sanguine Tear* over the ringing in his ears.

'The chalice,' Sanyctus says, finding he has to reach for words. For coherent thought.

'It is gone, Adiccio,' Darrago says. 'And it is for the better. It could not be saved.'

Sanyctus shakes his head, because that isn't what he was trying to say.

'I know,' he says. 'But it is not his legacy. We are. He told me so.'

Darrago puts his hand on his shoulder. 'Who, brother?' he asks.

Sanyctus feels the unmistakable chill of the teleport building around them. Hoarfrost crawls over his armour.

'Our father,' he says. 'He told me so.'

The last thing he sees is the concern in Darrago's dark eyes, and then the world lights white again.

The Sanguine Tear, now...

When Sanyctus finishes his retelling, there is a long moment of silence that is filled by the snarl of Astorath's armour. The High Chaplain's dark eyes are unreadable, as always. He has not removed his hand from the pommel of his executioner's axe.

'I spoke with your brothers before coming here,' Astorath says.

Those words are not the ones that Sanyctus expects, so he cannot help his reply.

'Why?' he asks.

'Because I am never asked for by those who are in need of judgement,' Astorath says. 'It is the dirge that calls me. The song of death. I hear it always.' He puts his free hand to his chest, over his hearts. 'No matter how far distant my brothers may be, I hear it and I answer. I do what must be done.'

Sanyctus knows what that means. He has known souls who have been granted redemption by Astorath's blade. Every Blood Angel has. It is what makes the High Chaplain both revered, and loathed. Sanyctus wonders for a moment at what a burden that is for Astorath to bear. To be so alone amongst brothers. He is a part of their father's legacy, too. The darkest part.

'But not this time,' Astorath continues. 'This time I was called upon not by the dirge, but by you. That is not the way of things, which is why I spoke with your brothers. They spoke highly of you, Adiccio Sanyctus,' he says. 'They named you as friend. A hero, and a brother. But they spoke honestly too of what they saw in the shrine. Of moments of fury and violence. You yourself have told me of the pull of the chalice. Of what you saw when you laid a hand upon it.'

Astorath narrows his dark eyes. An expression crosses his face that Sanyctus cannot name.

'You saw our father.'

Sanyctus glances down. He opens his hand again and looks upon the icon of the chalice that he holds. The burns on his hand have made patterns in his skin. They almost look as though they could be pressure marks, from the grip of another hand.

'Yes,' he says. 'That is what I saw.'

He looks back up at Astorath. The High Chaplain is still watching him in that same way, with his eyes narrowed.

'When the dirge brings me to a brother in need of judgement, they roar and scream in their delirium. They speak of our father, too. Of his death, and the arch-traitor who slew him. They see it. Experience it for themselves. They become trapped within it. It is agony, endless and tormenting. But you do not roar, or scream. You speak not of our father's death. You are not in agony.'

Sanyctus shakes his head. He feels no pain at all, though he should. Just that same distant calm.

'What you saw was something else,' Astorath says. 'This is neither the Rage, nor the Thirst.'

'Then what, High Chaplain?'

There is another heavy pause, in which Sanyctus recognises Astorath's expression, and understands why he found it so difficult to discern.

It is uncertainty.

'I do not know,' the High Chaplain says. 'A dream, perhaps. A vision. Something conjured by trauma. That I cannot say.' Astorath shakes his head. 'But I do not hear the dirge in you.'

Sanyctus becomes still. He feels as though his hearts have ceased.

'Then, the Flaw?' he asks.

'It lives in you still,' Astorath says. 'It is a part of you, and that cannot be changed. It is merely quieted, for now. Your descent arrested.'

Sanyctus thinks of his father's words.

The Flaw might tempt you and test you, but in those moments of being tested you will find strength.

'I understand,' Sanyctus says, and the words are only half meant for Astorath. 'Then what is your judgement, High Chaplain?'

Astorath finally moves his hand from the pommel of his axe.

'I have none to offer,' he says. 'I do not judge angels. Only the lost.'

Sanyctus blinks. Astorath deactivates and removes the manacles, setting him free.

'My thanks, brother,' Sanyctus says.

There is a subtle change in Astorath's face at the word 'brother'. He is quiet for a moment. Unlike the other pauses, it is not patient, or deliberate. It is a natural hesitation.

'I would ask you one final question,' the High Chaplain says.

'Of course,' Sanyctus replies.

That pause again.

'What was it like, to hear his voice?' Astorath asks.

Of all the questions, Sanyctus would never have expected this one. Not from Astorath. He thinks carefully about it, searching for words that can encompass the feeling of standing before his father, who was so very bright, like a noon sun. Words to capture seeing the glittering dunes of cast tears and hearing words spoken in a voice like molten gold.

My legacy remains in you, Adiccio.

You and every one of your brothers.

My Blood Angels.

'Perfect,' Sanyctus says, softly. 'It was perfect.'

IT BLEEDS

DAVID GUYMER

I don't know this world. I don't know this battle. There have been so many that one bleeds into the next, all the years of my life nothing more to me than a red smear across a hundred burning stars. I don't know this world, but I know that I hate it. Polluted rain patters against my armour like stub-rounds off a tank, acid run-off trickling through the maze of dents and scratches that have never been repaired. It winds down the rusted chains that drape my harness, scrubbing ineffectually at the tarry handprint that has been on my breastplate for longer than I can remember. At my hip, it pools in the eye sockets of a skull with the broad features and heavy structure of a transhuman. It's fixed to my armour by a bolt and a chain. A short passage of knife-cut symbols marks the frontal bone. I don't know what they mean, but looking at them fills me with a rage I struggle to contain.

Sometimes, I think–

Sometimes, I wonder–

'Hnnng.'

The sudden clenching of my brass teeth is a grating squeal vibrating through the base of my skull as the Nails whip my brain with pain agonists, cytokines and targeted electric shocks. My whole body spasms until the pad of my thumb finds the activation stud on my chainaxe. The motors send the belt-driven teeth whirring. I press it again, like a trained dog. Congealed lumps of flesh and chips of bone pelt my damaged faceplate, and I sigh in relief as the migraine eases, slightly.

With the red fog clearing, I experience a prickling sensation of lucidity and look around myself in disgust. The horizon is one of jagged manufactorum stacks, chimneys reaching up into the upper atmosphere to belch their pollutants into a nascent planetary ring system. The ground beneath me rumbles. The atmosphere weeps. Fiery red streaks run down its dirty, coal-black face, World Eaters drop pods and assault boats, falling out of orbit in crazy spirals into the vociferous welcome of flak guns and the sonic-boom shout of interceptors. I smell the promethium. I taste the fyceline.

I don't know this battle.

I wonder how I got here, and what happened to the rest of my squad.

The Space Marine stands huge in front of me.

'Hnnng.'

I cough up blood this time. It splats the inside surface of my helmet's snarling grille. I shake my head, and force myself to focus.

Space Marine.

He is one of the newer breed that emerged from Terra in the wake of the Blindness: taller, faster and stronger than those who had come before them. His armour is a metallic turquoise, but with a subtle, shifting tone that varies its hue for each sporadic burst of crossfire or passing gunship. His raiment is that of a Champion. A high gorget shields the vulnerable rotator cuffs around the neck joint and most of the helmet, up to a pair of golden, sharply accented lenses. A rain-sodden back banner flutters in the heat haze from his reactor pack, displaying what appears to be a heraldic sea dragon devouring a planet. The pain of the Nails settles into a dull throb, the implant's deceptively subtle machina animus placated by the hatred this symbol stirs in me.

I bare my teeth, confused, and enraged by my confusion.

'I have hunted you across three systems, *brother.*'

The Champion brings his sword into a two-handed guard, activating the disruption field as his alternating blue-green gauntlet closes over the grip and throwing off a cloudburst of flash-evaporated gore from the blade. The weapon emits a low-frequency hum that makes my eye twitch and triggers a shower of parasympathetic spite from the Nails.

His voice, though, is worse, as strident and hateful as a knife drawn across glass.

'Can you still speak? Or are you just another of the Foresworn's rabid beasts?'

I hate fighting Space Marines.

They are tough bastards to kill, and I would sooner spend the time it demands glorying Khorne with the butchery of weaker men. The Blood God has always favoured quantity over quality, and I am keen to oblige.

The Champion lowers his sword a fraction, as though the irritant hum of his weapon is preventing him from seeing me properly.

'Well?'

And Space Marines, for some reason, always want to talk.

Who does he think he is?

A mongrel infant. A Champion of genetic freaks.

I bare my cracked teeth in a snarl and shake my head as though that might be enough to dislodge the cybernetic pain device embedded there and let me just *think.* The rain fogs my lenses. One is cracked. The other has never worked properly.

I rev my chainaxe until red smoke bleeds from gore-clogged motors and reality fades...

I wake the way I always do: with screaming.

The carbon-alloy restraint bars pinning me to my upright cryo-slab tighten in response, row upon row of microscopically thin phlebotomy spikes puncturing my skin and dosing my veins with anticoagulants and counter-adrenals. Hundreds of tiny bleeds dribble down my horribly scarred nakedness, where they drip from my toes to the metal floor. To either side of me, as slow and crusted as a Death Guard's lungs, exsanguination pumps wheeze, drawing gurgling vitae out through bronze filtration loops, osmotically extracting the sus-an hormones from my system. The air is unpleasantly warm, and smells of blood and chemicals. I have been brought out of my nightmares into the madness of an asylum. The convalescent wails of my fellow maniacs, each one as damned and exalted as I, ring from the huge, hollow pipes that clutter the ceiling. They hang from cryo-slabs of their own. Carcasses in an abattoir. Waiting to be bled, ground or minced, depending on the whim of the Foresworn.

The Butcher's Nails affect us all differently. I know this. I know that I suffer it worse than most. There is a reason for that, niggling away somewhere inside my brutalised excuse for a subconscious. Wherever it hides, it daren't come out. The Nails make me dangerous, even by the standards of warriors who think nothing of training with live ammunition and active chainaxes. The warband's butcher-surgeons keep me cold until there is a real battle to fight, lest I satisfy the Nails with the blood of the ship's crew and my own brothers.

I try to remember how many times I have gone through the revivification procedure, but I can't. All I know is that it's been more than once.

'Brother...'

The word triggers something in my memory. The Nails jerk me fully conscious, and my eyes focus on the vulture that peers up at me from the gantry floor.

There are only a handful of names I can recall with ease. Most of them belong to dead men. Ghosts from another life. None of them are my own, but there are worse things to forget than your name.

Perun Tiyr, once Apothecary to the Eighth Company and now Chief Vivisector to the World Eaters warband calling themselves the Foresworn, is one I can remember.

'Brother.' His voice has a caustic tone that works through to the hyper-stimulated pain centres of my brain like an acid. The hand he places over my restrained wrist, level with his shoulder, is fever-warm and moist. He smiles at me the whole time and I bare my teeth back. The metal pegs are blunted from years of grinding. Even in my coma, I am told, I rage. 'It pleases me to have you back, brother. Your insanity is a source of endless blessing to me. The in-system deceleration should take several days, and my apprentices have been anticipating the chance to look inside your head one more time.'

He is not speaking figuratively. This, too, I know.

'B-b-b–'

I struggle to speak. My brain is misfiring and my mouth is still feeling the numbing effects of the torporific chemicals used to render me unconscious for warp transit.

'B-b-b-*hnnng*-blood.'

The Vivisector chuckles to himself. Like me, he no longer has his own teeth. Two rows of bolt shells have been carefully hammered into his gums in their place. He likes to tell us they are still live. I have no idea whether or not it is true, but can only assume that it is. It's the sort of insanity I would indulge in if I had his freedom. He turns from me to examine a screen bank that flickers with pictorial displays of my vital signs and a constant effluent of runic screed. The chirurgical appendages nerve-spliced to his thoracic spine twitch as they translate the angry impulses of his own Butcher's Nails. Bloody scraps of flesh and torn fabric hang from the metallic pseudo-limbs like scruffs of feather, which is why he has always put me in mind of a vulture: hunched and bloody, with keen eyes and wanton appetites.

'You will have it, brother,' he said. 'Very soon.'

'B-b-b-b–' The combined effort of thought and speech brings a rusty liquid dribbling from my nose. 'N-n-n-n–'

Tiyr grimaces, easily amused but just as quickly bored.

He gives the screens an impatient tap, watching as they fuzz out and then back in again, then turns back towards me. He leans in as though his bloodshot eyes aren't more than perfect enough to make me out from a safer distance. The Nails affect all of us differently, but they draw us all, to varying degrees, towards self-destruction. I'm thoroughly restrained, but the Nails flay my nervous system in defiance of it, and Tiyr knows full well that I would tear the meat from his face with my teeth if only he would come close enough.

'Blood,' I manage to spit.

'Soon,' he says.

'W-w-w–' I struggle to force the words through pain-clenched teeth. 'W-w-w-*where?*'

The Vivisector looks at me, blankly. 'Do you care?'

I try to shake my head. To clear it of the narcotic fog and the hideous, hideous scarring of my brain. But my head is held tight to the slab, the Nails sunk too deeply into my skull. There is a memory in there. A want. A need. An impulse. I remember a Space Marine, a warrior in turquoise armour on a conquered world, and suddenly nothing is more important to me than that memory. My fingers jolt, the combined effects of the Butcher's

Nails and the withdrawal of the tranquilisers making them tingle, but I resist them. A part of me has some pride. The butcher-surgeons haven't wholly robbed me of it yet.

'Where – *hnnng* – Where is my – *hnnng* – brother?'

Tiyr spreads his arms. His chirurgical harness twitches and jerks in a flutter of flayed skin. 'You are all brothers in here. And I love you equally.'

'Wh-wh-wh–' I try again. 'Wh-wh-*hnnnng*-wh–'

'Oh, who am I trying to fool?' Tiyr pushes the cold attachment head of his narthecium into my femoral artery. There is a spring-loaded hiss and then a sedative rush that slumps me back into my restraints. 'I love you most of all, you delightful wreck of an Astartes. Our transits through the warp have become so arduous, since the Despoiler managed to so foolishly rip the galaxy asunder. If it weren't for you and the fascinating nightmare of your neurochemistry, then I am sure I would be as insane by now as you are.' He reaches up and runs one gauntleted finger lovingly down the ventral ridge of my rib plate. Goosebumps spread outwards from his touch, but my numbing body barely feels it. 'The thought of your imminent and inevitable demise is the wound that never clots, my brother.'

Despoiler.

I feel as though this name should mean something to me.

'Your implants have been appended to your brain with a singular lack of skill,' the Vivisector goes on. 'Such incompetence is almost to be admired.'

Again, the brief sense that I remember the event Perun is describing, but it's fleeting, fleeing, and then it's gone, a scrap of oath paper flying loose in a narcotic fog. I try to remember what it was we were talking about, and in the moment I spend chasing after this thought the other one is well and truly lost.

All my oaths.

All my life.

It's all just paper, torn up and thrown away, flung into the uncaring vastness of the Emperor's galaxy.

Who am I? Where is my brother?

The questions gnaw at me.

If I were any less well restrained I would have been tearing my eyes out of my face with my own fingernails and screaming. As it is, all I can do is scream.

'Two more days of deceleration, brother, and then you will have your blood.' Tiyr smiles at me, indulgently. By the warp, how I loathe him. 'Until then, we have only time to kill.'

Is this peace?

My brain is swimming in an endorphin bath. My ears buzz in frantic syncopation to the howl of the chainaxe vibrating in my fist. The mutilated war cries of my brethren reverberate through my helmet vox. Mortals gurgle as they're ripped apart by once mortal beasts and have their innards strewn like null-G cargo netting across the ruined trench. The smell of guts, offal and the lubricant grease that someone once smeared into my chainaxe fills my nose and excites my genhanced senses, and I decide that truly, yes, this is peace.

I laugh like a brain-damaged god as my chainaxe rips into a Guardsman's vest, the ballistic weave providing scant protection. Adamantium teeth unpick it with relish, cutting through armour, through mustard-yellow fatigues, through flesh and then ribcage, until pulpy red lumps evacuate the screaming trooper's chest cavity and splatter over me.

It takes me less than a second to saw the man in half, but the chemical interplay between Space Marine neurology, the Butcher's Nails, and what I suspect to be my own underlying pathology have altered my perception of time.

The moment strings out indefinitely, and I'm thrilled.

Las bolts crack against my armour.

I laugh them off as time speeds back up, slows down, and settles on something linear and constant. This is what I was made for, after all, what I always craved, and what the Emperor, despite presiding over a galaxy forever wracked by war, could never provide enough of to satisfy my longings.

One of my brothers goes down.

He is practically unarmoured, an eight-foot-tall gladiator with a few non-functional plates of old-mark power armour hanging off a harness of chain. He jerks backwards, absorbing enough firepower to bring down a scout tank, foaming at the mouth whilst pulling frenziedly on the trigger of a pistol too gummed with gore to ever fire again before finally keeling over.

I admit to being envious.

I bellow, my voice amplified to ear-shattering volumes by the warped augmitter system built into my helmet, as my chain-axe saws through firing Guardsmen. I slay one, and toss her aside, setting upon the rest of her squad in a frenzy of arcing blood and flying limbs. Bayonets break against my armoured thighs. Las fire refracts, point-blank, off the encrusted grime. I shear a trooper's arm messily from his body even as he bends away from me. There is a grenade in it. My senses are sharp enough, and my mind still fast enough, for me to smile wryly in the split second before it explodes. The flying arm is eviscerated, flesh pulp and shrapnel scything wetly through the surrounding troops and gnawing toothlessly on my mistreated plate.

I don't know this world.

I don't know this battle.

If my leaders, whoever they are, have an objective for me beyond magnificent slaughter then I've forgotten it or was never told. It matters not. Whether we hold, conquer or ignominiously lose this world is of no concern to me at all.

Turning it red is all I wish for.

A kill counter blinks up across my visual screed. The one unbroken lens is intermittently functional. I don't remember the last time I had a serf to maintain it, or the last time I thought to switch it off, and so it has been running, on and off, since the Emperor alone knows when.

The Gothic numeral reads *692,284*.

I have no way of knowing if this is an excusable tally or a risible contribution to the eternal killing fields of Khorne's demesnes for which I am to be eternally damned. I don't even know if it has been counting as sporadically as it displays. All I can do is kill more.

The Guardsmen are falling back now, firing at me in disarray. Las fire lashes my armour as they turn and race across the no-man's-land to a prepared line of backup ditches and bunkers that my one working lens is just about able to resolve through the pall of smoke grenades and periodical artillery fire. I howl after them and give chase, hacking the fleeing Imperials down as I power through corpse-choked ditches and sink to the greaves in mud made soft by hours, days or weeks of slaughter.

I drive myself through, whipped on by the Nails for the mortal sin of losing ground and only distantly aware of my few remaining brothers struggling alongside me through the quagmire.

An autocannon, buried in a foxhole somewhere, thunders to life.

The warrior to my left is opened up like a can of sticky fluids. The one to my right is effectively shredded. Both roar for the final time as the blood leaks out of their broken armour, but my god has no interest in me today, and I run through with nothing more than scratches to jump up onto the sandbagged parapet of the second Imperial trench.

The sight of my cracked faceplate and sputtering eye-lens is enough to break the Guardsmen in the trench. They run, all except for one, an officer in a long black storm coat and peaked hat with a gold aquila across the brim. He raises his laspistol, then turns his head from me and, with oily calm, places shot after shot through his own fleeing soldiers' backs.

The Nails sing inside my skull.

They rejoice in this bloodshed, and there is no part of me that will accept the mortal doesn't feel it too. The universe revolves around us both, I feel it, gears of corroded brass greased by slaughter and ratcheting the eight cardinals into a rare conjunction.

It makes *sense.*

With the last of his unit shot dead or escaped, the officer finally deigns to look at me. 'Ave Imperator.' He spits on the ground. 'In the Emperor's name, I deny you.' With that, he presses the still-hot muzzle of his laspistol into the close-shaven underside of his chin and fires.

The las bolt blasts through the roof of his head, stippling the trench wall with steaming lumps of brain.

I look down at him, feeling amused but also profoundly cheated, and confused as to what I was supposed to feel. The Nails react to my uncertainty, as they do to everything that isn't hatred or killing, with a pounding headache.

Weapons fire from sentinel towers and concealed gun nests up and down the Imperial position continues to stitch across me. Strung out over several hundred yards of no-man's-land behind me, red-armoured legionaries are mown down by the hundred, not a one of them resenting the needlessness of it all.

Not a one of them thinks to pause, for a second, and wonder

at the sanity of rushing headlong into the entrenched guns of the Imperial Guard.

Death is the fate of all who choose to walk the bloody path and seek glory in the eyes of Khorne. For most of us, it comes sooner rather than later.

I know it.

They know it.

We can't all be Khârn.

A smile finds me then, in painful spite of the Nails: I just remembered another name.

With gunfire from a dozen different directions sparking across my pauldrons, I jump down into the trench. Even at a stoop my helmet is exposed to the occasional las bolt or auto-round crack that rings down through the Butcher's Nails and straight into my head. I squat, peeling the dead officer's head from the trench wall, and tilt it towards me.

I look down, through the scorched officer's cap, through the blown-out roof of his skull.

'Such a – *hnnng* – waste,' I growl, and go off in search of another.

The long, drawn-out *crack* of the trepanning tool breaking through my skull rings through the gloomily apportioned laboratorium. The diamantite drill bit, although specifically modified for Astartes surgery, has been making heavy work of it, and I suspect that my surgeon has been less than fastidious about maintaining its sharpness between uses. I have seen the state of his theatre, and the decrepit deep-void station he calls home, and there is nothing left here to surprise me.

Kritsyarrk Station is a skeletal claw of black metal, suspended in the twilight of the Obdurum Nebula, deep within the Halo Stars and thousands of light years from the nearest Imperial force. The name *Kritsyarrk* is, itself, a Low Gothic bastardisation of the name-sound applied to it by the sheed xenos species who claim to have built it. They may have done so, I'm no expert, but I suspect they were merely the first to discover it. A dozen renegade warbands of as many allegiances have their bases in its docking spines. There is a slaugth colony, somewhere deep in the cogitation sublevels, that I would have dismissed as a typical frontier myth had I not seen one of the hideous maggot-men for myself, preaching on the lower concourse. There are also numerous drukhari factions with embassies in veiled, difficult-to-access segments of the old base. I've observed them coming out from time to time to trade in narcotics and slaves.

There is no formal peace as such. I'm not even sure how one would go about talking with a slaugth or a sheed. But the mismatch of peoples and creeds somehow manages to rub along with only sporadic outbreaks of violence. This, it does, on the shared understanding that aggression begets retaliation and that, with no faction having the strength to wipe out all the others, open warfare would be a costly and tiresome affair.

My host's laboratorium is little more than a garderobe in the corner of a grimy little stall, sectioned off from the wildly variegated passing traffic by a photonic screen that, unfortunately, blocks none of the weird alien noises or their peculiar odours.

'Where did you find this butcher, brother?' I ask.

Tanikhor grins down at me.

His teeth are the white of plasma-scarred ceramite. His eyes are the blueish green of the ocean of a half-remembered birthworld. Knife-cut symbols, a few lines from a blood spell native to our home, trace his forehead, deep enough to mark the bone. 'He's the only medicae-trained renegade in the Obdurum Nebula. I heard from one of the Axelords' warriors that he performed the procedure many times for Lord Huron. Before being exiled from the Maelstrom and selling his services here in Kritsyarrk.'

'*This butcher* happens to be right here.'

My eyes swivel in their sockets, but Apothecary Bredek, better known to the Renegade Astartes that haunt Kritsyarrk Station as Bredek the Unburdened, is in the natural blind spot behind me. My right eyelid spasms, one of my fingers twitching furiously, as he draws the still-whirring drill back through the hole he had cut into my skull. With a greasy fluttering, a pair of servo-imps with forked tails and stretched, goatlike faces descend from hooks on the wall to spray the exposed brain matter with counterseptics and narcotic oils. There are no sense neurons in the brain, I know, but the imps do leave me with an unpleasant pins-and-needles sensation in various unexpected places.

I feel my breath quickening, my musculature tensing and, to my shame, I realise that I am having second thoughts about this procedure. This is the last step on the first path. It bears the hallmarks of a point of no return, but I know that there was never any turning back. My former brothers would not have me back now, and my new master would not relinquish me so easily, not after all the gifts he has already bestowed.

The only way now is forwards.

Always.

A Space Marine knows no fear, and in spite of everything I've already done, everything I'm in the process of becoming, I'm still a Space Marine. I fear no pain. I fear no death. Nor do I fear injury, but the grim likelihood of brain damage, paralysis or even some alien secondary infection on Bredek the Unburdened's garderobe gurney, I find, still terrifies me.

With an effort, I bring my breathing back under control. I work some moisture into my dry mouth. A constant, latent thirst has always been the burden of my gene-line. That and a doomed struggle against our inner rage. But it's too late to change my mind now.

'I'm here, brother,' says Tanikhor.

In spite of the surgical clamps holding my head in place, I make an attempt at a nod.

With a shriek of metal across metal, Bredek drags around a stool and sits himself down. I see him now. My Apothecary is a sallow, unkempt figure, downcast in every respect as though, from the moment that single-stranded nucleic acid chains in the chemical swamps of Old Earth first replicated themselves, the history of Terran life has been one of personal disappointment. Formerly of the Red Corsairs before his unspecified split from Lord Huron, his armour is a darker shade of red than Tanikhor's and mine, and encrusted with a more cosmopolitan splattering of gore.

I entertain the brief fantasy of breaking free, of overpowering the Unburdened and his imps, and then escaping the Obdurum Nebula to somewhere I might barter him to the Imperial authorities in exchange for my own life and Tanikhor's freedom.

I sigh.

It's still far, far too late.

Oblivious to the thoughts pulsing back and forth beneath his fingertips, Bredek conducts a cursory examination. He stares into my pupils under a bright light. He pricks my extremities with a pin, seeming to take grim satisfaction in watching me flinch, and sticks a finger far enough down my throat to make me gag. He looks contemplative as he licks the saliva from a dirt-encrusted fingernail, and then nods.

'Responses within the standard ranges. No significant trauma from the initial incision. Adequate. T-cell count responding to treatment and falling. More or less adequate. Now, remain still.'

The metal stool grinds across the floor again, and the Apothecary stands and walks out of sight. I hear the clatter of someone with large hands manipulating fine instruments.

'I don't know why we couldn't wait for a genuine World Eaters surgeon,' I hiss.

'He's all there is,' Tanikhor replies.

'Tell me again why Lord Huron exiled him.'

Tanikhor shakes his head, still smiling.

He is always smiling.

'If we're to be accepted by the Foresworn when we catch up to them, then you're going to need the implant.'

I lick my lips. I can almost taste the blood I'll shed.

Bredek the Unburdened returns before I can shape a reply. There is another scowl of metal, as though the alloy itself resents him, as he sits. With a sour look on his face, he holds up something that he has pinched between forefinger and thumb. It is about the size of a bolt shell, but there is something of the spider about it, if the common arachnid could be induced, through the fullness of mankind's perversity and genius, to become something even more conducive to nightmare. It is slender, almost inhumanly elegant in its obvious cruelty, its various nerve junctions fronded with barbs and electrodes.

My mouth is dry. 'Is… Is that…?'

'The Butcher's Nails,' he says. 'Yes.'

'How did one of Lord Huron's exiles come by such technology?'

Bredek frowns. He is the single most joyless individual I have encountered in the many years it took me to find this place. Those with such sterile desires, I find, tend to remain loyal to the Imperium they once served. 'They are really not so rare. Every would-be Tyrant and Despoiler craves berzerkers like those of Angron's Legion. But they burn themselves out so quickly.' It looks for a second as though he might break into a smile, but the temptation soon abandons him and his expression sinks towards one of even deeper melancholy than it had held before.

'Blood for the Blood God, brother,' says Tanikhor.

'Skulls for his throne,' I reply.

'I envy you, brother. Only one of us can have the honour of going first.'

Bredek looks up, as though seeking spirits in the air, and then back down. 'One last question,' he says, fiddling with the settings on his tools as he leans in. 'Before we begin.'

I give him a grunt.

'Who are you talking to?'

The thick, buttressing walls of the Dreadclaw assault pod shake around me. We're crossing atmospheric layers, hitting flak, the intense groan of an unsanctified heat shield and the bullet-rattle on the outer hull enough to convince the Nails that I'm charging joyously towards death. It dulls my head just enough for me to enjoy the descent. I always enjoy the descent. I shift in my restraint harness, but there are no consoles that still function and, of course, no windows. We could be hurtling through the white clouds of a maiden world, the toxic envelope of a hyper-industrialised hellscape, or even, as I seem to dimly recall once doing, plunging into the hydrogen layer of a gas giant towards the continent-sized extractor rigs that plied its electrical currents.

I've no preference, but I can't help but wonder.

Imperials. A rival Legion. Even xenos.

From ten thousand feet, they all sound the same.

Set against the trauma being meted out on the hull armour and the creak of the internal support rods, the growling of nine World Eaters Space Marines is white noise. We're not all set to the same vox-channel, and the snarls and hissing static of several near-neighbour frequencies trickles through my helmet like the mad whispers of the gods. None of them look alike. Some are armoured. Some are not. A handful have been altered with brutal mutations in recognition of their service, but most have not. Of those who are armoured, many do not even bear the World Eaters emblem on their shoulder. I strain my neck to look down at the state and age of my armour and the heraldry on my own pauldron, but my restraints deny me. The only uniting feature I can see is the singular lack of care we've put into ourselves and our wargear. We are abominations, scarred inside and out, hanging from hooks in the ceiling like carcasses. Where bare skin shows through broken armour it is mottled by internal bruising and swollen by mis-healed bone.

The pain of charging into battle on a shattered leg, of breathing through a ruptured lung, pales next to the torture of the Butcher's Nails. We don't even feel it.

Being blasted out of the sky by a Hydra battery would have been a mercy, but alas, it never comes.

The air we share is rancid.

It tastes of blood and sweat in equal parts, accentuated by cramped quarters and by other excretions that our broken nervous systems no longer have full control over. I smell the sour tang of Space Marine combat hormones, fast degrading, but each warrior's unique set of pheromones subtly tainted by his descent to corruption and lingering like a sense of guilt.

'I was there,' I hear one of them mutter, to himself, as though a daemon only he can see mocks him from an inch above his breastplate. 'I was there when the Red Angel descended on the Throneworld. I was there when the Eternity Gate fell.'

The berzerker beside him twitches in his restraints, like a cryo-sustained cadaver being force-fed the high-voltage spark of life.

'I saw the Angel fight the Angel,' growls another, contending with his own clenching teeth.

A World Eater dribbles into his harness as he tries to speak.

And so it goes, the boasts of madmen only superficially aware that they're not talking to themselves. I wonder how many of them really were there on Terra. I know how we World Eaters fight. I've seen how carelessly we throw our lives away. It is improbable to the point of absurdity that *any* veteran of Terra should still be fighting today, ten thousand bloody years on, without extraordinary luck or favour. It's said that a warrior who's fought in Angron's presence is indelibly marked by it. The primarch's fury forever darkens their soul.

I take in the twitching, growling, bitterly urgent nonsense being spouted by the warriors around me, and sense nothing.

I couldn't describe the sights and smells of Terra, or the sound of the Eternity Gate as it broke, how it felt in my insignificant battles even as the Angel duelled the Angel above my head. But I know I was there. I know it with such force and certainty that it doesn't matter that I can't explain it. My own rage-blackened spirit knows it. My two hearts know it. The blood of Angron pulsing through my veins *knows* it. I feel it every moment of my prolonged existence in the throbbing of the Nails. So what if I don't remember it? I don't remember yesterday. Or the battle before this one. Or how many mortal serfs had to die so that ten World Eaters could be strapped into a Dreadclaw assault pod.

I am an Eater of Worlds. I was there when the galaxy burned. We lost, I remember that, but the galaxy still burned and has not been doused since. That's what matters.

And I know *that*.

'I was there…' I mutter, my mouth wet where my metal teeth have again bitten through my tongue, sanctifying the absolute truth I sense in my words. 'I was there…'

* * *

The Space Marine comes at me with force, pushing momentum into that enormous frame in a way that logic dictates is impossible and which only another Space Marine can ever be fully prepared for. He ploughs through the intervening debris and scrap barricades, through the rain, pulverising every sludge-smeared obstacle under his enormous boots. I'm running too, but hardly aware of it, foaming at the mouth, chainaxe shrieking.

And then all of a sudden we're not running any more. We crash together with the sound of two tanks colliding. The rock beneath us ruptures, groundwater geysering up between us and threatening to hose the grime from our armour. Wet ceramite grinds the paint off wet ceramite, both of us clad in the same grey under the colours we choose to wear on top. The spiked ornamentation of my older battleplate gores deep into the sleek panelling of his Mark X armour. Scoring ceramite with bronze: that, too, is impossible. Terran primitives upgraded to iron for a reason. But appearances are nothing to Khorne and symbolism everything: my armour's embellishments are as much real bronze as I am human.

After the moment of collision, we come apart. The Space Marine's power sword is already well along its rising arc towards my neck, spitting in the rain. I turn my body aside and bludgeon my chainaxe through its path. Its teeth buzz like a horde of adamantium berzerkers as they try to chew through a molecular disruption field, spraying us both with metal shavings and energised particles. He throws a shoulder through the locked blades, forcing my chainaxe to bite into my own breastplate. I bellow in fury as it shrieks through the chains that bedeck my harness and starts on the ceramite underneath. A deep roar thunders from the Space Marine's augmitter housings as I stumble. He presses me, already recovering his grip on his sword and readying a backhand stroke. With a snarl, I grab him one-handed by the tabard and yank him towards me. My headbutt dents his gorget, but almost destroys my faceplate. My remaining eye-lens shatters, stranding me forever on a kill count of *982,001*.

Rain gets in my eye.

Spitting in blind fury, I let go of his tabard and shove back, taking my chainaxe in both hands like a club, and batter dementedly at the Space Marine's power sword. I barely even see him any more. Whether it's due to the rain in my eyes or the red mist clouding them from the inside, I don't know. He's nothing but a turquoise shade to me now, a figure of hate adorned with symbols I cannot bear to look at any longer. The Space Marine parries my blows with as much vehemence as I can deliver them. It gives me satisfaction to know he hates me as much as I hate him. All who fight praise Khorne, whether they intend to or not.

Hatred is the praise of the soul. With a bolter, I can kill a man once. With hate in my heart, I can kill him a million times over in my mind.

I wish he'd die now, though. I tire of the challenge and would sooner return to the slaughter elsewhere. The Nails urge me to go in harder, with even greater abandon. The skull nailed to my tasset plate gurgles and chatters with almost-words, as though it might speak if not for the rainwater flooding its eye sockets and spilling out through its forever-smiling mouth.

Even it hates this Space Marine and, unlike me, I'm almost certain it knows why.

With no thought left for defence, I hammer my chainaxe over and over across the Space Marine's guard. I smash, smash, smash until the armoured cowling housing the belt and motors splits open, my chainaxe's last action before the belt snaps being to throw adamantium in all directions. Several fragments score deep ricochets across my armour. One lodges itself between the eyes of the Space Marine's chest aquila.

That last blow, however, finally succeeds in overwhelming the energy field around the Space Marine's sword. He stumbles from the onslaught even as the weapon dies in his hands. My own weapon trails snapped belts and springs like a jester's marotte.

He's good, this Space Marine, this god amongst children. He throws a feint that I wholly misjudge, sending me the wrong way before using the edge of his de-energised sword to sweep out my legs and put me hard onto my back.

He pins my chest under his boot, tossing aside his cracked sword and drawing a bolt pistol from his mag-holster. The golden eye-lenses glare down at me, the Champion gleaming in the rain. I rage at the fact I'm not dead already, but for one tantalisingly lucid moment, I'm certain I've stared into eyes just like these before.

'Kurrinon,' he says. His use of that name, of *my name,* hits me like a punch to the conscience. A vestigial thing, but it still knows how to hurt. 'Captain of the Dragons Ardent.' I shake my head fiercely. No. *No.* I'm an Eater of Worlds. A legionary of the XII. *I was there.* I look down at my broken armour. There is another colour there, hidden between the red of blood and the grey of ceramite. Turquoise. He levels the pistol at me. My eyes cross down its wide-bore muzzle. 'I am Champion Su'ul Marhen of the Dragons Ardent, and I have come to administer the Chapter's judgement.'

'Brother.' The word catches in my throat the same way pink foam clumps in the rockcrete sea-armour of the fortress-monastery, borne aloft and abandoned by mile-high waves. 'We are victorious, brother.'

The waves of Nautilos, my birthworld, are true monsters. Without any significant land masses to check them, they are free to grow old and to grow huge. A rare few have been given names and a place in this world's primitive pantheon of gods, circling its endless ocean like the famous red spot of Jupiter in distant Sol. But even pups without names of their own are powerful enough to dash the half-ton corpse of a World Eater against the rockcrete.

Most of the dead I can see remain tangled in the tidal booms and netting that surround the monastery. Others are strewn over the lumpen rockcrete, heaped up against the cliff-edge walls of the Praecipitium where they were breached. I see a company's strength of the Traitor Astartes, floating face down and banging their dead heads in endless and repetitive purgatory against the unbroken adamantium portcullis of the sea-gate.

My voice becomes hoarse as I whisper, 'The fight is over.'

Mercy, restraint and forgiveness: these are uppermost amongst the Angel's Graces, the philosophy that the Dragons Ardent have inherited from our genetic predecessors. But I find myself wishing it was not so. One victory is not enough. One death, even administered over and over to a thousand fallen souls, is not a fitting punishment for what has been done here.

My world is dead.

And my brother...

My world is one of vast oceans, sparsely populated across tiny, heavily fortified islands harbouring the monastic facilities of the Dragons Ardent and the few scattered settlements that manage to persist here. It had never come under attack before and, for what little it offers in terms of wealth and resources, it is an Adeptus Astartes home world and well defended. The World Eaters had not been deterred. They had sailed out of the Blindness without warning, eschewing the conventional opening sorties of orbital bombardment and aerial assault and essentially ramming the mesopause in order to launch drop pods and assault boats as quickly as possible. The re-entry burn igniting the prows of two-dozen heretic warships had been visible to the unaugmented eye.

Several hundred berzerkers had survived the Praecipitium's air defences and the impact with the sea to make it onto the island. The wall guns had culled the survivors heavily, but they kept on coming.

The Dragons Ardent knew no fear.

But the World Eaters knew no sanity.

The walls had been broken, the guns had been silenced.

The Dragons Ardent were all dead.

Murmuring the calming mantras of the Solus Encarmine, I lean in with a bitter sense of purpose, and begin sawing at the neck of the Space Marine beneath me with my knife.

I cut slowly through the bundles and gorget rings until, with the gristly *wrench* of separating cartilage, half-congealed blood oozes up through the broken softseals.

My labours drawing to a close, I saw harder.

The Dragons Ardent have always consumed the flesh of their dead and claimed the heads of the slain as keepsakes and trophies. There are those who look askance at such practices, who whisper of gene-seed degradation or worse, but I have never cared for those who would sit in their palaces and pass judgement on things they do not understand. The skulls we take are destined to be etched, carved and engraved, made into objects of beauty to adorn the grand hall of the Praecipitium, where the Reclusiarch leads us in meditation on the humility we show in victory and the strength we draw on in defeat. Objects of a personal significance find their places instead on the bedstands and in the prayer cabinets of a warrior's cell.

This is the fate I have in mind for this head.

Except my cell is gone now.

The entire wing was reduced to rubble when the berzerkers undermined the citadel in their crazed efforts to break inside and butcher those of us that remained. All the skulls I have taken over two hundred and sixty years of battle: destroyed in a single hour of mad carnage.

I almost wish I had convinced the Chapter Master to go out and meet them in the open. We would have killed fewer. I could well be dead now alongside my brother. But my collection would be intact.

With a wet sucking noise and the snapping of the last few cables, the head comes away from the body.

I drop my knife. It clatters into the murky rock pool by my knee, and I hold the head aloft that I might better honour it.

The helmet is red, as mine too has no doubt become as well, the turquoise plate underneath all but totally obscured with the brutality of the fighting.

I push my hand into the helmet through the neck, squashing sinew and gristle, blood trickling down my vambraces as I work the severed head free. I let the helmet drop, holding the revealed head in my cupped hands, and look down into those familiar blue-green eyes.

Tanikhor.

My brother.

His favourite passage from the verses of the Moripatris is carved across his forehead, deep enough to mark the bone. It is a tradition observed by all Dragons Ardent on their ascension to the line companies from the Tenth. Whatever wisdom they have learned, whatever final message they wish to leave behind, it will be there, written in bone, when their brothers come for their heads.

I read the two lines and, as they were composed to do, I feel their invocation of the Black Rage in me and struggle more than ever to suppress it.

'This is not the end, brother,' I hiss.

I take his dead hand in mine and press it to my primary heart.

The tarry scum it has picked up from the many hours it has spent lying in a rock pool leaves a black print on my reddened armour. I move my head so that my ear is turned towards his cold lips, imagining almost that I can hear the Mass of Doom as his last testament to me. I remember how, when the orbital supply lighters came down for them, the local trawlermen would go aboard festooned in whelk shells and conches. The people of Nautilos had always believed that you could press your ear to such fetishes and hear the sea, as if, by some quantum entanglement or warp-bred witchcraft, the Nautilan pantheon could make their demands heard over any distance of airless space.

I hear now, and I listen, for there are gods speaking to me.

Both my hearts beat faster in my chest.

I vow to pursue the World Eaters into the Blindness. I will hound them to the edges of realspace and beyond, where I will slaughter them, and carry on slaughtering until the black of space becomes red.

I hold Tanikhor's head to my chest and say again, 'This is not the end.'

Champion Su'ul Marhen stands over me. The weight of his boot on my chest forces old blood and muck to ooze from the cracks in my breastplate. His high-calibre bolt pistol is trained on the short bridge of bone between my eyes, the expression on his turquoise faceplate glacial.

'The Dragons Ardent are dead,' I manage to spit. 'I was the last.'

I remember now, and the memory hurts. I had left Nautilos in a rage, determined to hunt down the Foresworn and punish every last one of them for the death of my brothers. I don't know how many World Eaters I managed to find and slay, but somehow, over countless light years, after decades of bloodshed in pursuit of vengeance, I managed to stray from the path.

Until I forgot it altogether.

'The Chapter was destroyed,' Su'ul Marhen confirms, with less emotion than I feel on hearing it. 'The Torchbearer fleet sent to relieve you instead founded a new Chapter to occupy the ruins of the fortress-monastery on Nautilos and rebuild. We adopted your name and, though we descended from a different gene-stock, we were proud to be the continuation of your legacy. But, soon after, we began to hear rumours. Two of the original Dragons Ardent had turned traitor, it was said, and joined with the warband that slaughtered your brothers. And so I and others were dispatched from Nautilos to learn the truth. It will be my honour alone to end you, *brother,* but it is a great wound you do me all the same. That I must be the one to bend my knee to the Chapter Master and present him the head of a traitor.'

I smile at that: there was a new lineage of Space Marine resident in the Praecipitium, but old customs died hard.

A fractional twitch of the bolt pistol hovering over me draws my attention back to the Dragon's gun.

'Repent now,' he says. 'Surrender the other who joined you in treachery, and I will be merciful. Or do neither, and face death without first allowing me to lift the burden of heresy from your soul.'

I think back, remembering the time I had lain on the table of Bredek the Unburdened as though I were living it again now. I'd doubted then. I'd been afraid. But it was too late for me then, and it is far, *far* too late for me now. The Nails are already throbbing against the inside of my skull, protesting the lack of battle with pain, and the Butcher's Nails have a way of purging the mind of such weaknesses as doubt.

Pain is coming back to me, the memories coming apart and scattering to the eight corners of my mind, and I feel lucidity passing away like the sun behind the bristling gothic prow of a warship.

I show the Dragon's gun my teeth. Drool fills my mouth and trickles slowly down the sides of my chin. 'I'm an Eater of Worlds.'

Su'ul Marhen sighs. His finger squeezes on the trigger.

'This is not the end,' Tanikhor whispers to me.

And I believe him. Vengeance exists in an eternal present, and so do I. For those who pledge their souls to Khorne, there can be no end.

THE PRICE OF MORKAI

MARC COLLINS

From out of the depths came they,
Greatest of the Allfather's challenges.
Set beneath the ice and salt
To test us again and forever.
Vast is the kraken, great its wrath.
And we? We fight on regardless.
Till we die in shame
Or are chosen by those who wait.

– Hunters of Beasts and Men, The Fenrisian Eddas

It is too late for the dead warrior by the time they bear him into what passes for Ivar Krakenblood's kingdom.

Ivar knows this, just as they know it. The pale skin of their faces is streaked with mourning tears, with ashes, with all the detritus of war and all the scars that Fenris etches upon its sons and daughters.

Four of the *Vlka Fenryka* bear their fallen brother into the halls of the slain, carrying him upon shields like a fallen chieftain of the ice. Fjolnir, proclaimed proudly by his armour as Fjolnir the war-wise, *mjod*-soaked and battle-drunk, lies cold and dead, never to rise again for feast or conflict.

They are called, he knows, *Wolf King's Call* and they have served Fenris and the Imperium with honour and glory. Fjolnir was their leader, a fine one at that, and now he has fallen.

Ivar looks upon him through the lenses of his wolf-skull helm and moves closer. In the cold of the apothecarion, deep in the bowels of the Aett, he knows that he looms like the very shadow of Morkai. Black-armoured, fur-wreathed, glaring at them from a mask of bone and cold iron. Such is the duty of the Wolf Priest – to judge and to test. To inspire fear and loyalty.

'Your brother has been taken from us,' Ivar intones simply.

'Upon the world of Winter and War, at the very hearth. Who will speak the saga of his passing?'

Silence reigns for but a moment, then all their eagerness crowds in. The restrained violence unleashes like a tidal surge and their voices rise, one above the other, clamouring for the honour.

Vili pushes forwards, so determined to be first, buoyed up by the impetuousness of youth. Ivar remembers what it was to be so keen, flush with all the freshness of near-death and after. The Blood Claw slaps his fist against his breastplate as though it were a tribal feast, and he were issuing a challenge.

Jolfr, by contrast, is a tightly wound knot with all his feelings locked within his heart. His scarred face is stony, as true and sure as Asaheim's soil. The only sign of his agitation is the flexing of his gauntleted fingers, still smeared with Fjolnir's blood. Ivar notes the trails that wind down his arm, from his shoulder, where he bore Fjolnir up as they left the field of battle. The warrior's own wounds are forgotten. Unimportant. There is only this final, onerous duty.

Orwandil and Hrungnir wait in mournful silence. Older warriors, more measured and surer. Theirs is the ice-grief, shared by all the tribes of Fenris, for a warrior taken too soon into the underverse.

'We will all speak his saga,' Vili says at last, and the others cheer with him. 'He was our brother and we all stood with him at the end.' Vili shakes with the effort of his words and fine grains of sand weep from his armour.

'As is proper,' Ivar says. There is no judgement in his words. He stands as a symbol of the Rout itself, as solid as the great iron ribs above them, rune-marked and potent. The marks of aversion are cut deep here, the better to ward the wounded and the dead from *maleficarum*. 'You have all shared in his passing.

You have carried him one last time into our halls. Now you will carry his saga down the ages, that the Rout might learn from it.'

The Fang of Morkai clicks at his wrist, blades stirring hungrily as Ivar pulls back the armour plates and exposes the wounds that ended Fjolnir's life. Great cuts and gouges have worked their way through the metal and into flesh, as inexorable as Fenris itself.

This is a killing world. They forget this absolute truth at their peril.

The blades bite, plunging like a seafarer's harpoons, prying and cutting at the bounty beneath. Ivar's other hand braces against Fjolnir's chest as he burrows through flesh and works at bone. The reductor element plunges inwards, and a crack echoes through the chamber as it finds its mark.

Ivar draws the first progenoid up and examines it, tilting it in the lights of the apothecarion, scrutinising it for any damage or defect. He reaches for the cryogenic canister, sliding the organ into the chill receptacle with exaggerated care. A small sensor flickers from crimson to green. Ivar nods to himself, lifts the canister, and lays it in a small chest of dark wood worked with silver and iron runes.

They watch as he turns back to Fjolnir and begins to work at his neck, seeking the second gland. The wolf-skull helm remains impassive, unjudging, seemingly unfazed by the dire work Ivar does. Congealed blood has stained his armour now, fingers and wrists slick with it, dappled across the black of his plate. In other Chapters, Ivar knows, those who tend to the body wear purest white – as though their souls could not be sullied by the duty. Those who are called to the Chaplaincy wear sacred black. It is not so amongst the Vlka Fenryka. The Wolf Priests of Fenris understand the weight of duty and feel Morkai's breath at their necks.

They are made death, judges of the slain and salvation of the living.

The second organ follows, and each warrior of the pack watches Ivar's respectful motions as he seals the casket and lifts it reverently.

'This is the legacy of our brother, Fjolnir. Tell me of him. Speak his saga that the Rout may know it. Let it carry through the hearth.'

'Fjolnir was mighty and wise,' Vili begins. 'Strong as the pillars of the Aett and his laughter was like thunder over the Aett's heights.' He pauses and considers his next words as, slowly, Ivar leads them out of the apothecarion's cold and downwards into the bowels of the world.

'It was the kraken that claimed him,' Jolfr continues. His dark hair is streaked with silver, old enough that Ivar does not doubt his words. Ivar Krakenblood pauses and raises his helm.

'How did the beast find him?' Ivar asks simply.

'We found it. The Kraken's Spur had risen from the depths,' Orwandil puts in, suddenly eager to say his part.

'Out of season,' Ivar muses. 'Out of its time.'

'The sorcerer's scars have unseated the world,' Hrungnir grumbles. 'That is what the Rune Priests say. Fenris' great soul sings and the seas rage. Land rises where it should not and even the strongest fastness might crumble.'

'The lies of the enemy, spread as though they were wisdom. Doubts are not our way,' Ivar says. 'Gird yourself against them. *Focus.*'

The word hangs in the cold corridors of the Aett as the stairs wind downwards into the deeper darkness, lit only by braziers. Bowls of oil and flame, clenched in the jaws of wolves, rendered in brass and iron. They stand, defiant against the shadow, as solid as the foundations of the world into which the procession descends.

'The Spur rose from the sea, Priest, like the knucklebone of a dead god.'

And Ivar listens and notes the saga, and remembers, in turn, when he had first seen the great Spur...

The Kraken's Spur rises from the sea like the knucklebone of a dead god.

Vast and wrathful, as all of Fenris' works are. Mighty as the All-father's fury. It looms over them with a predatory majesty, ringed and rimed with bones. Great plates of skeletal matter, of deep-forged chitin, spars of tooth and claw that grasp at the heavens. The heavens clutch back, tearing at the errant spire of rock, as though they could drive it back into the tumultuous sea.

Ivar watches as the storm rages, drawn by the world's bitter fury. Lightning crackles and dances, scything through the clouds to earth upon the kraken's graveyard. Death hangs heavy on this place, clinging to the black volcanic rock and the planes of ivory.

Before it, even the greatest of the gathered warriors feels small.

Ivar breathes a deep lungful of cold salt air and turns back to the others. They wait, standing or crouching upon a small rise smeared with tangles of deep seaweed and still crawling with withered and blinded beasts.

The storm lashes at him, tearing at his naked head. Rain spatters his dark skin, marked only by the pale scars of a youth spent at war. His tribal braids whip and dance, refracted lightning flickering along rings of copper and iron. His features are broad, as befits one raised up among the Sky Warriors.

The Trial is behind him now. The wolf is in his blood. When his senses taste the world, they are aflame with the savage strength of Fenris. No other breed of Astartes understands as he now does. None are as shaped by their crucible.

The first of his comrades looks at him with wary attention. Brynjar's skin is fish-pale and tattooed with winding blue ink, a drake-dance that coils up his neck to surround his right eye with fangs. The man scowls too easily, finding little joy in their task. Ivar smiles at him, baring his teeth with almost predatory relish.

'This is a rare honour,' Ivar says quickly and looks up. Somewhere in the storm, he knows the iron chariot circles.

No, *his subconscious mind whispers, purring with hypnogogic recall,* the Thunderhawk is circling...

Ivar banishes the thought and speaks again. 'We are watched by the Rout's favoured.'

He thinks again of the war-gnarled ancient who waits above, armoured in black and bone. His gaze winnowed Ivar to the core, judging him just as the glorious slain were judged. The living legend had scrutinised each of them in turn, no matter their origins.

They came from all over, Ivar had learned, drawn from different tribes and packs, drawn together to be assessed and tested. Brought across the tumultuous sea now that the Spur had once again revealed itself.

This is a fated moment, *he knows.* Now our *wyrds* reveal themselves.

'Let them watch,' Brynjar says, blustering.

The others watch impassively, caught half between scenting weakness and gravitating towards whoever proves themselves the dominant personality. Arkyn with his strawy hair and his pale eyes. Gudmund edges forwards, his chainsword raised and ready. Teeth bite the air, as true and hungry as his own fangs. Jolnyr is more cautious, dark eyes narrowed and uncertain.

'We earn their ire at our peril,' Ivar says, striding forwards, face to face with Brynjar now. 'This is not just a matter of packs and prestige. It is of rank.' The words hang in the air, cultivating import, becoming almost prophecy from his lips. 'When Grandfather Lupus holds you in his gaze, then you must bare your truest soul, and be judged.'

'This is kaerl work!' Brynjar laughs, practically braying. He sweeps an arm around at the graveyard as though he cannot see its worth.

Blinded by his own pettiness. 'We are to fetch claws and teeth for the armourers because they will not leave their halls of iron.'

'And why wouldn't they assign a simple pack to that task? Sworn brothers, true and tested. We are not bonded. Before this calling we did not know each other. There is a purpose here,' Ivar snarls.

The others grumble their assent. They have come from too far afield, all strangers, for it to be so low a task.

'We are caught in the wolf's attention now. Do your part. Prove yourself, and the rewards will make this bounty seem like the smallest of hoards.'

Brynjar moves to speak, but the world speaks first. Everything shudders and shakes. For a moment Ivar worries the island will sink once more into the depths and they shall drown, to be nothing more than underverse wights denied their glorious end.

The land does not move. Something hurls itself up, rising from the deep like legend, tendrils arcing up to eclipse the storm-streaked skies. The kraken rises from the frozen depths, ice-rimed and terrible, screaming in a voice like the howl of a thousand wolves, struck through with the roar of thunder and breaking glaciers.

All Ivar and his pack can do is howl back in defiance.

'We had never seen its like,' Vili says at last.

Ivar knows the youth speaks true, his own memories surging with thoughts of the kings of Fenris' seas.

The kraken has defined so much of their history, surging strong even in the time of Russ. Ivar knows the legends by rote, has studied every fragment of them, committed them to memory in the way of the *skjalds.*

Ancient and terrible, the bane of ship and sail, gnawing upon the world's roots when they were not stirred to the surface. The Wolf King himself had once caught the Father of Kraken and cast it to the depths.

Let us try again when it has grown a bit, eh?

Ivar suppresses a chuckle at the thought of the Wolf King's long-ago whimsy, echoing down the years, filling the Aett once again with his booming mirth and boundless melancholy alike.

He thinks of the vaults that hold the Chapter's legacy and of the Ancients who wait in the darkness, bound to the living death of the Dreadnought. Forever seeking to match that boundless heritage. To prove themselves to their fellows and to stand proud amongst the other brotherhoods of the Adeptus Astartes.

'Vast it was,' Hrungnir says, and interrupts Ivar's reverie. 'Greater than any beast of the sea that I have seen. It was like one of the Devourer's vast beast-ships, clawing its way up from beneath the ice, clawing at the heavens as though it could disgorge the Wolf's Eye from the firmament.'

The cold crowds in around them, through the dark and winding halls, almost radiating from the etched runes. Lumens weep pale blue light until all is tainted with an icy pallor. Even here, beneath the world, they cannot forget that this is Fenris. Winter and war touch all things, in time.

Ivar pictures the kraken anew, tearing through the frosty light, caught between their telling and his own memories. The beast in its rage and fury, tearing at the world itself. Lightning catching upon its hide, dancing with the firelight of old battles and distant stars. Spear-struck and scarred, yet never truly vanquished.

Only the greatest of heroes can risk its wrath and live, he thinks, and the thought curdles upon his mind, worried through with shame and false pride.

'But Fjolnir,' Jolfr continues, 'he did not pause beneath its gaze.' He pauses and slams his fist against his breastplate. 'Throne of the Allfather, but I have never seen its like. Axe raised, he spat his bile into the face of the great enemy, and we all saw its eye widen with mortal terror!'

Ivar lets himself laugh then. They all laugh with him. There is pride in the telling. Each warrior stands taller, despair fading as they remember the final stand of a brother.

Fjolnir, swaggering like a drunk, axe turning over and over in one gauntleted fist, grinning his defiance at the monster that rises to encompass all that is. For a moment standing as a totem against the firelight, blade raised to ward home and hearth against monsters.

'He died as he lived, then,' Ivar says. 'Honouring the spirit of Russ, the example set as the Imperium was born and the All-father's realm was carved out.' The Wolf Priest's hands close a little tighter about the sacred casket, fingers brushing over them with a wary reverence. 'That is all any of us can hope for, at the end.'

Pillars of basalt die in moments, swept away in the hurricane of scale and chitin, claw and fang.

All of them are firing madly, screaming their surprise and outrage. Scrambling up and over the ridge, turning to fire or to brandish their blades in hollow challenge. The dead ashes of fear flare in their hearts, kindling into a righteous fury.

They are Sky Warriors of the Rout. The Vlka Fenryka, and they shall not die a weakling's death at the teeth of a beast.

The kraken draws back in a rush of filthy water, shattered rock and bone dust. The deep reclaims it and they watch the ocean thrum and boil.

It waits. It lurks. They all know the hunter's ways, and they are defined by patience. They have not felt this way since they rose to rank and were chosen by the Rout.

They have not felt like prey.

'What do we do?' Brynjar hisses. He spins from side to side, turning his bolt pistol from a small, withered grove of macro-kelp to the west, to a vast cracked kraken skull that lies along the eastern shore, beak

and fangs digging into the volcanic sand as though devouring the world.

'Be still,' Ivar breathes. 'Be silent. Weapons ready. Watch the water for signs of the kraken... As though we were upon a sea ship.'

Ivar looks skywards, as if seeking an omen. The heavens keep their counsel. Demigods do not descend to save them. This is part of the test. The trial. This is the crucible through which they will be tested and shaped. The judgement of the Slayer.

He gestures for the rest to follow and slowly they begin to edge along the ridge, towards the shelter of the vast skull. Bone and rock crunch beneath their feet, the world's history dying in their advance.

Every growl and rumble of the tormented earth is another omen as Fenris speaks and the Blood Claws listen. Creaking, cracking, the roar of the ocean surging up and around them. Waves buffet the coast, rushing in with hungry inevitability.

'You all know the sea,' Ivar says. 'Whether you knew hard land or soft, you know the Worldsea's wrath. This is but another trial. We will be judged for what we do here. If not in the Aett then in the Halls of Russ that wait for us. No underverse death for us. No wight's fate.'

Gudmund laughs bitterly. 'The sea always takes its due, just as Morkai takes his price. The wolves of death are ever at our heels.'

'Let them come,' Arkyn growls. 'We've all passed through death and battle once already.' His blond hair is slicked to him with rain and sea salt. 'If I am to die then it will be with weapon in hand, as a true son of Russ.'

The sea roars up and onto the shore, driven by the vast force behind it, hurled against them with infinite strength and boundless malice. The tendril, wrought enormous, god-scale and terrible, slams through the crested ruin of bone and shatters it. The skull and beak explode, hurled apart with enough momentum to embed deep into the rock. They scar the obsidian with their passage.

The pack ducks low, instinct fuelling them as more tendrils rise from the deep. Bioluminescence flickers across their surface, a writhing and fitful colouration, almost gleeful at their suffering.

Jolnyr fires, roaring all the while. Shells burst and blossom along its armoured hide, flaring bright for mere moments. Fire wreathes its skin and then it stirs anew, coiling back before rushing forwards. A tendril larger across than a Thunderhawk falls towards them. The pack scatters, too slow, too late.

Jolnyr is there in one instant and then gone. A smear of blood and broken armour. He does not even have a chance to scream in sudden surprise. There is only his roared hate, and then silence, replaced by the howl of the storm.

They break for the shelter of the forest, barely even turning to look back as the monster busies itself with its meal.

'We do not survive this,' Gudmund murmurs. 'There is no way out. The monster is too great. We cannot outrun it. We have no way back to the ship. If we fight it – and skitja, but I do not shirk from that – then we will die. Glorious or unmourned, it will tear us from the rocks, one by one.'

'Peace, brother,' Brynjar whispers. 'No foe is our equal. No quarry is insurmountable.' He crouches low on his haunches, beneath the faded fronds and clinging muck of the dying plant life. 'We would not have been sent here without reason.'

'I thought you said this was kaerl work?' Arkyn says. 'A duty beneath us.'

Brynjar turns his eyes towards Ivar and then looks away, the drake a flash of blue around his eye, contracting as though hiding its face in shame. 'I was wrong, brother,' he says then. 'Ivar had the right of it. Perhaps he simply knows the sea and its seasons better than I do. He speaks with wisdom.' He fixes Ivar with his gaze once more. 'What do we do, brother?'

Their weapons have been set idle. There is only the low growl of their armour amidst the pulse and thrum of the sea. Something screeches across the volcanic shore, hungry and eager, seeking fresh prey.

Ivar can feel its eyes, questing. As savage and unceasing as any other thing of this world. Winter and war, eternal and all-consuming.

'It is a thing living,' Ivar says at last. 'It can be killed. Look around you. This is their graveyard. Perhaps it waits like Morkai's shadow, here. Grave-warded and deathsworn, guarding their dead. We are the Vlka Fenryka, and we fear nothing. No beast of the sea nor monster of the void.' He pauses and realises that the others hang on his every word. 'We are the Allfather's promise, carved into the galaxy's skin. Ever the guardian of humanity's dream. Executioners of the greatest of monsters.'

'Aye!' Arkyn hisses, his voice low. 'What next, brother?'

'What else?' Ivar asks with a grin. 'We slay the beast.'

They pause at last, their descent complete.

The cold beneath the earth is absolute now. They are pressed against the true soul of Fenris, the all-cold that will devour all but the worthy. Only the strong and the dead endure here.

'Your brother's journey nears its end,' Ivar breathes. 'He has passed through fire and ice, died and been born anew, only to die once more. That is our way. It is the way of Fenris. Sacred in a way that our cousins can never understand. They rob it of its power, by reducing it to the simple act.' He nods to the casket in his hands. 'Fjolnir is more than these organs. More than this rite.'

'He was our brother,' Vili says.

'Our friend,' Hrungnir says.

'A mentor,' Jolfr whispers.

'A leader,' Orwandil finishes.

'He is of the Rout and shall ever be so. The blood of Russ does not tire nor dull. It fights forever, no matter what is set against it.

His legacy returns to the Chapter. We commit it to the cold until it is needed. Then, in the sight of the Allfather and with the blessings of the priesthood, so shall Fjolnir's strength invigorate new sword arms. Raise up new valiant slain from their first deaths.'

'A great honour,' Orwandil says and nods. 'That our death is not the end. That our spirit endures, through new blood, and fresh rage.'

'Fjolnir's great strength, that cleaved into the crater-scarred beast, the one-eyed monster that rose from the deeps like the Cyclops' wrath itself.'

Ivar pauses. 'That was the beast he fought and slew?'

He leads them. It is somehow now as natural as breathing.

Desperation floods his marrow, the will to live caged in him like lightning from the storm-tossed skies. They will fight and perhaps they will die. That is nothing new. This is Fenris. Only the strong endure, be they man or kraken.

They forge north from the withered grove, ascending the base of the Kraken's Spur, committed to their course, set upon their duty. The storm speaks and earths itself into the rocks above, lighting all around them in flashes of phosphor-white.

It sees them. Its central eyes lock upon them and it moves in a sudden rush, like a landslip, akin to calamity. Great tendrils sweep up, demolishing ridges, tearing aside the kelp grove, slithering and flowing towards the beleaguered pack.

They scatter at Ivar's command.

Each warrior ducks and weaves beneath the questing tentacles, blades raised to tear at sucker and flesh. Chainswords whir and bite and the monster screams. Immense limbs whip back or hammer down. Volcanic dust kisses the air just as blood scents it. The warriors move, guided by Ivar's shouted instructions, blades and bolt pistols acting in perfect concert.

Death by a thousand cuts. Wound after wound, gouged into the beast.

'The eyes!' Ivar bellows. 'Aim for the eyes!'

Bolt shells detonate in a cluster of flame and shrapnel, tearing at the centre of the monster's mass. Eyes burst apart and the scream shifts up another octave. It lashes and howls, clawing at the land, scraping at the sky. Only one of its immense central eyes endures, glaring out from its flesh core, while the others weep ichor.

Brynjar falls.

A final whipping tendril drives him to the side, buckling his armour, till blood stains the salt-rock and bone. His howl of pain and rage cuts like a lash through the screaming tumult of the battle.

Ivar lunges through the fray. For a moment he understands the might and fury of Russ, the sagas and the traditions suddenly alive within him. Hearts thrumming, soul singing, he slides his body along the broken rock, hearing ceramite scrape against stone, like the whetting of a blade.

His own chainsword roars in sympathy, cleaving upwards, gouging at the biting flesh, forcing it back and away from his brother. Brynjar gasps and spits blood. He tries, vainly, to rise and continue his struggle.

Failure. Inaction. Death. All weights that will bear him down beneath the ice, pin him to his own red snow.

Ivar hews at the beast, screaming with all the hatred that Fenris can kindle. Rage sparks within him, surging upwards with volcanic choler, enough to split the very world. Ichor coats him, sizzling against his plate, hot blood against cold armour.

The beast lashes at him, thrashing and bellowing, till the teeth of the suckers clatter against his second skin. They bite. Bestial might meets its like, and they tussle like legends, demigod and monster, caught together in the timeless struggle. Man and beast, locked in conflict, each desperate for survival. For food, for shelter, for safety.

Blood chokes Ivar's throat as the kraken takes its price.

The others fire again and the limb judders, pulling back to coil protectively around one vast flank. Ivar snarls and buries his chainblade to the hilt in its flesh. He pulls his pistol free and sights, one-handed, his eyes meeting the beast's remaining orb. He tilts it down, just a fraction.

'Go back to the depths,' he growls. 'And when you have grown a bit more, then perhaps we shall try again.'

Ivar fires and the bolt shells strike the great beast around the yawning beak, scarring the hungry maw, tearing at it, without and within. The kraken screams. It recoils in one great motion, tendrils drawing in as it pulls itself back towards the safety of the ocean. There is a sudden peace, a moment where there is only the storm's wrath. Then a pulling, sucking sound, like a wound being finally and decisively drained. The kraken's vastness slinks back into the sea, drawn below, pouring itself back into the abyss.

The heavens speak again. Not in lightning but in fire.

Something streaks through the storm like a comet, howling its own rage against the roiling sea. Missiles scream through the tumult even as heavy bolters speak their fury. The waters churn, boiling and bleeding. The beast does not rise anew, driven deep by the gunship. By Ivar.

The Thunderhawk's fury is purgative, cleansing. Its engines are as one with Fenris' climactic anger, merely another gale amidst the tumult. The pack slinks forwards, almost cautious, as the Thunderhawk descends, casting up plumes of dust as its thrusters fire and its landing struts extrude.

The rear hatch clatters down, and the Slayer descends.

Ulrik fixes them with his skull-faced gaze, the impenetrable scrutiny of the Wolf Helm of Russ. Each feels its fell attention and reacts in turn. Gudmund flinches. Arkyn tenses. Brynjar tries to stand taller, to present himself. He can barely stand at all. Ivar returns the gaze evenly, as though he has seen all there is to be seen. Pain mars his visage, etched into him as surely as age. He sways, just for a moment, wounds already clotting, scars already cut into his flesh and soul.

'You have done well,' Ulrik intones at last. 'The Spur rises but once in a generation. The bounty it carries is profound, yes, but the test is the Spur itself.'

He pauses. They watch him, all eyes fixed upon him. The Wolf High Priest scrutinises them each in turn.

'We have monitored each of you, through your armour systems. There are none amongst you with cause for shame.'

The flame of his attention passes, and all fall silent.

'There is a place for all of you in the Chapter's ranks. You have each proven your skill and resolve.' The wolf-skull mask turns, and its eyes burn, locking Ivar in its sight. 'You have stood as the bane of kraken, and inheritors of the Spur's bounty. It is an omen, to be sure. In the sight of Russ and Fenris.'

Ivar falls to his knees. He gazes up at the Slayer himself, caught in the fire of his attention. In that moment he feels as though he will burn forever. Alight. Aflame.

'You shall all carve legends within the annals of the Rout.'

They are all silent as they advance into the vault.

The lumens are low, reverent as any ancient barrow crypt. There are no sconces or braziers here, no light, save for the chill glow of the lumens and the suspensor vaults. The light catches on the warriors and their armour, alighting on the etched oaths and boasts. It renders them almost as ice carvings, like ancient glacial monuments, like the statues of Asaheim.

There is only the dark and the cold beneath the earth. These are the vaults of eternity, where the Chapter's legacy is preserved and enshrined.

Here, in the depths, all pain and mourning has faded. They

are exalted in their brother's sacrifice; the fire of his deeds has kindled within them. The recounting has made them mighty.

'He is restored to the Chapter. Returned to the hearth, here at the end,' Ivar says.

They all bow their heads, silent. Waiting.

'Fjolnir,' Vili says at last. 'Fjolnir faced down the kraken and slew it. His axe was like the blade of Russ itself, hewing the beast apart. Ancient and unbowed, it was. A monster, marked by its previous struggles, yet rising to the challenge of the moment.'

Ivar nods. 'And he did not falter.'

'Aye,' Orwandil continues. 'As a champion and a hero. He stood against the kraken amidst the bones of its fellows. He has risen amongst the valiant slain, to fight at Russ' side come the Wolftime!'

They cheer, even in their mourning. Their brother is dead and yet they celebrate. Here, at the Aett's heart, the chill core of the gene-seed vaults. So far beneath the earth that Fenris' capricious spirit waxes strong.

'You have slain the kraken and proven its bane,' Ivar says at last. 'In this you are blessed. A brother has stood against the might of Fenris.' He pauses again. 'This is our cold cradle. The hearth from which the greatest warriors are raised up, to serve His great vision. A galaxy made ready for humanity. Broken beneath the blades and mauls of the worthy.'

He places the casket upon a plinth and opens it, reverence in every gesture and motion. He reaches out and activates the stasis vault. A section of the wall slides free, weeping pale light. He places each progenoid within.

'So does Fjolnir, war-wise, mjod-soaked, battle-drunk, kraken's foe, rise from the realm of men and gods. He has fought and warred in the Allfather's name, and has passed into the halls of the slain. Such is the glory of these times. The Era Indomitus rages. The galaxy burns.'

Ivar Krakenblood presses his hand to the ancient mechanisms of the vault and closes his eyes.

'Each of us is burdened with our wyrd. To fight and die at the whim of fate etched out before ever we were born.' He sighs. 'You have fought and bled for humanity's dream. You have suffered for your brothers. That is all that any son of Russ can ask. That is all that any trueborn heir of Fenris can seek as their destiny.'

And they cheer with him, voices raised for a brother's end and the victory he won there. His memory no longer a wound, or a burden.

But a blessing in the eyes of Morkai.

CONSECRATED GROUND

STEVEN B FISCHER

Blood pools atop the holy, golden aquila inlaid upon the chapel's onyx floor – a crimson stain spreading across its polished black surface like the scar that mars the God-Emperor's galaxy. It is an ill omen if I have ever seen one.

Beside me, Brother-Chaplain Dant falls to his knees before the small sanctum's altar. The reliquaries bound with consecrated golden cord to his black power armour rustle gently with the gesture. His lips move, though he is silent, whether so enraged by the obscenity of this scene that he cannot speak, or merely lost in prayer and meditation, as he is wont to be more and more in these dark days. With reverence, he unclasps the skull chained around his neck and begins the Sanctification of the Dying. Alvus, my stalwart Apothecary, surveys the flayed corpse atop the desecrated altar.

'This is a soiled world indeed, Brother Emeric,' he growls, 'if the enemies of the Throne are so emboldened they perform such atrocities on consecrated ground.'

I nod grimly and mutter my own prayer for the dead ecclesiarch's soul as I step up beside him. The priest's body is scarcely recognisable as human in the mess of flesh and offal he has become. His skin is flayed from head to toe, his entrails arranged in a grisly, indecipherable pattern.

'Burn it,' I call to the Neophytes at my back. Flamers roar to life at my command, engulfing the chamber in purifying fire.

Serraq's Reach. *Jewel of the Iliena Subsector*. A swarming, boiling corpse of a hive world, ruled by an unworthy, privileged fool. It has been decades since I set foot on this depraved planet, but the stench of its rot has only grown stronger, as has my revulsion for its decadent aristocracy, picking like bloated carrion birds at the corpse of the world they were entrusted to rule. If not for the debt of honour my Chapter holds to the lord governor's great-grandsire, I would have called myself blessed to never return.

But Marshal Laise's orders had been explicit.

Do not linger on that broken world, Brother Emeric. Fulfil the lord governor's request for aid, and burn out the cult she claims threatens her peace. Then return. The crusade cannot spare you for long, Castellan.

Castellan. The title feels strange to me, even in memory. Too fresh to be comfortable upon my shoulders, like the first time I wore my sacred power armour.

Rainbow-hued light fills the defiled shrine, flickering off a roof of the finest glassaic – a literal vision of the God-Emperor staring down over this abomination. I cannot fix this world. But perhaps, by His grace, I can purge it of one evil.

Flame swallows the sanctum and the despoiled altar, the priest's corpse crackling and hissing as his skin turns to ash.

'He was a loyal servant of the God-Emperor,' Brother-Apothecary Alvus remarks. 'Murdered first, then skinned. The purity of his soul shall usher in the reconsecration of this ground.'

I grunt. 'He was dead before he was mutilated, and therefore no use to any true servant of the Archenemy. What is more, the sacred relics and liturgical instruments that should adorn this chamber have been removed.'

Alvus nods. 'A poor effort by perpetrators of common theft

and murder to place the guilt of their sins upon more conspicuous transgressors.'

I turn from the altar and towards the door. Despite a week on this world, my fighting company has had no success hunting the cult we pursue. They have decimated a dozen of the lord governor's patrols in that span, then vanished like a shadow at the breaking of dawn.

'This seems another trail that leads us nowhere,' I say.

A figure stands in the gloom outside the chapel, and my hand falls unbidden to the power sword at my waist. Penitence drinks in the light of the conflagration and hums in my gauntleted grasp. Stepping from the blaze into the empty cold of the city, I face the interloper.

He stands half my height, short even for a mortal human, and wears his scalp bald and dyed a deep azure in the fashion of this system. A rusting bionic sits beside his single natural eye, and his left arm has been replaced by a prosthetic of marginal quality. A brutal shock maul and short-barrelled projectile shotgun hang from his belt, though he makes no move towards either.

'My lord,' he calls out before I reach him.

I stay my blade out of curiosity. 'These grounds are shut.'

The man trembles slightly, and I hear his heart hammer within his chest, but he masters his fear and holds it from his voice when he speaks.

'This is my stack, my lord, and therefore my jurisdiction.'

He moves aside, the silver crest of the local enforcers flashing on the lapel of his grey leather jacket. Beside him, a dark icon is scribed upon the chapel's stone exterior. A black silhouette stares down at me, roughly the shape of a man but winged, with a gleaming star at the centre of its chest. A coil of chain lies broken beneath its feet, masking an inlaid litany that is no longer legible.

'Vice-Regulator Kendam Ranp, my lord,' the enforcer says by

way of introduction. 'There's only one gang in this sub-stack bold and stupid enough to crack a priest and try to blame it on cultists. But they got their iconography right, and that alone is cause for concern.'

Penitence dances in my hand, a dimly flickering shard of retribution in the near-black. This blade has been held by Black Templars for so long that it scarcely needs my direction at all. The weapon is a thousand years old, at least, and has been borne by more than a dozen of my brothers before me.

I breach a narrow doorway in the dilapidated habitation stack, my pauldron shattering its decaying frame. I raise my storm shield and feel the soft shudder of repeated impacts. A moment later, two weapons fall to the floor, as do their wielders' hands as Penitence sings.

Alvus rushes past me and throws a pair of underhivers into the wall. One man's head cracks against the unforgiving rockcrete. The other screams but raises a wicked-looking billhook. The Apothecary's gauntlet pauses before the man's face, the small chainblade on his narthecium spinning before he grasps the man's head and smashes it into the floor.

'Better than to profane this holy instrument with his blood,' Alvus grunts, rising from his knees. He has served at my side long enough that I need not see his face to know his expression. It is one of bitter revulsion, and I wear the same.

'There is no glory in this, brother. Only killing. Yet honour demands that this sanction comes at our hands.'

'In the God-Emperor's name,' Alvus replies. That is answer enough for us both.

'Another anteroom, then the heart of this nest awaits, if the enforcer's information is as reliable as the vice-regulator believes.'

The small man follows me into the vestibule, breathing heavily and splattered with blood. His shock maul crackles in his augmetic hand, and he curses under his breath as he staunches a ragged wound on his leg. I had thought him a vulgar, irreverent man, but in battle he has proven adept at his craft.

We are the God-Emperor's sons. His most-favoured servants. We exist to bring war to His most fearsome enemies, not to sniff out the trails of petty criminals. I am content to allow the enforcer and his allies to fulfil that function on our behalf.

Alvus and I draw up before a sealed plasteel door. The chain-blade on the Apothecary's narthecium whirrs, adamantine teeth biting into the locking mechanism with ease.

'O Emperor,' Brother-Chaplain Dant cries in the small, naked space, his voice ringing clear with a hymn of battle.

I raise my foot and the plasteel door bursts inward. Smoke and fire greet us as we rush into the chamber. Dant's benediction surges before us.

'All stand unclean before your infinite perfection. All are sullied in the clarity of your unending light.'

The staccato impact of projectile rounds stitches a line across my storm shield and strikes my pauldron, vibrating through my bones. A dozen men huddle behind makeshift barricades, coughing in the smoke of their own obscura and fear.

'We, your sons, carry the ember of your all-consuming flame. Let us burn away the chaff without hesitation or weakness.'

Dant's righteous words echo through my soul, and there is zeal in my punishment now. The cleansing flame cares not for glory, it is content to devour any offering set within its reach.

Penitence shears a man's head from his shoulders, then drinks deeply from the chest of another. Something cracks against my shoulder and my grip slackens, my storm shield tumbling from my hand.

I turn to face a hulking mess of an abhuman grasping a length of plasteel bracing-beam. Confusion is writ across the ogryn's face at the fact that my arm is still linked to my body, and he mumbles a curse in broken Low Gothic. He raises his club again, and I step inside his swing.

There is no space to bring Penitence's blade to bear, but I drive its pommel into the ogryn's flank. He bellows as ribs crack beneath my blow, then the creature's stone-strong arms encircle me. For a terrible moment, my breath abandons my lungs and my bones groan. The abhuman's eyes shine with blank, animal fury. I pull my face away from his, then bring my helmet crashing into his nose.

The ogryn reels, his grasp slackening just enough for my left hand to reach my boltgun. A single shot rips through the ogryn's stomach, and the left side of his torso erupts in a plume of blood and bone.

I gasp as his vice-like arms fall from my chest and fire a second shot into the ogryn's chest to ensure his extinction. I stagger to the centre of the room, where Dant's crozius hangs over a kneeling man's head.

'In the Emperor's name, I condemn your body. By the Emperor's grace, I damn your soul. With my breath I declare you heretic, unworthy. With my hand, I deliver the God-Emperor's judgement.'

'Hold,' I call, and Dant pauses. The rest of the room is a mess of blood and corpses, our final living prisoner cowering beneath the Chaplain's gaze.

Towering over the prisoner, I see how truly small he is, both in size and in spirit compared to my brothers. At his feet lie stolen relics from the chapel, and a laspistol matching the dead priest's wounds.

'Speak,' I demand. 'Confess.'

'We are here to slay heretics,' Alvus grumbles. 'Not interrogate them.'

'Indeed. But first we must learn where they hide.'

The prisoner sweats, his weak flesh already failing as blood streams from his two shattered legs. He is too terrified of my brothers to open his mouth, and looks towards the only other mortal face in the room for deliverance. The enforcer glances towards me, then back at the man, dropping his speech into the local stack dialect.

'We ken you greased you that priest, frate. Donna bother sayin' nin. We ken you skin you'd 'im too, and scribe that pict on that the wall.'

Any colour left in the man's face fades, and he tries to mumble a denial.

Ranp spits to the side and motions towards me. 'Tell me true, frate. Where'd you ken that symbol? If you ain't spinning words, I swear I won't let this one 'ere crack you.'

The speech is broken and strange to my ears, but the enforcer's meaning is clear enough to us all.

'You cannot deny the God-Emperor justice,' Alvus protests, but I raise my hand and nod.

'I will not touch him. As you say.'

The prisoner swallows, a tear escaping his eyes. 'It weren't my plot, frate. We seen the symbol in the understack last week. By the cinch mill. I swear ya, I ain't spinnin'.' The man looks up anxiously at Penitence and then Ranp.

'That checks out, my lord,' the vice-regulator says.

'And you know where this cinch mill is?'

A small nod.

I look to Dant. 'The enforcer swore an oath on my behalf, Brother-Chaplain. He placed no such shackles on your hands, nor your honour.'

His crozius flashes as I turn towards the door.

* * *

'Breaker of chains.' The words fall bitter from my lips as I read them.

A dark figure twice my height is scribed before me upon a wall of crumbling rockcrete within the recesses of a waste-water alcove far beneath the main hive stacks. The silhouette floats on feathered wings of darkest black, and from the centre of its chest gleams the light of a burning star. Beneath its feet lies that same shattered pile of chains.

The sigil matches the mark on the profaned chapel, but almost a dozen identical forms are painted around it. The obscene mural is wreathed in a rotation of broken High Gothic, and I recognise the passage, though not in this form. Dant completes it for me.

'And He shall dispatch His angels to sever your bonds, to shatter your fetters and proclaim His power. Only in His service shall you discover liberation. Only in surrender shall you at last know peace.'

Something in those holy words juxtaposed upon this blatant sacrilege stirs me, and a deep disquiet settles on my soul.

'The artistry is impressive,' Dant remarks eventually.

Not the response I had anticipated. I turn away but do not disagree.

'We should destroy it,' a gruff voice greets me. Hadrick hefts his thunder hammer, volunteering.

'We will,' I reply. 'Though to do so now would risk attention that I would rather avoid.'

Hadrick's Crusader squad gathers behind him, four Initiates of fiercest zealotry and their Neophytes standing at their sides. Brothers Alvus and Dant and I make twelve. We are a small enough party to move with speed and silence, yet fierce enough that I am certain we can dispatch any foe.

I would prefer to simply storm these tunnels with the strength of my entire fighting company, but the vice-regulator assures me that the vaults of this underhive are nigh-endless and contain infinite, unmapped routes where our quarry could go to ground if startled. I do not doubt him, based on what I have so far seen.

Behind me, the enforcer paces nervously, two of his troopers milling at his side. A pair of cyber-mastiffs circle between them – he had insisted upon including the beasts in our number.

'We would not be the first to get lost where we're going, my lord,' he had told me. 'Might be they can smell fresher air if we do.'

'Carry on, vice-regulator,' I order him now, and he appears both more and less anxious to be moving.

'The cinch mill,' I ask, motioning to the dark structure that forms the base of the cyclopean tower beside us, 'what is it?'

No natural light penetrates this deeply into the stacks, and even the scattered torch lamps mounted on the hive's dilapidated foundation have faded from neglect untold aeons ago. I cannot see the soot and smoke spewing from the manufactorum, but I can taste their acrid flavour in the dank, sweltering air.

The little man laughs grimly. 'Ain't a proper mill, my lord, just what the underhivers call it. Sounds better than "crematorium". Lets you think a little less about what you're breathing in.'

My eyes make out a row of servitors pushing massive bins from a loading door behind the building and emptying them into a great mechanical lift, bearing their contents even deeper into the bowels of this world.

'For disposal?' Alvus asks.

'For construction.'

Vice-Regulator Ranp points to a titanic arch as we pass beneath it, one of a thousand such cantilevers – each the length of a Gladius frigate – supporting the towering stack above. Its surface is cracked and moth-eaten, patched with a stark white compound in a hundred places.

'Buildings, vessels, spoiled crops, corpses. The cinch mill burns it all, then sends the ash deeper down to patch crews who mix it with binders and use it to repair the hive's foundations. It's cheaper than shipping the waste off-world, and it keeps the stacks from collapsing. Usually.

'This cult began as a group of twists and renegades, by all reports, who deserted from those patch crews a few years back. They started hitting the crews shortly thereafter, but recently they've been moving upstack. Ambushed the Magistrate's convoy in stack nine last summer. Undermined and toppled half a precinct-fortress just last month. Been reports of them storming entire stack levels in some of the outlying sectors, though I'm not sure if that's truly to be believed.'

'The taint of heresy is like a festering wound,' Alvus replies. 'Let it sit unharried and it will seed this entire world.'

'If you say so, my lord. I sent an investigator down with a new patch crew last month, with orders to embed himself within the cult and try to learn something about their aims. Haven't heard from him since. Could be dead. Maybe worse.' The enforcer eyes Penitence at my side. 'Best be ready to use that, either way, my lord.' His gaze lingers on the stout black chain that binds the weapon to my gauntlet.

'It is a devotional chain,' I offer. 'It binds my weapon to my armour until victory is won.'

'Very well, my lord,' Ranp replies. 'Though it looks as if it has not been removed in some time.'

Beneath my helmet my face contorts into a grimace.

'I made a vow,' I reply coldly. That will have to be answer enough.

One of the cyber-mastiffs raises its snout as we reach another fork in the filthy catacombs.

'She wants to go right, my lord.' The beast's handler strokes its metallic plates affectionately, calming the primitive machine spirit within, though its serrated jaws still gnash with anticipation. 'I'd guess her auspex tells her the way ahead is more frequently travelled that direction.'

I pause. The same bitter iconography litters the walls of the cramped tunnel through which we tread. We walk miles below even the cinch mill now, and the underhive is absent of any true architecture, only the endless labyrinthine corridors of the Old City buried beneath Serraq's Reach.

'Left,' Dant says suddenly. He is lost deep in meditation, and I'm surprised to hear him speak, but I trust the Chaplain's guidance, as always.

'Left,' I reply. There is no argument. 'If our quarry is hiding they will avoid the well-travelled path.'

The tunnel narrows further ahead, partially collapsed beneath the hulking hive city above us. The air is thick and cloying. Millennia of waste and neglect make it burdensome to breathe. Vice-Regulator Ranp and his troopers cough uncomfortably beneath cheap respirators.

'To think that humans dwell among such squalor,' I subvocalise to Alvus. I was mortal once. Those memories are little more than a distant dream now, yet I am not so far removed from them that I cannot imagine what suffering such a life must be.

'The weight of the God-Emperor's Imperium lies heavy on us all, Brother-Castellan,' Alvus replies.

I do not sympathise with those who allow that force to crush their devotion to the Master of Mankind, but I am still human enough to understand the temptation to step out from beneath such a weight.

I lead the way beneath rubble into a dark anteroom. Even in the dimness the spectacle is clear. We stand in a hemispherical chamber, perhaps a dozen yards across. From floor to ceiling, its arching walls are bestrewn with rough petroglyphs carved by unskilled hands. All bear that same unsettling image of dark-winged angels perched atop broken chains.

At the far end of the room a shadow stirs.

I draw Penitence silently from its sheath and cross the distance to the cowering man without sound. He wears ragged clothes, his pale skin bulbous and deformed. His cracked, bleeding lips mutter a prayer towards the image illuminated in the stub of tallow candle that drips molten wax upon his callused fingers. Desperation laces his tone, bordering on hysteria.

A slight breeze disturbs the room's still air as my companions enter behind me. The man's candle flickers, and he turns. Penitence moves before he can fully face me, but not quickly enough to stifle his scream.

Blessed silence, for a moment, as my blade quiets his voice. Then a cacophony erupts from the cavern beside us.

Stealth and secrecy are not the strengths of my Chapter, and a weight falls from my shoulders with our presence revealed. A burning fervour envelops my limbs as I charge through the archway into a vaulted hall of immense proportions, lined with squalid dwellings and ancient habitations and pockmarked with the dark mouths of myriad shadowed passageways.

'Forward,' I cry to Alvus and Dant, raising Penitence over my head as the crack of startled weapon fire tears blindly through the large chamber towards us. Hadrick's Crusader squad splits from our vanguard and traces both flanks of our unprepared enemy. The vice-regulator's hounds keep pace at my side while their keepers and the enforcer fail to match my stride.

Dim torch lamps drinking from promethium vats light the chamber like a dying sun, its recesses and alcoves obscured by the smoke of cook fires and the stench of seething humanity.

Perhaps thousands of mortals dwell in this one hall, residing in remnant structures of the Old City around the base of an altar at its centre.

We charge towards that abomination as the cultists mount a desperate defence, firing wildly at this new, unseen threat. Penitence shears a twisted woman in half, the stub gun in her hands splitting beneath my blade, yet the power sword seems to resist me.

Behind her, a man with charred, flaking skin turns a mining laser in my direction. The tool whirrs as a blazing plume of yellow-white light erupts from its barrel. I leap to the side, and the beam grazes the edge of my poleyn. One of the enforcer's cyber-mastiffs evaporates, and a deep gouge appears in the chamber's floor, rimmed with the orange glow of molten stone.

Alvus descends on the cultist and his weapon. Both crumble beneath the weight of his fervour. The hall echoes with the din of battle, and the voices of my brothers are muffled even over the usual clarity of our vox-link.

'There is an idol,' Hadrick calls, 'at the centre of the chamber.' One of his Neophytes falls as his Crusader squad pushes the assault on my flanks.

'Press towards it,' I order. 'It shall be our first focus of holy destruction.'

I charge down a narrow passage between two dwellings, leaping over the rusted remnants of a construction sledge while Brother-Chaplain Dant cries a benediction at my back. As we pass the door of a darkened structure, a woman leaps out. She finds a seam in my armour with the blade of a twisted knife before I wheel and drop her with the back of my gauntlet.

As the woman crumbles, a mass of cultists converges upon us, well enough armed to bury me and my two brothers in searing las fire. But instead of firing their weapons, they gaze upon us, seeing their assailants clearly for the first time then falling to their knees.

My ardour falters.

I step towards the woman, a damaged, fragile thing. Her skin is pocked with scars and her hair sparse and broken, her face shattered and bleeding from a single blow of my fist. And yet, she has managed to wound me, though the price of her courage will be her life. She stares at me with rheumy eyes hooded by cracked and swollen lids, but does not break her gaze as I approach.

I raise my blade, but Penitence protests.

I am not certain if it is the woman's defiance or her words that stay my hand. She makes no movement save the churning of bloody lips, her arms crossed in the holy aquila before her. She speaks in stuttering, parsed Low Gothic, but I would recognise her prayer in any form.

'Love the Emperor, for He is the salvation of mankind. Obey His words, for He will lead you into the light of the future. Heed His wisdom, for He will protect you from evil. Whisper His prayers with devotion, for they will save your soul. Honour His servants, for they speak in His voice...'

'Tremble before His majesty,' Dant finishes for her, something akin to uncertainty in his tone. 'For we all walk in His immortal shadow.'

A terrible pit arises in my chest, as my mind falls back to the sigil scribed on the cinch mill wall. Twelve angels bearing swords and broken chains. Twelve destroyers carrying both salvation and death.

'Hold,' I order, as another group of cultists kneels beside the first. Dant stares at me and nods, though the sounds of death continue around me. 'Hold!' I bellow, my vox-amplified voice tearing through the vast hall like a peal of thunder.

The mortals before me collapse at the sound, and throughout the chamber, all movement stills. The sea of wretched humanity spreads slowly aside, men and women falling in reverence before my brothers now that their frantic defence has paused long enough for them to see whom it is that they war against.

'What in the God-Emperor's name?' Hadrick whispers over our vox-link.

'What, indeed?' I reply, though I fear I already know.

At the centre of the chamber, bathed in the warm glow of torch lamps, stands a pair of stone statues. One, tall and glorious, clearly depicts the Emperor of Mankind. Before Him, on his knees with wings outspread, holding a link of chains in his armoured hands, kneels a flawlessly carved Space Marine. The sigil upon his breastplate is not a star, but clearly the four-pointed cross of my Chapter.

'God-Emperor's grace,' Alvus mutters.

Between the two sculptures, an ancient man hobbles, a rusted chisel and mallet in his bony grasp. As my shadow falls upon him, he turns his clouded, blind eyes upon me and prostrates himself on the ground.

'Praise the Emperor,' he whispers. 'You have come at last.'

There is stark silence in the hall as my voice dies in my throat, all my fervour and rage turned to ash in my mouth. I have been used. My holy purpose subverted, turned against the meek and the faithful. The man crawls towards me, then pauses at my feet.

'I have dreamed of this day a thousand times, though I feared I would not live to see it.' Slowly, he lowers the hood of a roughspun cloak, revealing a scalp marred by tumours and the dark stains of bruising and blood.

'Brother Alvus. Brother Dant.' I call them both to my side.

The Chaplain gazes upon the blind man and his handiwork, then slowly speaks. 'This is unforeseen, Brother-Castellan. But I have viewed no image so far within this enclave that could not also adorn one of the God-Emperor's holy cathedrals. It is not heresy to long for the God-Emperor's deliverance, nor to treat with veneration the chosen instruments of His will.'

Alvus looks down at the diagnostor mounted beside his narthecium. He sets it against one of the deformities upon the man's neck.

'This is not the taint of Chaotic mutation,' he says. 'These masses are carcinoma, not the mark of the warp. They have been produced by exposure to radiative particles which have also poisoned this man's blood, and I suspect I will find the same pathology among his companions. The mutations within have spread no further than the tumours' borders, and if they are removed, the man himself will remain untainted. This is an infirmity. Nothing more.

'And, Brother-Castellan…' The Apothecary hesitates slightly. 'Any simple medicae with a bioscanner could have told you the same.'

I grunt, and turn from the kneeling man.

'My lord?' Vice-Regulator Ranp asks, approaching. 'I do not understand.'

Alvus kneels beside the blind sculptor as Dant begins to sanctify the stone icons.

'We have been used,' I reply. 'All of us. No deviant mutants lurk within these tunnels. The man before you leads no cult. In her hubris, the lord governor has tried – and failed – to direct our fervour upon her enemies, no doubt to conceal some dark trespass of her own. Find your agent, vice-regulator, if he is within this hall. I wish to know the lord governor's sins in their entirety.'

'We found it miles deep of here almost a decade ago, my lord,' the blind man says. His legs shiver with the weakness of age, but one of his acolytes holds him upright.

'Ezekial was the foreman of a patch crew at the time,' Vice-Regulator Ranp adds, handing me a dataslate from his agent. It bears grainy, dim picts of an immense, bizarre structure.

'I-I knew it weren't right,' Ezekial stammers. 'Especially once the blight began to take the weakest of us.'

Brother-Apothecary Alvus looks on beside me, and his face contorts into a bitter grimace beneath the flickering torch lamps of the subterranean compound.

'They're underhivers, my lord,' the vice-regulator replies. 'Mostly conscripts and indentureds. They don't know anything about archeotech or xenos machines, or whatever in the Emperor's galaxy that thing is. Ezekial reported it, and the next day a company of Lord Governor Agate's household guard swept through the tunnels and killed every patch crew in sight. Those that survived have been sabotaging excavation of the artefact ever since, despite increasing persecution from the lord governor's private institutions.

'It seems that recently, they've shifted their focus to preparing for the arrival of their prophesied messiahs and the overthrow of Lord Governor Agate's government. As far as their prophecy itself, my lord...' The vice-regulator looks with discomfort at the crest on my pauldrons and the two stone figures beside us. 'Well, I don't think I'm qualified to comment on that.'

I hand the pict-slate to the red-armoured warrior beside me. Barnard grasps it delicately in one of his multi-articulated servo-arms, and the augmetic fingers of the Techmarine's right hand dance in a fluid, writhing pattern as his neural network decodes the information within.

'It must be a powerful apparatus, whatever its source, to have produced such sickness by mere proximity. That the lord governor has sought to conceal its presence from us is reason enough to condemn her, no matter her purpose.'

I nod. Only the mad would dare deceive my brothers in

an attempt to use our order for their own vile aims. 'Greed. Sedition. Foulest heresy itself. Whatever her motives, the lord governor has damned herself a dozen times by virtue of her methods alone.'

I think back to the flayed priest and the shrine where I first met the vice-regulator, a dark suspicion taking root in my mind. To orchestrate such an atrocity would take nothing more than a word from the lord governor. And what quicker way to stoke my brothers' rage against her enemies? What better method to blind us to her own heresy?

'Aye, she's a right bastard,' Vice-Regulator Ranp offers. Not even the gaze of a dozen Space Marines seems enough to deter his impertinence. 'Just like the last one. Just like the next one will be.'

A stratagem forms in my mind.

'Vice-regulator, how many enforcers stand at the disposal of your magistrate who remain loyal to the God-Emperor's justice?'

'The God-Emperor's?' the little man asks. 'Or our own? I'm afraid I'm not certain how to tell the difference.'

My brothers flinch at his words, but I hold up my hand, noting for the first time the peculiar scar that encircles Ranp's neck like a collar. I have seen such a mark only once before, on the corpse of a penal legionnaire.

'There are times when those two are the same. How many, vice-regulator?'

The man bows his head, finally grasping my intent. 'In this stack? A few hundred. Across the whole hive?' He shrugs. 'Not enough for what you plan, my lord.'

'Have faith. The God-Emperor shall make do with whatever we offer. I swore an oath to the lord governor that I would purge a heresy from this world, and I intend, my brothers, to keep my word.'

A dozen Skyhammer missiles tear through the outer wall of the lord governor's palace spire, hulking chunks of gilded stone falling miles to the sun-starved earth below.

My three gunships dive through the resulting rift as sentry turrets target our vessels. There was no deception in our approach, but in her hubris the lord governor could not conceive of a reality where we would return bearing anything other than the tidings she sought.

Miles below, the surface shakes, vibrations amplified through soaring adamantine and rockcrete, the spire shivering like a tree in stiff wind. At the base of this tower, a hundred mining charges erupt, as the forces of the enforcers and Ezekial's enclave stream inside. In the streets, loyal Ministorum preachers shout calls to arms and holy retribution against the lord governor, inciting commoners to join a raging mob. Most of those masses will die before clearing the first few levels of the titanic palace spire, but more will take up their place like water filling a void.

'To the throne room,' I bellow, my brothers at my side. We are a score of black hammers pouring from the landing gunships, which then turn their cannons on the structure's innards.

Klaxons blaze within the tower, and blast doors slam shut across the spire level. Household guards adorned in ceremonial armour ready themselves too slowly to stymie our assault. Throngs of gilded, well-dressed courtesans and sycophants stumble through smoke-drenched corridors. The few who carry more than just ornamental arms draw their weapons with shaking, unpractised hands.

An indictment booms from Brother-Chaplain Dant.

'Lay down your arms!' he roars. 'And spill blood no longer in defence of your unholy sovereign! Fall on your face before the God-Emperor's vengeance, and pray He shields you with His undying grace.'

Few comply with the Chaplain's offer of surrender, and the refusal of the rest is enough to bathe them in the lord governor's guilt.

Penitence sings as a column of guards round a corner bearing hellguns. I see little and think even less before they fall still at my feet in a mist of blood.

Hadrick shatters a door with his thunder hammer, and death surges through the gap, devouring the troops that wait within. The searing light of a lascannon tears down an opulent corridor, shattering rows of intricately carved marble busts bearing the likeness of a hundred generations of lord governor. One of my brothers falls as the beam envelops him. The rest charge forward and tear the weapon apart.

For a blessed moment, the air around us quiets as we stand before the beautifully frescoed throne room door. Two of my Initiates step forward bearing meltaguns and begin to tear at the edges of the gate.

I drop to my knees, the glow and heat of molten metal washing over me, and my brothers follow suit. Dant rests his crozius upon my helmet.

'O, Emperor, in wrath rejoicing

At bloody wars, fierce and untamed,

Whose mighty power doth make the strongest walls

From their foundations shake.

All-conquering Master of Mankind,

Be pleased with this tumultuous roar. Delight in swords and fists red with blood,

And the dire ruin of savage battle.'

'Death, war, and blood!' my brothers roar behind me.

'In vengeance serve the Emperor, in the name of Dorn!'

We strike the door in unison, four abreast, and the bulwark bursts inward with a tremendous crash. We pour into the throne room like dark ink across its polished alabaster surface, and bloodshed consumes the lavish hall.

Here the traitors have mounted a more organised defence, and autoguns tear into our formation as we charge towards the dais at the centre of the room. An armaglass cupola encloses the hall, the glow of las munitions and power weapons flickering off its surface like reflections on water.

'Death to the traitor!' I roar as I crash into the massed guards before the lord governor's throne.

'Damnation to the heretic!' Brother-Chaplain Dant's crozius flashes as he strikes the defensive line by my side.

To their credit, the lord governor's soldiers do not retreat before us. Their hellguns roar into our charge. The searing heat of las fire burns across my shoulder as my storm shield catches the fury of a dozen other shots. Beside me, one of my brothers stumbles, brought down by the weight of fire burning through his armour. His sacrifice merely fuels my rage. I crush the next man who crosses my path, his skull bursting beneath my feet as I leap into a knot of his comrades. Penitence bites into a second guard's chest as I land, before a third slips the blade of his golden polearm between the ceramite plates of my plastron and greaves.

I roar, snapping the weapon's shaft as I turn on its bearer. Terror consumes the man's face for only a moment before a shot from Alvus' bolt pistol rips through his gut.

'You will survive, Brother-Castellan,' the Apothecary calls, after a cursory glance at the blade in my flank. He kicks a limp corpse into the wall of the cupola and turns back into the melee.

Another wave of household guards crashes against us as my brothers press forward towards the throne. Beneath the surging weight of our blades and our hammers, we force the host to take another step back. I drive into a gap and cut my way through a gleaming column of golden armour.

Suddenly, the heretic herself is in view.

The lord governor of Serraq's Reach cowers upon her gilded throne, clutching a small sceptre adorned with her emblem and pulsing with a strange, unholy power.

'Stop!' she shrieks over the roar of combat, her eyes wild with fear as the walls of her palace crumble. Such is the bitter face of hubris when forced to gaze upon true power. I hand my storm shield to Dant and raise my bolter, but with a crash my killing shot explodes against an unseen barrier. I fire again with the same result.

The air before the lord governor ripples as an energy field absorbs the blow. Feet away, my brothers force a column of guards to backstep onto the dais. As they cross that threshold, the soldiers' armour and flesh evaporates into the finest dust.

Only in the void shields of Imperial Titans and starships have I witnessed barriers more absolute.

I step towards the throne regardless.

'Brother-Castellan,' Dant calls at my side.

I pause.

He is ever my counsellor, and I await his wisdom, though I can already predict his words. Temperance. Caution. Fore-thought. These are the hallmarks of the ancient warrior, but no such warnings come from his lips. Bitter hatred creeps into his voice as he gazes upon the opulent woman on her throne.

'She spilled holy blood,' he says. 'On consecrated ground.'

His condemnation needs no reply.

'You fool!' Lord Governor Agate screams as my foot falls upon the edge of her dais.

A weight like the tide tries to drive me to my knees, and the sounds of battle fade away. The surface of my power armour boils as I step into the force field, ceramite subliming into a fine powder, torn apart by whatever forbidden energies she has summoned. Beneath, my skin begins to scream, my very flesh protesting as I carry it forward.

'You can feel the power of this one relic alone. What other miracles lie within those dark tunnels? What other gifts has the God-Emperor placed into our hands? Why would He grant me such power unless I was chosen? Why would He send you here but to secure my ascent?'

The lord governor's voice rages, but I hear little beneath the pounding in my ears and the hissing of my blood. My body wails, the concentrated energy of her looted archeotech pouring towards me like the heat of a star.

The madwoman shifts the sceptre in her grasp, and two of her guard evaporate at the base of her dais. I step through their ashes and face the lord governor, my flesh blistering beneath patches of fractured power armour.

'You damn yourself with every word,' I spit.

'I could save us!' Lord Governor Agate cries, raw terror shaking her voice in its jaws. 'From the xenos. From the heretics. From every evil that assails this system!'

This is the price of pride, always: the void it leaves when it collapses. To think oneself consequential, then to discover all at once that the God-Emperor's galaxy disagrees. I raise Penitence slowly, my limbs clumsy beneath the weight of all-devouring pain.

'I could be a god!' the lord governor shrieks.

Her final words strike me, the heresy in them more painful than any wounds. I bury Penitence in her throat, then grasp her sceptre and shatter it beneath my foot.

Gasping, I fall to my knees as the mind-rending agony of the force field dissipates. After a moment, I raise my head and survey a throne room now devoid of resistance. Beneath us, the palace spire still quakes with the unending impact of holy strife.

'Brother-Chaplain. Brother-Apothecary,' I call, my voice hoarse as they rush to my side. 'Our debt to this abhorrent world is repaid. Lead our brothers ahead, and when you reach the vice-regulator and his army, inform him that Serraq's Reach has been purged. Overseeing the search for a suitable replacement for the lord governor falls to them. We will tithe this planet for Expectanten, then depart promptly to rejoin the crusade.'

'Brother-Castellan,' Alvus protests. 'At least allow me to assess your–'

I raise my gauntlet and silence him. Between Penitence and my vambrace, my devotional chain still hangs, its iron moth-eaten but unbroken, like my will. The metal itself will have to be reforged, though I refuse to sever a single link.

'I will survive,' I reply, echoing his previous assessment. 'By the God-Emperor's grace.'

As I rise, I note the lord governor's crest inlaid upon the alabaster dais – a twisting serpent wrought from a golden chain. Blood pools atop the unholy icon, and as I stand the fragile stone shatters beneath my weight.

It is a pleasing omen if I have ever seen one.

HELL FIST

JUSTIN WOOLLEY

Nukreg pushed his way through the trees. He grabbed at the enormous leaves in annoyance as, heavy with the recent rain, they stuck to the green skin of his face. The dank leaves were sticky and almost as bad as those slimy little blood-sucking slugs he sometimes had to pull off his legs at the end of the day – at least those were tasty. Thinking about food made Nukreg remember the fungal beer he had stashed away back at their camp, and by *stashed away* he meant he'd found someone else's hidden barrel and was going to drink it just as soon as he got back from this patrol, which seemed to be taking forever.

The jungle was great for sneaking about like Warboss Nogrok Sneakyguts wanted, but that made it really hard to get around and there was hardly anywhere to get a good run-up for a proper charge.

The dense vegetation of Gondwa VI limited sight-lines, and arcs of fire were cut off by closely packed trees. It was all but inaccessible to vehicles and provided little opportunity for air support. Of course, Nukreg didn't know most of this. He didn't know this world was called Gondwa VI, he didn't know other worlds weren't covered in dense jungle in the same way, and he didn't give much thought to the strategic implications of the prevailing geography.

Nukreg was, as much as could be said for the greenskins, a native of this world. He had sprung from a fungal spore left behind in this very jungle by some previous ork infestation. To Nukreg this was probably what every planet was like, its name was simply Da Planet, and as far as warfare went, orks could and would fight anywhere.

As Nukreg cleared the rubbery leaves from his face he looked ahead into the shadowy green of the jungle. He was supposed to be following Zuglak, but he couldn't see Zuglak. Stupid Zuglak. How was he supposed to follow him if he kept getting too far ahead?

'Oi!' Nukreg yelled. 'Oi, Zuglak! Where are ya?'

It only took a moment for the dark shape of Zuglak to appear from the trees. The larger ork had backtracked, and emerged from the foliage with anger on his face. His fierce red eyes stared out at Nukreg through the black stripes painted over his green skin.

'Wot,' Zuglak said, his voice low, 'in Mork's name is you doin'?'

'I is tryin' to follow ya,' Nukreg said, not lowering his voice in the same way, 'but I can't follow ya coz you is gettin' too far ahead and I can't see ya through all the zoggin' trees. You is green. The trees is green.'

'Keep your zoggin' voice down,' Zuglak hissed through his teeth. 'Don't ya remember that Warboss Sneakyguts told ya to be proper sneaky and proper kunnin'?'

Nukreg shrugged. 'I s'pose.'

'You is learnin' to be a kommando,' Zuglak said, 'but you is out here bashin' through the scrub like a normal ork wot got no fungus in their 'ead. Now, stay close and stay quiet or I'mma have to tell Nob Ruktug and Nob Flik dat you ain't got the stuff to be a kommando, and do you know wot they do to feral orks wot ain't got the stuff to be a kommando?'

'No.'

'Why you think we got such big juicy squigs? It's coz they is well fed. Now come on, ya stupid git.'

Zuglak turned and moved off, pushing a branch out of his way. Nukreg, who was too busy mouthing an exaggerated imitation of Zuglak, didn't see the branch as it flicked back and smacked him right across the cheek. Nukreg growled and pulled out the thick-barrelled shoota he had holstered at his waist and fired it with a resounding boom to blow the guilty branch completely off the tree.

Zuglak once again appeared from the dense forest with his face painted both in camo and rage. He grabbed the barrel of the gun and used his superior strength to rip it from Nukreg's hand.

'I told you to zoggin' be quiet. Dat's da bloody opposite of bein' quiet. If ya don't shut up, you is gonna bring Da Hell Fist down on us.'

'Da Hell Fist,' Nukreg said. 'There ain't no such thing as a humie called Da Hell Fist. Plus, if there is, then let him find us. Dat would be a proper fight. I would krump dat Hell Fist and then it would be me teachin' stuff into your 'ead about krumpin' 'stead of you goin' on 'bout bein' kunnin' all da time.'

'You is a stupid git,' Zuglak said. 'You don't know nothin' about taktiks and you don't know nothin' about Da Hell Fist. You can't fight Da Hell Fist by yellin' "Waaagh!" and chargin' him.'

'Course ya can,' Nukreg said. 'Dat's how you do fightin'.'

'Nah,' Zuglak said, 'ya can't fight Da Hell Fist like dat coz he is incorp-or-real, like invisible but you can see 'im sometimes.'

'Orks can fight anythin' by yelling "Waaagh!" and chargin',' Nukreg said. 'Sounds like you is afraid of Da Hell Fist.'

Zuglak looked around, checking all directions multiple times before apparently satisfying himself that they were alone. 'I ain't afraid of Da Hell Fist,' he said, his voice back to that low hiss. 'I ain't afraid of no humie. But you don't know nothin'. I seen Da Hell Fist with my own two eyes back when I was a new kommando and you was still just a stupid feral ork who didn't know nothin'. Ya still don't know nothin'. Da Hell Fist ain't a normal humie. I was with my kommando mob when 'e appeared outta nowhere, like he just come up out of the ground.'

'I woulda krumped 'im,' Nukreg said.

'I'll tell ya wot it was like then, because you weren't there, ya git,' Zuglak said.

Colonel Haskell 'Hell Fist' Aldalon slipped through the thick branches without so much as disturbing the leaves. There was no other movement around him. No sounds but those of the jungle, the buzzing and chirping of insects, the dripping of wet leaves, birds somewhere in the canopy overhead. For all that he could tell, he might as well have been alone in the jungle – but he knew he was not. He did not need to see them or hear them to know that his Catachan 57th Jungle Fighters were out there. In fact, if he could have seen them or heard them he would have been annoyed. Squad Sappa were among the best he had and he would have chastised their movement discipline for so much as a cracked twig. The jungle hadn't revealed them yet but Aldalon suspected what else was out there, and he was about to have his intelligence confirmed.

Hell Fist stopped, looking ahead into the green darkness of the rain-soaked jungle. There were no obvious clues but he had something of a preternatural sense when in the jungle and he knew someone approached. He waited and then, sure enough, after a few moments there came a familiar sound. A click-clack, click-clack. A sound easily mistaken for something living in the jungle. Click-clack. Click-clack. Rhythmic and sharp.

Aldalon reached into a pouch at his waist and removed his own clicker – a small metal box whose top could be pressed, bending the springy metal with a click and releasing it to rebound with a clack. Aldalon responded. *Click-clack.*

From the gloom a figure rose from the undergrowth. Holt 'Poison Guts' Fletcha gave a lopsided grin as he approached, moving surprisingly casually for someone making barely any sound. Fletcha was something of an exception to the common perception of the permanently scowling Catachans. He enjoyed a good laugh where most Catachans seemed to just move forward with a grim determination. He was not, however, an exception to the rule when it came to moving wraith-like through the trees to kill you up close and personal with poison dripping from a serrated blade – in this respect he was all Catachan.

'Sir,' Poison Guts said in greeting, his voice low in a well-practised field whisper. 'Can confirm orks gathering five hundred yards ahead. Sneakyguts has been training the wild ferals. Looks like an initial strike on the southern entrance to the city.'

'Numbers?'

'I counted three distinct mobs, ten or twelve in each.'

'Weapons?'

'Blades and pistols mostly, a couple of heavier weapons.'

Hell Fist nodded. 'And is he there?'

'Sneakyguts?' Fletcha asked, but he knew this was who his commanding officer was asking about. 'No, he's not there. Just looks like one of the original ghost orks leading a bunch of green recruits – well, they're all green, but you know what I mean, sir.'

Aldalon sniffed. He, unlike Poison Guts, was the epitome of the scowling Catachan with no sense of humour. He pulled out his clicker and pressed out five clicks in quick succession. Then he took a knee, and brought his lascarbine up into a relaxed but ready pose. Poison Guts had already taken his position to watch the angle in front of him as, like the jungle itself had somehow sprung them forth, nine more Catachan Jungle Fighters eventually emerged, moving silently to take their place in a circle in front of Hell Fist – ready for a field briefing while maintaining a vigilant eye on every inch of the jungle around them.

'All right, listen up,' he said, as if his troops weren't hanging on his every word. 'We've confirmed the report of gathering orks, a mass of ferals grouping in the wilderness beyond the southern entrance to Karoo City. Our defences are strong there and should be able to stand against a group the size we're anticipating, but it's our job to make sure that happens. We know this warboss, and he's not like the others we've fought. Calls himself Sneakyguts so there's a chance he's planning something unexpected. We can't take them all with a single squad, but let's sow some disarray. I want to see how the greenskins react.' He turned to Lieutenant Sappa. 'Lieutenant.'

Lieutenant Learna Sappa looked expectantly at her father. 'Yes, sir?'

'Squad will split into fire-teams. You take Fire-team Alpha. I'll take Fire-team Bravo. Set up here on their eastern side. I'll head around to their western side. On my mark we strike, hard and fast. Once they look like they're getting their feet under them we'll withdraw under smoke. We're not going to give them the fight they want.' He looked at the troopers in front of him. 'We get into position, not just full silent but Catachan silent, you understand?'

The Jungle Fighters nodded.

'I want to scare these greenskins.'

'Sir,' Lieutenant Sappa said, 'what's your signal to engage?'

Aldalon looked at her, annoyed she had to ask.

'The same signal as always, lieutenant. Dying orks.'

'We was just standin' there,' Zuglak continued, 'gettin' ready to attack the big door to the humie city because Warboss Sneakyguts wanted some recon-o-sense. He wanted to know how much dakka the humies had protectin' da door and how many loads of orks would get krumped if we was gonna try and take the city.'

'Wotcha mean *if* he was gonna attack da city? Why didn't he just attack da city?'

'He was plannin', ya git.'

'Plannin',' Nukreg said, 'wot's plannin'?'

Zuglak shook his head. 'Look, don't matter why we was there, we just was. That's when Da Hell Fist appeared. I swear on Mork and Gork dat I was watching a spot on da ground and there was nothin' there and then 'e was there. I'm tellin' ya, he just come up out of the ground.'

Nukreg looked at him, obviously still not convinced. 'Wot did 'e look like then?'

'He was a big 'un,' Zuglak said. 'Biggest humie I ever saw. Big as a nob, and his big smashin' fist was as big as your 'ead.' Zuglak looked at Nukreg in some kind of crude evaluation. 'Bigger dan your 'ead. Plus, Da Hell Fist's other hand is metal too, like the humie painboyz 'ave been to proper work on 'im.'

'Wot?' Nukreg said. 'I thought 'e 'ad a klaw.'

''E does,' Zuglak said, 'a klaw on one arm and da other arm is metal too.'

'You makin' this up.'

'He came outta nowhere and started krumpin' orks all over da place. Then there was other humies too, I think, but I don't remember wot they did. Probably nothin'.'

Colonel Aldalon and Fire-team Bravo were in position near the gathered orks. The greenskins were in the centre of a small clearing and Aldalon had to wonder whether that was a purposeful decision to keep them away from the dense jungle, which provided ample ambush opportunity, or whether they had done it by accident. It was getting harder and harder to discern what was strategic and what was luck for the orks on this world. The influence of Warboss Nogrok Sneakyguts was undeniable and Aldalon wasn't ashamed to say the idea of orks thinking strategically on any level more than 'hit thing until dead' gave him pause. Either way, the position of the orks away from the cover of the trees meant they would have to assault across open ground rather than attempting a coordinated surprise attack from the jungle.

Hell Fist turned back to the five troopers with him. Each of them was a hardened veteran of the Catachan 57th. Even Trooper Torvin, a soft-worlder they'd been saddled with shortly after they'd arrived on Gondwa VI, had managed to earn his place. Aldalon silently grunted to himself. He had to be careful he wasn't turning soft with that line of thinking. Still, even including the soft-worlder, Aldalon knew that none of his troops would balk at the need to charge across the clearing. It wasn't ideal but they could still get in and out quickly with a proper application of Catachan shock and awe.

The crouching Jungle Fighters looked on as Aldalon shot out a series of hand signals – contact ahead, fifty yards, two together, concurrent strike, hold for mark. The meaning of all this was simple enough: the orks were fifty yards ahead, the Catachans were to fight in pairs to ensure they would not be overwhelmed by the superior strength of the greenskins. He knew that Lieutenant Sappa and her squad, who'd only needed to move a short distance to take position, would already be watching, waiting, and ready to strike.

The orks may have been standing some distance from the cover of the treeline, but where the Catachans would be constantly scanning the trees, on watch no matter how safely positioned they may have felt, the orks were doing what orks did when left for more than a minute without a larger ork breathing down their necks. They were squabbling with each other.

There may not have been tree cover between him and the orks but there was a not insignificant amount of smaller undergrowth, some of the large flat-leafed shrubs and thick-trunked ferns that were common across the jungle floor. Plus, even a clearing in the all-but-impenetrable jungle of Gondwa VI was crosshatched with shadow and cast in that ever-present green darkness, the canopy trying to reach up and close any gap overhead.

With the orks being so distracted, Aldalon could see an approach that would bring him closer. It was risky using such little cover to move in through the clearing, but if he could use the shadows and the foliage to get close enough to the orks, he could strike before they knew he was there. The initial moment of confusion would provide a distraction for both fire-teams to charge. The orks would focus on him and his troops could close the distance before the greenskins managed to get their shootas up and start firing.

Aldalon dropped into a prone stance and began crawling forward. Just before he reached the edge of the ork-filled clearing he stopped and turned back. He flashed the hand symbol for *hold for mark* again, just to make sure none of his troopers would attempt to follow. This first strike would be him alone. This wasn't some Emperor-damned desire for the first kill, or some heroic act of the sort other Imperial Guard soldiers might be desperate to brag over. Certainly, he always wanted to kill orks, but this was a well-planned move to protect his soldiers, not some lunatic dash for glory. He was a Catachan commander, and unlike many so-called commanders in the rest of the Astra Militarum, he would not hang at the back to give orders over vox; he would take the devil's share of the risk, because that's what he was: a Catachan Devil.

Once he'd received the signal of acknowledgment from Fireteam Bravo, Aldalon moved forward, out of the loving embrace of the jungle and into the dangerous open space of clear ground. He followed the path he'd spotted earlier, slipping across the earth like a serpent to reach cover behind the thick trunk of a fern. Ahead of him was the most dangerous moment, another yard of open ground between him and thick scrub and undergrowth dense with a tangle of dead vines. It would only take an ork deciding to actually keep watch for once to notice shadowy movement, no matter how low he kept. It would not be much, but a Catachan Jungle Fighter would spot him, and perhaps even the most perceptive of Nogrok Sneakyguts' ghost orks would too.

He paused, deathly quiet, purposefully slowing his heart rate, which adrenaline was beginning to speed up. Then he moved. He didn't look up; he concentrated on keeping himself in the darkest shadows until he reached the cover of the dense bush. He hadn't heard the boom of an ork weapon, hadn't heard a shout of warning. These feral orks, young and less focused than Nogrok's more elite greenskins, hadn't spotted him.

Unable to see much through the vine-laced bush, he listened intently. Sure enough, orks argued about when they were going to attack and who was going to kill the most humies and whether they should just kill each other while they were waiting, but there was nothing to indicate he'd been spotted. After a moment Aldalon moved again, crawling beneath the huge flat leaves that covered much of the ground, each several yards in diameter. The leaves should cover the rest of his approach, all the way to the closest of the orks.

The leaves were only just high enough for Aldalon to lie pressed face down against the moist dirt, dragging himself forward with his left elbow while trailing his power-fist-wielding right arm along behind him. For Aldalon, crawling beneath the heavy leaves was reminiscent of basic training back on Catachan, when they would force all potential Jungle Fighters to crawl for almost a mile beneath a criss-cross of necrotising ivy – a plant native to Catachan which secreted a sticky sap that caused flesh to disintegrate. During that training, if a Jungle Fighter touched the ivy it would adhere to them, burning through clothes, skin and flesh. The more they struggled the more the ivy would wrap around them. The result was permanent disfigurement or, in the worst cases, a slow and painful death.

A mistake in Hell Fist's current situation would have similar repercussions. Even the most inattentive ork would notice an enormous leaf rattling next to their foot and would execute whatever was underneath with a booming shot from their oversized pistol.

When Aldalon saw the heels of two heavy ork boots just beyond the edge of the leaf he crawled beneath, he paused for a moment to prepare before using the power of his augmetic arm and power fist to push himself explosively upwards.

The leaf above him tore from its twisting, vine-like stem as Aldalon leapt to his feet. The ork in front of him had been facing the other direction, engaged in a lively discussion with another greenskin about whose choppa was bigger, but turned swiftly at the sudden disturbance behind him.

What greeted him was the power fist of Colonel Haskell 'Hell Fist' Aldalon rushing towards him in a mighty right hook. In the moment before the strike Aldalon took great pleasure in the wide-eyed look of surprise on the ork's face.

Their intimidating size, their impressive strength, and their enviable inability to weather pain and recover from the most outrageous injuries, plus of course their sheer numbers, made orks among the gravest threats to the Imperium of Man. It was always nice to catch one completely unaware and be reminded that, though they ordinarily swarmed in a green tide crazed with primal rage, they could be surprised and could even, at least momentarily, feel fear.

For this ork, his fungal brain was too slow to replace shock and confusion with snarling anger. The creature was only just feeling the joy that he was about to get to have a fight when Aldalon's power fist struck him in the side of the head. The disruptive energy field that crackled and buzzed around Aldalon's massively oversized fist ripped the ork's flesh to its component atoms and then pummelled his thick skull, crushing it inwards. The greenskin's neck snapped with the force of the impact.

There was a beat of silence from the orks as their slower-than-normal brains processed the sudden appearance of an enormous power-fist-wielding human from seemingly out of the ground. The Catachans hiding in the trees all around them took this moment of confusion to attack. They transitioned from deathly silent to all-out roaring war cries as they charged at the gathered orks. Aldalon, seeing the eyes of the orks all around him grow wide and flick between the soldiers running from the trees, roared even louder, a booming shout to rival even an ork warboss. He charged his power fist with crackling energy again and dashed forward, clamping it around the neck of the nearest ork and squeezing. He felt the distinctive sensation of flesh disintegrating under his grip and then the crushing of windpipe and spine.

Ork shouts sounded through the clearing as their synapses finally registered a fight. The ever-familiar guttural shouts of 'Waaagh!' filled the air, but Aldalon also heard several ork voices call out variations of 'It's Da Hell Fist!' in tones ranging from joy, to rage, to fear, and he couldn't help but smirk. *Good,* he thought, *they'll know me even more after this.*

Hell Fist's wild attack had worked as intended. Most of the orks nearby turned their furious desire for a fight on him.

The whine-crack of lascarbines filled the air as the Catachans ran in, loosing as many shots as they could before switching to their vicious blades, known as Catachan Fangs. The smell of burning and cauterised ork flesh filled the humid air. It was a disgusting smell that Aldalon still found satisfying for its meaning, and it was enough to spur him on.

He lashed out with unbridled fury again, swinging his power fist at the first of the orks, who had pulled its rusty cutta. He battered the ork's weapon aside with his augmetic arm before uppercutting the ork under its protruding jaw with his power fist, sending the greenskin howling off its feet.

It was then that the confusion of the attack began to wane. A nearby ork took the opportunity to lash out at Aldalon. He saw the attack coming and managed to dodge to the side, but not far enough. The point of the ork's blade sliced across his exposed upper arm above his augmetic, leaving a nasty gash that caused a sudden sensation of weakness and left his arm hanging limp. Even through the adrenaline he knew some damage had been done: tendons or muscle had been cut. This left him no choice but to fight one-handed as the orks began to swarm towards him.

Luckily, this was when the rest of the Catachans charged in. There were only eleven Catachans in the fight but they hit the orks with as much of their own medicine as they could, ploughing in, swinging blades and roaring their lungs out.

The Catachans followed their orders to perfection, sticking in pairs as they hit the orks. One of the Jungle Fighters would engage the ork aggressively enough to draw the majority of its attention while the other would strike the killing blows, or at least blows enough to incapacitate.

Catachan Jungle Fighters were human beings at peak physical fitness – they weren't known as 'baby ogryns' for nothing. Even with that they were at a disadvantage in single combat against the ripplingly muscled orks. It was certainly possible for a Catachan to kill an ork one-on-one, but they preferred to do it with the aid of stealth. In a situation like this, in fiery face-to-face melee, a Catachan might get a greenskin kill, but the odds were too high that they would be killed in the process. Pairing up had long been the Catachan approach to fighting the greenskins hand-to-hand. It levelled the playing field and meant the Catachans could take down orks without too many losses of their own. The downside of this approach was that, at those times when they were heavily outnumbered – which was almost all the time against the orks – the numerical disadvantage was worsened by focusing two-on-one.

Hell Fist Aldalon watched his Catachans fight with ferocity. In the chaotic minutes following their charge he saw several orks go down in sprays of ichor drawn by the serrations of Catachan Fangs. He backhanded a snarling ork with his power fist and roared. He would not let the orks see he was injured. If they were going to fear him then he couldn't show weakness.

Still, even though the Catachans fought like monsters Aldalon knew it was time to withdraw. The initial shock of his sudden appearance and then that of his troops had put the orks on the back foot and had rattled them, but now the green tide was turning.

'Torvin!' Aldalon shouted.

Nearby, Trooper Torvin, who fought in partnership with Poison Guts, turned.

'Sir?'

'Now!'

'Yes, sir! Cover me,' Torvin said to Poison Guts as he reached down and pulled several smoke grenades off his webbing.

'Oh, sure,' Poison Guts said as he parried a wild ork swing, ducking low as the ork blade sailed overhead. 'Easy.'

Aldalon watched as Torvin pulled the pin on one, two, three grenades, tossing them out in several directions. One of the grenades rolled towards Aldalon. Hell Fist planted his foot on the grenade, bringing it to a stop beneath him. Several high-velocity sprays of thick grey smoke burst out and rapidly began rising.

'Catachans!' Aldalon roared to be heard over the fighting. 'Withdraw!'

Plumes of smoke billowed upwards from the grenades and rapidly filled the clearing with thick white-grey haze. Smoke grenades were designed for exactly this type of application, creating a rapid blocker to enemy line of sight to allow cover for infiltration or extraction, and soon, in a matter of seconds, Aldalon could barely see the greenskins in front of him, let alone those who had been massing to rush forward and join the fight.

He disengaged from combat with a final swipe of his power fist that sent an ork stumbling to the side, several fat teeth spraying across the ground. All around him the other Catachans began to do the same, a fighting retreat away from the orks until they were at a distance safe enough to make a break for the trees. The orks, previously shocked by their sudden appearance, were left equally shocked by their sudden disappearance.

'Oi!' Aldalon heard as he backed into the trees. 'Where did da humies go?'

'So, just as I was gonna charge Da Hell Fist,' Zuglak was explaining, ''e just turned into smoke and vanished.'

'Wot? You mean da big scary Hell Fist ran away?'

'Nah, 'e didn't run away. 'E done taktiks. 'E killed loads of orks and then when it looked like 'is humies might get krumped, they done fallin' back. But you ain't listenin'. I ain't said 'e ran away, I said 'e turned to smoke.'

'Wot you mean 'e turned to smoke?'

'I mean it 'appened so fast 'e must 'ave turned into smoke. 'E was there krumpin' orks and then next minute there was just smoke floatin' about and all da boyz wot weren't krumped was just standin' around.'

Nukreg stared at Zuglak for a long, long moment before finally breaking into a short laugh. 'Ha,' Nukreg said, 'I get it. You is doin' a joke.'

'I ain't.'

Nukreg stared at Zuglak again. 'Well, if you ain't doin' a joke you is crazy. Did Da Hell Fist knock you on da skull? You should be called Zuglak Busted 'Ead. I ain't believin' a word of nothin' you been sayin'. If there is humies out 'ere, if there is a Hell Fist out 'ere then let 'em find us. I want to fight 'em 'stead of listenin' to you make up stories coz you too scared.'

Nukreg, only able to cope with so much un-orky behaviour for one afternoon, reached out quickly and, catching him by surprise, managed to snatch back his shoota from Zuglak's hand. He lifted the heavy, short-barrelled pistol into the air and fired.

BOOM BOOM BOOM.

Three rattling shots erupted with the glorious sound of dakka that reverberated through the jungle.

'Come on, Da Hell Fist!' Nukreg screamed. 'I'm ready for a proper fight!'

'You git,' Zuglak hissed. 'You is not bein' kunnin'!'

'Kunnin' is about gettin' into a fight, ain't it?' Nukreg replied before turning his attention back to the thick jungle around them. 'I said I is ready for Da Hell Fist!'

Nothing happened. For a long moment there was silence in the jungle.

Nukreg turned to Zuglak. 'See, you is full of–'

With the zap-crack of a humie lasgun Nukreg stumbled back. He looked down at his shoulder and saw that his crudely stitched leather armour had been burned through; and because orks do not feel pain – at least not in the same way as most species in the galaxy – it also took this glance down at his shoulder for him to realise his flesh beneath the armour had been left a blackened crater.

Nukreg growled and lifted his shoota in the direction the shot had come from. The jungle was so thick he couldn't see anything, but that didn't stop him, with the joy of an imminent fight flooding through his ork body, from firing wildly into the trees.

'Waaagh!' he roared as his booming shoota blasted into the jungle, doing little but blow holes in tree trunks and cut down hanging vines.

Despite Zuglak's insistence they follow the orders given to them by Warboss Sneakyguts that they were supposed to be proper kunnin' kommandos, he was still an ork, and the sound of gunfire stirred something primal within him. He pulled his cutta from where it hung at his waist and readied himself for some humie krumpin'.

He moved to Nukreg's side, his eyes squinting into trees now full of smoking holes courtesy of his acquaintance. There was no movement, and even beneath the overwhelming ecstasy that came from the anticipation of a fight he felt a sense of unease, perhaps only experienced by those orks that followed the way of Mork.

Suddenly there was movement off to the right side of the pair of orks. Complete silence had been replaced by the sound of charging footfalls and growling – weak humie growling, but growling nonetheless. Nukreg and Zuglak turned just in time for Nukreg, the closer of the two, to raise his shoota, which was fitted with a small, dented and rusty bayonet. He managed to block the arcing swing of a Catachan humie's knife. Zuglak roared and attacked as well, but two more humies were there to meet him. He swung his cutta wildly, a blow which the first of the humies ducked. The second one lashed out and his humie knife sliced across Zuglak's side. As Zuglak swung again both the humies darted away. They moved into the trees, pushing back through a curtain of vines.

Nukreg was being similarly frustrated. He stabbed out at the humies with the blade on his shoota, but they had sidestepped quickly out of the way, and just like the two that had attacked Zuglak, they both vanished into the oppressive trees. At the sight of the disappearing humies Nukreg roared in rage.

'Oi! Fight proper, you gits!' he shouted into the trees as he lifted his shoota and began blasting aimlessly into the jungle again.

Zuglak looked around wildly. 'I told you, Nukreg, you git. You can't fight da Catachan humies like an idiot ork.'

Nukreg turned to Zuglak. 'You is a stupid git! I'mma krump da humies. You wait and see.'

'I'mma krump you for bein' stupid enough to bring da humies 'ere in da first place! If you 'ad shut up and done as–'

Nukreg watched as Zuglak's shouting was cut short as his head snapped back. The crack of a humie lasgun sounded as it blasted a craterous hole open, right in the middle of his forehead.

'Oi!' Nukreg said, looking down at Zuglak. A thin trail of smoke was rising up out of the black hole in the middle of his head, and his red eyes were staring at the canopy above. 'Get up, ya git, the humies are gonna come back!'

'Already here.'

Nukreg turned at the voice. What he saw in front of him was

a looming humie who must have appeared out of nowhere. A humie with one augmetic arm and one power fist crackling with building energy, already swinging for him. He didn't even have time to yell 'Waaagh!' before the enormous power fist smashed him directly in the centre of his face. As the Hell Fist liquefied his skin, and started to burn through the front of his brain, Nukreg's joy disappeared as he realised there wasn't going to be much of a fight.

He was dead before he hit the floor.

SARCOPHAGUS

DAVID ANNANDALE

The true measure of my enemy's threat isn't just in the brute force at his disposal. Nor is it fully captured in the tally of victories and defeats. What lies behind events? Why are some actions taken and others not? The answers to those questions can reveal a power even more deadly than armies of millions could imply. Ghazghkull Thraka had annihilated our forces on Golgotha. What that showed of his means and ability was bad enough, but that he released me had even worse implications.

Sometimes questions alone point to dark revelations.

I was in Anaon, south of Hive Tartarus. It was a smaller hive on the coast of the Tempest Ocean. I had come for two reasons. One was to inspect the maritime defences. The fate of Helsreach still hung in the balance, and we had to prepare against the possibility of a second invasion from the water. The other reason was symbolic. That had always been an integral part of my duties as a commissar: to represent something more important than the individual in the uniform.

I never meant to become an icon, but circumstances were circumstances. The Second War for Armageddon had changed the meaning of my name. 'Yarrick' now meant 'the Saviour of Armageddon'. My thoughts about the truth of the matter were irrelevant. The legend existed. And now the Third War had come.

My duty was to use every weapon at my disposal against the enemy. So if my presence was enough to motivate a population to a greater effort, then I would make sure I was seen. The people of Anaon had to be willing to sacrifice everything, down to their lives. Every single one. No one person, group or hive was more important than Armageddon.

So I flew in from Tartarus. I made my inspection. I met with the commanders of the military forces charged with the hive's defence. I made myself visible. Anaon had suffered a few bombing raids, but had been spared a major assault. The people felt safe enough to take to the streets. I spoke to them. I exhorted. I made sure of their commitment to the war.

All was well and good, but the problems began when I had to return to Tartarus. A massive aerial battle was underway between the two hives. Air transport back to Tartarus was out of the question. I had to travel using terrestrial means.

I climbed out of my command car just inside the outer gate of Anaon, a massive configuration of entwined metal columns that resembled a fused manufactorum. I greeted Captain Veit Morena of the Steel Legion's 12th Company, 22nd Regiment. He was a short man and wiry. A good build for a tanker.

'Captain,' I said. 'I understand your squadron is being recalled to Hive Tartarus.'

'That's correct, commissar.'

'I would like to accompany you.'

He seemed taller suddenly. 'I would be honoured if you rode with me,' he said.

'Thank you.'

He led me to his Leman Russ Vanquisher, *Storm of the Wastes*. His driver, Alna Klaren, and gunner, Jaro Berne, snapped to attention. Like Morena, they were compact soldiers. They looked as if they had been born in the tank, their bodies shaped to its confines. Oil was so deep in the folds of their skin, it might as well have been pigmentation. The hull of *Storm* bore similar marks. It had been scored by centuries of exposure to the acidic rains of Armageddon.

The long line of tanks rolled out of Anaon at dusk with *Storm* at the head. The toxic cloud cover was heavy with the threat of rain. We made good time for the first few hours, rumbling along the pitted, cracked rockcrete route that linked Anaon to Tartarus. Morena and I alternated riding the hatch. At the northern horizon, in the direction of Tartarus, the night sky flashed and burned with reflected explosions. I saw the streaks of missiles, and the spiralling flame of stricken aircraft falling to earth. War's steady, pulsing thunder rolled over us, all the sounds of conflict melding into a muffled, arrhythmic, stuttering – *boom, b-boom-boom, b-b-boom*.

When I traded places with Morena, he looked into the distance. 'I make it another two hours before we're under the worst of the fighting,' he said.

'Agreed.'

I thought that would be the point of greatest vulnerability for the squadron, but I was wrong.

An hour later, when I was again at the hatch, the beat of the war drum changed. A layer detached itself from the rest. It was more regular, and sounded closer. It was slow, deep as a continent. Even over the rattling of the Vanquisher, I could feel the beat's vibrations in my chest. It came from north-east of our position.

I peered into the dark as points of light appeared. They confused me at first. They looked like stars, an impossible sight on Armageddon; the planet's polluted sludge of an atmosphere was impenetrable. Then I realised that the stars were moving. The ground shook at measured, relentless intervals. The stars drew nearer. They were in pairs and a red the colour of flames. I could make out massive shadows in the night as we came closer. Mountains were slouching towards the road to Tartarus.

I dropped back down the hatch. 'Gargants!' I warned.

Even in the red illumination of the tank's interior, I saw Morena turn pale. His fear was not cowardice. It was an entirely rational response to the presence of the ork monsters of war. 'We can't fight those,' he said. Those words weren't cowardice either. They were the judgement of a commander who knew the limits of his force's strength. War will call upon us to do the impossible. It will force us to fight when there is no chance of survival, let alone victory. But we were not in a position where choice had been taken away from us. Duty calls for sacrifice, not stupidity.

'Berne,' Morena told the gunner. 'Vox Tartarus Command. Warn them.'

I climbed out of the hatch entirely to make room for Morena, riding on the turret and grasping the cupola with my power claw. We watched the progress of the Gargants. There were three of them, each a hundred metres high. They were still far from us, but we could see them more clearly now. They were lumbering, wide-bodied products of diseased invention; they had none of the majesty of Titans. But they provoked awe all the same. They gouted flame and smoke, towering over the landscape like brutal, shambolic gods. A single one could destroy a city. And they would reach the road long before we had passed them.

We looked further to the east. The land was dark, and there were no further signs of ork forces accompanying the Gargants.

'That way seems clear,' Morena said. 'I wish the terrain was better.'

We were in a region of bare, rocky hills. Perhaps at some

point in Armageddon's distant, eroded past, they had been verdant. The millennia had stripped them of all vegetation and worn them down until they had the dead, rounded shapes of bone. The tanks could handle their slopes, but we wouldn't be able to see far ahead. Obstacles in the form of boulders would be common, and we'd be encountering them in the dark. Progress would be slow.

'We have no other option,' I said. If we stayed on the road, annihilation was a certainty. 'We'll need to make a wide sweep.' Even more time lost.

Morena nodded and disappeared inside the tank to issue the commands.

We turned off the road onto terrain that was uneven, broken, hostile to our passage. It was riddled with the cracks of dried stream beds. Forward visibility in the tanks' lamps shrank to the crest of the next hill. We headed east and did not turn until the earthquake rumble of the Gargants faded, their flames only pinpricks in the dark again. I guessed we were twenty kilometres off the road when Morena finally ordered a northward course again.

The hours passed. Dawn was still a long way off when the Gargants were finally to our south. Though we had been slowed, we were still faster than they were. I was so focused on the Gargants' position that I barely noticed how close we had come to the aerial battle.

It came to us with a high-pitched snarl. I looked up. More lights in the dark, a swarm of them racing in from the north-east: two ork bomber squadrons, and ten aircraft that I could count. There was no question of evasion – we had been spotted and the bombers were coming right for us.

They were still some distance away when they began to release their incendiary bombs. The land vanished in a billowing cloud of flame. The night burned, heat racing ahead of the fire. My face blistered. The holocaust marched towards us, and there would be no escape.

I went down into the tank again and sealed the hatch. The others were already reacting to the threat. Morena was at the vox, coordinating the response. Heavy bolter turrets along the entire line of the tank squadron were turning to fire at the enemy fliers. Klaren gunned the engine, pushing *Storm* to full speed, terrain be damned. We had little defence against what was coming. If we were lucky, heavy bolter-rounds or a miraculous cannon shot might bring down a couple of planes. Speed was a gesture more than a strategy. The weapons that were about to hit us did not require accuracy.

I braced, grasping the hatch ladder with my claw.

The booming voice of war had arrived and the bombs continued to fall. The light of sudden day burst though the driver's viewing block, bright enough to illuminate the full interior of *Storm*. Then the full force of the bombardment arrived and we drove into a high-explosive firestorm.

The vox exploded with cries. Morena was shouting into it. *'Tartarus Command, this is Scorched Earth Squadron, Twelfth of the Twenty-Second out of Anaon, transporting Commissar Yarrick. Our position–'*

The world erupted beneath *Storm of the Wastes*. For a moment, I had the impression of a gunship lifting off. Then we were turning end over end, and everything was violence and ruin.

And then everything was darkness.

Waking was a transition from one darkness to another. I left oblivion for pain and crushing pressure on my legs. Something was pushing my head and neck forwards, forcing me into a harsh bend. The blackness swam with sparks, but they were all from behind my eye. I could hear metal ticking, creaking and settling. Somewhere, a circuit crackled and fell silent. I didn't know where I was or why I hurt.

Nothing moved. Nothing changed. There was only the pain, growing worse, and the weak muttering of wreckage. Then my head cleared and I knew what had happened.

It's not important, I told myself. *What's important is knowing what is happening now.* Did I even know which way I was facing? No. Was I the only survivor?

'Captain Morena,' I called. 'Klaren. Berne.'

No answer.

I waited a minute before trying again, several more times, and louder. Nothing.

They're dead, then. What about the rest of the squadron? Learn the situation.

I kept quiet and listened. Beyond the groans of the dead tank, there were sounds from the outside world. The war thunder continued. It was distant once more. No combat in the immediate vicinity. I kept listening, straining to focus beyond my pain and interpret what I could hear and what I could not. There were no engines or guns. No hammering of tools. No sounds at all of any activity in the close proximity of the hull.

The conclusion was a simple one. The ork bombers had done their job well. The tank squadron had been destroyed.

A further conclusion: I was alone.

I confronted the temptation to close my eye and return to the deeper dark. I judged it unworthy. I had not earned the right to rest. Not yet. After Golgotha, when Thraka had taken me captive to his space hulk, he had thrown me into a pit. I had had every reason to believe I was about to die. During my fall, that was when I had known several seconds of rest. Those moments would still have to suffice. Perhaps, once Thraka was dead, I would win the reward of the truest sleep. Not now, though. My duty was far from discharged. Armageddon called.

Besides, I was very uncomfortable.

I tried to move. I could turn my head from side to side, for all the good it did me. I was still hunched, my back protesting and darkness was everywhere. My legs were pinned. My left arm was blocked if it moved more than a few centimetres to my side. My right, though, had a good degree of range. I raised the claw up and down, left and right. I imagined that I was caught in a fold of the wreckage. My right arm reached into what had been the open space of the tank's interior.

Though my legs were trapped, I didn't think they were broken. They hurt, and I wasn't going anywhere. But I could feel and move my toes. When I struggled, there was no sudden burst of fresh agony.

You're intact. The Emperor protects. He truly does. So how will you use His blessing, old man? Show your gratitude. Get out.

I reached forwards with the claw and struck crumpled metal right away. Keeping its digits closed, I brought it next to my side, then slid it up and down against the barrier. My legs were held, not pulped, so there had to be a gap, small though it was, in the wreckage that gripped me. It took me several attempts. I was trying to accomplish a task by touch with a hand that was not mine. At last, though, the claw slid forwards a few centimetres. I worked it forwards until it was wedged. Then I paused.

Are you sure you want to do this? You have no idea of the condition of the wreckage. You don't know what will happen if you disturb the present equilibrium.

True. I might contrive to crush myself properly. Then again, did I have a choice?

No. You don't.

I opened the claw as slowly as I could. Metal protested. I pried the three metal digits apart. The corpse of the Vanquisher cried out. The pressure eased on my legs. I pulled. My feet moved. I lurched my torso to the right while keeping the claw in place. I was pivoting on my own arm, and now I did get some new bursts of agony.

I didn't stop. I risked opening the claw all the way. The wreckage shrieked. I heard snaps. I bent my legs and threw all my weight to the right, moving a bit further. I tested it, scrabbling with my feet until I found a purchase and making sure my boots wouldn't slip.

Ready?

I whispered, 'The Emperor protects.'

I shut the claw with a snap and propelled myself to the side, sliding out of the trap a second before it slammed shut.

I tumbled free through the space, landing on hard angles. I bought myself some new bruises.

I sat up, working the kinks out of my neck. Feeling around with my left hand, I learned the contours of my prison. Jagged angles and heavy masses pressed in on me. Not everything I found was metal. I discovered a leg that appeared to be sticking out of a solid mass of metal and broken bodies. My hand sank into something that felt like a broken sphere. It was very wet. I didn't know whose head it was.

I had room to crouch, but not stand. I could move a few steps in any direction. In the centre of the space, I found a cylindrical depression. This, I guessed, had been the turret hatch. *Storm of the Wastes* was upside down. I would not be leaving that way.

I sat down on something level and rested, thinking. Trying to make my way up would mean going through the chassis. There was little hope there, unless it had already been split open. Was it night or day? I had no idea how long I'd been unconscious. A few more hours and I could assume there was daylight outside the tank. I'd know then if there were any tears in the armour I could exploit. I didn't feel any stirring of air, though. Upwards did not seem like a fruitful route.

The flanks, then. For the time being, I put aside considerations of where the armour was thickest or thinnest. I could punch through a lot with the claw. But not anything. And my leverage was limited.

I thought about the driver's compartment. The viewing block was too small to crawl through, but any gap might be something I could enlarge. I worked my way around the circumference of the space again and tried to orient myself. Where was the gunner's seat? Which way was the cannon? Which way were the engines?

I failed. The damage was too severe. Nothing was recognisable. Whatever direction I chose could lead me towards the engines, and I had no desire to start pounding at them. I was lucky that they had not exploded, and that I wasn't wading through promethium waiting for the first spark. I was already entombed. I was not ready to be cremated.

The thought of *Storm of the Wastes* as a coffin gave me pause. I stopped moving and made myself take the time to work through that possibility. The air smelled of grease and blood. There was a trace of smoke. I was not short of breath; the space was small. Enough time had passed, and I had exerted myself enough, that my lungs would be labouring if I were sealed in hermetically.

Air was getting in. That did not imply I would be getting out. It could mean that I would be able to breathe until I died of thirst.

What about rescue?

I chose not to work through those possibilities just yet. I would have to rely too much on outside circumstances. I was already at the mercy of plenty. Time enough to think about that later.

Up, then? I thought.

Yes. Up.

That was the only direction of which I had any certainty.

I felt above my head, looking for any hint of weakness. I found an area where the wreckage seemed a bit more sparse. I swiped at it with the claw. A metal tangle came down on me. I brushed it off, then began in earnest. I pulled my arm back as far as I could. The energy of the claw built up. I punched upwards.

The bang shook the entire vehicle. I paused, waiting for the explosion or the final collapse. When neither occurred, I struck again. Then again. And again.

I settled into a rhythm. Each blow worked out a bit more frustration. For the first few minutes, I made progress. The decking buckled under my attacks. I had to reach higher. Soon I could straighten up.

That was the extent of my victories. Though I was tearing through layers of metal, I was also smashing the plating, mechanism and armour together to create a denser mass. A moment came when I could no longer reach my target. I tried to climb, but there was nothing I could perch on with enough stability to punch again. Even if I clung to the edge of the hole in the decking, there wasn't enough room to get the claw past my own arm.

I sat back down. I had gone as far as I could in this direction. My options had been reduced to one, and it was poor one: rescue.

I examined the facts. Remaining dispassionate was not difficult. Between the battering I had taken and the one I had just given, I was exhausted.

There would be a search for me, and to the degree that was possible in the middle of the worst ork assault in Armageddon's history. I had last been seen in Anaon, and it was known that I was travelling with the tanks of Sixth Company. Morena's route was known too.

But we had gone many kilometres off that route to avoid the Gargants towards the region of the air war. I could still hear the sounds of conflict, though I couldn't tell from that rumble how close the battle was to my position, nor its nature. Was the struggle for control of the airspace near Tartarus still ongoing? Or was I hearing the siege of the hive itself by the Gargants? I had no beacon. The vox was in fragments. There would be no transmission coming from the destroyed squadron.

So where did that leave me? I would have to count on the burned squadron being spotted by an overflight of this particular patch of hills. From the air, I doubted there would be anything to suggest the chance of a survivor. I was also having to count on *Storm of the Wastes* not having met its end so far from the rest of the squadron that it would be missed. How far had we rolled? How far had the others travelled? There was no way to know.

But *if* someone were to see the wrecks, and a land-based search followed, there would be nothing to say there was a survivor. Nothing to suggest that prying open the destroyed armour would be worthwhile. Unless there was an unmistakeable signal.

That was the one thing I could do. I couldn't reach high enough to strike and do any damage, but I could ring the hull like a bell. So I did. Three rhythmic blows. I stopped to listen, counting to twenty, then three more blows.

I fell into the new rhythm. I might very well not be able to hear searchers until they were actually working on the tank. For all I knew, I could be the last human on Armageddon, fruitlessly hitting the interior of his coffin. But I could not risk silence, in case there *was* help nearby. So I hit three times and listened. Hit three times, listened.

On and on. For hours. How many, I had no way of telling. My existence reduced itself to this one task of striking metal in pitch blackness, a task I had no reason to expect would be successful. I refused to accept the likelihood of failure. If I did, the temptation to rest would become overwhelming. I lived from second to second. I found the energy to strike the hull three times, and then again for another three. I tried to shut out all thoughts of the past and future. The eternal present was all that mattered. Despite my efforts, though, I could not ignore the irony of my situation. The Saviour of Armageddon, dead in an overturned tank. A glorious end, truly.

I did laugh a bit. That helped.

Time wore on, and my bursts of dry laughter died away. My throat was parched. I could barely move my arm. My body demanded sleep, but I refused. Then, quite suddenly, I heard noises outside. Engines. Loud, coughing, rattling engines. And over their din, closer to the hull, voices. Guttural. Savage.

Orks.

I had poor options. A choice of deaths, but the decision was an easy one. I would go down fighting. I smashed at my tomb with renewed force. After another three blows, I heard pounding from the other side. And then the unmistakeable grind of metal cutting metal. The greenskin voices sounded excited.

I reached to my belt and activated my shield generator. The air around me thrummed as the power field sprang into being. I drew my bolt pistol, building up the charge of my bale eye. I waited. I was eager to begin. The moment the orks broke through, the situation would change. I had no illusions about my chances, but I would make the best of them.

Sparks showered into my cell. The pitch of the grinding rose to a scream, and a chainblade broke through.

Still I waited for the enemy to free me and provide a clear shot at his bestial face.

The blade worked its way around in a rough circle about a

metre wide. The cuts joined. The blade withdrew. A heavy blow from the other side knocked the sliced plating inside.

Armageddon's grey daylight was blinding after the hours of total darkness.

I fired my eye as the ork poked its head through the hole. The las-burst shot through the greenskin's right eye, incinerating its brain, and it fell away. There was a growl, and then another ork appeared. I blew its skull off with the pistol.

The orks roared with outrage. Fists pounded against the hull. For the moment I saw nothing except a circle of brown sky. Heavy booted feet thudded across the hull towards the hole. Firing again, I took off the brute's arm just as it began to aim.

The attack began in earnest now. They fired around the hole at every angle. Bullets ricocheted around the interior. My shield absorbed their kinetic energy and they fell. A grenade arced in. I caught it and threw it back outside. It exploded in mid-air, and I was rewarded with roars of outrage that turned into roars of pain.

The orks kept coming and I kept shooting them. I was trapped, but they couldn't come at me where they could see me more than one at a time. I could hold them off indefinitely… until I ran out of clips for the pistol. Even then, I would take them apart with the power claw if they tried to come inside.

Indefinitely. Not infinitely.

I knew what the end was. I dismissed it. I would kill them one by one in the same eternal present as when I had banged my claw against the hull. They kept coming, wearing me down closer and closer to final exhaustion.

As I fought, and shot, and killed, I wondered why their attacks were so limited. I didn't hear any engines, so perhaps these orks were without heavy armour. But none of them tried to burn me out with flamers. A well-placed rocket would have ended the struggle in an instant. Instead, they appeared to be limiting themselves to shotguns and blades.

But in the end, they tired of the game, and decided to change the rules. The grinding started up again. When the blade poked through, it began to cut the outline of a much larger hole. I would lose my shelter. I would be cornered with no protection except my power field, and concentrated fire would overwhelm it.

I changed my bolt pistol's clip and waited for the endgame.

The huge roar of an approaching aircraft shook the air. I heard the shriek of launched missiles. Explosions. Howls from the orks. A confused stampede. The aircraft came closer. There was the blast of retrorockets as it landed. And then the sounds of a perfect, cleansing slaughter.

I leapt and grabbed the edge of the gap with my claw. Hauling myself up, I climbed out of the coffin.

Storm of the Wastes had come to rest in a narrow plain between the hills. The wreck of one of the other tanks lay on the slope to my left. A dozen metres to my right, an obsidian Thunderhawk gunship sat on level ground. A squad of Space Marines marched through the battlefield. It was full day, but they looked like darkest thoughts of the night. They were horned monsters. Though they carried bolters, most of them were killing orks with blades that grew out of their forearms.

Black Dragons.

Judging from the number of bodies I saw, there had been a few hundred orks to start with. I had lost track of how many I had killed. In the initial moments of their attack, the Black Dragons had cut them down by half. The rest fought back, but not for long.

The massacre was over in just a few minutes.

The captain of the Black Dragons came to meet me as I jumped down from the Vanquisher's upturned hull. He towered over his battle-brothers. The adamantium edge of his crescent horn gleamed in the sun. The coating of his bone blades was dark with greenskin blood. His flesh seemed more reptilian than human. In appearance, the Space Marine approached the daemonic.

This being too, I reminded myself, had a role to play in service to the Emperor.

The Black Dragon nodded. 'Volos,' he said. 'Second Company. An honour, commissar.'

'My thanks, Captain Volos. I am greatly in your debt. How did you find me?'

'If we had flown through this area before you were attacked, I don't think we would have,' he said. 'We spotted the orks.'

I took in the bodies stretching away on all sides. 'So large a group in the middle of nowhere would have caught the eye,' I agreed.

'A large raiding party, yes,' he said. 'I am puzzled by their overall weakness, though. There are no warlords here. And their weapons...'

'...are very limited,' I finished.

He must have seen something on my face. 'Commissar?' he asked.

An ork force weak in strength but large in numbers. Easily spotted. One that could not simply blow up the tank they were attacking; one that would be just possible for a single human being to hold off. And why were the orks here? I had called them to the specific tank, pinpointing my location for any searching eyes, but I could not understand why this force had been in the area at all. After the bombers did the job, there was little to scavenge. There would have been no reason for any infantry to be diverted to this location.

Unless *I* was the reason.

I remembered Morena's last vox transmission, alerting Imperial forces to my presence. I wondered now if someone else had heard it, if my enemy had sent this force knowing I was here. If they had sent these orks, whose constant fire showed they were not trying to capture me and also did not have the means of an assured kill.

I had no answers, only possibilities. But the questions were enough.

They were their own revelations, and they gave me that much more of the measure of my enemy.

I finally answered Volos. 'I was just gathering my thoughts, Captain Volos,' I said. 'Learning what I must to win this war.'

ABOUT THE AUTHORS

Dan Abnett has written over fifty novels, including the acclaimed Gaunt's Ghosts series and the Ravenor, Eisenhorn and Bequin books. His work for the Horus Heresy includes the first book in the series, *Horus Rising*, and the three-volume-long conclusion, *The End and the Death*. He also wrote several novels in between: *Legion, The Unremembered Empire, Know No Fear, Prospero Burns* and *Saturnine*. He scripted *Macragge's Honour*, the first Horus Heresy graphic novel, as well as numerous Black Library audio dramas. He recently penned the Warhammer 40,000 novel *Interceptor City*, the eagerly awaited sequel to fan-favourite *Double Eagle*. Dan lives and works in Maidstone, Kent.

Chris Wraight is the author of the Horus Heresy novels *Warhawk, Scars* and *The Path of Heaven*, the Primarchs novels *Leman Russ: The Great Wolf* and *Jaghatai Khan: Warhawk of Chogoris*, the novellas *Brotherhood of the Storm, Wolf King* and *Valdor: Birth of the Imperium*, and the audio drama *The Sigillite*. For Warhammer 40,000 he has written the Space Wolves books *Blood of Asaheim, Stormcaller* and *The Helwinter Gate*, as well as the Vaults of Terra and Watchers of the Throne series, *The Lords of Silence* and the Dawn of Fire novel *Sea of Souls*. Additionally, he has many Warhammer Fantasy novels to his name, and the Warhammer Crime novel *Bloodlines*. Chris lives and works in Bradford-on-Avon, in south-west England.

Guy Haley's work for Black Library spans the depth and breadth of the Warhammer universes. He is the author of several Horus Heresy novels, including *The Lost and the Damned, Titandeath, Wolfsbane* and three titles in the Primarchs series. He has also written many Warhammer 40,000 books, including *Dawn of Fire: Avenging Son,* the Dark Imperium trilogy, and the Belisarius Cawl novels *The Great Work, Genefather* and *Archmagos.* For Age of Sigmar he has penned the Drekki Flynt novels *The Arkanaut's Oath* and *The Ghosts of Barak-Minoz* as well as many other stories. He lives in Yorkshire with his wife and son.

Mike Brooks is a science fiction and fantasy author who lives in Nottingham. His recent work for Black Library includes the Warhammer 40,000 novels *Brutal Kunnin, Da Big Dakka, Harrowmaster, Voidscarred, Huron Blackheart: Master of the Maelstrom* and *Lelith Hesperax: Queen of Knives.* He has also written the Horus Heresy Primarchs novel *Alpharius: Head of the Hydra,* the Necromunda titles *Road to Redemption* and *Wanted: Dead,* and the Warhammer 40,000 titles *The Lion: Son of the Forest, Rites of Passage, Da Gobbo's Revenge* and *Warboss.* When not writing, he plays guitar and sings in a punk band, and DJs wherever anyone will tolerate him.

Nate Crowley is an SFF author and games journalist who lives in Walsall with his wife, daughter, and a cat he insists on calling Turkey Boy. He loves going to the zoo, playing needlessly complicated strategy games, and cooking incredible stews. His work for Black Library includes the Twice-Dead King duology, the novel *Ghazghkull Thraka: Prophet of the Waaagh!*, the novella *Severed* and the short stories 'Empra' and 'The Enemy of My Enemy'.

Rachel Harrison is the author of the Warhammer 40,000 novel *Honourbound,* featuring the character Commissar Severina Raine, as well the accompanying short stories 'Execution', 'Trials', 'Fire and Thunder', 'A Company of Shadows', and 'The Darkling Hours', which won a 2019 Scribe Award in the Best Short Story category. Also for Warhammer 40,000 she has written the novel *Mark of Faith,* the novella *Blood Rite,* numerous short stories including 'The Third War' and 'Dishonoured', the short story 'Dirty Dealings' for Necromunda, and the Warhammer Horror audio drama *The Way Out.*

David Guymer's work for Black Library includes the Warhammer Age of Sigmar novels *Kragnos: Avatar of Destruction,* and the Gotrek novels *Realmslayer: Legend of the Doomseeker* and *Verminslayer.* For The Horus Heresy he has written the Primarchs novels *Ferrus Manus: Gorgon of Medusa* and *Lion El'Jonson: Lord of the First.* For Warhammer 40,000 he has written *Angron: The Red Angel* and *The Eye of Medusa,* amongst others. He is a freelance writer and occasional scientist based in the East Riding, and was a finalist in the 2014 David Gemmell Awards for his novel *Headtaker.*

Marc Collins is a speculative fiction author living and working in Glasgow, Scotland. His first works for Black Library were the Warhammer Crime novel *Grim Repast,* and the short story 'Cold Cases'. Since then he has written the Warhammer 40,000 novels *Void King, Helbrecht: Knight of the Throne, Krakenblood,* the Dawn of Fire title *The Martyr's Tomb,* and the Horus Heresy novel *Eidolon: The Auric Hammer.* When not dreaming of the far future he works in Pathology with the NHS.

Steven B Fischer is a physician living in the Southeastern United States. When he's not too busy cracking open a textbook, he can be found exploring the Appalachian Mountains by bike, boat, or boot. Steven's work for Black Library includes the novels *Witchbringer* and *Broken Crusade*, and several short stories.

Justin Woolley hails from the bottom of the world in Tasmania, Australia and is an author of science fiction and fantasy. In his other life Justin has been an engineer, a teacher, and at one stage even a magician. A long-time fan of Warhammer 40,000, he has written the novel *Catachan Devil*, the novellas *Prisoners of Waaagh!* and *Long Live Da Red Gobbo*, and the many short stories including 'Redemption Through Sacrifice' and 'Night Shriekers'.

David Annandale is the author of the Warhammer Age of Sigmar novels *Callis & Toll* and *A Dynasty of Monsters*, and the Neferata titles *Mortarch of Blood* and *The Dominion of Bones*. His work for Warhammer 40,000 includes *Apostle*, *Ephrael Stern: The Heretic Saint*, *Warlord: Fury of the God-Machine*, the Yarrick series, and several stories involving the Grey Knights. His Horus Heresy titles include the novels *Ruinstorm* and *The Damnation of Pythos*, and the Primarchs novels *Roboute Guilliman: Lord of Ultramar*, *Vulkan: Lord of Drakes* and *Mortarion: The Pale King*. For Warhammer Horror, he has written the novels *The House of Night and Chain* and *The Deacon of Wounds*, as well as the novella *The Faith and the Flesh*. David lectures at a Canadian university, on subjects ranging from English literature to horror films and video games.

MORE FROM BLACK LIBRARY

DARK IMPERIUM
by Guy Haley

The first phase of the Indomitus Crusade is over, and the conquering primarch, Roboute Guilliman, sets his sights on home. The hordes of his traitorous brother, Mortarion, march on Ultramar, and only Guilliman can hope to thwart their schemes with his Primaris Space Marine armies.

An extract from
Dark Imperium
by Guy Haley

The void is impossible for the human mind to encompass.

Within the galaxy mankind calls home there are three hundred billion stars. Around these revolve hundreds of billions of worlds, and the spaces between are crowded by a diversity of objects that defy enumeration. Mankind's galaxy is but one of trillions of galaxies in a universe of unguessable size. The distances between even proximate astronomical bodies are inconceivable to creatures evolved to walk a single, small world.

This is why the void cannot be understood. Not by men, nor by their machines.

And when one considers the warp, that nightmare realm skulking behind that of touch, sound and sight, well... any being who claims comprehension of that is either deluded or insane.

Among the higher races there are those that grasp their limitations better than mankind. They understand that the cosmos is ultimately unknowable; they accept their lack of insight. By comparison, the creatures of Terra are so crude in thought that – in the opinion of these more enlightened civilisations – it is a wonder humanity can understand anything at all.

Humans are beings of short reach. Give them voidships, change their shape by gene-forge and augmetic, provide them with weapons of sufficient power to break a star, and the children of Old Earth are still but apes removed from the savannah. Just as an ape's mind cannot hold an ocean, and the notion of a whole world is inexplicable to it, so a man's mind cannot hold the void, and the layered infinities of the warp are beyond him entirely.

The Imperium claims a million worlds as its own. It is an empire spread gossamer-thin across the run of stars, its worlds so far removed from one another that it requires the bloody effort of countless men and women to sustain. In the grand flow of history, the Imperium is the greatest galactic empire of its day. To the people that populate it, it is the most powerful ever to have existed.

To the uncaring universe, it is nothing – the latest in a line of such realms that stretches back to the days of the first thinking beings, when the stars were young and the warp was calm and horror had yet to uncoil its tendrils into the material realm.

There are philosophers that argue war is man's natural state, and to the inhabitants of this era of blood it is a proven hypothesis. War is everywhere. Peace is the dream of a silent Emperor, broken by His treacherous sons.

Those sons continued to fight.

Over the green gas giant of Thessala, two battlefleets engaged. Titanic energies snapped and blinked in the eternal night of space.

The total efforts of star systems went into the construction of these fleets. Neither was free of the taint of blood: not in their construction, nor in their usage. The resources of planets had been poured entire into the forging of their frames; tens of thousands of lives had been expended in their making, and the secrets of ancient sciences plundered to bring them to life. Both had been responsible for the levelling of civilisations.

The fleets differed in only two regards. First was in their appearance. One was a gaudy assault on the senses, the other a motley collection of sober liveries. The more fundamental difference was in their allegiance. The sober fleet fought for the continuation of humanity's great stellar empire; the gaudy one was dedicated to its extinction.

The battlefleets pursued each other in a slow dance through Thessala's rings, hundreds of vessels ploughing gaps in the dust that would take centuries to close. The voiceless lightning of their guns filled the skies of Thessala's inhabited moons. The lives of millions below depended on the outcome of the battle, but the consequences would ripple much further.

At the centre of this iron storm there was no calm, no eye in which respite might be found. Instead, there was a pair of leviathans: the Ultramarines battle-barge *Gauntlet of Power* and the Emperor's Children battleship *Pride of the Emperor*. Two vessels, forged in a common cause but now implacable enemies, locked together in mortal combat only thirty miles apart – no distance at all in void war.

Each was the flagship of a primarch, genetically engineered demigods crafted by the Emperor of Mankind. Aboard the *Gauntlet of Power* stood Roboute Guilliman, the foundling of Ultramar, the Avenging Son. The *Pride of the Emperor* was home to Fulgrim – the traitor, the fallen exemplar, the blighted phoenix. Once covered in his Emperor's blessings, Fulgrim had followed the arch-traitor Horus and pledged his allegiance to dark gods.

In fighting for their father, both primarchs were made fathers themselves. Through the application of arcane science, they were the sires of two of the Space Marine Legions, mankind's greatest warriors. The Space Marines were lords of the galaxy, designed to reunite the human race and shepherd it to a glorious future. They had failed and turned upon one another, and their war had nearly destroyed the galaxy. They fought still.

Such fury a battlefleet can unleash!

It can cow a world without a shot. It can extinguish the life of a species. Battlefleets are the tools of tyrants, whomever they fight for. Whether their admirals espouse salvation or damnation matters not to the execution of their purpose. Death follows in their wake.

To those participating, a void war is a terrifying, roiling chaos of violence. It is the pinnacle of mankind's destructive ingenuity, a whirl of gigantic explosions where lives are snuffed out by the hundred. In such combat, a single person is nothing; they are but part of the machine of the ship they serve, only as essential as a steel cog or an indicator lumen. They can do nothing but work their appointed task and pray their life will not end, or if it must end, that it does so in painless disintegration. A single crewman's task dominates everything, even their fear of death. There is no escape from service. War and their part in it are the totality of their existence.

Yet what is a void war to the timeless blackness that envelops the footling motes of inhabited worlds? A void war is twinkles in the distance. It is silence. It is infinitesimals of matter sparking and dying, scintillas of metal and flesh consumed by transient fires. The detonation of a battleship miles long is insignificant to a cosmos where the deaths of suns are mere blinks. On a galactic scale, the loss of a warship is a nugatory flash, outshone by the billion-year candles of the stars.